THE STORY SHOP

Stories for
Literacy

D1385893

Nikki Gamble is a lecturer, writer and directs the Write Away education consultancy. She is editor of Write Away! www.writeaway.org.uk, a reader development and creative writing website for teachers. Nikki is an evaluator for the Literature Matters project, which aims to promote children's literature in initial teacher training courses. She has written extensively about children's literature and reading including teachers' materials for Booktrust, and she is co-author of *Exploring Children's Literature* (Paul Chapman) and *Guided Reading at KS2* (University of London, Institute of Education). Nikki currently teaches the Advanced Diploma in Language, Literature and Literacy at the University of Cambridge, Faculty of Education, and contributes to the CPD and PGCE programmes at the University of London, Institute of Education.

THE STORY SHOP

Stories for
Literacy

COMPILED BY
NIKKI GAMBLE

WAYLAND

This compilation copyright © Nikki Gamble 2006

First published in Great Britain in 2006
by Hodder Children's Books

Reprinted in 2007

Reprinted in 2008 and 2010 by Wayland

The right of Nikki Gamble to be identified as the compiler
has been asserted by her in accordance with the Copyright,
Designs and Patents Act, 1988

All rights reserved. Apart from any use permitted under
UK copyright law, this publication may only be reproduced,
stored or transmitted, in any form, or by any means with
prior permission in writing from the publishers or in the case
of reprographic production in accordance with the terms of
licences issued by the Copyright Licensing Agency.

A Catalogue record for this book is available
from the British Library.

ISBN 978 0 340 91104 4

Typeset in Palatino by Avon DataSet Ltd,
Bidford on Avon, Warwickshire

Printed in the UK by CPI Bookmarque, Croydon, CR0 4TD

The paper used in this book is a natural recyclable
product made from wood grown in sustainable forests.

Wayland
A division of Hachette Children's Books
338 Euston Road, London NW1 3BH
An Hachette UK company
www.hachette.co.uk

Contents

Introduction ix

Traditional Stories 1
Myths: how it all began
How Fire Came to Earth   Lucy Coats   1
The Seven Pomegranate Seeds   Anthony Horowitz   4
Maui and the Great Fish   Kiri Te Kanawa   12

Legends: hero tales
Father of Stories, Horse of Songs   Sally Pomme Clayton   16
How Cúchulainn Got His Name   Una Leavy   20
The Grendel   Anthony Horowitz   26

Legends: fabulous beasts
Saint George and the Dragon   Margaret Clark   33
The Fire-bird, the Horse of Power and the
Princess Vasilissa   Arthur Ransome   37

Folk tales
The Three Tests   James Riordan   49
Two Giants   Edna O'Brien   53
The Wise Men of Gotham   Kevin Crossley-Holland   63
The Storm Child   Nancy Cutt   68
The Girl from Llyn Y Fan Fach   T Llew Jones   72

Fables: tales that teach

Town Mouse and Country Mouse	*Aesop*	78
A Blind Man Catches a Bird	*Alexander McCall Smith*	80
The Dream	*Robert Leeson*	83
The Remarkable Rocket	*Oscar Wilde*	85

Tricksters

Head Over Heart	*Martin Bennett*	99
Tiger Story, Anansi Story	*Philip Sherlock*	105
Brer Rabbit to the Rescue	*Julius Lester*	117

Stories with Familiar Settings   120

Holly and the Skyboard	*Ian Whybrow*	120
Moonflower	*Pippa Goodhart*	127
Jacinta's Seaside	*Marilyn McLaughlin*	135
The Happy Team	*Alan Gibbons*	139
The Gang Hut	*George Layton*	149
Mozart's Banana	*Gillian Cross*	159

Humour in Different Guises   170

Jack and the Tinstalk	*Michael Rosen*	170
A Career in Witchcraft	*Kaye Umansky*	176
Olympic Marathon	*Morris Gleitzman*	185
That's None of Your Business	*Kevin Crossley-Holland*	189
The Fallen Angel Cake	*Maggie Pearson*	191
In the Shower with Andy	*Andy Griffiths*	193
Grimble's Monday	*Clement Freud*	202
How Not to be a Giant Killer	*David Henry Wilson*	209

Adventure Stories   215

Mackerel and Chips	*Michael Morpurgo*	215
The Leopard	*Ruskin Bond*	219

How Little John Came to the Greenwood

                                      Roger Lancelyn Green   227

The Picnic   *Penelope Lively*   234

Mystery Stories   251

The Happy Alien   *Jean Ure*   251

Moving House   *Louise Cooper*   260

Mrs Chamberlain's Reunion   *Philippa Pearce*   262

Ghost Trouble   *Ruskin Bond*   275

Nule   *Jan Mark*   287

Historical Stories and Fantasies in Bygone Times   298

The Fugitives   *Rosemary Sutcliff*   298

London Rises from the Ashes   *Jeremy Strong*   310

Toinette   *Adele Geras*   317

A Lighthouse Heroine   *Henry Brook*   325

Upon Paul's Steeple   *Alison Uttley*   334

Robert the Bruce and the Spider   *Geraldine McCaughrean*   342

Fantasy: Imagined Worlds and Fantastic Adventures   346

Thumbelisa   *Hans Christian Anderson*   346

Sailor Rumbelow and Britannia   *James Reeves*   359

The Smallest Dragonboy   *Anne McCaffrey*   372

Ully the Piper   *Andre Norton*   390

Wheelbarrow Castle   *Joan Aiken*   403

Science Fiction: Robots, Space and Virtual Reality   412

Oddiputs   *Nicholas Fisk*   412

Virtually True   *Paul Stewart*   438

All Summer in a Day   *Ray Bradbury*   451

Barry   *Stephen Bowkett*   459

Stories About Issues 471
Jessica's Secret *Malorie Blackman* 471
The Paradise Carpet *Jamila Gavin* 479
That Bit of Sule *Chika Unigwe* 485
Out of Bounds *Beverley Naidoo* 489
The World Next Door *Joan Aiken* 505

Acknowledgements 514

Introduction

Can you remember the most embarrassing thing that has ever happened to you? Have you ever been so frightened that you could feel your heart pounding in your chest and goose bumps creeping across your skin? Can you recall being reprimanded for something that wasn't your fault? Do you remember receiving news that made you want to jump in the air, shout at the top of your voice and run down the street in your pyjamas? If so, then you certainly have some good stories waiting to be told. That's where stories come from – harvested from everyday experiences and transformed through the imagination and well chosen words into something quite magical.

'Once upon a time, in a far off land . . .'; so begins the storyteller, transporting us in the twinkle of an eye to distant lands. Story travellers can visit Aotearoa, 'Land of the Long White Cloud', to watch Maui catch the big fish that becomes New Zealand, or the haunting Orkney Islands where a storm child might be found, washed ashore by the turbulent stormy seas. They can travel through time: one turn of the page is a step back to ancient Greece, Roman Britain or revolutionary France. Or perhaps a story might be found somewhere closer to home: in the classroom, at the seaside, in the house next door.

Stories have the power to change us, to make us see things differently. In 'Jessica's Secret', Malorie Blackman reminds us that, while it is easy for a victim to become a bully, we can all make positive choices. Not all stories have happy endings; they can help us face the darker side of life too. Through the lens of a story we can appreciate what life might be like for children living in difficult circumstances or in conflict-torn areas of the world.

Myths are the oldest stories and connect us to the ancient world. They were the means by which people explained the natural wonders: the coming of night and day, the formation of the landscape and the creation of animals. In 'The Seven Pomegranates', Anthony Horowitz retells the ancient Greek myth of Persephone and how the seasons came about. Many modern writers have reworked these old tales and you too might be inspired to write a story, poem or lyrics based on a favourite tale.

Legends offer us the chance to escape into an extra-ordinary world. Action-packed tales about superheroes like Cúchulainn or Beowulf tell of larger than life exploits in which heroes can seemingly achieve anything. But even these heroic giants have human failings; they may lack compassion or break a promise with devastating consequences. Why not collect stories about other heroes and heroines from your wider reading? Do most heroes share similar qualities? Do they always have to be brave and strong? What makes a good hero story? Strange, exotic creatures also make regular appearances in legend: feared monsters, like St George's dragon, have to be conquered; beasts with rare qualities can bestow immortality or help in times of peril. Did legendary fire-breathing dragons exist? Did mermaids once lure sailors onto rocks with their singing? What may have inspired the travellers returning home with tales of fabulous beasts?

All around the world people have told stories about the trickster, a cheeky, cunning and wily character who often outwits a stronger opponent. You have to admire plucky Anansi when he captures the stories from much-feared Tiger.

If you enjoy writing stories, encounters with these master storytellers will help you hone and perfect your writing skills. When you have read them, think about the stories that you most enjoy. What makes them successful? Is it the sting-in-the-tale of Maggie Pearson's 'The Fallen Angel Cake', the build up of tension in Jan Mark's 'Nule' or the word play in Michael Rosen's 'Jack and the Tinstalk'?

Short stories from every genre are collected together in *The Story Shop*. There are mystery stories populated with ghosts, detectives and aliens; historical stories about events that really happened and others about events that could have happened. There are jungle adventures, time-slip adventures, fantastic adventures and everyday adventures. There are fantasies set in imagined lands and miniature worlds, animal fables and anti-fables. There are laugh-out-loud stories and wryly humorous stories. Enjoy!

NOTE FOR TEACHERS

The stories in this collection are intended for children aged 7–11. They are diverse in their appeal and in the level of linguistic and thematic challenge. The stories in each section vary in accessibility and sophistication to allow the selection of stories for reading aloud and for group or independent reading. The stories have been organised into sections that correspond with the range of fiction outlined in the Literacy *Framework for Teaching*. However, a story might easily fit into several sections: 'How Little John Came to the Greenwood' is an adventure story but it is also a legend from the Robin Hood cycle; 'Jessica's Secret' has an important issue at its heart but it also takes place in a familiar setting; 'All in a Summer Day' is Science Fiction but it has some interesting issues for reflection and discussion.

TRADITIONAL STORIES

How Fire Came to Earth

Lucy Coats

ZEUS WANTED to reward Prometheus and Epimetheus, the two Titans who had helped him in battle. So he gave them the job of making new creatures to scamper over the earth, and fill her woods and meadows with songs and joyful sounds once more.

'Here are the things you will need,' he said, pointing to a row of barrels. 'There's plenty for both of you.' And he flew off back to Olympus.

Prometheus set about making some figures out of the first barrel, which was full of clay. He shaped two kinds of bodies, and rolled out long sausages of mud and pressed them against the bodies to make arms and legs. Then he made two round balls, and stuck them on the tops. He hummed as he worked, and his clever fingers shaped ears and eyes and hair and mouths until the figures looked just like tiny copies of Zeus and his wife. It took him a very long time, because he wanted his creations to be perfect.

In the time that Prometheus had made his two sorts of figures, Epimetheus had made many. First he used up the barrels of spots, then he used all the stripes; he simply flung handfuls of bright feathers about, and as for the whiskers and claws he gave them out twenty at a time! By the time Prometheus had finished his men and women there was not a thing left to give them other than some thin skin, and a little fine hair.

Prometheus went straight to Zeus.

'My creatures are cold!' he said. 'You must give me some of your special fire to warm them up, or they will die!' But Zeus refused.

'Fire is only for gods. They will just have to manage,' he said. 'You shouldn't have been so slow in making them.'

Now this annoyed Prometheus a lot. He had taken such care, and his creations had things inside that Epimetheus could never even have *thought* of. So he decided to steal Zeus's fire for them. He sneaked up to Olympus, carrying a hollow reed, and stole a glowing coal from Zeus's hearth. Then he flew down to earth.

'Keep this sacred fire of the gods burning always,' he commanded his creatures. And they did. They looked deep into the flames and saw just what they should do. They built temples, and in each temple was a fire. And on the fires they placed offerings to the gods, and the smoke of them reached right up to Zeus's palace on Olympus.

Zeus liked the delicious smell. But when he looked down to earth and saw the fires burning everywhere like little red stars, he was not happy at all.

'Prometheus!' he bellowed. 'I told you not to take that fire! I'll make you regret your stealing ways!' He swooped down on the back of a giant eagle and carried Prometheus away to the Caucasus Mountains, where he chained him to the highest peak. And Zeus sent the giant eagle to visit him every morning and tear enormous chunks out of his liver. Every night the liver magically regrew, so that poor Prometheus's punishment was never-ending.

But Zeus never took back the gift of fire from the earth, and we have it still to warm us on cold winter nights.

The Seven Pomegranate Seeds

Anthony Horowitz

DEMETER WAS one of the more gentle goddesses who inhabited Mount Olympus. Not for her were the jealous rages of Hera, the whip-like chastity of Artemis or the burning passions of Aphrodite. Demeter was the goddess of agriculture and of marriage. Her hair was the colour of wheat at harvest-time and her eyes were a pastel blue. She delighted in bright colours, often wearing brilliant ribbons and carrying a golden torch.

Only once did she really lose her temper. This was when she discovered that the beautiful trees in a grove that was sacred to her were being cut down by a foolhardy young man called Erysichthon. Perhaps he was some sort of early town planner, but whatever his reason for this act of vandalism, Demeter appeared to him disguised as a mortal and asked him if he would be so kind as to stop. His answer was short and unfriendly.

Then Demeter assumed her own form and punished Erysichthon in a way that was truly horrible. She condemned him to remain hungry for ever, no matter how much he ate. From that moment on, he seldom stopped. At dinner that same night, he astonished his parents by eating not only his food but theirs too – as well as that of their seventeen guests. In the weeks that followed, he ate so much that his weeping father was forced to throw him out of the house, no longer able to afford his keep. And yet the more he ate, the thinner and hungrier he got until, in the end, he became a beggar, shuffling pathetically along in rags, still stuffing himself with the filth he found in the streets.

This, then, was the full extent of Demeter's anger. But most people would agree that Erysichthon only got what he deserved. For the unnecessary destruction of a tree is a terrible crime.

Demeter had a daughter called Core (later on, her name was changed to Persephone) whom she loved more than anything in the world. Unfortunately, another of the gods also loved the girl, although in a very different way. This was Hades, the shadowy lord of the Underworld, the god of death. Hades had spent virtually his whole life underground and his skin was pale and cold. No light shone in his eyes, eyes that had seldom seen the sun. And yet he had seen an image of Core, magically reflected in an ebony pool and he had lost his heart to her. So great was his love that he took a rare leave of absence from the Underworld, travelling to Olympus. There he came before Zeus and demanded that he give Core to him as a wife.

The demand somewhat embarrassed the king of the gods. For although he did not want to offend Hades, who was his brother, Zeus could not let him have what he wanted. For Core was his daughter. He had fallen in love with Demeter some years before and Core had been the result. If he were to send the girl to the Underworld, Demeter would never forgive him. Moreover, it would hardly be fair to condemn his own daughter to such a gloomy place – for the kingdom of Hades was such a dull and dismal land. But on the other hand, what was he to say to Hades, who was older than he and . . . ?

'I'll think about it,' Zeus said.

And promptly forgot all about it.

When it became clear that he was not going to get a satisfactory answer out of Zeus, Hades decided to take things into his own hands.

'He did not say I could have the girl,' he reasoned to himself. 'But nor did he say that I could not. And surely, if something is not forbidden, then it must be allowed. Of course it must! In which case, Core shall become Persephone and as Persephone she will be my wife.'

And so it was that two days later, Core found herself kidnapped by the grim god of death. She was living in Sicily at the time and was out in the fields with some of her friends, collecting wild flowers for a feast that same evening. Noticing a particularly bright narcissus, she leant down to pick it. Suddenly the ground trembled. As the blood drained from her face and her friends screamed, dropping their baskets and scattering in all directions, a great chasm appeared in front of her, yawning like a black mouth. Desperately, Core tried to keep her balance. But then a white hand that smelt of damp earth stretched out and grabbed hold of her, pulling her forward. With a hopeless cry, she tumbled forward, disappearing into the chasm. The ground trembled again, then closed up as suddenly as it had opened. Only a jagged line, zig-zagging through the flowers, showed what had happened.

When Demeter discovered that Core was missing, her grief was overwhelming. Almost overnight she changed. No longer did she wear ribbons and bright colours. No more was her laughter heard in the fields. Covering herself with a dark veil, she flew round the world on a search that would take her nine days and nine nights.

Not once did she stop for food or for drink – nor even to rest. Her only thought was for her daughter. She visited Sicily, Colonus, Hermione, Crete, Pisa, Lerna . . . nobody had seen the girl, nor was there any sign that she had been there.

At last she went in desperation to Helios, the god who every day followed the sun, riding across the heavens in a golden chariot drawn by four white horses. Nothing ever escaped the eye of Helios. Soaring in an arc, high above the world, he could see everything. And what he had to tell Demeter chilled her heart.

'You must forget Core,' he said. 'Core exists no longer. Look, if you will, for Persephone – destroyer of men – for that is what she has become as wife of the king of death. Yes! Hades has stolen her from you. Never again will you see her. Where she is now, deep in the shadows of the Underworld, she is lost even from the sight of Helios.'

At once Demeter went to Zeus. White with anger and haggard after her nine days of fasting, she was almost unrecognizable and the king of the gods squirmed in front of her.

'I didn't say Hades could take her,' he muttered.

'Did you say he couldn't?'

'Well . . .'

'I want her back, Zeus. You will return her to me!'

'I can't!' The king of the gods almost wept with frustration. 'You know the rules. If she has eaten so much as a mouthful of the food of the dead, she is stuck in the Underworld for ever.'

'She won't have eaten. She can't have eaten.'

'And anyway,' Zeus went on, 'you know Hades. There's no arguing with him. He has to have his own way . . .'

'Very well,' Demeter cried. 'Until my daughter is returned to me, no tree on earth will yield fruit. No plants will grow. The soil will remain barren. The animals will starve. Such is the curse of an unhappy mother. Bring her back, Zeus. Or mankind will perish!'

So began a year of unrelenting famine. The crops withered and even the grass turned brown and rotted. As Demeter had promised, the animals, unable to find fodder, died by the hundred, their bloated carcasses dotting the arid landscape.

At last the situation became so desperate that Hermes, the messenger-god, was sent down to the Underworld to bring Persephone back.

'Never!' Hades exclaimed. 'I love her. I will never relinquish her.'

'But does she love you?' Hermes asked.

'She . . . she will learn to. In time.'

'But there is no time,' Hermes said. 'Her mother, Demeter, is destroying the world in her grief. If you do not release Persephone, mankind will come to an end.'

'Why should the extinction of mankind be of any concern to the god of death?' Hades asked.

'Because even death depends on life. Nothing can continue without it.'

The king of the Underworld thought long and hard but then he nodded his head.

'You speak the truth,' he said. 'Very well. It seems that I am defeated. My wife, my Persephone . . . she must go.'

And he turned his head, bringing his hand up to cover his eyes.

When Persephone heard that she was to be returned to the world of the living, she was so happy that she laughed and cried at the same time. But one of the gardeners of Hades, a man by the name of Ascalaphus, also heard the news and at once he crept off and, changing into his best clothes, knelt before Hades.

'Oh ghastly and glorious master!' he said, rubbing his hands together in front of his chin. 'Dread lord of the Underworld, grotesque king of the dead, sovereign of the . . .'

'Get on with it!' Hades commanded,

'Of course! Of course!' The gardener laughed nervously. 'I just thought you'd like to know that your wife, the good and delicious lady Persephone, has tasted the food of the dead.'

'That's impossible,' Hades said. 'She has refused to eat since the day I brought her here. Not so much as a crust of bread has passed her lips.'

'I'm sure. I'm sure. But something less than a crust of bread has, noble king. With my own eyes I saw her eat seven pomegranate seeds. In the garden. I saw her.'

Then the eyes of Hades lit up. 'If this is true,' he said, 'you shall be rewarded.'

'Rewarded?' Ascalaphus licked his lips. 'Well, I didn't *do* it for the reward. But if there is a reward. Well . . .'

'Follow her to the surface,' Hades said. 'Do what must be done.'

So when Hermes took Persephone with him in his chariot, Ascalaphus rode on the back, unseen by either of them, dreaming of his new career (for he had never liked gardening very much) perhaps as secretary to Hades or perhaps as palace librarian or even – who could say? – as the next prince of Hell. And no sooner had Demeter received her daughter in a joyful embrace than he stepped forward with a crooked smile.

'Persephone has eaten the food of the dead,' he cried. 'She must return with me to the Underworld. There's nothing any of you lot can do about it. It's the law.'

'Is this true?' Demeter asked.

Then tears sprang to Persephone's eyes and she sank to her knees.

'Yes, mother,' she whispered. 'I ate seven pomegranate seeds. But that was all I ate. Although I was one year in that horrible place, that was the only food that passed my lips. Surely it doesn't count. Surely . . .'

But by now Demeter was weeping too.

'You have eaten the food of the dead,' she said. 'Though mankind will die when they take you from me, there is nothing I can do.'

When the gods heard what had happened, they held a great conference to discuss what should be done. On the one hand, nobody wanted the world to end. But nor could they allow Persephone to remain in the land of the living. At last, a compromise was reached and both Persephone and Demeter were called before the throne of Zeus.

'We've come to an agreement,' Zeus explained. 'And I hope it satisfies you because it really is the best we can do. Listen. What would you say if we allowed Persephone to stay in the world for six months of the year, provided she spent the other six months with Hades in the Underworld?'

Demeter thought for a moment. 'Make it nine months with me and three months with Hades and I will agree,' she said.

'Very well. You've got a deal.'

At once the famine ended. Nine months later, Persephone went back to begin her spell in the Underworld, and although she was never a truly loving wife to Hades, she was never unkind to him.

The miserable Ascalaphus never received the reward he had been hoping for. For Persephone punished him for his treachery by pushing him into a small hole and covering him with an ornamental rockery complete with flowering hibiscus border and fish-pond. In this way he was condemned to spend the rest of eternity not only in the garden but under it too.

This myth explains why it is that for three months every year, the cold season comes and it looks as though the world has gone into mourning. Then the trees lose their leaves, nothing will grow and, like Demeter, we look forward to the spring. For it is only in the spring, when Persephone is released from her dark confinement, that the warmth and the colours will return and we can all – god and man – celebrate the return of life.

Maui and the Great Fish

Kiri Te Kanawa

THIS IS the story of how Maui caught the Great Fish of New Zealand. When I was very young I imagined that Maui was very young too and I was very impressed that such a young boy could catch such a great fish.

When I look at my maps of New Zealand, I can see that it is in fact the North Island that is in the shape of a fish. However, I always imagined it was shaped like a shark, not a fish, because when I first heard the story I was terrified of sharks and thought that the shark was the only fish that would fight so violently against Maui's god-like powers.

The Maori name for the North Island is still *Te Ika A Maui*, meaning the fish of Maui.

Maui was, they say, half man and half god. He knew many magic spells and had many magic powers that his older brothers didn't know about, or if they did they pretended to ignore.

One day, when he heard his brothers talking about going fishing, Maui decided that he wanted to go too. So, before his brothers had woken up he went down to where the canoe was, carrying his special fishing hook. Hearing his brothers approach he quickly hid under the floorboards of the boat.

The brothers arrived and they were laughing about having managed to escape without Maui. They were looking forward to having a good day's fishing without being bothered by their young brother.

They pushed out from shore and were still laughing when suddenly they heard a noise.

'What was that?' asked one of them.

Then they thought they heard someone talking. They couldn't see anyone; they couldn't see anything except for the water.

'Oh, it must have been a seagull or something screeching in the distance,' suggested another of the brothers.

Then they heard the sound again. It was Maui, laughing and saying in a strange voice, 'I am with you. You haven't tricked me at all.'

The brothers were becoming quite scared now. It sounded like muffled speech but there was no one to be seen.

On they paddled into the deep waters. Again they heard the voice and this time one of the brothers said he thought the noise was coming from under the floorboards so he wrenched up a few. There was Maui, laughing loudly and boasting, 'I tricked you! I tricked you!'

The brothers were amazed to see Maui there. They decided to turn back immediately. 'You are not coming with us,' they said. 'You're far too young and our father doesn't want you to come with us.'

But Maui said, 'Look back! Look back to the land! Look how far away it is!'

He had used his magic powers to make the land seem much further away than it really was. The brothers, not realizing that it was a trick, reluctantly agreed to take Maui with them.

They paddled on for a while and then stopped. Just as they were about to throw over the anchor and start their fishing, Maui said, 'No. Please don't do that because I know a much better place further out, full of fish – all the fish you could want. Just a little while longer and you'll have all your nets filled in half the time.'

The brothers were tempted by this promise of fish and paddled out a little further when Maui stopped them and told them to start fishing. So they threw over their nets which within a few minutes were overflowing. They couldn't believe their luck.

Their boat was lying low in the water with the weight of their catch so the brothers told Maui that they were going to turn back. But Maui said, 'No, it's my turn. I haven't had a chance to do my fishing.'

'But we have enough!' they replied.

'No! I want to do my fishing,' insisted Maui.

With that, he pulled out his special fishing hook made of bone, and asked for some bait. The brothers refused to give him any so Maui rubbed his nose so hard that it began to bleed. Then he smeared the hook with his own blood and threw it over the side.

Suddenly the boat was tossed about, and Maui was thrilled because he was sure he had caught a very big fish. He pulled and pulled. The sea was in a turmoil and Maui's brothers sat in stunned silence, marvelling at Maui's magic strength.

Maui heaved and tugged for what seemed like an age until at last the fish broke the surface. Then Maui and his brothers could see that what he had caught was not a fish but a piece of land, and that his hook was embedded in the doorway of the house of Tonganui, the son of the Sea God.

Maui's brothers couldn't believe their eyes. This beautiful land pulled up from the sea, was smooth and bright, and there were houses on it and burning fires and birds singing. They had never seen anything so marvellous in their whole lives.

Realizing what he had done Maui said, 'I must go and make peace with the gods because I think they are very angry with me. Stay here quietly and calmly, until I return.'

As soon as Maui had gone the brothers forgot his instructions and began to argue for possession of the land.

'I want this piece,' said one.

'No! I claimed it first. It's mine!' shouted another.

Soon the brothers began to slash at the land with their weapons. This angered the gods even more and its smooth surface was gashed and cut. It could never be smoothed out again.

To this day, those cuts and bruises of long ago can still be seen in the valleys and mountains of New Zealand.

Father of Stories, Horse of Songs

Sally Pomme Clayton

Oh my Khan,
under blue skies
beneath spreading trees
beside swift rivers
surrounded by strong horses
sitting on carpets of felt,
our ancestors drank tea.

IN THIS time, Korkut was a young man. He was just sixteen years old when he had a dream. He dreamt that Death was looking for him.

Korkut woke with a start. 'I am too young to die!' he cried. 'Death can take me when I'm old. Death can take me when I'm ready.' And he leapt on to his beautiful chestnut horse. 'Carry me, horse,' he cried, 'carry me away from Death.'

Korkut had not ridden far when he came to some people digging a hole in the ground.

'What are you digging?' he asked.

'We are digging the grave of Korkut,' they replied.

Korkut turned his horse and rode in the other

direction. He came to some more people digging a hole.

'What are you digging?'

'We're digging the grave of Korkut.'

Korkut rode fast. But everywhere he rode, there were people with spades, digging his grave.

Korkut did not stop riding. The chestnut horse galloped through sun and wind, stars and snow, looking for a place where there was no Death.

Korkut asked a tree, 'Do you know the place where there is no Death?'

'Death is here,' whispered the tree. 'Birds peck me, leaves fall from me.'

Korkut asked the steppe, 'Do you know the place where there is no Death?'

'Death is here,' moaned the steppe. 'Sheep graze me, horses' hooves pound me.'

Korkut asked the mountain, 'Do you know the place where there is no Death?'

'Death is here,' rumbled the mountain. 'Rain lashes me, wind howls around me.'

Suddenly Korkut's horse stumbled. Its legs gave way and it fell to the ground. The chestnut horse was worn out. Korkut ran to the river to fetch water, but the horse was too tired to drink. Korkut watched as his beautiful horse closed its eyes and died.

'Death is here,' wept Korkut. And he buried his face in his horse's mane. 'My beloved horse, there must be a place where there is no Death.'

Korkut took his knife and cut a branch from a tree. He began to carve a pear-shaped box. He stripped some skin from his horse and stretched it over the box. He twisted hairs from his horse's mane into two long strings, and tied them to each end of the box. Then he cut hair from his horse's tail, and stretched it along a stick.

Korkut made a musical instrument, a horsehair fiddle and a horsehair bow.

Korkut waded into the river and stood on a stone. He rested the fiddle in the cuff of his boot and began to play. He drew the horsehair bow across the strings. Music filled the air. Korkut began to sing a song about the life and death of his beautiful chestnut horse. The sound of Korkut's music echoed across the steppe.

Children stopped playing, old men stopped working, women put down their embroidery. They all ran to the river and stood silently, listing to Korkut's music.

Korkut sang of warriors and princesses, eagles and wolves. The horsehair fiddle resounded and everything listened. The rocks listened. The wind fell silent. The river stopped babbling. The birds were still. The flowers moved closer. All creation listened to Korkut's songs.

At the back of the crowd there was a shadowy figure. It was Death. Death had come to listen to Korkut's music. Death listened in wonder as Korkut sang of heroes and monsters, saints and devils and magic horses. Korkut sang and sang, and Death listened. Death was so entranced by the stories, he forgot his work. And all the time that Korkut sang, nobody died. Korkut's songs and stories held back death.

Many, many years passed. And there was no death. Korkut grew old, his hair turned white and his back bent.

'Now I am ready,' said Korkut. He stepped out of the river, put his instrument on the ground at the feet of all the people who had been listening, and let Death take him.

The people buried Korkut on the banks of the river. Then they picked up his horsehair fiddle and began to play. They sang his stories and played his tunes. Korkut and his horse lived on, in the place where there is no death – the place of stories.

The people called the horsehair fiddle the *kobiz*. And they carved a horse's head on top of the kobiz, remembering how the horse of songs helped make the first fiddle.

Korkut's grave is on the banks of the Syr Darya river, in Southern Kazakhstan. And it is said that if you sleep beside Korkut's grave, you will become a poet.

Korkut became known as Dede Korkut, Father Korkut, father of all the stories he had created – stories still being sung by storytellers today.

> Dede Korkut sang the stories
> of all the Central Asian peoples.
> Like them,
> we come to this world and leave it,
> camp and move on.
> For if we did not die
> the earth would not be made.
> When Death comes
> may he give you fair passage.
> May your firm-rooted mountain never crumble.
> May your great shady tree never be cut down.
> May your clear-flowing river never run dry.
> May your horse never stumble.
> May your sword never be notched in the fray.
> May your lamp,
> which God has lit,
> never be put out.
> Oh my Khan.

How Cúchulainn got his Name

Una Leavy

LONG AGO, there lived a king in Ulster called Conor Mac Nessa. His warriors were known as the Red Branch Knights. The king himself trained them in his own special school. They could run faster, jump higher and fight more fiercely than anyone else.

The king had a nephew named Setanta. Ever since he was little, the boy had heard about the Red Branch Knights. He could hardly wait to grow up so that he could become one himself.

'I am tall and strong,' he said to his mother one day. 'I want to go to Ulster to join the Red Branch Knights.'

'No, no, my son!' his mother answered. 'You are still only a little boy. I cannot let you go. I would miss you too much.'

For a while, Setanta was happy. He tracked wild animals in the woods and knew the song of every bird. Sometimes he made hurley sticks from the springy ash wood. He and his friends played together, whacking a ball with their sticks. Setanta's team always won – he hit the ball harder than anyone else and could run like the wind.

A year passed and Setanta grew restless again.

'I am ten years old now,' he said to his father one day. 'I can run fast and I am very strong. I want to go to Ulster to join the Red Branch Knights.'

'No, no, my son!' his father answered. 'You are still too young. You must wait until you are older.'

For a while, Setanta was content. He milked the cows and kept the sheep from straying. He gathered firewood and carried water for the house. When winter came, there were games of chess that went on for hours. At night he listened to the old people telling their ancient tales.

One autumn evening, a stranger came to the gate.

'I have come from the north,' he said, 'from the court of Conor Mac Nessa. I seek shelter for the night.'

Setanta was delighted. Quickly he took the stranger to his father.

'Of course! You are a thousand times welcome! Come and sit by the fire. We will have music and storytelling this night!'

Soon the house was packed with neighbours and relations. Everyone wanted to hear the traveller's news. All he talked of was King Conor Mac Nessa and his brave warriors. His songs praised them and he recited the history of the king's family for many generations.

Setanta listened, his heart thumping with excitement. In his ears he could hear the roar of battle and the warriors' fearless cries.

'I must go and join the Red Branch Knights!' he burst out at last. 'My uncle needs me! I am old enough now! I am strong enough now!'

But the stranger laughed.

'You are only a child!' he said. 'You would be smashed to pieces in battle and thrown aside!'

At last everyone settled down for the night. Setanta could not sleep. He lay watching the sparks as they flew up into the darkness and were lost among the stars . . .

'It's no good,' he thought at last. 'I just can't wait another night.'

Silently he rolled on to his feet, stopping only to pick up his hurley and ball. Outside was the first hushed light of a misty dawn.

All day he travelled, taking directions from the sun. He did not go by the usual paths but kept to remote hills and sheep tracks. Now no one could follow him.

It was evening when he reached King Conor Mac Nessa's fort. Just in front of it swept a great wide lawn. There was a hurling match going on and, almost at once, the ball dropped at Setanta's feet. He scooped it up with his hurley and ran. The players were all big boys. They tried to tackle him but he was too fast, whirling past them till the ball was in the goal!

There was a mighty roar. A row broke out among the boys. Some of them attacked him. Setanta defended himself as well as he could.

'Stop!' shouted the king's voice. 'What's happening here? And who is this child?'

'I am your nephew,' Setanta replied. 'I have come to join the Red Branch Knights.'

'Well!' laughed King Conor. 'You are only a little man. But if you always fight as bravely, some day you'll be the leader of my army.'

So Setanta was allowed to stay.

Setanta soon settled in to his new life. He learned to fight like a stag and to move as silently as the clever red fox. But he learned too about loyalty, honour and truth. Conor was a strict master and only the most promising boys were allowed to remain.

One evening Setanta was hurling with his new friends. King Conor called to him.

'Culann, the blacksmith, has prepared a feast,' he

explained. 'I am going there now. Would you like to come?'

Setanta had heard a lot about Culann. He was as strong as a giant, the greatest blacksmith in the land. He gave wonderful feasts. It would be nice to hear some music and have a little fun.

'I would love to come,' Setanta said, 'but I am in the middle of a game. I will follow you later – it won't be dark for a long time.'

'Very well,' said the king, and off he went in his royal chariot.

The game was long and hectic. Setanta quite forgot about the time. The sun was going down when he scored the winning goal.

'I must hurry,' he thought, as he washed and changed. 'It will soon be dark and it's a long walk. I'm not even sure of the way.'

He set off, following the tracks of the chariot wheels. There was no proper road and soon it was almost dark. Trees creaked eerily in the shadows and rocks took on strange shapes. Old tales of ghosts and spirits whispered in his head. Once or twice a wolf howled and owls skimmed overhead. But Setanta would not admit that he was afraid. He whistled a cheerful tune and tried to see how well he could balance his hurley and ball.

It began to rain. A shivery wind trembled in the trees as the last of the light disappeared. Setanta grew cold and wet. He wished he was at home . . .

Meanwhile, at Culann's house, there was music and dancing. Mead and wine flowed from every cup. Roast pig and fresh oatcakes were piled at every place. The room was smoky and hot. Culann's beautiful sisters tended the guests. The king could not take his eyes off them. As the night went on, he grew sleepy with food and wine. He did not notice the rising wind or the rain that poured down outside.

'It's a terrible night,' Culann said. 'I will call in my sentries. All my guests are here. My hound will guard instead. He is a vicious killer and no enemy will enter my gates.'

But King Conor was not listening. His eyes were on the beautiful girls . . .

At last Setanta saw lights ahead. He was cold, tired and hungry. He could not wait to be inside. He smiled to himself as the noise and music flowed out across the night. The gates were closed but he climbed easily over and dropped into the yard.

Immediately there was a murderous snarl. Setanta stood absolutely still. Two wicked eyes glittered in the shadows – it was Culann's dog, half hound, half wolf! Setanta gripped his hurley. Wild thoughts tumbled through his head. He knew that this dog would eat him alive. There was only one chance . . .

As the dog hurtled towards him, eyes raging, mouth snarling, Setanta took careful aim – and rammed the ball down the hound's gaping throat. With a fearful screech, the dog crashed to the ground. Choking and gasping, he tried to cough up the ball, but it was firmly stuck. With one last mighty shudder, he tossed his head and died.

The door crashed open. Culann and King Conor had heard the dog's wild cries.

'My hound!' shouted Culann.

'Setanta!' yelled the king, suddenly remembering. He dashed out, afraid of what he might find. But there was Setanta with the dog dead at his feet.

'I am glad you are safe,' said Culann at last, 'but I am sad to lose my poor faithful hound. He served me long and well.'

Setanta stepped forward.

'I am sorry I had to kill your dog,' he said. 'But if you will let me, I will be your hound. I will guard your home with my life.'

King Conor and Culann agreed. Soon Setanta had another name. He was called Cúchulainn, which means Culann's hound. This was his name, ever after, when he became the best and most famous warrior of the Red Branch Knights.

(From *The O'Brien Book of Irish Fairy Tales and Legends* by Una Leavy, The O'Brien Press Ltd)

The Grendel

Anthony Horowitz

WHEN KING Hrothgar came to the throne of Denmark (in the fifth century after Christ), he decided to build a great banqueting hall in which he would entertain all his friends. And as he was a popular king, who had fought bravely and won many fierce battles, and as he had more friends than most kings tend to have he decided that the hall would have to be larger and more splendid than any in the land of Denmark. This was how Heorot came into being. Heorot the mead-hall, the home of feasting and of singing and of storytelling.

Thatched with heather and decorated by blazing beacons and gilded antlers, the hall would fill every day with warriors and travellers, musicians and poets. King Hrothgar himself would sit at the very end of the hall on a raised dais and sometimes his wife, the fair queen Wealtheow, would take the seat beside him. The servants would race past the roaring fires carrying steaming plates of eel pie and roasted boars' flesh to the trestle tables that ran the full length of the room. Hunting dogs, lying on the straw, would raise their heads as the meat went past, their tongues hanging out, and by the end of the feast, they too would have been rewarded with scraps of meat and marrow bones. The mead would never stop flowing. And as the sun reached out to claim possession of the night sky, the music from the harps would still ring out across the fields along with the laughter and the chatter of old comrades at ease.

Grendel heard that sound.

Curled up in the darkness of the swamp, it heard and one poisoned eye flickered open. Softly it growled to itself. For Grendel understood nothing of pleasure and so hated it. Hatred ruled its life. It was descended from Cain – the same Cain that had been cast out of Eden for the murder of his brother. Grendel blamed all mankind for the sin of its ancestor and its own fall from grace. The bitterness of centuries ran in its veins, congealing its blood. In its every waking moment it writhed in a torment of self-pity and half-formed dreams of revenge. Now, hearing the sound, it slithered through the mud and began to limp towards the hall.

It was at that grey time between night and day when it reached Heorot. Now, at last, the revellers were asleep, intoxicated by the wine and good companionship. Grendel struck quickly and greedily. Thirty warriors were snatched up from where they lay. Thirty brave men met a brutal, cowardly death. Glutted with blood, Grendel slunk away, back to the solitude of the swamp. Even in its victory, it knew no pleasure. It had done what it had set out to do; neither more nor less.

The next morning, when King Hrothgar awoke, the sweetness of the banquet turned in an instant to the bitterness of betrayal and death. Blood was everywhere, splattered on the walls and in pools on the flagstones. Nobody had woken up, so stealthily had the Grendel come, and now they found that their clothes were stained with the blood of their friends. Bones and twisted scraps of armour lay on the floor, grim reflections of the debris of the night's feasting. At once a great cry of anger and outrage went up. Spears were seized, swords unsheathed. But it was useless. How could they fight an enemy they could not see – an enemy they had never seen?

Twice more the Grendel came to Heorot, each time returning in the twilight hours to claim another thirty Danish warriors. After that, the hall was closed, and with the booming of the door it was as if all happiness had come to an end in the reign of King Hrothgar. A shadow had fallen not only across Heorot but across the whole country and the emptiness of the banqueting hall soon came to be a fitting image for the hollowness in the heart of all Denmark.

Sometimes, King Hrothgar would return alone to his beloved Heorot. He would sit on his raised dais, drawing patterns in the dust with one finger. Then he would search with his eyes to see memories of firelight in the darkness and strain with his ears to hear echoes of laughter in the silence. He was an old man now. Twelve whole winters had passed since the Grendel had come to plague him.

It was at Heorot that he met Beowulf.

He was sitting in his chair, muttering to himself, when the door of the banqueting hall crashed open. He squinted as bright sunlight flooded in, capturing a million motes of dust within its golden beams. A figure stepped forward, silhouetted against the light which could almost have been emanating from his own body. The dust formed a shimmering aura around him. The king trembled. Never had he seen a warrior so tall, so strong.

The stranger approached and fell onto one knee. He was dressed in a blue cloak over a silvery mail-shirt. In one hand he carried a richly decorated shield, in the other a spear. His helmet masked his face but it could not hide the fair hair that tumbled down onto his shoulders nor the bright blue eyes that shone despite the shadows.

'Your majesty!' the figure said.

'Who are you?' Hrothgar demanded, recovering himself.

'My name is Beowulf,' the warrior replied. 'I come from the land of the Geats. I have crossed a great sea to come before you, to serve you. And I do not come alone.'

There was a movement at the door and fourteen more men entered the hall, bringing with them – or so it seemed to the old king – the light that had for so long been absent. As one they knelt before him, forming a semi-circle around his throne.

'We are soldiers of King Hygelac,' Beowulf continued. 'My noble father was Edgetheow, a famous fighter amongst the Geats. I too have found fame in my lifetime, and seek to add to that fame by destroying the beast that has emptied this most stately hall. My own sovereign, ever a friend of the Danes, bids me wish all health to your majesty. He too will be glad to see this monster die.'

'Noble Beowulf!' the king replied. 'Well is your name known to me – and that of your father. I bid you welcome. But this creature has already taken ninety of my finest warriors. I fear your quest is hopeless.'

'Not so!' Beowulf said with a grim smile. 'Tonight, as we feast once again in great Heorot, I will tell you something of my past exploits which will remove your fears for the present.'

And so it was that the servants returned to Heorot and swept the floors and cleaned the tables and relit the beacons and fires. For that one night, Heorot relived its former glory, only this time it was not Danes who filled and refilled their goblets, but Geats. This time the stories were all tales of the exploits of Beowulf, how he had enslaved the five giants and destroyed the seething mass of sea-serpents.

'Your monster comes here unarmed,' he told King Hrothgar, 'so unarmed will I fight it. Yes! Neither sword nor spear will I carry. With my bare hands will I fight and defeat the beast.'

The Geats raised their goblets and broke out in song. The notes were carried by the wind away from Heorot, out and across the fields. Fainter now, they travelled over the swamp until at last they reached the lair of the Grendel. Once again, the poisonous yellow eye flickered open. Its brain turned the information over as though it were chewing a piece of meat. Music. Heorot. Man. It reached out with one hand and pulled itself to its feet.

In the banqueting hall, the Geats had finished eating and were lying on their rugs, their eyes closed. Only Beowulf remained half-awake. He had taken off his coat of mail and helmet and given his sword to his attendant. Unarmed, he lay beside the door, listening to every breath of the wind, to every leaf that rustled on the ground outside.

Gliding through the shadows, the Grendel came. Pushing through the mists that shrouded the moors, it pressed on towards Heorot. When at last it saw the mead-hall, its pace quickened. One scaly foot came down on a twig, snapping it. Beowulf heard the sound and opened his eyes.

The Grendel reached the door of Heorot.

At the touch of its hands, the solid wood crumpled like paper. Two flames ignited in its eyes as it stepped inside, seeing for the first time the fifteen Geats. Saliva dripped from its mouth.

Beowulf had expected it to make straight for him. But one of the young soldiers had chosen to sleep on the other side of the door and it was this unfortunate youth that the monster seized first, tearing him into pieces and swallowing them whole.

Only then, driven to a brutal frenzy by the taste of blood, did the Grendel stretch out its hands and seize Beowulf.

At once it knew that it had made a fatal mistake. Even as its claws tightened, it found itself grasped with a strength that it would have thought impossible in a human. Suddenly afraid, it tried to pull away, to slither back into the darkness in which it had been born, but it was too late. Its whole arm was frozen in Beowulf's grip. Struggle though it might, it could not escape.

It howled. It howled in terror and sobbed in pain. Hearing the sound, the remaining Geats awoke, reaching for their weapons. But although they could make out the shape of a huge bulk beside the door, it was still too dark to see the Grendel, and when they stabbed at it with their swords, somehow their blades passed straight through it, as if through a shadow.

The Grendel screamed at Beowulf, their heads so close that they almost touched. The monster who had never once in its life known fear had now discovered terror. It had to get away, away from the impossible man who still held it in a savage grip. And away it went – snapping the tendons in its own shoulder, unlocking the bones and tearing the skin. Howling with pain, it fled from Heorot, back into the night, blood gushing from the horrible wound that it had inflicted on itself.

And inside the hall, Beowulf held the dreadful trophy of his victory. It was the monster's hand, its arm, its entire torn-off shoulder. These he hung beneath the gable of the roof. Heorot was cleansed. Never again would the creature return.

For the Grendel was dying. Even as it fled, sobbing,

through the night, its life-blood was flowing out of it. By the time it reached its home in the swamp, it was cold, colder than it had ever been before. Tears flowed from its eyes as it buried its raw, jagged shoulder in the mud, trying to ease the pain.

When dawn finally came it was dead. It had died miserably, alone in its lair, and its soul had been welcomed in Hell.

Saint George and the Dragon

Margaret Clark

L ONG, LONG ago there was a city whose inhabitants
lived in constant fear of a dragon. This dragon had
wings as big as a ship's sails and when it flew it
cast a gigantic shadow that terrorized everyone in its
path. In its gaping mouth were three rows of iron teeth,
and its eyes blazed like two bright suns.

No one knew where the dragon had come from. One
morning the people of the city had been woken by a
noise like a roll of thunder and when they rushed out of
their houses to see what had happened they found flocks
of birds screeching and squawking and flying in all
directions, while their animals – cows, sheep and goats –
were running in terror from the pasture by the lake.

After that day the citizens kept their animals safe
within the city walls and bolted the city gates. The
dragon spent most of its time sleeping in the murky
depths of the lake not far from the city walls, but at dusk
it would heave its great body out of the water and
lumber off in search of food. It ate every living thing it
could find and with the flames that roared from its
mouth it charred every tree and blade of grass for miles
around. Then in its fury the dragon came right up to the

city walls and breathed fire and poison into the streets so that all the men, women and children, with the cows, the sheep and the goats, had to shelter wherever they could to escape the heat and the stench of its breath.

'What are we to do?' said the king, who was the most frightened of them all. 'Who is brave enough to go out and fight this dragon?' When no one answered him, he groaned. 'Then if we cannot kill the dragon, we must try to keep it away from our city by leaving food for it near its sleeping place in the lake.'

So they began by dragging two sheep to the lake, where they tethered the animals to a tree-trunk while the dragon slept. That night it did not come near the city and the citizens felt safe in their beds. They did this until there were no more sheep left. Then they took the cows and the goats, and even the cats and the dogs to the dragon, but still its hunger was not satisfied.

At last they realized there was nothing more to offer to the dragon except themselves. But who should be the first? They decided to draw lots. They collected all the small white pebbles they could find and put them in a bag with just one black stone. They tied a string round the top of the bag and pulled it tight until there was only room to put in a hand. Then each citizen in turn, as well as the king and his daughter, picked out a stone. Whoever got the black one was taken out to the dragon's lair so that the rest could live in safety and at peace.

Every day there was much weeping as children lost their fathers, mothers lost their sons and babies lost their grandparents. Then one morning it was the king's daughter who found the black stone in the palm of her hand. The king shouted out in his grief. He loved her so much that he told the people he would give them all his gold and silver in return for her life. But they said, 'No, why should she be spared when so many of *our* children have been sacrificed?'

The princess herself was a good girl and although she was very frightened she knew that her father must share the suffering of his people. So when the king kissed her and said goodbye, she held her head up bravely as she was led out of the city to the dragon's lair. She never looked back and did not flinch as she was bound with ropes to the tree-trunk. But when she was left alone to wait for the moment when the dragon would wake up, she began to cry very quietly.

Then she heard a sudden noise – the sound of a horse's hooves – and across the charred ground came a knight. His horse was pure white, his shield bore a red cross, and his armour was so highly polished that it glittered in the setting sun.

'Why are you weeping?' asked the knight.

'Oh, don't stop,' answered the princess. 'Go on your way quickly or you will surely die, as I shall, very soon.'

'Why are you going to die?' said the knight, and when the princess told him about the dragon he drew his sword from its scabbard and held it above his head. 'Don't be afraid,' he said. 'By the vows I took when I became a knight, I promised to help anyone in distress and to fight evil wherever I find it. Trust me! I shall fight the dragon and I shall win.'

Immediately there was a stirring in the lake as the dragon began to haul itself out of the water. The knight's horse reared in terror as the dragon opened its hideous mouth and roaring flames appeared. But the knight swung his sword against the dragon's wing and when it lifted the wing in pain the knight flung himself against the dragon's body and plunged his sword into its side. The dragon fell to the ground and the knight swiftly freed the princess from the ropes that held her. 'Give me your girdle,' he said, 'and I will bind it round the dragon's neck.'

And when he did this, the dragon closed its cruel jaws, picked up its feet and followed the princess and the knight meekly into the city. The people looked out of their windows and could not believe their eyes. Then the king saw his daughter and rushed to embrace her, shouting for joy that she was alive.

When at last the people dared to creep out of their homes, the knight cut off the dragon's head so that they all knew it was dead and they could live at peace once more. They threw the dragon's body into the lake where it sank and was never seen again. Gradually the grass and trees began to grow and the people returned to enjoying life as they had done before.

The king offered the knight a reward of many gold pieces but the knight would have none of it and asked that it should be given to the poor. Then he left the city and rode away in search of more adventure.

The name of this good knight was George and he became the patron saint of England, being renowned for his courage and devotion. St George's Day is celebrated each year on 23 April, when a feast is given for members of the Order of the Garter, the highest order of knighthood, founded in 1348 by King Edward III, in honour of St George.

The Fire-Bird, the Horse of Power and the Princess Vasilissa

Arthur Ransome

ONCE UPON a time a strong and powerful Tsar ruled in a country far away. And among his servants was a young archer, and this archer had a horse – a horse of power – such a horse as belonged to the wonderful men of long ago – a great horse with a broad chest, eyes like fire, and hoofs of iron. There are no such horses nowadays. They sleep with the strong men who rode them, the bogatirs, until the time comes when Russia has need of them. Then the great horses will thunder up from under the ground, and the valiant men leap from the graves in the armour they have worn so long. The strong men will sit on those horses of power, and there will be swinging of clubs and thunder of hoofs, and the earth will be swept clean from the enemies of God and the Tsar. So my grandfather used to say, and he was as much older than I as I am older than you, little ones, and so he should know.

Well, one day long ago, in the green time of the year, the young archer rode through the forest on his horse of power. The trees were green; there were little blue flowers on the ground under the trees; the squirrels ran in the branches, and the hares in the undergrowth; but no birds sang. The young archer rode along the forest path and listened for the singing of the birds, but there was no singing. The forest was silent, and the only noises in it were the scratching of four-footed beasts, the dropping of fir cones, and the heavy stamping of the horse of power in the soft path.

'What has come to the birds?' said the young archer.

He had scarcely said this before he saw a big curving feather lying in the path before him. The feather was larger than a swan's, larger than an eagle's. It lay in the path, glittering like a flame; for the sun was on it, and it was a feather of pure gold. Then he knew why there was no singing in the forest. For he knew that the fire-bird had flown that way, and that the feather in the path before him was a feather from its burning breast.

The horse of power spoke and said:

'Leave the golden feather, where it lies. If you take it you will be sorry for it, and know the meaning of fear.'

But the brave young archer sat on the horse of power and looked at the golden feather, and wondered whether to take it or not. He had no wish to learn what it was to be afraid, but he thought, 'If I take it and bring it to the Tsar my master, he will be pleased; and he will not send me away with empty hands, for no tsar in the world has a feather from the burning breast of the fire-bird.' And the more he thought, the more he wanted to carry the feather to the Tsar. And in the end he did not listen to the words of the horse of power. He leapt from the saddle, picked up the golden feather of the fire-bird, mounted his horse again, and galloped back through the green forest till he came to the palace of the Tsar.

He went into the palace, and bowed before the Tsar and said:

'O Tsar, I have brought you a feather of the fire-bird.'

The Tsar looked gladly at the feather, and then at the young archer.

'Thank you,' says he; 'but if you have brought me a feather of the fire-bird, you will be able to bring me the bird itself. I should like to see it. A feather is not a fit gift to bring to the Tsar. Bring the bird itself, or, I swear by my sword, your head shall no longer sit between your shoulders!'

The young archer bowed his head and went out. Bitterly he wept, for he knew now what it was to be afraid. He went out into the courtyard, where the horse of power was waiting for him, tossing its head and stamping on the ground.

'Master,' says the horse of power, 'why do you weep?'

'The Tsar has told me to bring him the fire-bird, and no man on earth can do that,' says the young archer, and he bowed his head on his breast.

'I told you,' says the horse of power, 'that if you took the feather you would learn the meaning of fear. Well, do not be frightened yet, and do not weep. The trouble is not now; the trouble lies before you. Go to the Tsar and ask him to have a hundred sacks of maize scattered over the open field, and let this be done at midnight.'

The young archer went back into the palace and begged the Tsar for this, and the Tsar ordered that at midnight a hundred sacks of maize should be scattered on the open field.

Next morning, at the first redness in the sky, the young archer rode out on the horse of power, and came to the open field. The ground was scattered all over with maize. In the middle of the field stood a great oak with spreading boughs. The young archer leapt to the ground, took off the saddle, and let the horse of power loose to wander as he pleased about the field. Then he climbed up into the oak and hid himself among the green boughs.

The sky grew red and gold, and the sun rose. Suddenly there was a noise in the forest round the field. The trees shook and swayed, and almost fell. There was a mighty wind. The sea piled itself into waves with crests of foam, and the fire-bird came flying from the other side of the world. Huge and golden and flaming in the sun, it flew, dropped down with open wings into the field, and began to eat the maize.

The horse of power wandered in the field. This way he went, and that, but always he came a little nearer to the fire-bird. Nearer and nearer came the horse. He came close up to the fire-bird, and then suddenly stepped on one of its spreading fiery wings and pressed it heavily to the ground. The bird struggled, flapping mightily with its fiery wings, but it could not get away. The young archer slipped down from the tree, bound the fire-bird with three strong ropes, swung it on his back, saddled the horse, and rode to the palace of the Tsar.

The young archer stood before the Tsar, and his back was bent under the great weight of the fire-bird, and the broad wings of the bird hung on either side of him like fiery shields, and there was a trail of golden feathers on the floor. The young archer swung the magic bird to the foot of the throne before the Tsar; and the Tsar was glad, because since the beginning of the world no tsar had seen the fire-bird flung before him like a wild duck caught in a snare.

The Tsar looked at the fire-bird and laughed with pride. Then he lifted his eyes and looked at the young archer, and says he:

'As you have known how to take the fire-bird, you will know how to bring me my bride, for whom I have long been waiting. In the land of Never, on the very edge of the world, where the red sun rises in flame from behind the sea, lives the Princess Vasilissa. I will marry none but her. Bring her to me, and I will reward you with silver and gold. But if you do not bring her, then, by my sword, your head will no longer sit between your shoulders!'

The young archer wept bitter tears, and went out into the courtyard where the horse of power was stamping the ground with its hoofs of iron and tossing its thick mane.

'Master, why do you weep?' asked the horse of power.

'The Tsar has ordered me to go to the land of Never, and to bring back the Princess Vasilissa.'

'Do not weep – do not grieve. The trouble is not yet; the trouble is to come. Go to the Tsar and ask him for a silver tent with a golden roof, and for all kinds of food and drink to take with us on the journey.'

The young archer went in and asked the Tsar for this, and the Tsar gave him a silver tent with silver hangings and a gold-embroidered roof, and every kind of rich wine and the tastiest of foods.

Then the young archer mounted the horse of power and rode off to the land of Never. On and on he rode, many days and nights, and came at last to the edge of the world, where the red sun rises in flame from behind the deep blue sea.

On the shore of the sea the young archer reined in the horse of power, and the heavy hoofs of the horse sank in the sand. He shaded his eyes and looked out over the blue water, and there was the Princess Vasilissa in a little silver boat, rowing with golden oars.

The young archer rode back a little way to where the sand ended and the green world began. There he loosed the horse to wander where he pleased, and to feed on the green grass. Then on the edge of the shore, where the green grass ended and grew thin and the sand began, he set up the shining tent, with its silver hangings and its gold-embroidered roof. In the tent he set out the tasty dishes and the rich flagons of wine which the Tsar had given him, and he sat himself down in the tent and began to regale himself, while he waited for the Princess Vasilissa.

The Princess Vasilissa dipped her golden oars in the blue water, and the little silver boat moved lightly through the dancing waves. She sat in the little boat and looked over the blue sea to the edge of the world, and there, between the golden sand and the green earth, she saw the tent standing, silver and gold in the sun. She dipped her oars, and came nearer to see it better. The nearer she came the fairer seemed the tent, and at last she rowed to the shore and grounded her little boat on the golden sand, and stepped out daintily and came up to the tent. She was a little frightened, and now and again she stopped and looked back to where the silver boat lay on the sand with the blue sea beyond it. The young archer said not a word, but went on regaling himself on the pleasant dishes he had set out there in the tent.

At last the Princess Vasilissa came up to the tent and looked in.

The young archer rose and bowed before her. Says he:

'Good day to you, Princess! Be so kind as to come in and take bread and salt with me, and taste my foreign wines.'

And the Princess Vasilissa came into the tent and sat down with the young archer, and ate sweetmeats with him, and drank his health in a golden goblet of the wine the Tsar had given him. Now this wine was heavy, and the last drop from the goblet had no sooner trickled down her little slender throat than her eyes closed against her will, once, twice, and again.

'Ah me!' says the Princess, 'it is as if the night itself had perched on my eyelids, and yet it is but noon.'

And the golden goblet dropped to the ground from

her little fingers, and she leant back on a cushion and fell instantly asleep. If she had been beautiful before, she was lovelier still when she lay in that deep sleep in the shadow of the tent.

Quickly the young archer called to the horse of power. Lightly he lifted the Princess in his strong young arms. Swiftly he leapt with her into the saddle. Like a feather she lay in the hollow of his left arm, and slept while the iron hoofs of the great horse thundered over the ground.

They came to the Tsar's palace, and the young archer leapt from the horse of power and carried the Princess into the palace. Great was the joy of the Tsar; but it did not last for long.

'Go, sound the trumpets for our wedding,' he said to his servants, 'let all the bells be rung.'

The bells rang out and the trumpets sounded, and at the noise of the horns and the ringing of the bells the Princess Vasilissa woke up and looked about her.

'What is this ringing of bells,' says she, 'and this noise of trumpets? And where, oh, where is the blue sea, and my little silver boat with its golden oars?' And the Princess put her hand to her eyes.

'The blue sea is far away,' says the Tsar, 'and for your little silver boat I give you a golden throne. The trumpets sound for our wedding, and the bells are ringing for our joy.'

But the Princess turned her face away from the Tsar; and there was no wonder in that, for he was old, and his eyes were not kind.

And she looked with love at the young archer; and there was no wonder in that either, for he was a young man fit to ride the horse of power.

The Tsar was angry with the Princess Vasilissa, but his anger was as useless as his joy.

'Why, Princess,' says he, 'will you not marry me, and forget your blue sea and your silver boat?'

'In the middle of the deep blue sea lies a great stone,' says the Princess, 'and under that stone is hidden my wedding-dress. If I cannot wear that dress I will marry nobody at all.'

Instantly the Tsar turned to the young archer, who was waiting before the throne.

'Ride swiftly back,' says he, 'to the land of Never, where the red sun rises in flame. There – do you hear what the Princess says? – a great stone lies in the middle of the sea. Under that stone is hidden her wedding-dress. Ride swiftly. Bring back that dress, or, by my sword, your head shall no longer sit between your shoulders!'

The young archer wept bitter tears, and went out into the courtyard, where the horse of power was waiting for him, champing its golden bit.

'There is no way of escaping death this time,' he said.

'Master, why do you weep?' asked the horse of power.

'The Tsar has ordered me to ride to the land of Never, to fetch the wedding-dress of the Princess Vasilissa from the bottom of the deep blue sea. Besides, the dress is wanted for the Tsar's wedding, and I love the Princess myself.'

'What did I tell you?' says the horse of power. 'I told you that there would be trouble if you picked up the golden feather from the fire-bird's burning breast. Well, do not be afraid. The trouble is not yet; the trouble is to come. Up! into the saddle with you, and away for the wedding-dress of the Princess Vasilissa!'

The young archer leapt into the saddle, and the horse of power, with his thundering hoofs, carried him swiftly through the green forests and over the bare plains, till they came to the edge of the world, to the land of Never, where the red sun rises in flame from behind the deep blue sea. There they rested, at the very edge of the sea.

The young archer looked sadly over the wide waters, but the horse of power tossed its mane and did not look at the sea, but on the shore. This way and that it looked, and saw at last a huge lobster moving slowly, sideways, along the golden sand.

Nearer and nearer came the lobster, and it was a giant among lobsters, the tsar of all the lobsters; and it moved slowly along the shore, while the horse of power moved carefully and as if by accident, until it stood between the lobster and the sea. Then when the lobster came close by, the horse of power lifted an iron hoof and set if firmly on the lobster's tail.

'You will be the death of me!' screamed the lobster – as well he might, with the heavy foot of the horse of power pressing his tail into the sand. 'Let me live, and I will do whatever you ask of me.'

'Very well,' says the horse of power, 'we will let you live,' and he slowly lifted his foot. 'But this is what you shall do for us. In the middle of the blue sea lies a great stone, and under that stone is hidden the wedding-dress of the Princess Vasilissa. Bring it here.'

The lobster groaned with the pain in his tail. Then he cried out in a voice that could be heard all over the deep blue sea. And the sea was disturbed, and from all sides lobsters in thousands made their way towards the bank. And the huge lobster that was the oldest of them all and the tsar of all the lobsters that live between the rising and the setting of the sun, gave them the order and sent them back into the sea. And the young archer sat on the horse of power and waited.

After a little time the sea was disturbed again, and the lobsters in their thousands came to the shore, and with them they brought a golden casket in which was the wedding-dress of the Princess Vasilissa. They had taken it from under the great stone that lay in the middle of the sea.

The tsar of all the lobsters raised himself painfully on his bruised tail and gave the casket into the hands of the young archer, and instantly the horse of power turned himself about and galloped back to the palace of the Tsar, far, far away, at the other side of the green forests and beyond the treeless plains.

The young archer went into the palace and gave the casket into the hands of the Princess, and looked at her with sadness in his eyes, and she looked at him with love. Then she went away into an inner chamber, and came back in her wedding-dress, fairer than the spring itself. Great was the joy of the Tsar. The wedding feast was made ready, and the bells rang, and flags waved above the palace.

The Tsar held out his hand to the Princess, and looked at her with his old eyes. But she would not take his hand.

'No,' says she, 'I will marry nobody until the man who brought me here has done penance in boiling water.'

Instantly the Tsar turned to his servants and ordered them to make a great fire, and to fill a great cauldron with water and set it on the fire, and, when the water should be at its hottest, to take the young archer and throw him into it, to do penance for having taken the Princess Vasilissa away from the land of Never.

There was no gratitude in the mind of that Tsar.

Swiftly the servants brought wood and made a mighty fire, and on it they laid a huge cauldron of water, and built the fire round the walls of the cauldron. The fire burned hot and the water steamed. The fire burned hotter, and the water bubbled and seethed. They made ready to take the young archer, to throw him into the cauldron.

'Oh, misery!' thought the young archer. 'Why did I ever take the golden feather that had fallen from the fire-bird's burning breast? Why did I not listen to the wise words of the horse of power?' And he remembered the horse of power, and he begged the Tsar:

'O lord Tsar, I do not complain. I shall presently die in the heat of the water on the fire. Suffer me, before I die, once more to see my horse.'

'Let him see his horse,' says the Princess.

'Very well,' says the Tsar. 'Say good-bye to your horse, for you will not ride him again. But let your farewells be short, for we are waiting.'

The young archer crossed the courtyard and came to the horse of power, who was scraping the ground with his iron hoofs.

'Farewell, my horse of power,' says the young archer. 'I should have listened to your words of wisdom, for now the end is come, and we shall never more see the green trees pass above us and the ground disappear beneath us, as we race the wind between the earth and the sky.'

'Why so?' says the horse of power.

'The Tsar has ordered that I am to be boiled to death – thrown into that cauldron that is seething on the great fire.'

'Fear not,' says the horse of power, 'for the Princess Vasilissa has made him do this, and the end of these things is better than I thought. Go back, and when they are ready to throw you in the cauldron, do you run boldly and leap yourself into the boiling water.'

The young archer went back across the courtyard, and the servants made ready to throw him into the cauldron.

'Are you sure that the water is boiling?' says the Princess Vasilissa.

'It bubbles and seethes,' said the servants.

'Let me see for myself,' says the Princess, and she went to the fire and waved her hand above the cauldron. And some say there was something in her hand, and some say there was not.

'It is boiling,' says she, and the servants laid hands on the young archer; but he threw them from him, and ran and leapt boldly before them all into the very middle of the cauldron.

Twice he sank below the surface, borne round with the bubbles and foam of the boiling water. Then he leapt from the cauldron and stood before the Tsar and the Princess. He had become so beautiful a youth that all who saw cried aloud in wonder.

'This is a miracle,' says the Tsar. And the Tsar looked at the beautiful young archer, and thought of himself – of his age, of his bent back, and his grey beard, and his toothless gums. 'I too will become beautiful,' thinks he, and he rose from his throne and clambered into the cauldron, and was boiled to death in a moment.

And the end of the story? They buried the Tsar, and made the young archer Tsar in his place. He married the Princess Vasilissa, and lived many years with her in love and good fellowship. And he built a golden stable for the horse of power, and never forgot what he owed to him.

The Three Tests

James Riordan

I N THE lands of the Sioux, upon the right bank of what is now the Mississippi River in Dakota, there was once a village of the Dakota people. And in that village lived a young woman of great grace and beauty. So lovely was she that suitors came from far and near to win her love. But, besides being very beautiful, she was also extremely difficult to please: she set such hard tests for would-be lovers that none could win her heart.

Not far off in what is now the Missouri Valley lived a young brave who came to hear of the maid's great charms; and he made up his mind to woo and win her. The difficulty of the task did not daunt him, and he set off upon his journey full of determination.

On his way he climbed a hill and saw in the distance a mighty mountain. Imagine his surprise when that mountain suddenly crumbled to dust and a level plain appeared in its place. As he came closer, he noticed a man with a long rake levelling the soil.

Realizing the man was so strong he could move mountains, the young brave immediately invited him to join his quest; perhaps the Strong One could help him in his mission. The man agreed and on they went together.

They had not gone far when the young brave saw in the distance a man with great rocks tied to his ankles.

'Why have you tied these great stones to your ankles?' he asked.

'Oh,' replied the man, 'every time I chase buffalo, I run so fast I overtake and lose them; so I tie stones to my ankles to slow me down.'

The young suitor at once invited the Swift One to join him on his mission, and the fellow readily agreed.

The three companions were walking along when they spied two great lakes beside which sat a man who kept bowing his head to drink the water. Surprised that he did not quench his thirst, the young brave asked, 'Why do you sit there drinking so much water?'

'Because,' said the man, 'I can never drink enough water; once I have finished this lake, I shall start on the other.'

Straightaway, the young suitor invited the Thirsty One to join them on their mission. So now there were four companions walking along. They had not gone far when they noticed a man with his eyes raised to the sky. Curious to know why he was looking up, the young brave approached and asked, 'Why do you walk with your eyes turned skywards?'

'I have shot an arrow into the sky and am waiting for it to fall,' the man said.

Such a Skilful Archer could well be useful in their mission; so he, too, was invited to join the group.

Not long after, the band of companions was making its way through a forest when it came upon a strange sight: there before it was a man lying on the ground with his ear pressed to the soil.

'Friend,' asked the young brave, 'what are you doing?'

'I am listening to the plants breathing,' replied the man.

'Who knows,' thought the suitor, 'perhaps Keen Ear will be of help to me in my mission?'

So he, too, was invited to join the band.

In the course of time the six companions arrived at their destination, and the young brave explained his mission. The villagers shook their heads: did he not know how impossible was his task?

When they realized he would not be dissuaded, they led him and his companions to a great boulder that overshadowed the village.

'If you wish to win the beautiful maiden,' they said, 'you must first remove this boulder; it keeps the sunlight from us.'

'But that is impossible,' muttered the young brave in despair.

'Not so,' said the Strong One. 'Nothing could be simpler.'

So saying, he put his shoulder to the boulder and, with a terrible crash, it crumbled into many pieces, strewing rocks and stones across the plain.

For the second test, the villagers brought great baskets of food and cauldrons of water.

'You must eat every crumb and drink every last drop of water,' they said.

Being hungry, the travellers managed to consume all the food. But the poor suitor gazed sadly at the great cauldrons of water.

'Alas,' he said, 'no one can drink all that.'

'Not so,' said the Thirsty One. And in the twinkling of an eye, he had drunk it all, every last drop.

The villagers were amazed.

'But the last test is the hardest,' they declared.

At that, the lovely maiden herself stepped forward.

'You must run a race with me,' she said to the young brave. 'But I warn you: no one has ever beaten me.

Should you do so, you will have passed the three tests and I shall marry you.'

Naturally, the young brave chose the Swift One for this test. As the runners started, the onlookers watched them until they disappeared out of sight, surprised that there was nothing between them. Gradually, however, the maid began to tire. She had never been challenged by such a fast runner, and she turned to the Swift One, saying:

'Come, let us rest awhile before we complete the final leg.'

The man agreed, but no sooner had he sat down than he fell asleep. The young woman seized her opportunity: she raced off back to the village, as hard as she could go.

In the meantime, the five companions were anxiously awaiting the return of the two runners. Great was their disappointment when they saw the woman come into sight on her own.

Keen Ear at once pressed his ear to the ground, listening hard.

Looking up, he told his companions:

'He is fast asleep. I can hear him snoring.'

At that the Skilful Archer stepped forward and loosed an arrow from his bow. So accurate was his aim that it just nipped the sleeper's nose as it landed, rousing him from his slumbers. At once he jumped to his feet, looking round for the woman. Realizing he had been tricked, he raced away to try to catch up with her.

Just as she was about to pass the winning post he surged past her and won the race.

So the young brave had passed all three tests and, to great rejoicing from his companions, he and the lovely maid were married. And the two lived together in peace and happiness, producing many children to tell their story throughout the nations of the Sioux.

Two Giants

Edna O'Brien

FINN WAS the biggest and the bravest giant in all of Ireland. His deeds were known far and wide, lions lay down before him, his chariot flashed like a comet through the fields of battle, and with his 'Venomous' Sword he lay low a hundred men while with the other hand casting his sling at a troop of deer or a herd of wild boar. Along with that he had a thumb of knowledge and when he sucked his thumb he could tell what was happening anywhere in Ireland and he could foretell the future encounters. Now when Finn was no longer young, the rumour went about that there was a giant in Scotland who was Finn's equal and his name was McConigle. McConigle was not only fierce in battle, but when he walked up a hill the earth trembled under his feet, the trees wobbled, and the wild game fled to their lairs. By one blow of his fist he flattened a thunderbolt one day, turned it into the shape of a pancake and kept it in his pocket as a souvenir. He too had a way of prophecising by putting his middle finger into his mouth and sucking on it. Now the two giants had never met but it was reported that McConigle intended to come over to Ireland, to fight Finn and to give him a pasting.

It so happened that one day Finn and his men were away from home and were busy making a bridge across the Giant's Causeway. In the distance they could see a messenger galloping towards them and Finn wondered if his wife Oonagh had taken sick or if there had been some breach in their fortifications at home. The messenger announced that Finn was to come home at once and then whispered something in Finn's ear that made him tremble with rage.

'So he's on my trail,' said Finn as he stood up and with that he pulled up a big fir tree, banged the clay off it and with his knife snedded it into a walking stick, so that it was both a walking stick and an umbrella. To see Finn walk was like seeing a mountain move and in no time he was across one county and heading towards home. He was going up a slope when in the mud he saw footmarks which were as big as his own. In fact they were the exact shape as his own and Finn thought 'Lo' and had his first feeling of terror and doubt. Never before had he come across a giant the length and breadth of whose feet were as enormous as his own. He widened his chest and let out an almighty roar just to make his presence felt and it echoed all over the valley and was heard by his wife in her own home.

Finn's palace was on the top of a hill called Knock-many and it looked out on another mountain called Culamore and there was a deep gorge in between. Finn had settled here so that he could see his enemies a long way off and as well as that he could throw the bodies of his prey into the gorge for the crows to fatten themselves on.

'Oh my bilberry,' said Finn as he saw his wife Oonagh who had plaited her hair and put on a silk dress to please him. At once Finn asked if the reason she had sent for him was true.

''Tis true, Avick,' said Oonagh and went on to tell him how McConigle had pitched tent at the far side of the province and had his famous thunderbolt in the shape of a pancake in his pocket, and called himself The Invincible. Finn put his thumb into his mouth to verify all these things and found that they were true. He could only use his gift of prophecy on very trying and solemn occasions such as this was.

'Finn darling, don't bite your thumb,' said Oonagh very sweetly as she led him into the house where there was a dinner prepared. Finn squatted at one end of the low table, Oonagh at the other and along with maidens to wait on them there were harpists playing in order to soothe Finn. He started by having sixteen duck eggs, eight pig's crubeens and three raw onions for his digestion. The main course was a haunch of roast venison and it was so long that it stretched between them down the length of the table, a sizzling roast dotted with berries and all sorts of herbs. But no matter how much he ate or drank there was a frown on Finn's forehead and a big brown ridge like a furrow on the bridge of his nose because of his thinking.

'Dearest,' said Oonagh as she bobbed along and began to stroke his great naked back. Finn always removed his cloak before he sat down to eat.

'You'll best him, you always do,' said Oonagh, but Finn shook his head and said it was perilous because according to this thumb he and McConigle had equal amounts of strength, ate the same amount of food, weighed the same, and were equally matched in daring, wisdom and cunning.

'What else does it say?' Oonagh asked and Finn put his thumb right inside his mouth and shut his eyes in order to concentrate.

'Take care you don't draw blood,' said Oonagh.

'He's coming,' said Finn, 'he's below in Dungannon,' and at that he jumped up.

'When will he be here?' said Oonagh.

'He'll be here before long,' said Finn and he began to put his vest and his jacket on. He looked at his wife and for the first time she saw fear and apprehension in his eyes. She decided that she would have to help him and make use of her own enchantments. Oonagh was in with the fairies too and with her wand had once turned a hussy into a hound. She told Finn that she would help him to succeed.

'How, how?' said Finn, hitting the table and sending delph in all directions.

Oonagh hurried out of the doorway in order to give a message to her sister who lived on the opposite mountain at Culamore.

'Grania,' said Oonagh, 'are you at home?'

'I'm in the kitchen garden,' said Grania, 'I'm picking berries for a tart.'

'Run up to the top of the hill and look about you and tell us if you see anything untoward,' said Oonagh. They waited for a few minutes with Finn pacing up and down and servants fanning him with great leaves.

'I am there now,' said Grania.

'What do you see?' said Oonagh.

'Oh lawsie me,' exclaimed Grania, 'I see the biggest giant I've ever seen coming out of the town of Dungannon.'

'What is he like?' said Oonagh.

'He's something terrible to behold,' said Grania and went on to describe a giant of about twelve feet in height, his hair all the way down to his waist, his face ruddy like any giant's except that he had daubed blood over it and, most unnerving of all, his three eyes. He had an eye in the middle of his head that was rolling round like the hands of a clock. Not only was the ground shaking beneath him but the birds in the trees were dying of fright. Along with that he was laughing out loud as if he had just heard the most hilarious joke.

'He's coming up to leather Finn,' said Oonagh to her sister.

'Finn has my sympathy,' said Grania and then she just announced that the giant had picked up a white goat and was wringing its neck and was obviously going to eat it raw.

'I'll tell you what,' said Oonagh, 'call down to him and invite him up to your place for a bite to eat.'

'Why so?' said Finn, unable to follow his wife's drift of thought.

'Strategy,' said Oonagh, 'strategy.'

Grania called across to say she'd be glad to oblige and she'd entertain the monster but she was a bit short of bacon and of butter.

'I'll fling you some across,' said Oonagh and she snapped her fingers for a servant to bring a flitch of bacon and a firkin of butter. However, before throwing them she forgot to say her charms and didn't the butter and the bacon fall into a stream and get carried away.

'Never mind,' said Grania, 'I'll give him heather soup and I'll put shredded bark in it to give him indigestion.'

'Good on you,' said Oonagh and she winked at Finn.

'He'll skewer me,' said Finn.

'Don't be ridiculous,' said Oonagh, although to tell you the truth she could see a situation where she herself might be a dainty morsel, a little fritter for the giant's supper.

'My courage is leaving me, I'll be disgraced,' said Finn.

'Two heads are better than one,' said Oonagh as she went towards the place where she kept her magic threads. She drew nine woollen threads of different

colours, she plaited them into three plaits, with three
colours in each one; she put a plait on her right arm,
another round her right ankle, a third round her heart,
and in that way Oonagh was protected. Then she got
going. She asked the servants to go up in the loft and
bring down iron griddles and a child's cradle. She got
them to make cakes but she hid the griddles inside the
cakes and then baked them in the fire in the usual way.
When they were done she dusted them over with flour so
as to hide any protuberances and she put them on the
window to cool. Then she put down a large pot of milk
which she later made into curds and whey and showed
Finn how to pick up a curd in his hand and make it
smooth as a stone. Then she got a nightgown and a shawl
and dressed Finn in it and put a nightcap on his head.
She told him that he would have to get into the cradle
and completely cover himself with clothes, with only his
two eyes peering out.

'I can't fit in a cradle,' said Finn.

'You'll have to double up,' said Oonagh.

'I'll have to triple up,' said Finn as she pushed him
towards it.

'You must pass for your own child,' said Oonagh.

'But I'm not a child,' said Finn and he was afraid that
he had taken the cowardice too far. Oonagh ignored his
mutterings and just put him into the cradle and covered
him up with great wool blankets and red deerskins.

'What do I do?' said Finn.

'Whist,' said Oonagh because they could hear the
bruiser coming up the hill and giving a skelp of his axe
to the dogs to shut them up. He strutted across the
courtyard and when he arrived at their door he put a
hand around either oak pillar and bellowed 'Anyone
home?'

Oonagh came forward all shy and mincing and gave a

little gasp to signify to him how formidable he was. He had rat skins and coon skins dangling from his ears and his third eye was rolling about like a spinning top.

'Mr McConigle,' said Oonagh.

'The great McConigle,' said the giant and then asked if he was in the house of Finn.

'Indeed you are,' said Oonagh and gestured towards a chair to make him welcome.

'You're Mrs Finn, I suppose,' said the giant.

'I am,' said she, 'and a proud wife at that.'

'Thinks he's the toughest giant in Ireland,' said McConigle.

'It's a proven fact,' said his wife proudly.

'There's a man within three feet of you that's very desirous of having a tussle with him,' said McConigle and he looked around in order to sniff out his rival.

'Is he hiding from me?' he asked.

'Hiding?' said Oonagh. 'He left here frothing, he's gone out to find you and it's lucky for you you didn't meet him, or you'd be a dead man now, your head on his pike as an ornament.'

'You vixen,' said McConigle and he roared with rage but Oonagh was in no way dismayed.

'He's twice your height and much better built,' said she.

'You don't know my strength,' said McConigle.

'In that case would you turn the house,' said Oonagh.

The giant stood up, put his middle finger in his mouth, thought for an instant, then went out, put his arms around the house, picked it up and put it facing a different way. Finn in his cradle was now facing in a different direction and there was sweat pouring out of him with heat and nerves.

'You're a handy giant,' said Oonagh and then told him that she was short of water, but that there was a fine spring under some rocks and that if he could split the rocks she'd be most obliged. He took his axe out from under his leather apron, struck at the rocks and tore a cleft that was hundreds of feet deep. Oonagh began to have doubts.

'Come in and eat,' said she and added that although her husband would make mince of him, the laws of hospitality must be observed.

She placed before him six cakes of the bread and a mound of newly churned butter and she sat down pretending to be polite. He put one of the cakes in his mouth, took a bite and let out the most terrible growl.

'What kind of bread is this?' he said fiercely.

'Fresh bread,' said Oonagh, cool as a breeze.

'And here are two teeth of mine gone,' said he as he hauled out two big molars that were grey in colour and shaped like drinking horns.

'Why,' said Oonagh, 'that's Finn's bread, the only bread that he eats, him and the child there.' At that she offered another cake. As soon as he put it in his mouth another great crack was heard and he let out a yell far fiercer than the first, so that the baby mewled. 'Thunder and giblets,' said he as he pulled out two more teeth with bits of gum on them.

'Well, Mr McConigle,' said Oonagh, 'if you can't manage the bread, don't bother with it but don't be disturbing my child.'

'Mammy, mammy, can I have some bread?' said the baby from the cradle and its voice gave McConigle a start. Oonagh very cleverly handed a cake that had no griddle in and McConigle was flabbergasted as he watched the child gobble it up.

'I'd like to take a glimpse at that lad in the cradle,' said he.

'Certainly,' said Oonagh and she told the little baby to

get up and prove himself the worthy child of his father. Now the baby stood up, looked at McConigle and said, 'Are you as strong as me?'

'Thundering giblets,' said McConigle, 'how dare you insult me.'

'Can you squeeze water out of a stone?' said the child, and he put a stone into McConigle's hand. McConigle squeezed and squeezed but not a drop of liquid came out.

'Watch me,' said the child and he put his hands under the covers, took out one of the white curds that looked exactly like a stone and squeezed until the liquid came out in a little shower from his hands.

'My daddy is training me,' said he, 'but I have a lot to learn yet.'

McConigle was speechless,

'I'll go back to sleep now,' said the child, 'but I'd hate to waste my time on anyone that hasn't my daddy's strength, that can't eat daddy's bread or squeeze water out of a stone.' Then he slipped down and as Oonagh was pulling the covers up over him he raised his index finger and gave a word of warning to McConigle. 'I'd be off out of here if I were you as it's in flummery my father will have you.'

'What he says is a fact,' said Oonagh as she tucked Finn into the cradle and patted him to let him know how proud she was.

'I'm thinking it is,' said McConigle.

'You're not in his league at all,' said Oonagh and went on to remind McConigle that if the child was that strong he could only guess at the immensity of the father.

'Will you let me feel the teeth of that infant?' said he still in a quandary.

'By all means,' said Oonagh and she took his hand and she stuck it straight into Finn's mouth explaining that the child's best teeth were in the back of his head. McConigle was amazed to find a baby with a full set of grinders and more amazed when he felt something snap and then felt his finger detach itself and when he pulled out his hand there was a big wound where his finger of knowledge had been. Finn had eaten it. So shocked was he and so horror-stricken that he fell down. Finn rose from the cradle and laid roundly on the monster with his bare hands. He could easily have killed him with his sword but that McConigle begged for his life and Finn being a chivalrous hero gave it to him. After that McConigle made his peace, picked up his teeth and his accoutrements and promised to go home to Scotland and never set foot in Ireland again.

The Wise Men of Gotham

Kevin Crossley-Holland

1 TWO MEN from Gotham met on Nottingham Bridge.
One of them was on his way to the market to buy
sheep and the other was on his way home.

'Good morning!' said the man coming from the village.

'Where are you going?' said the man coming from the
market.

'Market!' said the first man. 'I'm going to buy some
sheep.'

'Sheep!' said the other. 'How will you get them home?'

'Over this bridge, of course,' said the first man.

'By Robin Hood,' said the second man, 'you will not!'

'By Maid Marian,' said the first, 'I certainly will!'

'You will not,' said the second man.

'I will,' said the first.

Then the two men began to hammer the ground with
their staves. They pounded the cobbles and the bridge
boomed.

'Keep your sheep back!' the first man shouted.

'Beware!' yelled the second. 'Beware or mine will leap
over the parapet!'

'My sheep will all come home this way,' bawled the
first man.

'They will not!' shouted the other.

While they were arguing, another wise man from Gotham rode up to the bridge on his way home from the market. He had a sack of meal up in the saddle behind him.

For a while this man listened to his neighbours arguing about their sheep, with not one sheep in sight. Then he jumped down from his horse. 'You fools!' he called. 'Will you never learn sense?'

The man's two neighbours turned and looked at him.

'Come on!' he said. 'Help me get this sack up on to my shoulder.'

When the man with the meal had shouldered his sack, he went over to the parapet, untied the sack's mouth, and shook out all the meal into the river. 'How much meal is there in this sack?' he asked.

'None,' said the first man.

'None,' said the second man.

'There's just as much meal in this sack,' said the wise man, 'as you have wit in your two heads, arguing over sheep you don't even own.'

So which of these three men was the wisest?

2 'That cuckoo,' said the boys of Gotham. 'Let's capture it and then we'll be able to hear it sing all year round.'

So the boys made a circular hedge and then they caught the cuckoo and put her into it.

'Here you are,' said one.

'And here you'll stay,' said another, 'and sing all the year round.'

'Otherwise,' said a third, 'you'll have nothing to eat or drink.'

The cuckoo looked at the boys. She looked at the circuit of the hedge, and spread her wings and flew away.

'Curses!' shouted the boys. 'We'll get her! We didn't make our hedge high enough.'

3 Twelve men from Gotham made up a fishing party. Some of them fished from the bank of the stream; a few of them waded into the water – right up to their shins.

Before they left for home, one of the men said, 'What an adventure we've had today, wading and all! I hope to God none of us have been drowned.'

'Let's check before we leave,' said another man. 'There were twelve of us set out from home.'

So each man counted his neighbours and every one of them counted up to eleven.

'One of us is missing,' they said. 'One of us has been drowned.'

The men walked up and down the little stream where they had been fishing, looking for the missing man, wringing their hands, and sighing and moaning.

At this moment, one of the king's courtiers rode up. 'What's wrong?' he asked. 'What are you looking for?' 'Oh!' cried the men. 'We've been fishing here today. Twelve of us! One of us has been drowned.'

'You count,' said the courtier. 'One of you count again and I'll check.'

So one man walked round and counted his neighbours. But he did not count himself.

'Well!' said the courtier. 'Well! Well! What will you give me if I can find the twelfth man?'

'All the money in my pocket!' said one man.

'All mine too!' cried another.

The wise men of Gotham promised to give the courtier every coin they had on them.

'All right!' said the courtier. 'Give me the money!'

As the courtier walked round the group, collecting the

money, he thwacked each man over the shoulders with his whip and began to count, 'One, two, three . . .' When the courtier came to the last man, he thwacked him especially hard and called out, 'Here he is! Here's the twelfth man!'

The wise men rubbed their shoulders. 'God bless you!' they said. 'You've found our friend and neighbour.'

4 A man from Gotham was on his way to the market at Nottingham to sell his cheeses. On his way down the hill to Nottingham Bridge, one of the cheeses toppled out of his shoulder bag and ran down the hill.

'Ah!' said the man. 'So you're able to run down the hill on your own.' He looked at the cheese, rolling and cart-wheeling down the slope, and it started him thinking. 'In that case,' he said, 'I expect the other cheeses can run too. I'll get them all to run down the hill.'

So the wise man swung the heavy bag off his shoulders, and took out the cheeses, and sent them tumbling down the hill one after another. One disappeared into a thorn bush, one rolled into a rabbit-hole, one ran into a thicket. The man wagged a finger at the disappearing cheeses. 'Make sure,' he shouted, 'that you all meet me in the market-place.'

The man stayed at Nottingham market until it was almost over. Then he made his way round, asking friends and strangers alike whether they had seen his cheeses.

'Why?' asked another man from Gotham. 'Who is bringing them?'

'They are!' said the man. 'They're bringing themselves.'

'Bringing themselves!'

'And they know the way well enough, damn them!' exclaimed the man. 'When I saw my cheeses running so fast, I was afraid that they would overrun this marketplace. I should think they're almost in York by now.'

So the man spent what money he had with him on the loan of a horse. He rode after his cheeses. He galloped all the way to York.

But no one has been able to find out where the cheeses got to, not from that day to this.

5 A woman of Gotham was walking home from a neighbour's cottage late at night. In fact, it was after midnight.

As she passed the horse-pond, she saw a whole green cheese floating just under the surface.

'My word!' she exclaimed. 'This is worth some effort.'

She ran back to her cottage, shouting as she went. Her husband heard her and all her neighbours, lying in their beds, heard her too. They jumped up, they opened their little windows.

'There's a green cheese in the pond,' bawled the woman. 'Come and help me rake it out!'

The woman's friends and neighbours hurried out of their little cottages in their nightshirts and nightcaps. They all brought their rakes and began to drag the surface of the pond.

Just then a passing cloud sank the cheese. The woman sighed a deep sigh and all her neighbours went back to their beds, disappointed.

The Storm Child

Nancy Cutt

I N STORM she came, and in storm she went. Washed up on the ness many, many years ago, the Storm Child was plucked from a rock pool by Jamie Dass, the crofter. The gale that cast her ashore had, in the same night, scattered the wreckage of a great Indiaman along the island skerries; Jamie Dass lost a chance at some good driftwood while he took the foundling home to his wife.

Nothing was ever discovered about her. No women survived the wreck of the Indiaman; none of the half-dozen men who came ashore knew of there being an infant aboard. And so James and Mary Dass kept the Storm Child.

She was tiny: by her size, perhaps a year old. Mary Dass warmed her and coaxed her to drink a little milk. Then she carefully cut away the thin, soaked, greenish scraps like tatters of seaweed that clung to the fragile limbs. All the while the babe skirled tearlessly, high and thin like a seagull's wail. But Mary persevered, cleaning away the ragged wisps until only a fine dark line remained down each leg from hip to heel. These she could not wash away, so like a wise woman – or a fool – she said nothing about them. Wrapping the babe in a bit of linen cloth, she rocked it gently and it slept. In a few days it was thriving, a silent little creature who never cried.

They called her Sibilla. Their only child, a grown man by now, lived away from the island, and Mary Dass was glad to have this one for company. Not much company, said the neighbours: indeed, Sibilla did not speak until she was near ten years old by Mary's reckoning. She was a delicate-looking girl, pale and thin, with long lank fair hair. Most of the time she was gentle and biddable, though absentminded.

She did little enough to help her foster parents. She would feed the hens and tend the cow, or gather a little driftwood if Mary or Jamie were with her. Left to herself on the sands, she was forgetful, returning, most likely, with only a handful of shells. She shrank and shuddered away from the fire and never learned to cook. But Mary made much of her and would hear no word against her.

Others looked askance at Sibilla. Why, they asked, did she not play with other children? Why did she slip away whenever possible from her foster mother, on the way to kirk? And hide from the minister? They recalled that her christening had put her into convulsions . . . It was uncanny too, the way she listened by the hour to the murmur of a large, spotted cowrie shell that some earlier oceangoing Dass had brought home.

'What do you hear, Sibilla?' said Mary casually one day when the child had laid the shell down for a moment. Surprisingly, Sibilla answered.

'My sea,' she said clearly in a sweet, caressing voice. She picked up the cowrie again, and her clear, light blue eyes once more gazed vacantly past her foster mother.

Delighted and amazed, Mary poured forth a torrent of questions and exclamations. But Sibilla did not reply. Pressed, she withdrew into a corner, her downcast eyes greenish and evasive in the shadow.

Mary did not give up.

'You can go down to the shore and hear the sea, Sibilla,' she said another day. 'You do not need the shell to listen to the sea.'

Sibilla shook her head. '*My* sea,' she said again, and ran her delicate hand over the spotted curves of the cowrie.

'What does the whelk say?' asked Mary, thinking to humour her. Sibilla did not reply. She never listened to the murmur of the whelk.

Having found that her foster child could talk, Mary Dass tried in vain to provoke further speech. Sibilla said nothing more for months. She was growing fast, and growing very pretty. Her limp fine hair had lost its faint greenish sheen and glinted gold in the sunlight. The pallor of her skin was now delicately rose-tinted, her thin face rounding out.

When by Mary's reckoning Sibilla was about twelve, one of the island families moved away. Among the dispersed contents of their cottage was a handsome shell, a nautilus, all spiral coils and pink pearly mouth. Thinking to please Sibilla, James Dass brought it home and put it into her hands. The colour ran up into her face, and her blue eyes came suddenly to life. She sat down, entranced, and raised it to her ear.

'What do you hear, lassie?' asked James, who had doubted Mary's account of Sibilla's speech.

'*My* sea!' said Sibilla. 'My sea calling.'

'There, James!' said Mary triumphantly. She turned to Sibilla. 'What does it say?'

'It says *listen*,' replied Sibilla.

And she spoke no more, shrinking away unhappily when questioned.

Day after day thereafter she listened intently to the new shell, often with signs of pleasure. Then came an equinoctial gale with high wind and rain squalls alternating with sun. All day Sibilla moved restlessly about the cottage from window to door, careless with her little tasks. Towards evening, Mary chided her gently.

'Put the shell up, Sibilla. You must do your work first.'

But the girl clutched the nautilus fiercely and backed away. Her eyes gleamed a cold blue-green, and her hair seemed to crackle and glint of itself.

'No,' she cried. 'No!'

'Sibilla!' said her foster-mother anxiously, 'What is wrong? What do you hear?'

The Storm Child had raised the shell and was listening with parted lips. Her eyes blazed eerily with lambent fire.

'My sisters!' she cried shrilly. 'My sisters are calling! Now I can find the way!'

Flinging off her woollen shawl and tearing at the neck of her shift, she whirled and ran out into the gale, moving clumsily in her long homespun skirt. Mary followed as fast as her stiff limbs permitted. Sibilla made for the ness where the water was breaking white. She paused at the edge of the rocks to shed her shift and drop her heavy skirt. Then, golden hair flying, she ran swiftly, her back and shoulders gleaming white in a momentary ray of sunlight. From the waist down, flowing green folds rippled around her as she fled across the rocks. At the edge, she bent, and swept the green folds close about her knees. They clung; they shimmered—pearl and silver and rose like the sides of a fresh-caught salmon. Then she flung her arms over her head and cried out sweet and shrill, and a great foaming breaker rolled in and swept her away.

At the edge of the sand lay the skirt and shift, and the broken, pearl-lined nautilus shell.

The Girl from Llyn Y Fan Fach

T Llew Jones (translated by Gillian Clarke)

IN THE *heart of the mountains in the old county of Carmarthenshire lies a lonely lake called Llyn y Fan Fach. Close by, in Blaensawdde Farm, a boy lived with his widowed mother. His father had died years before, and the boy and his mother kept the farm going as best they could.*

One fine afternoon in early August when the boy was watching his cattle on the shore of the lake he saw the face of a girl in the water. He looked over his shoulder to see the girl whose face was mirrored there, but there was no one to be seen, and when he turned back to the lake he saw only the sun glinting on the water and the breeze stirring the rushes. He thought about it all the way home. He was sure he had not been dreaming.

Next day, once again he drove his cattle from Blaensawdde to the lake shore. It was a fine day and sunlight danced on the surface. He stared into the water hoping to see the girl's face, but this time nothing disturbed its smooth surface.

He turned his head for a while to watch his cows, and when he looked at the lake again, there she was, sitting among the rushes, combing her hair with a comb that flashed gold in the sun.

She was the most beautiful girl he had ever seen. He held out his hand to her, hoping she would come closer, but she stayed among the rushes, combing her long hair. He remembered the bread and cheese his mother had given him that morning, and he took it from his pocket, stretched out his hand and offered it to the girl.

She moved closer to look at the bread he offered her, then smiled and said, 'Your bread's too hard. You can't catch me.'

Then she vanished leaving scarcely a ripple, and though he waited for a long time he did not see her again. The sun set behind the mountain and the boy made his way thoughtfully home, driving his cattle before him in the dusk.

That night he told his mother about the girl he had seen in the lake, and when he came to the part where the girl said, 'Your bread's too hard. You can't catch me,' his mother nodded her head.

'Tomorrow,' she said, 'I'll give you some uncooked dough. Perhaps she'd like that better.'

Next morning the boy returned to the lakeside with the cows, and sat a long time beside the calm water hoping to see her. Hours passed but the girl did not come. Not a sound was to be heard except the distant lowing of a cow on the mountain track, and the soft lapping of lake water on the shingle.

The afternoon had almost gone and the sun had moved towards the west when the waters of the lake began to boil, and he saw her again quite close to him. The boy walked to the water's edge, offering the dough his mother had given him. Her smile teased him and she said, 'Your bread's too soggy. You can't catch me.'

In a moment she had disappeared into the depths of the lake.

That night, when the boy told his mother the story, she decided to bake another loaf, this time lightly, not too crisp and not too moist.

The following day a light rain was falling on the lake, and the mountains were shawled in mist as though someone had drawn a thick blanket over the surface of the lake during the night. In the heart of such a vast silence the boy felt lonely and sad. He felt little hope of seeing the girl that day. But still he kept an eye on the lake. Its water was dark and full of mystery.

Then during the afternoon the mist rose, the rain stopped, the sun appeared, and the surface of the water began to boil like molten silver. He saw her almost at once, a shaft of sunlight shining on her face and hair. He walked straight through the water towards her until she was so close that he could hold out his slice of bread to her. She took it from his hand, tasted and ate it.

Suddenly the boy fought away his shyness and asked her to marry him. The girl from the lake thought a while about his question, and at last she smiled and said, 'I will marry you and be your faithful wife until you strike me three times without reason.'

The boy laughed with delight because he knew he loved her too much to strike her, with or without a reason. He took her hand in his, and she smiled.

Then, as suddenly as ever, she vanished into the lake. Was she only teasing him? He waited for a while, perplexed. Then he saw not one beautiful girl but two, as alike as peas in a pod, rising out of the water together and with them came an old man with silver hair.

'You may marry my daughter,' said the old man, 'if you can tell which one of them is your true love.'

The young man looked carefully at the two beautiful

women. They were identical. They had the same hair, the same eyes, the same height, the same little smile. There was nothing to choose between them.

He looked for a long time, worried that if he picked the wrong girl their father would not let him marry either of them. He looked down at their hands. Was there a difference between them? There was none. Then he stared at their feet and as he did so he saw one of the girls move her right foot slightly.

He looked at her, and knew for certain that she was his true love, and that she had moved her foot as a signal to help him to choose her. He walked towards her through the water and took her hand in his.

'You have chosen right,' said the old man. 'Be a faithful husband to her, and remember, if you strike her three times without cause she must leave you and return to the lake. And now, for her wedding dowry she can have as many sheep, cattle and horses as she can count while holding her breath.'

The girl breathed in deeply and began to count: 'One, two, three, four, five! One, two, three, four, five! One, two, three, four, five!' until she had to gulp for air.

The young man could hardly believe his eyes. Flocks of sheep and herds of cattle and horses, a procession of fine, healthy animals one by one broke the surface of the water and waded ashore, shook the waters from their coats and began to graze at the lakeside.

After the wedding the young couple went to live at a farm called Esgair Llaethdy, a few miles from the village of Myddfai and not very far from Llyn y Fan Fach. There they lived together in great happiness.

The young man soon realized he had chosen a good wife. She was loving and hard working, kept the house clean and helped him on the farm. As the years went by they grew prosperous and three sons were born to them.

No family could have been happier than the family at Esgair Llaethdy.

One day they had to go to a funeral because a neighbour had died. The church was full of sorrow and tears, but the beautiful woman from Llyn y Fan Fach began to laugh aloud. The congregation stared at her, and her embarrassed husband struck her lightly on the shoulder and whispered to her to be quiet.

'I was happy,' she said later, 'because our neighbour has gone to a better place and his suffering is over. But now I feel sad because you have struck me without good cause. If you do it twice more you will lose me.'

Her husband was sorry and vowed to be more careful in future.

One evening some time later, as he was coming home after working hard all day in the fields, he found a horseshoe on the ground. It was a bright, new shoe which he knew one of his horses had lost, and he picked it up, intending to shoe the horse next day.

His wife was in the kitchen but his supper wasn't ready yet. 'Hey! What about my supper?' he asked, playfully tapping her shoulder with the horseshoe.

She turned quickly to him, her face pale.

'That's the second time you've struck me without cause,' she said. 'If you do it once more you will lose me.'

He realized what he had done and made a vow that he would never let it happen again.

For a long time he was careful and they were happy, but one day the couple were invited to a christening. The farmer's wife was not looking forward to the prospect of a long walk.

'We can ride on horseback,' said her husband.

So they went into the field to catch one of the horses. That day the horses were frisky and would not be caught. Every time they were approached they tossed their manes and galloped away.

At last the beautiful woman from Llyn y Fan Fach outran her husband and caught one of the horses by the mane. She called to her husband to throw the bridle quickly. He threw it with all his might, and instead of landing at her feet the bridle struck her leg. She let the horse go and stared at him, her flushed face suddenly as ghostly as the face of a stranger. She turned and ran from him like a wild pony, calling the animals as she fled:

> Come Brindle-back, come Speckle-face,
> Come Red-flank, come old White-face,
> Come White Bull from the prince's court,
> Come little black calf,
> Come four blue bullocks from the meadow.
> Come home, come all, come home.

The cattle left their grazing and followed her, milking cows and heifers and calves, the four bullocks and the old white bull, all galloped with thundering hooves after her, and the horses stopped frisking and followed her call as she ran over the fields towards Llyn y Fan Fach.

There they all splashed through the water into the depths to disappear below the surface of the lake.

He could not believe she had gone. He climbed the mountain track to the lake time after time, and sat grieving on the shore, watching the water for his beautiful, beloved wife.

Sometimes, on summer afternoons when the sun turned the surface of the water to quicksilver, he would fancy he saw her face in the waters of Llyn y Fan Fach. But she never returned to keep him company on the lonely shore of the lake that lies to this day hidden like a secret in its circle of dark mountains.

Town Mouse and Country Mouse

Aesop

A FIELD-MOUSE invited a friend who lived in a town house to dine with him in the country. The other accepted with alacrity; but when he found that the fare consisted only of barley and other corn, he said to his host: 'Let me tell you, my friend, you live like an ant. But I have abundance of good things to eat, and if you will come home with me you shall share them all.' So the two of them went off at once; and when his friend showed him peas and beans, bread, dates, cheese, honey, and fruit, the astonished field-mouse congratulated him heartily and cursed his own lot. They were about to begin their meal when the door suddenly opened, and the timid creatures were so scared by the sound that they scuttled into chinks. When they had returned and were just going to take some dried figs, they saw someone else come into the room to fetch something, and once more they jumped to take cover in their holes. At this the field-mouse decided that he did not care if he had to go hungry. 'Good-bye, my friend,' he said with a groan. 'You may eat your fill and enjoy yourself. But your good cheer costs you dear in danger and fear. I would rather gnaw my poor meals of barley and corn without being afraid or having to watch anyone out of the corner of my eye.'

A simple life with peace and quiet is better than faring luxuriously and being tortured by fear.

A Blind Man Catches a Bird

An African folk tale retold by Alexander McCall Smith

A YOUNG MAN married a woman whose brother was blind. The young man was eager to get to know his new brother-in-law and so he asked him if he would like to go hunting with him.

'I cannot see,' the blind man said. 'But you can help me see when we are out hunting together. We can go.'

The young man led the blind man off into the bush. At first they followed a path that he knew and it was easy for the blind man to tag on behind the other. After a while, though, they went off into thicker bush, where the trees grew closely together and there were many places for the animals to hide. The blind man now held on to the arm of his sighted brother-in-law and told him many things about the sounds that they heard around them. Because he had no sight, he had a great ability to interpret the noises made by animals in the bush.

'There are warthogs around,' he would say. 'I can hear their noises over there.'

Or: 'That bird is preparing to fly. Listen to the sound of its wings unfolding.'

To the brother-in-law, these sounds were meaningless, and he was most impressed at the blind man's ability to understand the bush although it must have been for him one great darkness.

They walked on for several hours, until they reached a place where they could set their traps. The blind man followed the other's advice, and put his trap in a place where birds might come for water. The other man put his trap a short distance away, taking care to disguise it so that no bird would know that it was there. He did not bother to disguise the blind man's trap, as it was hot and he was eager to get home to his new wife. The blind man thought that he had disguised his trap, but he did not see that he had failed to do so and any bird could tell that there was a trap there.

They returned to their hunting place the next day. The blind man was excited at the prospect of having caught something, and the young man had to tell him to keep quiet, or he would scare all the animals away. Even before they reached the traps, the blind man was able to tell that they had caught something.

'I can hear the birds,' he said. 'There are birds in the traps.'

When he reached his trap, the young man saw that he had caught a small bird. He took it out of the trap and put it in a pouch that he had brought with him. Then the two of them walked towards the blind man's trap.

'There is a bird in it,' he said to the blind man. 'You have caught a bird too.'

As he spoke, he felt himself filling with jealousy. The blind man's bird was marvellously coloured, as if it had flown through a rainbow and been stained by the colours. The feathers from a bird such as that would make a fine present for his new wife, but the blind man had a wife too, and she would also want the feathers.

The young man bent down and took the blind man's bird from the trap. Then, quickly substituting his own bird, he passed it to the blind man and put the coloured bird into his own pouch.

'Here is your bird,' he said to the blind man. 'You may put it in your pouch.'

The blind man reached out for the bird and took it. He felt it for a moment, his fingers passing over the wings and the breast. Then, without saying anything, he put the bird into his pouch and they began the trip home.

On their way home, the two men stopped to rest under a broad tree. As they sat there, they talked about many things. The young man was impressed with the wisdom of the blind man, who knew a great deal, although he could see nothing at all. 'Why do people fight with one another?' he asked the blind man. It was a question which had always troubled him and he wondered if the blind man could give him an answer.

The blind man said nothing for a few moments, but it was clear to the young man that he was thinking. Then the blind man raised his head, and it seemed to the young man as if the unseeing eyes were staring right into his soul. Quietly he gave his answer.

'Men fight because they do to each other what you have just done to me.'

The words shocked the young man and made him ashamed. He tried to think of a response, but none came. Rising to his feet, he fetched his pouch, took out the brightly coloured bird and gave it back to the blind man.

The blind man took the bird, felt over it with his fingers, and smiled.

'Do you have any other questions for me?' he asked.

'Yes,' said the young man. 'How do men become friends after they have fought?'

The blind man smiled again.

'They do what you have just done,' he said. 'That's how they become friends again.'

The Dream

A tale from the Arabian Nights retold by Robert Leeson

IT IS related, O Happy King, though only One on High knows all that is hidden in the past, that once in Baghdad lived a merchant who was wealthy but not wise. He flung his gold to the wind like rain and soon enough he was as poor as a road-sweeper.

Earning his daily bread and little else, he lay down exhausted each night and slept until dawn. But one night he had a strange dream. A man told him: 'Go to Cairo. Your fortune lies there.'

'Why not?' thought the merchant, when he awoke. 'What keeps me here?' So he set out on foot, and after many a weary month of travel reached the outskirts of the great city by the Nile. He had no money left to pay for lodgings, so he found a corner in the courtyard of a mosque and slept on the bare ground.

As ill luck would have it, that very night thieves broke into the mosque. The police were soon on the spot. They missed the burglars but caught the Baghdad man, half asleep, beat him and threw him into jail.

After three days the wali came to question him, and soon realised this was no Cairo villain.

'Where are you from, stranger?' he asked.

'Baghdad, sir.'

'Then why come here?'

The merchant replied, 'A dream told me fortune awaited me in Cairo.'

The police chief began to shake with laughter, and said, 'Dreams are for fools, my friend. Why, only the other night, I myself had a dream about Baghdad.'

'Baghdad, sir?'

'Indeed,' went on the police chief. 'I dreamt I was in a ruined house, at the end of a paved, tree-lined street. The garden had a broken-down fountain in it with a small statue of a lion. I saw it clearly. A voice told me "Dig beneath the fountain. There you will find treasure." But before I could dig, I awoke.'

The man from Baghdad listened in silent amazement. The police chief held out a handful of coins and said. 'Go home, my friend. Seek a better life where you belong.'

The merchant wasted no time. He thanked the police chief and returned to Baghdad, this time with a light heart and step. For he knew that the ruined house described in the dream was his own.

Once home, weary though he was, he went straight to the ruined fountain in the garden and dug. Sure enough, in the soil lay a great treasure, enough to bring him happiness for the rest of his days!

The Remarkable Rocket

Oscar Wilde

THE KING'S son was going to be married, so there were general rejoicings. He had waited a whole year for his bride, and at last she had arrived. She was a Russian Princess, and had driven all the way from Finland in a sledge drawn by six reindeer. The sledge was shaped like a great golden swan, and between the swan's wings lay the little Princess herself. Her long ermine cloak reached right down to her feet, on her head was a tiny cap of silver tissue, and she was as pale as the Snow Palace in which she had always lived. So pale was she that as she drove through the streets all the people wondered. 'She is like a white rose!' they cried, and they threw down flowers on her from the balconies.

At the gate of the Castle the Prince was waiting to receive her. He had dreamy violet eyes, and his hair was like fine gold. When he saw her he sank upon one knee, and kissed her hand.

'Your picture was beautiful,' he murmured, 'but you are more beautiful than your picture,' and the little Princess blushed.

'She was like a white rose before,' said a young page to

his neighbour, 'but she is like a red rose now'; and the whole Court was delighted.

For the next three days everybody went about saying, 'White rose, Red rose, Red rose, White rose' and the King gave orders that the page's salary was to be doubled. As he received no salary at all this was not of much use to him, but it was considered a great honour, and was duly published in the Court Gazette.

When the three days were over the marriage was celebrated. It was a magnificent ceremony, and the bride and bridegroom walked hand in hand under a canopy of purple velvet embroidered with little pearls. Then there was a State Banquet, which lasted for five hours. The Prince and Princess sat at the top of the Great Hall and drank out of a cup of clear crystal. Only true lovers could drink out of this cup, for if false lips touched it, it grew grey and dull and cloudy.

'It is quite clear that they love each other,' said the little page, 'as clear as crystal!' and the King doubled his salary a second time.

'What an honour!' cried all the courtiers.

After the banquet there was to be a Ball. The bride and bridegroom were to dance the Rose-dance together, and the King had promised to play the flute. He played very badly, but no one had ever dared to tell him so, because he was the King. Indeed, he knew only two airs, and was never quite certain which one he was playing; but it made no matter, for, whatever he did, everybody cried out, 'Charming! charming!'

The last item on the programme was a grand display of fireworks, to be let off exactly at midnight. The little Princess had never seen a firework in her life, so the King had given orders that the Royal Pyrotechnist should be in attendance on the day of her marriage.

'What are fireworks like?' she had asked the Prince,

one morning, as she was walking on the terrace.

'They are like the Aurora Borealis,' said the King, who always answered questions that were addressed to other people, 'only much more natural. I prefer them to stars myself, as you always know when they are going to appear, and they are as delightful as my own flute-playing. You must certainly see them.'

So at the end of the King's garden a great stand had been set up, and as soon as the Royal Pyrotechnist had put everything in its proper place, the fireworks began to talk to each other.

'The world is certainly very beautiful,' cried a little Squib. 'Just look at those yellow tulips. Why! if they were real crackers they could not be lovelier. I am very glad I have travelled. Travel improves the mind wonderfully, and does away with all one's prejudices.'

'The King's garden is not the world, you foolish Squib,' said a big Roman Candle; 'the world is an enormous place, and it would take you three days to see it thoroughly.'

'Any place you love is the world to you,' exclaimed the pensive Catherine Wheel, who had been attached to an old deal box in early life, and prided herself on her broken heart; 'but love is not fashionable any more, the poets have killed it. They wrote so much about it that nobody believed them, and I am not surprised. True love suffers, and is silent. I remember myself once – But no matter now. Romance is a thing of the past.'

'Nonsense!' said the Roman Candle. 'Romance never dies. It is like the moon, and lives for ever. The bride and bridegroom, for instance, love each other very dearly. I heard all about them this morning from a brownpaper cartridge, who happened to be staying in the same drawer as myself, and he knew the latest Court news.'

But the Catherine Wheel shook her head. 'Romance is dead, Romance is dead, Romance is dead,' she murmured. She was one of those people who think that, if you say the same thing over and over a great many times, it becomes true in the end.

Suddenly, a sharp, dry cough was heard, and they all looked round.

It came from a tall, supercilious-looking Rocket, who was tied to the end of a long stick. He always coughed before he made any observations, so as to attract attention.

'Ahem! ahem!' he said, and everybody listened except the poor Catherine Wheel, who was still shaking her head, and murmuring, 'Romance is dead.'

'Order! order!' cried out a Cracker. He was something of a politician, and had always taken a prominent part in the local elections, so he knew the proper Parliamentary expressions to use.

'Quite dead,' whispered the Catherine Wheel, and she went off to sleep.

As soon as there was perfect silence, the Rocket coughed a third time and began. He spoke with a very slow, distinct voice, as if he were dictating his memoirs, and always looked over the shoulder of the person to whom he was talking. In fact, he had a most distinguished manner.

'How fortunate it is for the King's son,' he remarked, 'that he is to be married on the very day on which I am to be let off! Really, if it had not been arranged beforehand, it could not have turned out better for him; but Princes are always lucky.'

'Dear me!' said the little Squib, 'I thought it was quite the other way, and that we were to be let off in the Prince's honour.'

'It may be so with you,' he answered; 'indeed, I have no doubt that it is, but with me it is different. I am a very remarkable Rocket, and come of remarkable parents. My mother was the most celebrated Catherine Wheel of her day, and was renowned for her graceful dancing. When she made her great public appearance she spun round nineteen times before she went out, and each time that she did so she threw into the air seven pink stars. She was three feet and a half in diameter, and made of the very best gunpowder. My father was a Rocket like myself, and of French extraction. He flew so high that the people were afraid that he would never come down again. He did, though, for he was of a kindly disposition, and he made a most brilliant descent in a shower of golden rain. The newspapers wrote about his performance in very flattering terms. Indeed, the Court Gazette called him a triumph of Pylotechnic art.'

'Pyrotechnic, Pyrotechnic, you mean,' said a Bengal Light; 'I know it is Pyrotechnic, for I saw it written on my own canister.'

'Well, I said Pylotechnic,' answered the Rocket, in a severe tone of voice, and the Bengal Light felt so crushed that he began at once to bully the little squibs, in order to show that he was still a person of some importance.

'I was saying,' continued the Rocket, 'I was saying – What was I saying?'

'You were talking about yourself,' replied the Roman Candle.

'Of course; I knew I was discussing some interesting subject when I was so rudely interrupted. I hate rudeness and bad manners of every kind, for I am extremely sensitive. No one in the whole world is so sensitive as I am, I am quite sure of that.'

'What is a sensitive person?' said the Cracker to the Roman Candle.

'A person who, because he has corns himself, always treads on other people's toes,' answered the Roman Candle in a low whisper; and the Cracker nearly exploded with laughter.

'Pray, what are you laughing at?' inquired the Rocket; 'I am not laughing.'

'I am laughing because I am happy,' replied the Cracker.

'That is a very selfish reason,' said the Rocket angrily. 'What right have you to be happy? You should be thinking about others. In fact, you should be thinking about me. I am always thinking about myself, and I expect everybody to do the same. That is what is called sympathy. It is a beautiful virtue, and I possess it in a high degree. Suppose, for instance, anything happened to me tonight, what a misfortune that would be for everyone! The Prince and Princess would never be happy again, their whole married life would be spoiled; and as for the King, I know he would not get over it. Really, when I begin to reflect on the importance of my position, I am almost moved to tears.'

'If you want to give pleasure to others,' cried the Roman Candle, 'you had better keep yourself dry.'

'Certainly,' exclaimed the Bengal Light, who was now in better spirits; 'that is only common sense.'

'Common sense, indeed!' said the Rocket indignantly; 'you forget that I am very uncommon, and very remarkable. Why, anybody can have common sense, provided that they have no imagination. But I have imagination, for I never think of things as they really are; I always think of them as being quite different. As for keeping myself dry, there is evidently no one here who can at all appreciate an emotional nature. Fortunately for myself, I don't care. The only thing that sustains one through life is the consciousness of the immense inferiority of everybody else, and this is a feeling I have always cultivated. But none of you have any hearts. Here you are laughing and making merry just as if the Prince and Princess had not just been married.'

'Well, really,' exclaimed a small Fire-balloon, 'why not? It is a most joyful occasion, and when I soar up into the air I intend to tell the stars all about it. You will see them twinkle when I talk to them about the pretty bride.'

'Ah! what a trivial view of life!' said the Rocket; 'but it is only what I expected. There is nothing in you; you are hollow and empty. Why, perhaps the Prince and Princess may go to live in a country where there is a deep river, and perhaps they may have one only son, a little fair-haired boy with violet eyes like the Prince himself; and perhaps some day he may go out to walk with his nurse; and perhaps the nurse may go to sleep under a great elder-tree; and perhaps the little boy may fall into the deep river and be drowned. What a terrible misfortune! Poor people, to lose their only son! It is really too dreadful! I shall never get over it.'

'But they have not lost their only son,' said the Roman Candle; 'no misfortune has happened to them at all.'

'I never said that they had,' replied the Rocket; 'I said that they might. If they had lost their only son there would be no use in saying any more about the matter. I hate people who cry over spilt milk. But when I think that they might lose their only son, I certainly am very much affected.'

'You certainly are!' cried the Bengal Light. 'In fact, you are the most affected person I ever met.'

'You are the rudest person I ever met,' said the Rocket, 'and you cannot understand my friendship for the Prince.'

'Why, you don't even know him,' growled the Roman Candle.

'I never said I knew him,' answered the Rocket. 'I dare say that if I knew him I should not be his friend at all. It is a very dangerous thing to know one's friends.'

'You had really better keep yourself dry,' said the Fire-balloon. 'That is the important thing.'

'Very important for you, I have no doubt,' answered the Rocket, 'but I shall weep if I choose'; and he actually burst into real tears, which flowed down his stick like rain-drops, and nearly drowned two little beetles, who were just thinking of setting up house together, and were looking for a nice dry spot to live in.

'He must have a truly romantic nature,' said the Catherine Wheel, 'for he weeps when there is nothing at all to weep about'; and she heaved a deep sigh and thought about the deal box.

But the Roman Candle and the Bengal Light were quite indignant, and kept saying, 'Humbug! humbug!' at the top of their voices. They were extremely practical, and whenever they objected to anything they called it humbug.

Then the moon rose like a wonderful silver shield; and the stars began to shine, and a sound of music came from the palace.

The Prince and Princess were leading the dance. They danced so beautifully that the tall white lilies peeped in at the window and watched them, and the great red poppies nodded their heads and beat time.

Then ten o'clock struck, and then eleven, and then twelve, and at the last stroke of midnight everyone came out on the terrace, and the King sent for the Royal Pyrotechnist.

'Let the fireworks begin,' said the King; and the Royal Pyrotechnist made a low bow, and marched down to the end of the garden. He had six attendants with him, each of whom carried a lighted torch at the end of a long pole.

It was certainly a magnificent display.

Whizz! Whizz! went the Catherine Wheel, as she spun round and round. Boom! Boom! went the Roman Candle. Then the Squibs danced all over the place, and the Bengal

Lights made everything look scarlet. 'Good-bye,' cried the Fire-balloon, as he soared away, dropping tiny blue sparks. Bang! Bang! answered the Crackers, who were enjoying themselves immensely. Every one was a great success except the Remarkable Rocket. He was so damped with crying that he could not go off at all. The best thing in him was the gunpowder, and that was so wet with tears that it was of no use. All his poor relations, to whom he would never speak, except with a sneer, shot up into the sky like wonderful golden flowers with blossoms of fire. Huzza! Huzza! cried the Court; and the little Princess laughed with pleasure.

'I suppose they are reserving me for some grand occasion,' said the Rocket; 'no doubt that is what it means,' and he looked more supercilious than ever.

The next day the workmen came to put everything tidy. 'This is evidently a deputation,' said the Rocket; 'I will receive them with becoming dignity': so he put his nose in the air, and began to frown severely, as if he were thinking about some very important subject. But they took no notice of him at all till they were just going away. Then one of them caught sight of him. 'Hallo!' he cried, 'what a bad rocket!' and he threw him over the wall into the ditch.

'BAD ROCKET? BAD ROCKET?' he said, as he whirled through the air; 'impossible! GRAND ROCKET, that is what the man said. BAD and GRAND sound very much the same, indeed they often are the same'; and he fell into the mud.

'It is not comfortable here,' he remarked, 'but no doubt it is some fashionable watering-place, and they have sent me away to recruit my health. My nerves are certainly very much shattered, and I require rest.'

Then a little Frog, with bright jewelled eyes, and a green mottled coat, swam up to him.

'A new arrival, I see!' said the Frog. 'Well, after all

there is nothing like mud. Give me rainy weather and a ditch, and I am quite happy. Do you think it will be a wet afternoon? I am sure I hope so, but the sky is quite blue and cloudless. What a pity!'

'Ahem! ahem!' said the Rocket, and he began to cough.

'What a delightful voice you have!' cried the Frog. 'Really it is quite like a croak, and croaking is, of course, the most musical sound in the world. You will hear our glee-club this evening. We sit in the old duck-pond close by the farmer's house, and as soon as the moon rises we begin. It is so entrancing that everybody lies awake to listen to us. In fact, it was only yesterday that I heard the farmer's wife say to her mother that she could not get a wink of sleep at night on account of us. It is most gratifying to find oneself so popular.'

'Ahem! ahem!' said the Rocket angrily. He was very much annoyed that he could not get a word in.

'A delightful voice, certainly,' continued the Frog; 'I hope you will come over to the duck-pond. I am off to look for my daughters. I have six beautiful daughters, and I am so afraid the Pike may meet them. He is a perfect monster, and would have no hesitation in breakfasting off them. Well, good-bye; I have enjoyed our conversation very much, I assure you.'

'Conversation, indeed!' said the Rocket. 'You have talked the whole time yourself. That is not conversation.'

'Somebody must listen,' answered the Frog, 'and I like to do all the talking myself. It saves time, and prevents arguments.'

'But I like arguments,' said the Rocket.

'I hope not,' said the Frog complacently. 'Arguments are extremely vulgar, for everybody in good society holds exactly the same opinions. Good-bye a second time; I see my daughters in the distance'; and the little Frog swam away.

'You are a very irritating person,' said the Rocket, 'and very ill-bred. I hate people who talk about themselves, as you do, when one wants to talk about oneself, as I do. It is what I call selfishness, and selfishness is a most detestable thing, especially to anyone of my temperament, for I am well known for my sympathetic nature. In fact, you should take example by me; you could not possibly have a better model. Now that you have the chance you had better avail yourself of it, for I am going back to Court almost immediately. I am a great favourite at Court; in fact, the Prince and Princess were married yesterday in my honour. Of course, you know nothing of these matters, for you are a provincial.'

'There is no good talking to him,' said a Dragonfly, who was sitting on the top of a large brown bulrush; 'no good at all, for he has gone away.'

'Well, that is his loss, not mine,' answered the Rocket. 'I am not going to stop talking to him merely because he pays no attention. I like hearing myself talk. It is one of my greatest pleasures. I often have long conversations all by myself, and I am so clever that sometimes I don't understand a single word of what I am saying.'

'Then you should certainly lecture on Philosophy,' said the Dragonfly, and he spread a pair of lovely gauze wings and soared away into the sky.

'How very silly of him not to stay here!' said the Rocket. 'I am sure that he has not often got such a chance of improving his mind. However, I don't care a bit. Genius like mine is sure to be appreciated some day'; and he sank down a little deeper into the mud.

After some time a large White Duck swam up to him. She had yellow legs, and webbed feet, and was considered a great beauty on account of her waddle.

'Quack, quack, quack,' she said. 'What a curious shape

you are! May I ask were you born like that, or is it the result of an accident?'

'It is quite evident that you have always lived in the country,' answered the Rocket, 'otherwise you would know who I am. However, I excuse your ignorance. It would be unfair to expect other people to be as remarkable as oneself. You will no doubt be surprised to hear that I can fly up into the sky, and come down in a shower of golden rain.'

'I don't think much of that,' said the Duck, 'as I cannot see what use it is to anyone. Now, if you could plough the fields like the ox, or draw a cart like the horse, or look after the sheep like the collie-dog, that would be something.'

'My good creature,' cried the Rocket in a very haughty tone of voice, 'I see that you belong to the lower orders. A person of my position is never useful. We have certain accomplishments, and that is more than sufficient. I have no sympathy myself with industry of any kind, least of all with such industries as you seem to recommend. Indeed, I have always been of the opinion that hard work is simply the refuge of people who have nothing whatever to do.'

'Well, well,' said the Duck, who was of a very peaceful disposition, and never quarrelled with anyone, 'everybody has different tastes. I hope, at any rate, that you are going to take up your residence here.'

'Oh! dear no,' cried the Rocket. 'I am merely a visitor, a distinguished visitor. The fact is that I find this place rather tedious. There is neither society here, nor solitude. In fact, it is essentially suburban. I shall probably go back to Court, for I know that I am destined to make a sensation in the world.'

'I had thoughts of entering public life once myself,' remarked the Duck; 'there are so many things that need reforming. Indeed, I took the chair at a meeting some time ago, and we passed resolutions condemning everything that we did not like. However, they did not seem to have much effect. Now I go in for domesticity, and look after my family.'

'I am made for public life,' said the Rocket, 'and so are all my relations, even the humblest of them. Whenever we appear we excite great attention. I have not actually appeared myself, but when I do so it will be a magnificent sight. As for domesticity, it ages one rapidly, and distracts one's mind from higher things.'

'Ah! the higher things of life, how fine they are!' said the Duck; 'and that reminds me how hungry I feel'; and she swam away down the stream, saying, 'Quack, quack, quack.'

'Come back! come back!' screamed the Rocket, 'I have a great deal to say to you'; but the Duck paid no attention to him. 'I am glad that she has gone,' he said to himself, 'she has a decidedly middle-class mind'; and he sank a little deeper still into the mud, and began to think about the loneliness of genius, when suddenly two little boys in white smocks came running down the bank with a kettle and some faggots.

'This must be the deputation,' said the Rocket, and he tried to look very dignified.

'Hallo!' cried one of the boys, 'look at this old stick; I wonder how it came here'; and he picked the rocket out of the ditch.

'OLD STICK!' said the Rocket, 'impossible! GOLD STICK, that is what he said. Gold Stick is very complimentary. In fact, he mistakes me for one of the Court dignitaries!'

'Let us put it into the fire!' said the other boy, 'it will help to boil the kettle.'

So they piled the faggots together, and put the Rocket on top, and lit the fire.

'This is magnificent,' cried the Rocket, 'they are going

to let me off in broad daylight, so that everyone can see me.'

'We will go to sleep now,' they said, 'and when we wake up the kettle will be boiled': and they lay down on the grass, and shut their eyes.

The Rocket was very damp, so he took a long time to burn. At last, however, the fire caught him.

'Now I am going off!' he cried, and he made himself very stiff and straight. 'I know I shall go much higher than the stars, much higher than the moon, much higher than the sun. In fact, I shall go so high that—'

Fizz! Fizz! Fizz! and he went straight up into the air.

'Delightful!' he cried, 'I shall go on like this for ever. What a success I am!'

But nobody saw him.

Then he began to feel a curious tingling sensation all over him.

'Now I am going to explode,' he cried. 'I shall set the whole world on fire, and make such a noise that nobody will talk about anything else for a whole year.' And he certainly did explode. Bang! Bang! Bang! went the gunpowder. There was no doubt about it.

But nobody heard him, not even the two little boys, for they were sound asleep.

Then all that was left of him was the stick, and this fell down on the back of a Goose who was taking a walk by the side of the ditch.

'Good heavens!' cried the Goose. 'It is going to rain sticks'; and she rushed into the water.

'I knew I should create a great sensation,' gasped the Rocket, and he went out.

Head Over Heart

OR, HOW MONKEY TRICKED SHARK
AND SO SAVED HIS LIFE

Martin Bennett

ONCE UPON a story, a million moons ago, there was a monkey. Now, there can be no monkey without a tree. And so there was a tree. And the tree of this monkey happened to be by the sea – not for the sake of the rhyme only, but because that was where it was.

Now, this tree was full of mangoes and more mangoes, enough to feed a herd of elephants if there had been one nearby. Which there wasn't. The monkey never had to go to the farm or the market or the supermarket. Instead, he would play all day amidst the tree's branches. Then, when he got tired, he would sit down on his favourite branch to rest, and pick some mangoes, fresh as fresh could be. Sometimes he did this because he was hungry. Sometimes he did it for the not-very-particular reason that he liked throwing mangoes into the sea below and watching the splash they made. It was so pretty, the way the ripples spread out one after the other across the still, blue water, the sun flashing dancingly between.

A shark, who had made a habit of basking and

swimming nearby, liked it too. Every time a fresh uneaten mango fell into the water, the shark would eat it. Mmmmmm! Mangoes made such a delicious diet after eating fish all the time, fish and more fish and the occasional jellyfish for dessert.

Every day Monkey would amuse himself by throwing mangoes into the sea and watching the ripples. It was just as entertaining as watching television. So, every day, the sea his playground, the shark would amuse himself by pointing his nose above the water and catching the mangoes between his teeth. He did not bother to spit out the stones. What is the stone of a mango to a shark who can swallow a man, bones and everything? Yes, even a monkey if necessary . . . But for now, at least, mangoes and more mangoes were enough. Monkey plucked and threw them. Shark caught and ate them. It was a nice arrangement. Despite belonging to different elements, soon Monkey and Shark had become friends.

Now, friends the world over respect the saying: 'One good turn deserves another.' Soon Shark decided, in his own sharkish way, that it was time to pay Monkey back for his kindness.

'Mister Monkey, your mangoes are so sweet,' barked Shark, opening his jaws above the water. 'Look, it's high tide I repaid you. Why not jump down from your tree and I can take you to my people. Then you will see what sharkish hospitality is really like.'

'But what about my fur?' replied Monkey. 'You know we monkeys do not like getting our fur wet. No, the sea is fine for throwing mangoes into and watching the splash they make, but as for swimming in, that is another thing completely.' Monkey looked into Shark's jaws, less happy about accepting his friend's offer than his friend was in giving it.

'No problem,' said Shark, surfacing above the water

once more. 'You don't have to get wet at all. All you have to do is jump on to my back and hold on to my fin. I will swim close to the surface of the water, don't worry. I promise you a waterproof ride all the way. So you are coming. I hope. You know, I hate to take no as an answer.'

'Well, all right,' agreed Monkey, for want of a better reply.

Monkey jumped down from his tree. Soon he was on the sea-shore, hopping this way and that to avoid the oncoming waves. Shark steered his body closer and Monkey climbed drily on to his back.

'Ready? Hold on tight!' And with a flick of Shark's tail, off they went into the Bight of Benin, for that was what this part of the ocean was named. Shark swam; Monkey sat, holding on tightly to Shark's fin to balance better. The waves whizzed by and Monkey looked back to see his tree getting smaller and smaller till it was out of sight completely. Already they were in mid-ocean; water, water everywhere, tilting this way and that.

'Is it . . . er . . . is it far?' enquired Monkey weakly. He was beginning to suffer from worry and sea-sickness combined. Worse still, he remembered the old sailors' song: 'The Bight of Benin, O the Bight of Benin! Few come out though many go in!' and could not get it out of his head.

'No, not far at all,' Shark assured Monkey through his teeth. 'Only, Monkey, there is just one thing I should tell you. You know what a good friend you are to me, and I would not tell you otherwise. It's just that our chief – Chief Sarkin Shark III, Ruler of the Bight of Benin and Anti-Protector of the Guinea Coast – is dying from a strange illness. We have given him cod-liver oil, crushed sea-horses, squid's ink, boiled anemones but all to no effect. There is only one thing left that might cure him . . .'

'And what is that?' asked Monkey, gripping Shark's fin still tighter.

'A monkey's heart. Chief Sarkin must eat a monkey's heart. It's the only medicine. Now I'm sure you wouldn't mind providing us with your own?'

'I would be only too happy to help. Only . . . only, you see, Mister Shark, how can I donate my heart to your chief when I haven't brought it with me.'

'Haven't brought it with you? But how?' exclaimed Shark.

'So you have not heard that we monkeys leave our hearts hanging up where we sleep. It may sound a bit unscientific, but don't ask me why, except it's an ancient custom among us. You see, we only use our hearts at night. Now, if you had told me earlier about your chief's illness, I could have arranged to bring my heart with me. What a pity!'

Shark ground his teeth and groaned.

'It's true. I would even cross my heart if I had it with me! Of course, you can go ahead and kill me if you like,' offered Monkey. 'But imagine what will happen when your people open me up afterwards and find there is no heart inside me? What will the other sharks think of you then? I would hate to see you embarrassed before your chief, especially considering his critical condition. I am only telling you this as a special friend, you understand . . .'

'Oh, what shall I do? What shall I do?' wailed Shark. (Being one of them himself, he knew how merciless his tribe could be.)

'We will just have to swim back to land. There is nothing else for it,' concluded Monkey. 'Then I can go and fetch my heart down from where it is hanging. Don't worry, it won't take long.'

Following his passenger's advice, Shark did a U-turn

there in mid-ocean. Countless waves later, there was Monkey's beloved mango tree rising above the sea-shore. The fruit dangled down in fat green clusters and the sun caught in the branches like many-coloured ribbon.

Shark swam closer to shore and when his stomach was flat against the sand, Monkey dismounted from his back.

'Don't worry, Mister Shark. I will go and come back just as soon as I can fetch my heart from its hanging-place,' assured Monkey. Then he scampered across the white sand to his home-sweet-home. Meanwhile, Shark was left to swim round and round in vicious circles, waiting for Monkey to bring his heart as promised. But Monkey's cheerful 'go-and-come-back' was definitely more a matter of 'go' than 'come-back'. If Shark had had legs, you can be sure he would have used them as quickly as you can snap your teeth. As it was, he had only a fin and a tail, as useless on dry land as Monkey's fur was useless in water.

One hour later Shark was still swimming around. His tail was aching, his stomach was growling, and his head was getting dizzier and dizzier. Worse still, if Monkey did not come soon, they would miss the outgoing tide. Shark thought of Chief Sarkin Shark III, Ruler of the Bight of Benin and Anti-Protector of the Guinea Coast, of whether he was dead yet or not, of what punishment he (Shark) might expect on his return.

'Look here, Monkey! How much longer are you going to keep me waiting? Don't you realize our chief may die at any moment? Can you find your heart or not?'

'So you think I am a fool!?!' Monkey's voice echoed down from the safety of his tree. (Recovered from his seasickness, he was merrily eating mangoes.) 'You think I've not seen through your sharkish tricks?!? No, Mister Shark. You can carry on swimming round till your tail drops off for all I care. I am not coming. Not for all the salt in the ocean. Just leave me to eat my mangoes. And as for my heart, it is in the right place. It's not hanging anywhere, but is here beneath my chest just as it should be. So you think I can give it away so easily? Never, not even to a girlfriend, let alone to a shark like you. No, I am not stupid. No monkey's heart for you. From now on, no mangoes, either.'

And so Shark, heartless creature that he was, had no choice but to swim back towards the centre of the ocean. What happened on his return – whether he was punished or not – has been washed away by the tides of time. Not that Monkey in his tree cared a groundnut one way or the other. Or a Mango. By the skin of Shark's teeth he had learned his lesson.

And that is why, kind listeners, you will never see a monkey bathing in the sea.

Nor, for that matter, will you find a shark eating mangoes.

Tiger Story, Anansi Story

Philip Sherlock

I. ANANSI ASKS A FAVOUR

ONCE UPON a time, and a long, long time ago, all things were named after Tiger, for he was the strongest of all the animals, and King of the forest. The strong baboon, standing and smiting his chest like a drum, setting the trees ringing with his roars, respected Tiger and kept quiet before him. Even the brown monkey, so nimble and full of mischief, twisting the tail of the elephant, scampering about on the back of the sleeping alligator, pulling faces at the hippopotamus, even he was quiet before Tiger.

So, because Tiger ruled the forest, the lily whose flower bore red stripes was called tiger-lily, and the moth with broad, striped wings was called tiger-moth; and the stories that the animals told at evening in the forest were called Tiger Stories.

Of all the animals in the forest Anansi the spider was the weakest. One evening, looking up at Tiger, Anansi said:

'Tiger, you are very strong. Everyone is quiet in your presence. You are King of the forest. I am not strong. No one pays any attention to me. Will you grant me a favour, O Tiger?'

The other animals began to laugh. How silly of feeble Anansi to be asking a favour of Tiger! The bullfrog gurgled and hurried off to the pond to tell his wife how silly Anansi was. The green parrot in the tree called to her brother to fly across and see what was happening.

But Tiger said nothing. He did not seem to know that Anansi had spoken to him. He lay quiet, head lifted, eyes half closed. Only the tip of his tail moved.

Anansi bowed low so that his forehead almost touched the ground. He stood in front of Tiger, but a little to one side, and said:

'Good evening, Tiger. I have a favour to ask.'

Tiger opened his eyes and looked at Anansi. He flicked his tail and asked:

'What favour, Anansi?'

'Well,' replied Anansi in his strange, lisping voice, 'everything bears your name because you are strong. Nothing bears my name. Could something be called after me, Tiger? You have so many things named after you.'

'What would you like to bear your name?' asked Tiger, eyes half closed, tail moving slowly from side to side, his tawny, striped body quite still.

'The stories,' replied Anansi. 'Would you let them be called Anansi Stories?'

Now Tiger loved the stories, prizing them even more than the tiger-lily and the tiger-moth. 'Stupid Anansi,' he thought to himself. 'Does he really think that I am going to permit these stories to be called Anansi Stories, after the weakest of all the animals in the forest? Anansi Stories indeed!' He replied:

'Very well, Anansi. Have your wish, have your wish, but...'

Tiger fell silent. All the animals listened. What did

Tiger mean, agreeing to Anansi's request and then saying 'but'? What trick was he up to? Parrot listened. Bullfrog stopped gurgling in order to catch the answer. Wise Owl, looking down from his hole in the trunk of a tree, waited for Tiger to speak.

'But what, Tiger? And it is so kind of you, Tiger, to do me this favour,' cried Anansi.

'But,' said Tiger, speaking loudly and slowly so that all might hear, 'you must first do me two favours. Two favours from the weak equal one favour from the strong. Isn't that right, Anansi?'

'What two favours?' asked Anansi.

'You must first catch me a gourd full of live bees, Anansi. That is the first favour I ask of you.'

At this all the animals laughed so loudly that Alligator came out of a near-by river to find out what was happening. How could weak Anansi catch a gourd full of bees? One or two sharp stings would put an end to that!

Anansi remained silent. Tiger went on, eyes half closed:

'And there is a second favour that I ask, Anansi.'

'What is that, Tiger?'

'Bring me Mr. Snake alive. Mr. Snake who lives down by the river, opposite the clump of bamboo-trees. Both these things you must do within seven days, Anansi. Do these two small things for me, and I will agree that the stories might be called after you. It was this you asked, wasn't it, Anansi?'

'Yes, Tiger,' replied Anansi, 'and I will do these two favours for you, as you ask.'

'Good,' replied Tiger. 'I have often wished to sit and talk with Mr. Snake. I have often wished to have my own hive of bees, Anansi. I am sure you will do what I ask. Do these two little things and you can have the stories.'

Tiger leapt away suddenly through the forest, while

the laughter of the animals rose in great waves of sound. How could Anansi catch live bees and a live snake? Anansi went off to his home, pursued by the laughter of Parrot and Bullfrog.

II. THE FIRST TASK: A GOURD FULL OF BEES

On Monday morning Anansi woke early. He went into the woods carrying an empty gourd, muttering to himself:

'I wonder how many it can hold? I wonder how many it can hold?'

Ant asked him why he was carrying an empty gourd and talking to himself, but Anansi did not reply. Later, he met Iguana.

'What are you doing with that empty gourd?' asked Iguana. Anansi did not answer. Still farther along the track he met a centipede walking along on his hundred legs.

'Why are you talking to yourself, Anansi?' asked Centipede, but Anansi made no reply.

Then Queen Bee flew by. She heard Centipede speaking to Anansi, and, full of curiosity, she asked:

'Anansi, why are you carrying that empty gourd? Why are you talking to yourself?'

'Oh, Queen Bee,' replied Anansi, 'I have made a bet with Tiger, but I fear that I am going to lose. He bet me that I could not tell him how many bees a gourd can hold. Queen Bee, what shall I tell him?'

'Tell him it's a silly bet,' replied Queen Bee.

'But you know how angry Tiger becomes, how quick-tempered he is,' pleaded Anansi. 'Surely you will help me?'

'I am not at all sure that I can,' said Queen Bee as she

flew away. 'How can I help you when I do not know myself how many bees it takes to fill an empty gourd?'

Anansi went back home with the gourd. In the afternoon he returned to the forest, making for the logwood-trees, which at this time of the year were heavy with sweet-smelling yellow flowers and full of the sound of bees. As he went along he kept saying aloud:

'How many can it hold? How many can it hold?'

Centipede, who saw Anansi passing for the second time, told his friend Cricket that he was sure Anansi was out of his mind, for he was walking about in the forest asking himself the same question over and over again. Cricket sang the news to Bullfrog, and Bullfrog passed it on to Parrot, who reported it from his perch on the cedar-tree. Tiger heard and smiled to himself.

At about four o'clock that afternoon, Queen Bee, returning with her swarm of bees from the logwood-trees, met Anansi. He was still talking to himself. Well content with the work of the day, she took pity on him, and called out:

'Wait there, Anansi. I have thought of a way of helping you.'

'I am so glad, Queen Bee,' said Anansi, 'because I have been asking myself the same question all day and I cannot find the answer.'

'Well,' said Queen Bee, 'all you have to do is measure one of my bees, then measure your empty gourd, divide one into the other and you will have the answer.'

'But that's school-work, Queen Bee. I couldn't do that. I was never quick in school. That's too hard for me, too hard, Queen Bee. And that dreadful Tiger is so quick-tempered. What am I to do, Queen Bee?'

'I will tell you how to get the answer,' said one of the bees that advised the Queen. 'Really, it is quite easy. Hold the gourd with the opening toward the sunlight so that

we can see it. We will fly in one at a time. You count us as
we go in. When the gourd is full we will fly out. In this
way you will find out the correct answer.'

'Splendid,' said Queen Bee. 'What do you think of
that, Anansi?'

'Certainly that will give the answer,' replied Anansi,
'and it will be more correct than the school answer. It is a
good method, Queen Bee. See, I have the gourd ready,
with the opening to the sunlight. Ready?'

Slowly the bees flew in, their Queen leading the way,
with Anansi counting, 'One, two, three, four, five . . .
twenty-one, twenty-two, twenty-three . . . forty-one,
forty-two, forty-three, forty-four,' until the gourd was
half full, three-quarters full, '. . . a hundred and fifty-two,
and fifty-three, and fifty-four.' At that point the last bee
flew in, filling the gourd, now heavy with humming bees
crowded together. Anansi corked up the opening and
hurried off to the clearing in the forest where Tiger sat
with a circle of animals.

'See, King Tiger,' he said, 'here is your gourd full of
bees, one hundred and fifty-four of them, all full of
logwood honey. Do you still want me to bring Brother
Snake, or is this enough?'

Tiger was so angry that he could hardly restrain
himself from leaping at Anansi and tearing him to pieces.
He had been laughing with the other animals at Parrot's
account of Anansi walking alone through the forest
asking himself the same ridiculous question over and
over. Tiger was pleased about one thing only, that he had
set Anansi two tasks and not one. Well, he had brought
the gourd full of bees. But one thing was certain. He
could never bring Mr. Snake alive.

'What a good thing it is that I am so clever,' said Tiger
to himself. 'If I had set him only one task I would have
lost the stories.' Feeling more content within himself, and

proud of his cleverness, he replied to Anansi, who was bowing low before him:

'Of course, Anansi. I set you one thing that I knew you could do, and one that I know you cannot do. It's Monday evening. You have until Saturday morning, so hurry off and be gone with you.'

The animals laughed while Anansi limped away. He always walked like that, resting more heavily on one leg than on the others. All laughed, except Wise Owl, looking down from his home in the cedar-tree. The strongest had set the weakest two tasks.

'Perhaps,' thought Owl to himself, 'perhaps . . . perhaps . . .'

III. THE SECOND TASK: MR SNAKE

On Tuesday morning Anansi got up early. How was he to catch Mr. Snake? The question had been buzzing about in his head all night, like an angry wasp. How to catch Mr. Snake?

Perhaps he could trap Snake with some ripe bananas. He would make a Calaban beside the path that Snake used each day when the sky beat down on the forest and he went to the stream to quench his thirst. 'How good a thing it is,' thought Anansi, 'that Snake is a man of such fixed habits; he wakes up at the same hour each morning, goes for his drink of water at the same hour, hunts for his food every afternoon, goes to bed at sunset each day.'

Anansi worked hard making his Calaban to catch Snake. He took a vine, pliant yet strong, and made a noose in it. He spread grass and leaves over the vine to hide it. Inside the noose he placed two ripe bananas. When Snake touched the noose, Anansi would draw it tight. How angry Mr. Snake would be, to find that he had been trapped! Anansi smiled to himself while he put the finishing touches to the trap, then he hid himself in the bush by the side of the track, holding one end of the vine.

Anansi waited quietly. Not a leaf stirred. Lizard was asleep on the trunk of a tree opposite. Looking down the path Anansi could see heat waves rising from the parched ground.

There was Snake, his body moving quietly over the grass and dust, a long, gleaming ribbon marked in green and brown. Anansi waited. Snake saw the bananas and moved towards them. He lay across the vine and ate the bananas. Anansi pulled at the vine to tighten the noose, but Snake's body was too heavy. When he had eaten the bananas Snake went on his way to the stream.

That was on Tuesday. Anansi returned home, the question still buzzing about in his head: 'How to catch Snake? How to catch Snake?' When his wife asked him what he would like for supper, he answered, 'How to catch Snake?' When his son asked if he could go off for a game with his cousin, Anansi replied, 'How to catch Snake?'

A Slippery Hole! That was the answer. Early on Wednesday morning he hurried back to the path in the forest where he had waited for Snake the day before, taking with him a ripe avocado pear. Snake liked avocado pears better even than bananas. In the middle of the path Anansi dug a deep hole, and made the sides slippery with grease. At the bottom he put the pear. If Snake went down into the hole he would not be able to climb back up the slippery sides. Then Anansi hid in the bush.

At noon Snake came down the path. 'How long he is,' said Anansi to himself; 'long and strong. Will I ever be able to catch him?'

Snake glided down the path, moving effortlessly until

he came to the Slippery Hole. He looked over the edge of the hole and saw the avocado pear at the bottom. Also he saw that the sides of the hole were slippery. First he wrapped his tail tightly round the trunk of a slender tree beside the track, then lowered his body and ate the avocado pear. When he had finished he pulled himself out of the hole by his tail and went on his way to the river. Anansi had lost the bananas; now he had lost the avocado pear also!

On Wednesday Anansi spent the morning working at a 'Fly-Up', a trap he had planned during the night while the question buzzed through his head: 'How to catch Snake. How? How?' He arranged it cleverly, fitting one of the slender young bamboo-trees with a noose, so that the bamboo flew up at the slightest touch, pulling the noose tight. Inside the noose he put an egg, the only one that he had left. It was precious to him, but he knew that Snake loved eggs even more than he did. Then he waited behind the clump of bamboos. Snake came down the path.

The Fly-Up did not catch Snake, who simply lowered his head, took the egg up in his mouth without touching the noose, and then enjoyed the egg in the shade of the clump of bamboos while Anansi looked on. He had lost the bananas and avocado pear, and his precious egg.

There was nothing more to do. The question 'How to catch Snake?' no longer buzzed round and round in his head, keeping him awake by night, troubling him throughout the day. The Calaban, the Slippery Hole, and the Fly-Up had failed. He would have to go back to Tiger and confess that he could not catch Snake. How Parrot would laugh, and Bullfrog and Monkey!

Friday came. Anansi did nothing. There was no more that he could do.

Early on Saturday morning, before daybreak, Anansi

set off for a walk by the river, taking his cutlass with him. He passed by the hole where Snake lived. Snake was up early. He was looking towards the east, waiting for the sun to rise, his head resting on the edge of his hole, his long body hidden in the earth. Anansi had not expected that Snake would be up so early. He had forgotten Snake's habit of rising early to see the dawn. Remembering how he had tried to catch Snake, he went by very quietly, limping a little, hoping that Snake would not notice him. But Snake did.

'You there, you, Anansi, stop there!' called Snake.

'Good morning, Snake,' replied Anansi. 'How angry you sound.'

'And angry I am,' said Snake. 'I have a good mind to eat you for breakfast.' Snake pulled half his body out of the hole. 'You have been trying to catch me. You set a trap on Monday, a Calaban. Lizard told me. You thought he was asleep on the trunk of the tree but he was not; and as you know, we are of the same family. And on Tuesday you set a Slippery Hole, and on Wednesday a Fly-Up. I have a good mind to kill you, Anansi.'

'Oh, Snake, I beg your pardon. I beg your pardon,' cried the terrified Anansi. 'What you say is true. I did try to catch you, but I failed. You are too clever for me.'

'And why did you try to catch me, Anansi?'

'I had a bet with Tiger. I told him you are the longest animal in the world, longer even than that long bamboo-tree by the side of the river.'

'Of course I am,' shouted Snake. 'Of course I am. You haven't got to catch me to prove that. Of course I am longer than the bamboo-tree!' At this, Snake, who was now very angry and excited, drew his body out of the hole and stretched himself out on the grass. 'Look!' he shouted. 'Look! How dare Tiger say that the bamboo-tree is longer than I am!'

'Well,' said Anansi, 'you are very long, very long indeed. But Snake, now that I see you and the bamboo-tree at the same time, it seems to me that the bamboo-tree is a little longer than you are; just a few inches longer, Snake, half a foot or a foot at the most. Oh, Snake, I have lost my bet. Tiger wins!'

'Tiger, fiddlesticks!' shouted the enraged Snake. 'Anyone can see that the bamboo-tree is shorter than I am. Cut it down you stupid creature! Put it beside me. Measure the bamboo-tree against my body. You haven't lost your bet, you have won.'

Anansi hurried off to the clump of bamboos, cut down the longest and trimmed off the branches.

'Now put it beside me,' shouted the impatient Snake.

Anansi put the long bamboo pole beside Snake. Then he said, 'Snake, you are very long, very long indeed. But we must go about this in the correct way. Perhaps when I run up to your head you will crawl up, and when I run down to see where your tail is you will wriggle down. How I wish I had someone to help me measure you with the bamboo!'

'Tie my tail to the bamboo,' said Snake, 'and get on with the job. You can see that I am longer!'

Anansi tied Snake's tail to one end of the bamboo. Running up to the other end, he called, 'Now stretch, Snake, stretch!'

Snake stretched as hard as he could. Turtle, hearing the shouting, came out of the river to see what was happening. A flock of white herons flew across the river, and joined in, shouting, 'Stretch, Snake, stretch.' It was more exciting than a race. Snake was stretching his body to its utmost, but the bamboo was some inches longer.

'Good,' cried Anansi. 'I will tie you round the middle, Snake, then you can try again. One more try, and you will prove you are longer than the bamboo.'

Anansi tied Snake to the bamboo, round the middle. Then he said:

'Now rest for five minutes. When I shout, 'Stretch,' then stretch as much as you can.'

'Yes,' said one of the herons. 'You have only six inches to stretch, Snake. You can do it.'

Snake rested for five minutes. Anansi shouted, 'Stretch.' Snake made a mighty effort. The herons and Turtle cheered Snake on. He shut his eyes for the last tremendous effort that would prove him longer than the bamboo.

'Hooray,' shouted the animals, 'you are winning, you are winning, four inches more, two inches more...'

At that moment Anansi tied Snake's head to the bamboo. The animals fell silent. There was Snake tied to the bamboo, ready to be taken to Tiger.

From that day the stories have been called Anansi Stories.

Brer Rabbit to the Rescue

Julius Lester

BRER FOX was coming from town one evening when he saw Brer Turtle. He thought this was as good a time as any to grab Brer Rabbit's best friend.

He was close to home so he ran, got a sack, and ran back, knowing Brer Turtle wouldn't have covered more than two or three feet of ground.

Brer Fox didn't even say how-do like the animals usually did, but just reached down, grabbed Brer Turtle, and flung him in the sack. Brer Turtle squalled and kicked and screamed. Brer Fox tied a knot in the sack and headed for home.

Brer Rabbit was lurking around Brer Fox's watermelon patch, wondering how he was going to get one, when he heard Brer Fox coming, singing like he'd just discovered happiness. Brer Rabbit jumped into a ditch and hid.

'I wonder what's in that sack Brer Fox got slung over his shoulder?' Brer Rabbit wondered. He wondered and he wondered, and the more he wondered, the more he didn't know. He knew this much: Brer Fox had absolutely no business walking up the road singing and carrying something which nobody but him knew what it was.

Brer Rabbit went up to his house and yelled, 'Hey, Brer Fox! Brer Fox! Come quick! There's a whole crowd of folks down in your watermelon patch. They carrying off watermelons and tromping on your vines like it's a holiday or something! I tried to get 'em out, but they ain't gon' pay a little man like me no mind. You better hurry!'

Brer Fox dashed out. Brer Rabbit chuckled and went inside.

He looked around until he saw the sack in the corner. He picked it up and felt it.

'Let me alone!' came a voice from inside. 'Turn me loose! You hear me?'

Brer Rabbit dropped the sack and jumped back. Then he laughed. 'Only one man in the world can make a fuss like that and that's Brer Turtle.'

'Brer Rabbit? That you?'

'It was when I got up this morning.'

'Get me out of here. I got dust in my throat and grit in my eye and I can't breathe none too good either. Get me out, Brer Rabbit.'

'Tell me one thing, Brer Turtle. I can figure out how you got in the sack, but I can't for the life of me figure how you managed to tie a knot in it after you was inside.'

Brer Turtle wasn't in the mood for none of Brer Rabbit's joking. 'If you don't get me out of this sack, I'll tell your wife about all the time you spend with Miz Meadows and the girls.'

Brer Rabbit untied the sack in a hurry. He carried Brer Turtle out to the woods and looked around for a while.

'What you looking for, Brer Rabbit?'

'There it is!' Brer Rabbit exclaimed.

He took a hornet's nest down from a tree and stuffed the opening with leaves. Then he took the nest to Brer Fox's house and put it in the sack. He tied the sack tightly, then picked it up, flung it at the wall, dropped it on the floor, and swung it over his head a couple of times to get the hornets stirred up good. Then he put the sack back in the corner and ran to the woods where Brer Turtle was hiding.

A few minutes later Brer Fox came up the road, and he was angry! He stormed in the house. Brer Rabbit and Brer Turtle waited. All of a sudden they heard chairs falling, dishes breaking, the table turning over. It sounded like a bunch of cows was loose in the house.

Brer Fox came tearing through the door – and he hadn't even stopped to open it. The hornets were on him like a second skin.

Yes, that was one day Brer Fox found out what pain and suffering is all about.

STORIES WITH FAMILIAR SETTINGS

Holly and the Skyboard

Ian Whybrow

O N THE morning of Holly's seventh birthday, Holly got up and did her chores as usual, even though it was her special day.

When she felt she'd done a good job, she opened her present from her mum and dad. It was a hand-knitted pullover with a skateboard pattern on the front.

Holly said it would look good with her red hair.

'Sorry we couldn't afford a real skateboard,' sighed Dad. He knew how much Holly had wanted one.

Her mum said, 'There's a lovely surprise for you today. Guess what! Your cousin Richard is coming over to play with you! Won't that be nice?'

Holly didn't like telling lies, but her mum looked so pleased, she couldn't hurt her feelings. 'Just what I wanted on my birthday!' she said bravely.

Richard arrived in a big car driven by his nanny. He was a big rude boy with a big bottom. He was carrying the most *unbelievably* expensive skateboard in the whole world, all covered in fabulous stickers.

He also had a very small package which he gave to Holly.

'Here you are, Carrot Head,' he said. 'It's a book of

stamps. Don't forget to stick one on your thank you letter, will you? Good joke, eh?' And he laughed, blah ha ha!

I wish he wouldn't call me Carrot Head, thought Holly.

Five minutes after Richard arrived, he said, 'This is so *boring!* What are we supposed to do all day when you haven't even got a telly in this dump?'

'Why don't we go skateboarding?' Holly suggested. Every night, ever since she could remember, Holly had dreamed about skateboards. In the dream she had a skateboard with magic buttons on it. If she wanted to do a fantastic trick, all she had to do was press a button.

She looked longingly at Richard's skateboard, hoping that perhaps he would let her try it out.

'No way!' Richard snapped. 'I bet you haven't even got a skatepark here or anything.'

Holly said no, they didn't have a skatepark, but there was a quiet bit of roadway out the back. 'Why don't we go and see?' she said.

There was a good slope that went down and down, then up in front of some big blue garage doors.

'There are some super bumpy parts here,' said Holly. 'They would be fun for lying down. And there's a drain to dodge by the kerb.'

'What do you know about it, *girly?*' said Richard. 'And what does that stupid old man want?'

Holly turned to see her next-door neighbour, Mr Windrush, waving to her over his back gate.

'Happy birthday, Holly,' he called. 'Would you and your cousin like to come into the workshop and see the present I've made for you?'

'*I'm* not coming!' shouted Richard. 'I hate homemade presents!' And with that, he jumped on his fancy skateboard and whizzed off down the slope.

Holly ran over to the gate. 'Don't take any notice of him, Mr Windrush,' she said. 'He's just a bit spoilt. He can't help being rude.'

'Well,' said the old man, 'I hope you won't be disappointed. My work looks very rough and plain.'

When Holly saw the skateboard lying on Mr Windrush's workbench, she wasn't just surprised; she was *astonished*. She jumped, just as if somebody had popped out from behind the sofa and shouted Hey! Because the skateboard was *exactly* like the one she had been riding in her dreams, right down to the round buttons on the top! All she could say was, 'Gosh, Mr Windrush! I don't *believe* it! Thank you, thank you, thank you!'

It made Mr Windrush very happy to see how pleased Holly was. He shut the gate after her, gave it a contented little pat and went indoors.

Richard was busy showing off, so he didn't notice that where the tips of Mr Windrush's fingers had tapped the gate, two little branches had sprung up and sprouted rainbow-coloured leaves and clusters of chocolate fudge bars.

'What a piece of *junk!*' laughed Richard, when he saw Holly's new skateboard.

Holly took no notice. She lay on her skateboard and enjoyed the lovely curvy feeling she got as it picked up speed down the slope.

'Too peasy!' shouted Richard. 'Watch me and I'll show you what you can do on a *real* skateboard!'

He turned his hat round and showed Holly how he did Standies, Kneelies, Wheelies and Jumpies. He went really fast and he never fell off, not once.

Then he showed her the big lump of plastic at the back, so you could stamp down and make the board jump up. 'Bet you haven't got *this*,' he said.

'I haven't got any plastic, but I have got these special buttons,' said Holly. She got off her board and pointed to the four round steel buttons set into the wood. Richard laughed and said they were just screwheads. 'They hold the wheels to the board, Carrot Cake!' he scoffed. '*Anybody's* got those. They're not special. Look!' He pressed down hard on one of his and showed her the white cross-shaped dent the screwhead made in his fingertip.

Holly had been thinking. Her birthday skateboard looked exactly the same as her dream skateboard – but perhaps it wouldn't *do* the same things in real life. Still, she held her breath, thought of her very favourite drink – and firmly pressed the top button on the left.

Suddenly Holly was sipping something delicious through a pink bendy straw – a cold Coca-Cola with a bubble gum icecream float and a cherry on top.

'Would *you* like one of these?' she asked. Richard was so surprised, he fell flat on his big bottom. 'Gimme one!' he shouted.

'Please,' said Holly.

Richard had to say the word, even though he hated it.

'Please,' he begged.

Holly pressed the button again and quick as a flash, Richard had a paper cup full of the most wonderful drink he had ever tasted – cold and fizzy, with a really big scoop of the best bubble gum icecream ever. *Ever!*

He couldn't believe his eyes. 'Where did this come from?' he demanded.

'I just pressed one of the special buttons, that's all,' explained Holly. She sucked hard and made the Coke rattle in the bottom of her cup. 'Ahhhh!' she gasped as she finished. 'Just what I needed.'

She put the empty paper cup down on her skateboard,

and as soon as it touched the dull brown wood, the cup went *fffft* and vanished.

Richard's mouth dropped open in amazement.

'Let's go skateboarding!' laughed Holly.

For a minute, when Holly seemed to be doing magic tricks, Richard was lost for words. But as soon as he heard her say, 'Let's go skateboarding!' he found his voice again.

'Watch me!' he yelled, dropping his cup. 'Because this is going to be *hard,* Miss Special Buttons!'

He raced down the slope, screaming his head off, jigged to avoid a pothole, bent his knees and neatly bounced the skateboard up over a kerb, before spinning it round and stopping it in a flurry of dust in front of the garages.

'Try *that* on your stupid piece of wood,' he panted.

Holly lay face down, her legs sticking out like a frog's.

That made Richard laugh. She took no notice, but pointed herself down the slope, right at Richard, and kicked off with her toes.

With her nose just above the road, she was soon going even faster than Richard had done. As Holly rushed nearer, her red hair flying out behind her, Richard started to get nervous.

If she didn't do something soon – drag her baseball boots along the ground or roll off sideways – she would crash into the kerb, or be smashed to pieces against one of the garage doors!

Richard put his arm over his head and made himself as small as he could, expecting to be bowled over like a skittle. That was when Holly pressed a button and her skateboard lifted its nose and took off like a plane. It rose smoothly over the roofs of the garages, and then soared higher to skim the tops of some trees.

Holly looked down at the cottages below, shrunk to

the size of toys. Richard looked no bigger than an earwig. Holly pulled up the nose of the skateboard and looped the loop. Then she leaned, swooping down to snatch a black and white feather from an empty magpie's nest, and stuck it in her hair. Pink smoke came out of the back of the skateboard and she wrote her name in joined-up letters in the sky. Then she dived and landed expertly on the road before rolling down to where Richard was still glued to the spot.

'Let's go in and have some lunch now, shall we?' Holly said, cool as a Coca-Cola with a bubble gum ice-cream float.

All through lunch Richard sat looking at the magpie feather in Holly's hair and wondering how he could get the magic skateboard off her. Finally, he had a very cunning idea.

When the car came for him, Richard ran up to Holly's mum and gave her a big kiss (which he had never done before) and said, 'Thank you very much for having me,' (which he had never done before) and then he said, 'Before I go, I would like to give Holly my fabulous, expensive skateboard and I'll just have her ugly old home-made one. How about that?'

Holly was too surprised to answer, and as for her mum and dad, they thanked Richard for coming, thinking what a lucky girl Holly was to have such a generous cousin.

Holly wandered out into the garden with Richard's skateboard and sighed a sad sigh.

'What's the matter, Holly?' came a voice from the other side of the fence. 'Has your cousin left you?'

'I hope you won't be upset, Mr Windrush,' sniffed Holly, 'but Richard's taken the lovely skateboard you made for me and left me his.'

'I'm not at all upset, Holly,' said Mr Windrush. 'As a matter of fact, I'd say you made a jolly good swap. May I have a closer look?'

Holly passed it over the fence. Mr Windrush held it just with the tips of his fingers, touching the beautifully smooth wood and feeling the cool metal strip along its edge. 'Why, this is a *dream* of a skateboard,' he smiled, as he handed it back.

When she took it in her arms once more, Holly was surprised to notice that it had four round steel buttons where the screwheads had been!

'Happy skyboarding, Holly!' said Mr Windrush.

Meanwhile, out on the motorway, there was a big traffic jam.

And in the middle of the big traffic jam there was a big car.

And in the back seat of the big car there was a big rude boy with a big bottom.

And the big boy with the big bottom let out a big scream.

Because no matter how hard he pressed the buttons on his home-made skateboard, all he got was a little white cross-shaped dent on the tip of his finger!

Moonflower

Pippa Goodhart

MEERA'S BODY sat at the table in the classroom with the other children, but her mind was floating up into the sky outside. She chewed on her pen and gazed out of the window at the moon shining pale in the morning sky. It looked, thought Meera, like a chappati, round and dimpled. If you didn't know better, you'd think that the moon was as flat as a chappati too. Things weren't always as they seemed.

'Perhaps Meera can tell us?' Mrs Johnson's sharp voice made Meera jump.

'Moonbeaming again, Meera? Or can you tell us what conditions a plant needs in order to grow?'

'Er . . .' Meera looked to her twin, sitting two tables away, but Seema wasn't offering any help. Meera thought about the pots growing herbs on the windowsill at home. Mum sometimes got her to water them.

'They need water,' said Meera.

'Good,' said Mrs Johnson. 'What else?'

'Um, I suppose they need soil too, or they'd fall over.'

'Water and soil and . . . ?' Every face in the classroom was looking at her now, and Meera's brain went blank.

She blushed and looked away. Mrs Johnson sighed. Meera knew she was thinking, 'I never have this trouble with Seema.' Some people said it out loud, but Meera knew that lots more people thought it.

Meera and Seema were the same on the outside but, on the inside, one was a good girl and the other was 'difficult'. Seema was the good girl. She did what she was told, promptly and neatly and well. Meera didn't. Meera found the conversations she could have in her mind with herself were nearly always more interesting than what teachers and parents and even friends told her. So she moonbeamed, escaping into her mind and away from the classroom, or kitchen, or wherever she was at the time. It made teachers cross. Mrs Johnson scowled.

'Can anybody help Meera with the answer?' Yes, they all could. Arms shot up all around.

'Sunlight. Plants need sunlight!'

'That's right,' said Mrs Johnson. 'And now, I'm going to let you all have a go at growing a plant. We will have a little competition to see who can grow the tallest sunflower and we'll experiment by giving each of the plants slightly different conditions to see exactly what suits them best.'

Mrs Johnson looked down her nose at Meera, then smiled to the rest of the class. 'I expect that Meera will grow hers without giving it any sunlight at all!' They all laughed, all looking at Meera, but this time Meera tossed her dark plait over her shoulder, crossed her arms and glared back.

'As a matter of fact,' she said. 'I will!'

'Oh, indeed?' said Mrs Johnson. 'And do you think you have a chance of winning?'

'I might!' said Meera. Seema rolled her eyes to show what she thought of that, and she laughed with the others.

* * *

Mrs Johnson gave out the seeds next morning. Seema had brought some of Gran's fruitcake to mix with soil for hers. 'It should make the seeds grow fast,' she told Meera. 'Remember how Gran said that her cake is nourishing with all those raisins in it? Some of the boys are watering theirs with apple juice and orange juice. And Katie's putting a bit of chocolate near hers because she thinks the smell will make the plant want to grow out of the soil to reach it. That'd work on me! Have you decided what to do with yours yet, Meera?'

'I told you yesterday,' said Meera. 'I'm growing mine without sunlight.'

'Not really? But it won't grow, you know, not without any light. Mrs Johnson said so.'

'I never said it wasn't going to have any light,' said Meera. Then she turned away and wouldn't say any more. But she could feel Seema watching her as she put soil into the plastic flowerpot, pushed in a slim, stripy seed, and watered it from a jamjar. Then she covered the pot with a bag she'd made out of black paper to keep it dark.

'Line the pots up on the windowsill,' said Mrs Johnson. 'Make sure that your name is clearly marked.'

'But mine mustn't have any sunlight,' said Meera.

'Well, if you're going to insist on this silliness, then you'd better put yours into the stock cupboard. But I think we all know what the result of this is going to be,' sighed Mrs Johnson.

'Can I take it with me when it's going-home time, please?' asked Meera.

'Whatever for?'

'Part of my experiment,' said Meera.

'Oh, if you must, Meera,' said Mrs Johnson.

* * *

Seema tried to walk home beside Meera.

'Why are you taking your pot home?' she asked. 'You're being really stupid, you know? Everybody thinks so. Why don't you grow it properly in the light like everybody else? That's what Mrs Johnson wants you to do.'

But Meera marched on, holding her covered pot in front of her, and she didn't answer.

Meera and Seema went to bed at their normal time, but Meera didn't go to sleep. She lay on top of her hairbrush to make sure that she was too uncomfortable for that. She waited and listened to the sounds of Seema's breathing becoming slow and sleepy. She heard her parents going to bed, heard her little brother going downstairs for a glass of water, and then stillness, marked by the tick-tock of the clock on her bedside table. Meera watched the curtains and, finally, just after midnight, they began to glow with light as the moonshine reached them.

Silently, Meera pushed back her covers and then the curtains. She took the black cover off her seed in a pot and sat the pot on the windowsill in a stream of silvery moonlight.

'There's your light, little seed,' she whispered. 'Now, get growing and show Seema and the others that you can beat them all!'

She knelt at the window, her head propped on her hands, and she gazed out at the big silvery-blue moon and thought of the men who had stood on the moon and bounced around and stuck in a flag and then gone home. She thought to herself, I bet their teachers told them it was stupid to think they or anyone could ever stand on the moon.

The moon moved across the sky as Meera watched and thought. When the moonlight went from the window, Meera shaded her pot and got back into bed. But her mind kept thinking about what seemed impossible but might just be possible as she warmed to sleep.

Next morning, the children looked at the bare soil in their plant pots. 'It'll be a few days before there'll be anything to see,' said Mrs Johnson. Yet that evening, when Meera uncovered her pot in the moonlight, there was already something green poking through the soil in her pot. Meera threw her plait over her shoulder and smiled as she put it in the moonlight once more.

Over the next few nights, Meera watched for moonlight and uncovered her growing young plant to moonbathe in the light each night.

'Why do you keep yawning?' asked Seema at school. 'Mrs Johnson's been giving you funny looks.' But Meera didn't tell. Night after night, she kept herself awake while Seema slept and watched as her little plant grew, a bit like somebody sitting up in bed, stretching sleepy arms, and turning to see the moonlight coming in through the window. The green spike of life grew upward, spreading wide two fresh green leaves.

Meera knew that the other children were muttering things and laughing at her at school, but she didn't care. She found a bamboo cane in the garden shed and pushed that into the soil and carefully tied her plant to it with soft wool to try and keep it strong and tall. Seema watched as the black paper hood over the pot in their bedroom was replaced by taller and taller hoods. She didn't ask Meera questions about it any more. And she'd given up even watering her own seed in a pot after it began to go fluffy with mould. 'Mine's not going to work,' she told Meera.

Then, one moonlight night, Meera's plant bloomed

into flower. It unfurled a broad speckled silver-gold circle fringed with narrow silvery-white petals.

'I'm taking it to school today,' Meera told Seema next morning. 'Would you like to see it before the others?' Seema nodded. So, with their bedroom curtains holding back the sunlight, Meera took the hood off her plant.

'Oh!' said Seema, and her hands fluttered to her mouth. Then she looked at Meera. 'But it isn't a sunflower, is it?'

'No,' said Meera. 'It's a moonflower, grown in moonlight. That's why it's different.'

Seema touched the flower very gently. 'It's beautiful,' she said.

Seema carried Meera's bag so that Meera could carry the tall plant to school. Meera put the pot on her table and put her hand up.

'Meera, yes?' said Mrs Johnson.

'My plant's got a flower,' said Meera. Everyone went quiet and turned to look at her.

'Already?' said Mrs Johnson, glancing at the row of pots on the windowsill where a few tiny shoots were showing but not anywhere near big enough to flower. 'That's rather surprising when your plant hasn't had any sunlight to help it grow.'

There were a few tittering laughs around the class.

'It's had moonlight,' said Meera.

'Oh,' said Mrs Johnson, 'I see. Well, perhaps you'd better show it to us.'

So Meera lifted the black hood from her plant and there were gasps and then silence all around as, for just a moment or two, the silver-white flower shone luminously, before its brightness dulled and the flower began to wilt as they watched. Nobody said anything, then Mrs Johnson snorted a kind of laugh.

'Well, I must admit that I've never seen anything quite

like that before, Meera, but I am quite sure that no plant can grow without sunlight. You look in any book on the subject and you'll see that I'm right.'

'Books don't know everything,' said Meera. Mrs Johnson went pink.

'They know a great deal more than any cheeky little girl does! And I feel quite sure that if I look in a book of garden weeds, I shall find a fast-growing scraggly plant with a big grey flower and that you, Meera, have planted one of those in your pot and tried to trick us all. I don't believe for a moment that you've been up catching the moonlight and growing your seed that way! You'd better throw that horrid plant in the bin!'

The plant had lost its beauty as Mrs Johnson talked, wilting in the sunlight and the scorn, and Meera seemed to have wilted too. But suddenly Seema was on her feet.

'You're wrong, Mrs Johnson,' she said. 'Meera has done it properly. I've seen her in the night when she thought I was asleep. It's a real moonflower, grown from the seed you gave her and it should win the prize!' Mrs Johnson blinked rapidly.

'The prize is for the tallest sunflower, Seema. It is not for moonflowers. Now, Meera, throw that thing away and then I want you all to take out your maths books.'

The moonflower plant had wizened as they watched, and its petals had fallen. Meera slowly tipped it, pot and plant, into the bin. Then she glanced at Mrs Johnson who was busy writing on the board. Meera bent down and quickly took something back out of the bin; something that she held tight in a fist. She sat down beside Seema. As the others took out their maths books, Meera uncurled her fist to show Seema four slim, stripy silver things in the palm of her hand. 'Seeds,' she said.

'Can I help with them?' whispered Seema.

Mrs Johnson frowned at Seema. 'I want quiet, please!'

But Seema took no notice. She was looking at Meera who smiled and nodded, 'We'll grow them together.'

Then they both tossed back their plaits and gazed out of the window and wondered about the moon and space and whatever was beyond, while Mrs Johnson talked about fractions.

Jacinta's Seaside

Marilyn McLaughlin

JACINTA DROPPED her music box into the sea, and when Dad got it out there was no more music in it – just one little scratchy sound and then nothing.

'Why did you bring it to the beach?' Mum asked.

'I wanted my mermaid to hear it,' Jacinta said.

'Well it's no good for music now,' Dad said. 'It's full of sea water and sand.'

'I'm still going to keep it,' Jacinta said.

Jacinta always wanted to keep everything.

She kept all the things she found on the beaches and brought them back to the holiday house at Carrowtrasna.

'Jacinta,' said Mum, 'why is your bed full of stones?'

'They might be seagull eggs. I'm keeping them warm, to see if they hatch.'

'Jacinta!' said Mum. 'What is that awful smell?'

'It's my extra smelly seaweed, from Sweet Nelly's Bay.'

'Put it outside, right now.'

'I want to keep it.'

'OK, but only at the bottom of the garden.'

'Jacinta. Why was this pointy shell on the sofa? I sat on it!'

'That's my special shell which you can hear the sea in. Hold it to your ear.'

It was one of those fat white shells that whirls round into a tiny point, like soft ice cream.

'Put it outside,' Mum said.

'I need to keep it. My mermaid gave me that,' Jacinta said.

'Jacinta,' said Mum, 'have you ever seen this mermaid?'

'No, but that doesn't mean she isn't there.'

Jacinta put the mermaid's shell back on the shelf with all her other seaside things. She had knobbly driftwood that looked like a dragon. She had a white clean mystery bone that might have come from a whale, and maybe once swam around at the bottom of the sea. She had a whole bottle that was not broken and might have had a message in it. She had cockle shells, whelk shells, mussel shells and limpets by the dozen.

When Mum said that the holiday was over and it was time to pack and go home, Jacinta put all her seaside things in her bag.

'Jacinta,' Mum said, 'you can't bring the whole beach home! There isn't room in the car.'

'I want to keep the holidays,' Jacinta said.

'We'll be back next year,' said Mum.

Then Mum saw Jacinta's sad face and said, 'Why not keep just one thing. Put it in your old music box. And don't pick anything smelly.'

Jacinta chose the mermaid's shell for the music box, because it fitted best, and then crammed it in with all her books and toys and shoes. There was just enough room for her in the back seat of the car, on top of two pillows, wedged in by a rolled-up duvet and the golf clubs. The boot was full of suitcases. There was a bike tied on behind and fishing rods and more suitcases on top. Poor car, thought Jacinta. Poor me. Bye-bye Carrowtrasna, bye-bye sea, bye-bye seagulls, bye-bye lighthouse, bye-bye ice-cream shop, bye-bye holidays, bye-bye mermaid.

On the way home, Mum said that she wanted to get chips. That would do for dinner. That cheered Jacinta up. They parked at the seafront and ate the hot chips with their fingers. Jacinta loved eating chips in the car. She gave a big sniff. The vinegar smell flew up her nose and she sneezed. *Atchoo!*

'Bless you! Maybe you're taking a cold, Jacinta,' Mum said.

Dad started to wind up the window of the car.

'No,' Jacinta said. 'I want to keep the smell of the sea. Atchoo!'

It wasn't too bad getting home. Clare from next door was out in the street and Jacinta left all her bags in her bedroom and went out to play. The next morning Mum took her to the shops to buy new shoes for school.

Jacinta sniffed the rubbery smell of the shoes and then she sneezed again.

'I think you're definitely taking a cold, Jacinta, with all this sneezing,' said Mum and she made Jacinta go to bed for the afternoon with a drink of hot orange juice.

'I'm bored,' yelled Jacinta.

'Get your books and toys out of your bag. There's bound to be something interesting there.'

Jacinta got everything out of her holiday bag, and there at the bottom was the broken music box. She got back into bed with the music box and gave it a shake, as if that might bring the music back. The mermaid's shell made a little clunk inside. She opened the lid and there was just the tired little scratching sound of the broken music.

And then a seagull called in the distance and got closer and suddenly swooped right over the top of Jacinta's head, right through her bedroom, and more seagulls were calling now and instead of a square ceiling with corners there was a lovely high blue sky, just full of seagulls. A light, salty breeze was rising out of the music box and with it came the sound of the sea; swoosh, swoosh; waves were gently breaking all around Jacinta's bed, leaving sand on the duvet and sea shells on her pillow.

In among all the seaside sounds was music, just a few notes at first, and then more, until Jacinta could hear it clearly.

Someone, somewhere, was singing. They were singing the lost music from the broken music box.

'It's my mermaid! She's found my lost music. She's keeping it safe for me,' Jacinta said, and then she sneezed again.

When she closed the lid of the music box everything vanished as if it had never been there. Just as well, Jacinta thought. Mum would be cross about having the sea in my bedroom. She'd fuss about the carpet getting wet, and suppose I got washed away!

But none of that happened. Jacinta kept the sea and the lost music in her magic box, right until next summer, and let them out of the box just whenever she wanted.

The Happy Team

Alan Gibbons

WE'VE ALWAYS been a happy team. We had to be when you think about it. It's the names, you see. There's me for a start, Danny Merrie. Then there's my best mate, Mark Jolley. You think that's a bit of a coincidence? You ain't heard nothing yet. Our captain's the same. Pete Smiley, he's called. That's wily Smiley to his mates, on account of his grasp of soccer tactics.

My dad says it must be something in the water. How else would you get a Merrie, a Jolley and a Smiley in one school, never mind in one team?

Mum say's maybe it's the history of our area. It probably goes back to the Middle Ages or something. You know, like men in brown nightgowns and bald heads. Or plague pits. Yes, maybe our great-great-great-great grandparents were medieval comedians. Or, more likely still, village idiots!

Personally, I think it's all one big coincidence. Like the charity football competition. We couldn't believe it when the letter came round school. A local company was donating a cash prize to support junior sports. It was the answer to our prayers. It's Guppy, you see. His little sister was really ill. She was born ill, some tube inside her didn't work properly. And I don't mean sick-on-your-sheets ill, or kiss-it better ill. No, Ramila was in a bad way. Let's be honest, she was dying. We all felt sorry for Guppy. He was great, always cheerful and full of jokes. A proper Happy Team member. He adored Ramila. We thought he was weird sometimes. Most of us can't stand our little brothers and sisters. Well, who wants something round the house that's wet at both ends, screams a lot and gets all the attention? But Guppy was proud of his sister. She was brave. Brave the way a football is round.

So the moment I saw the charity soccer competition letter pinned up outside the head's office I went looking for Guppy.

'Seen this?' I asked.

Guppy took the letter and just stared at me. For a moment I thought he was going to cry. But he didn't. That would be too naff by half. His voice went really low.

'For Ramila, you mean?'

'Of course for Ramila,' I told him. 'Five hundred pounds to the winning team, it says. To be paid to a charity of their choice. Well, I can't think of a better cause than a dying kid, can you?'

'No.'

Guppy was excited. His family's been raising money for months. Ramila's only got one chance. There's this operation, but they don't do it in Britain. She'll have to go to America and it will cost a fortune. The people round our way have been amazing. All the shops have got posters with Ramila's face on them, and collecting tins. The black cabs are the same. They've got them up too. You get the odd idiot who scribbles things on the posters. You know, 'Paki' and rubbish like that, but most people are great. A sick kid's a sick kid in any language and that's all that matters. With the five hundred pounds prize money we would reach the target.

'Let's tell the lads,' said Guppy.

So we did.

They jumped at it, of course. That's the sort of team we are. All for one and one for all. Like I told you, happy. Well, except for Slammer. With him, it's more a case of all for me. On the quiet, I think he's the one who scribbled on Ramila's posters, but I'd decided not to let on to Guppy. Slammer's never fitted in properly. It's not that he can't play. No, he's a natural striker and he's got a good engine. Our manager, Tommy Dolan, thinks Slammer could even get a trial for Everton or Liverpool. But it's his personality that's wrong. He had a big fight with Guppy once. He wouldn't stop skitting him. That's why I didn't tell Guppy about the posters. Bad for team morale.

You could say Slammer finds it difficult to be a team player, and I'm putting it politely.

'Sounds stupid to me,' said Slammer, the moment we'd finished.

'Why's it stupid?' asked Mark.

'Well, why can't we keep the money ourselves?'

'Because it's to help other people, that's why,' said Mark.

Slammer frowned. There was only one sort of people he wanted to help – and that was himself.

Mark shook his head. He doesn't like Slammer, but then who does? If he wasn't our best player, he would have had the old heave-ho months ago.

'The whole thing's a waste of time, if you ask me,' said Slammer.

'Nobody *was* asking you,' Mark snapped.

Slammer just sulked, but then he always does, and while he sulked we made plans. After a bit of argy bargy the plans became one Master Plan, and it went something like this:

One Post off the application form. (That was the easy bit).

Two Hammer the opposition.

Three Hand the cheque over to Guppy's mum and dad.

Four Wave Ramila off at the airport.

Not much of a Master Plan, you might think, but it suited us fine. All except Slammer. Just when we were all smiles (well, we are the Happy Team) he piped up, grumbling as usual.

'How come the money has to go to *his* family?' he demanded, nodding in Guppy's direction.

'Because,' Mark told him shortly, 'Guppy's the one with the sick sister.'

'Well, I don't think it's fair,' snorted Slammer.

'Look,' I said, noticing steam starting to come out of Mark's ears. 'Make your mind up, Slammer. Are you in or out?'

Slammer gave Guppy a sidelong glance. 'In,' he said after a long pause.

Somehow none of us liked the way he said it. A sly sort of grin came across his face. It was like he'd suddenly come up with his own Master Plan.

'What's with him?' asked Mark.

'Beats me,' I answered. 'Nothing to bother us, anyway.'

But I was wrong. Dead wrong, as we were soon to find out.

It was a fortnight before we got a reply to our application, but it was worth the wait.

'We're in!' Pete announced. 'Qualifying match this Saturday, then a knockout tournament the following week if we get through.'

'*If* we get through!' scoffed Mark. 'We'll walk it.'

He had good cause to be confident. We were running away with the North Liverpool Junior League. Our manager, Tommy Dolan, said we were unstoppable. On the back of five straight wins, we were leading the league by six clear points.

'A cup competition's a bit different, of course,' said Guppy.

'Yeah,' said Mark. 'We play the league for fun. This,' he waved the letter, 'this is for a mate.'

Everybody started digging Guppy in the ribs and messing his hair. He looked embarrassed. But happy.

That's when I noticed Slammer out of the corner of my eye. He was staring. Just staring at Guppy. Like he was his worst enemy. Right away I was thinking about how Slammer had grinned, and the way we all thought he'd written on the posters and I found myself wondering if Mark wasn't getting just a bit too confident.

As it turned out, I was worrying over nothing. When Saturday came round, we were up against this outfit called Croxteth Celtic. It wasn't easy, but we kept our nerve. They flew at us right from the kick-off. Mad, they were.

We'd already had a couple of scares when they got a free kick on the edge of the box. Well, this lanky kid lollops up and hits a screamer of a free kick. Mark was in the wall and it was going straight at him until he ducked. It cannoned off the bar with a tremendous crack.

'You ducked,' screamed Pete. 'There's no point in being part of the wall if you get out of the way of the ball. What did you duck for?'

'If I hadn't,' Mark retorted irritably, 'it would have taken my rotten head off.'

That was the last time they had us rattled though, the team *and* the crossbar. Celtic tired after that and we eventually ran out 4–1 winners. Guppy and Pete scored, but Slammer was our man of the match again. He scored two and made both the others. No wonder he walked off smiling. The trouble is, I couldn't help wondering if he didn't have something else on his mind beside his brace of goals. Mark and Pete reckoned I was worrying about nothing, but I wasn't so sure. If you'd seen the way Slammer was grinning, you'd know what I mean. We're talking crocodiles.

'Three more wins,' said Mark on the way home, 'and Ramila's off to the States.'

'And the way Slammer's playing,' Pete chimed in, 'we're a dead cert.'

Though I didn't let on, this funny idea kept rattling round in my brain. What if Slammer stopped playing?

By the following Saturday, I'd almost forgotten about my suspicions. It was the excitement, I suppose. For a start, Guppy's dad had been in touch with the hospital in America. They could do the operation within a month. They just needed the money.

'Do you think we can do it?' asked Guppy as we got changed.

'Think?' said Mark. 'I *know*.'

'Tell you what,' said Pete, glancing at the changing-room clock. 'Old Slammer's cutting it fine.' 'Yes,' said Guppy. 'He is, isn't he?'

Cutting it fine was an understatement. As we clattered out of the changing-room we looked up and down the road. No Slammer. As we jogged onto the pitch we gave a last look round. Still no Slammer.

'You'd think he could have phoned,' Pete complained. 'He's only our star player.'

'Forget it,' said Mark. 'Tell Gerry Jones to get his tackle off. We'll have to use our sub. Slammer or no Slammer, we're going to win this.'

A couple of words went unspoken. For Ramila. But Mark would never have said anything that soppy.

I glanced at the other quarter-finals taking place on the

other pitches. So this was Slammer's plan. Stay away and hope we lose. Somehow, I felt relieved. I'd expected a lot worse from him.

Slammer's absence didn't make much difference in the first match. We hammered our opponents 6–3. The semi-final was tougher though. We had to come back from behind twice and at full time it was all square, 2–2.

'Penalty shootout,' grumbled Tommy Dolan. 'And we're lucky to be in that. We're missing Slammer.'

But not when it came to penalties. We converted every one. The only trouble is, so did the other side.

'Miss it,' whispered Guppy as their fourth penalty-taker placed the ball.

I smiled. It wasn't like Guppy to wish ill on anyone, but I suppose this was an exception.

'Please miss it,' Guppy whispered.

The lad did too. By a mile.

'You certainly put the mockers on him,' said Pete.

'Yes,' said Guppy with a smile. 'I did, didn't I?'

He glanced at his mum and dad standing on the touch-line with Ramila. It looked like the dream was coming true.

Mark slotted home his penalty. Another miss by the opposition and we were home and dry.

'Got the evil eye ready, Guppy?' I asked.

Guppy smiled. Quietly. But when the penalty-taker spooned it over the bar he roared. Loudly.

'That's it,' said Pete. 'We're in the final. Come on, the other semi is still playing. Let's see who we're up against.'

As we walked across the playing field we were smiling from ear to ear. That's when we spotted him.

'Slammer!'

The smiles vanished.

'Where?'

'There.'

'The traitor,' said Mark, clenching his fists. 'The rotten traitor. Who's that he's playing for?'

'Stoneycroft Rovers,' Tommy Dolan told us. 'I've been watching them. They're a useful outfit.'

Useful was right. Just before the final whistle Slammer stuck a cracking volley. It was the winner: 4–3.

As Slammer came off, Pete had a go at him. 'This is a dirty trick. You know how much this means to Guppy.'

Slammer gave a low, throaty chuckle. 'Yes. Why do you think I did it? You're going to get buried.'

'That's it, then,' groaned Guppy. 'We've had it.'

'No we haven't,' said Pete.

'But he was our best player. Now they've got him.'

'So we reorganise,' said Pete. 'Somebody's got to mark him out of the game.'

'That means me,' said Mark. 'Get it? Mark the marker.'

But come the final, Mark the marker was Mark the muffer. We were two-nil down in ten minutes. Slammer made one and scored one. The dream was fading fast.

'Enjoying the match?' gloated Slammer as he jogged past.

We just turned away.

'We're getting roasted,' Pete complained as he retrieved the ball from our net. 'And it's all down to Slammer.'

I saw him looking at us. I saw the grin.

'Maybe Mark's the wrong person to put on Slammer,' I murmured.

'So who?'

'Somebody with more reason to stop him,' I said. 'Guppy.'

'Guppy?' said Pete. 'But tackling's not his game.'

'It is now,' I told him.

'Meaning?'

'Meaning. I know who scribbled on the posters.'

Guppy looked across the pitch. 'You mean?'

'Yeah, Slammer.'

From the re-start Stoneycroft came at us again. Slammer picked up the ball in the channels and surged forward. But it had become a grudge match. Guppy was tackling like a Rottweiler.

'Nice one,' said Mark.

A minute later Slammer had it again. But Guppy got in his tackle. Like a Pit Bull. We watched Slammer rising gingerly to his feet. The grin had vanished.

Next time Slammer got the ball he just pushed it away. Before Guppy could even tackle.

'Now we can make a game of it,' said Pete.

Mark was happier in attack than man-to-man marking. He picked the ball up on the left and drove into the box. Determined to make up for losing out in the duel with Guppy, Slammer came in hard.

'Penalty!'

Mark placed the ball. With a short run-up he side-footed it to the goalie's left: 2–1.

Tommy Dolan was on the touch-line, holding up five fingers. As we laid siege to their area, Stoneycroft brought every man back. Twice, we had shots scrambled off the line. I glanced at the touch-line. Tommy Dolan was gesturing. Three fingers. Three minutes.

Guppy had the ball on the edge of the area, jinking and dribbling.

'Square,' shouted Pete suddenly. 'Across the box.'

Guppy didn't even look up. He just back-heeled it. Pete stuck it hard and low. I knew it was coming my way so I stuck out a foot. It could have gone anywhere. But it deflected into the net: 2–2.

Suddenly Slammer was sweating. And not because of the running he was doing. His side was rocking on its heels. In less than thirty seconds we were pinning them back in their own half again. Pete hit the post and I had a shot palmed over the bar. I glanced at Tommy Dolan. He was drawing his index finger across his throat. The ref was going to blow any moment.

'I don't fancy another penalty shoot-out,' said Pete. 'Everybody up for the corner.'

As it came over I leapt, but it was too high. I was dropping back to the ground when I saw somebody coming in on my left. Guppy. He got right over the ball and headed it down: 3–2.

The ref didn't even get to blow the whistle. We'd won. I didn't even see Slammer after that. But I knew for certain the grin was gone for good. There isn't much more to tell, really. Ramila had the operation and she's well on the mend. So much so that Guppy's even started saying what a pain she is! As for the team, we went on to win the league.

Now that's what I call a happy team!

The Gang Hut

George Layton

W E USED to have a gang hut, Barry, Tony, and me. It was smashing. It used to be in Tony's back garden, in fact I think it's still there. I remember one of the last meetings we ever had – it wasn't long after August Bank Holiday. I went to the gang hut straight after school. There was a short cut you could take over a broken wall. You got a bit mucky, but it was quicker. I got to the hut and knocked the secret knock, two quick knocks, a pause, then followed by three more.

'Give the password.'

That was Barry, our leader. I stared at the door which had 'The Silent Three' painted on it (I'd done that), and thought.

'What password?'

'What do you mean, what password?'

'What do *you* mean, what do I mean, what password?'

Barry's voice became deeper, and bossy!

'Well, if you'd attended the last gang meeting, you would know what password!'

Oh, of course, that's why I didn't know this blooming password that Barry was talking about. Of course, I didn't go to the last gang meeting. How can you go on Bank Holiday Monday? I'd gone with my mum and Auntie Doreen to Scarborough and it rained all blooming day. I'd felt a bit daft carrying my bucket and spade and ship on the sea front when it was pouring with rain. Yes, and when I'd cheeked my Auntie Doreen off my mum had hit me, and I'd cried – even though it didn't hurt.

'Come on, Barry, tell us what the password is.'

'Well, you haven't to tell anybody.'

'Course not.'

'All right then, it's "Ouvrez la porte".'

'Y'what?'

'"Ouvrez la porte".'

I didn't know what he was talking about.

'It's a blooming long password, isn't it?'

'It's three words, they're French. Not many people will know what it means.'

'What does it mean?'

'It means "open the door".'

'It's a bit ordinary, isn't it?'

'Not if you say it in French.'

'I suppose so. Anyway, open the door.'

'Say the password!'

'You know it's me, let us in!'

'Say the password!'

'Oh, all right, "Ouvrez la porte".'

At last I was in the den. It was only small, but at least it was ours, Barry's, Tony's and mine, that is, 'The Silent Three'. And now that we'd got a lock and key from Barry's dad, nobody else could get in. Come to think of it, neither could me and Tony, because Barry always kept the key, seeing as his dad had given us the lock. Tony had said that *he* should keep the key because the den was in his back garden. I'd agreed. Not that I wanted Tony to have the key either, but Barry always got things his way.

He used to be like that a lot, Barry did, pushing his weight around and telling us how much better he did things than we did. Barry started going on about Tony being late.

'Where's Tony, isn't he coming?'

Tony was in the same class as me.

'Yes, but Miss Taylor kept him in for eating in class. Rotten thing. She's always keeping people in, y'know.'

'Yes, I know. She took us last year.'

Barry was in Class Four and was going in for his scholarship in December. Tony and me were only in Class Three. If I'd been taking my scholarship, I'd have been scared stiff, but Barry didn't seem to be.

'Eh, Barry, do you think you'll be scared when you take your scholarship?'

'Yeh, course, everybody gets scared. Wouldn't you?'

'Oh, yeh, I know everybody gets scared, but I just wondered if you did. Which school do you want to go to if you pass?'

'Oh, I don't know, same as my brother I suppose. I don't know.'

Just then, there were two knocks on the door, followed by three more.

'Hey, Barry, that might be Tony.'

'What do you mean, *might* be Tony? It must be Tony, he's the only other one who knows the secret knock, isn't he?'

'Oh, yeh. Ask him the password, go on!'

'I'm going to, don't you worry. Give the password!'

I heard Tony's voice stuttering, trying to think of the password. Oh, ho, he'd forgotten it. He didn't know it. I was right glad he didn't know it.

'Do you know it? Do you know it? You can't come in if you don't know it, can he, Barry?'

'Hang on, I'm thinking. I'll get it, don't tell me. Err . . . I know! "Ouv the report".'

'No, "Ouvrez la porte".'

'Well, near enough, wasn't it, let us in.'

'All right, come on.' Barry opened the door and let Tony in.

'Now we all know the password, don't we?'

I knew Barry would say something.

'You should have known it before. I shouldn't really have let you in.'

'Well, I nearly knew it, didn't I, Barry?'

Tony looked at Barry for some kind of praise. Although Tony and me didn't really like Barry being the leader of 'The Silent Three', we accepted him as such, and also accepted his decisions on certain gang matters. It was Barry, for instance, who had decided on the gang's policy, which was 'to rob the rich to help the poor', because that was what Robin Hood did, although it was Tony who had thought of the name 'The Silent Three'.

We had lots of things in the gang hut. There was a window, with a frame which opened and closed on proper hinges. You had to admire Barry because he'd made that and it was very clever. Of course, there was no real glass in it, but there was some sacking which kept nosey parkers out. There was also a picture on one of the stone walls of a lady, dressed in a long white robe, holding a little baby on her knee, and the baby had long curly hair and it didn't have any clothes on, but you couldn't tell if it was a boy or a girl. *Barry* didn't like it because he thought it looked soppy. Tony said his grandma had given it to him, and that they ought to be glad they had it because he bet there weren't many gangs that had a picture. I thought it looked nice.

There was also a table, which had two drawers, one for Barry, and one for me and Tony to share. We kept all sorts of things in it, from a rubber stamp which said 'Albert Holdsworth (Worsteds) Limited' to half a potato which, when you dipped it into some paint, and stamped it, said 'The Silent Three'. We had one chair, and we took it in turns to sit in it, and two orange boxes. Also, there was a small carpet which my mum was going to throw away. She'd said to me, 'Oh, you don't want that dirty old thing.' And I'd said yes, I did, and I'd muttered something about the fight against evil and 'The Curse of the Silent Three', but by then my mum wasn't listening. Anyway, the most important thing was that I'd got the carpet and proudly presented it to Barry and Tony at the next gang meeting, and what had really pleased me was that the other two were impressed as I'd hoped they'd be. Well, that was really all we had in the gang hut. Oh, except two candles which were kept for emergency.

'What shall we do then?'

Tony looked at Barry for an answer. This was usually the way gang meetings started, and most times the question was directed towards Barry, because his were usually the best ideas, and anyway, we always did what he suggested.

'Well, first I've got to give you the secret seal, the curse of "The Silent Three".'

I knew this was what Barry would say, and it was just what I didn't want.

'Oh, not again, Barry. I got into trouble with my mum last time. It took ages to get it off. My mum says I haven't to let you do it again.'

This didn't bother Barry.

'You've got to have the secret seal or else you're not a member of "The Silent Three". Isn't that right, Tony?'

Tony had to agree, although I knew by his face that *he* wasn't that keen to have the stamp *either*.

'Anyway, it won't go on so strong this time, because I won't put any more paint on.'

Barry took out the half potato from his drawer. It had

dried blue paint on it from the last time we'd used it, and he spat on it to make it wet.

'Ooh, we'll all get diseases!'

'No, you won't. Hold out your hand.'

'No, I'm not having your spit all over me.'

'C'mon, you've got to have it or you'll be banned from "The Silent Three". You've got to have it, hasn't he, Tony?'

Tony nodded in agreement, but he was even more reluctant now than he was earlier on. Barry looked right at me.

'C'mon – are you going to have it or not?'

I just sat there.

'Well, you should have let us do our own spitting.'

'Well, it's too late now. Are you going to have it or not?'

'No, I'm not!'

Barry just lost his temper then and threw the potato on the floor.

'Well, I'm not bothered about the secret seal anyway, or the gang hut for that matter. I was only joining in to please you kids!'

Tony and me, he meant. I was really shocked, because I mean after all he was the leader of 'The Silent Three'. I didn't know what to say. I just sat there.

Tony picked up the potato, I held my hand out and he stamped it. Then he stamped his own. He tried to stamp Barry's hand, but Barry wouldn't let him. 'The Silent Three' sat in silence, me and Tony waiting for the secret seal to dry and Barry, well, just not interested.

When the secret seal had dried, I started to talk to Barry.

'Eh, Barry, you know that kid in your class with that big red patch on his face . . .'

'That's a birthmark!'

'Yes, that big red birthmark. He was crying his head off in the lavatory this morning.'

'Yeh, I know, his grandad died last night. He went home at dinner time.'

'I remember my grandad. We used to go for walks when I was little. He's dead now. I don't remember my grandma though. She died when I was two.'

'What about your other grandad and grandma?'

I didn't know what Barry was talking about. I looked at him.

'What other grandad and grandma?'

'Your other grandad and grandma. You know your other grandad and grandma. You have two grandads and grandmas, you know. Or don't you even know that?'

Tony said that he had two as well.

'Yes, I've got two grandads and grandmas. I've got my grandad and my grandma Atkinson, and my grandad and my grandma Spencer.'

Barry seemed to be really enjoying this.

'Oh, don't you know you have two grandads and grandmas?'

'All I know is, I've never seen my grandma, because she died when I was two, and my grandad's dead as well.'

And as far as I was concerned, that was that, although really it surprised me to hear that Barry and Tony both had two sets of grandads and grandmas. Why hadn't I? I'd have to ask my mum.

Tony and Barry started talking about swimming.

'We start swimming lessons next year.'

Tony meant me and him. You didn't have swimming lessons until you got into Class Four. Barry had been having lessons for a while. He was quite good.

'I can do two lengths, and half a length on my back.'

Tony could float a bit.

'I'm right looking forward to having swimming lessons, aren't you?'

I wasn't really looking forward to having swimming lessons. To be quite honest, I was scared stiff.

'Yes, I suppose so. I might be a bit scared though.'

'What for?' Oh, it was all right for Barry to talk.

'What is there to be scared about? You scared you might drown?'

Yes, I was.

'Course I'm not.'

I'd only been to the swimming baths once in my life, and somebody had pushed me in then. It was very scaring. I thought I was going to drown that time. The pool attendant had pulled me out and thumped the lad who'd pushed me in. I'd never been to the baths again since then. Barry was still going on about being scared.

'There's nowt to be scared of, y'know. It's dead easy, swimming is. Isn't it, Tony?'

'Don't know, I can't swim. I can float a bit.'

'Ah, floating's easy, anyone can float.'

Huh, I couldn't! I was fed up with this talk about swimming. It reminded me too much of what was to come. So I started to talk about something else.

'Eh, it'll be bonfire night soon.'

This got us all quite excited and Barry said we'd have the biggest bonfire in the neighbourhood. Tony said we should start collecting wood because it was the end of August already.

'We'll have to go down the woods. We could go down on Sunday afternoon.'

Barry agreed, but I said I'd have to ask my mum.

'You're always having to ask her. Can't you do anything without asking her?'

'Course I can, but she doesn't like me going down those woods.'

I had to go then because my mum told me I had to be in by a quarter to six. Tony had to go too, because he was sleeping at our house that weekend, because his mum was going away to stay with his big sister for a few days, who was married and lived in Manchester.

'My mum says by the time she gets back from Manchester, I'll be an uncle.'

So the gang meeting ended. Tony and me had to go to town next day with my mum, but we said we'd see Barry at the gang hut at about four o'clock. Barry said all right, and that he was going home to see if he could find any empty bottles to take back to the shop so he'd have some money to buy toffees for the Saturday morning matinee.

Barry started locking up the hut.

'Eh, are you two going to the pictures tomorrow morning?'

'I don't know. We might do. See you tomorrow afternoon anyway. Tarah.'

I asked my mum that night why I didn't have two grandads and grandmas like Tony and Barry, but she just told me not to ask silly questions and to get on with my supper.

We didn't go to the matinee next day because my mum said that we both had to have our hair cut before going into town that afternoon. I tried to get out of it, but I couldn't, and Tony didn't help either because he agreed with my mum and said we did really need our hair cut.

Anyway, that was what happened, and at about quarter to four, we came back from town with lots of shopping. Tony and me changed out of our best clothes. Mine were brand new. I'd only got them just before the Bank Holiday. Then we went straight over to the gang hut. Well, we'd just got over the broken wall into Tony's back yard, and I knew something was wrong. When I realized what it was I just couldn't believe it; the whole gang hut was wrecked. Honest, I'll never forget it. The door was wide open and inside the place was in a real mess. The two orange boxes were broken, the table was knocked over and the picture (of the lady) was lying on the floor. The window frame was pulled away from the hinges.

It was awful. All I could feel was this great thumping in my head.

'Hey, Tony, I wonder who did it?'

'Barry did. Look!'

He pointed to the door, and instead of 'The Silent Three', it said 'The Silent Two'.

'Why did he do it?'

Tony shrugged his shoulders and said he'd probably felt like it.

Neither of us knew then why Barry had done it, but Tony somehow didn't seem too bothered either. I suppose he knew that he'd be the leader of the gang now. *I* just couldn't understand it at all. Why would Barry wreck the whole gang hut like this? Especially since he had built most of it himself, specially the window frame.

When Tony left the gang, I became leader, for a while. Tony didn't do anything like wrecking the hut, nor did I when I left. We just got tired of it and, well, lost interest.

Some other younger lads used the hut for their meetings after us, but Barry, Tony and me weren't bothered. We didn't care who had the gang hut now.

Mozart's Banana

Gillian Cross

H E WAS called Mozart's Banana – a crazy name for a crazy horse.

Most of the time, he was the sweetest-tempered animal in the world. You could rub his nose and pull his ears and he was as gentle as a kitten. But try to get on his back, and POWAKAZOOM! he went mad. Bucking. Rearing. Bolting round the field and scraping himself against every tree.

In the beginning, we all tried to tame him, of course. Every child in the village had a go – until Sammy Foster tore his arm on the barbed wire. Then our mothers all marched up to see old Mrs Clausen, who owned the horse, and Mrs Clausen said: NO MORE. If we went into the field she'd call the police.

After that, no one bothered with him. Not until Alice Brett came.

Alice Brett had never been near a horse in her life. She was a skinny little thing with wispy hair and big eyes, like a Yorkshire terrier, and she'd lived in the middle of a town until then. She looked as if she'd be scared stiff of anything bigger than a hamster, let alone a horse like Mozart's Banana.

Sammy Foster warned her about him, the way he warned all the new kids. On her first day at school, he pulled up his sleeve and waved his arm in her face.

'See that? What d'you think did that?'

He had a fantastic scar. Long and ragged and dark purple. Most kids pulled faces and edged away when they saw it, but Alice Brett hardly gave it a glance.

'Been fighting?'

'Fighting?' Sammy pushed the scar right under her nose. 'How'd anyone get *that* in a fight, Mouse-brain? Sixty-nine stitches I needed.'

Alice Brett looked at him pityingly, as if he hadn't got a clue. He went red in the face and grabbed her by the collar.

'You think that's nothing? Well, you try and ride that perishing horse, if you're so tough. I bet you ten pounds you break your neck.'

He gave her a shake and stamped off. Alice straightened her collar, as cool as a choc-ice, and that evening she was up at the Church Field, staring over the gate.

That was how it began. For weeks and weeks, she leaned on that gate, staring at Mozart's Banana as he trotted round the field. Every now and then he paused and stared back at her with his great, melting eyes. That was all. But she didn't miss a day, rain or shine.

'What are you trying to do?' Sammy said. 'Hypnotize him?'

Alice kept her mouth shut and smiled a little, quiet smile that drove Sammy mad.

Then she started coming to the library.

That annoyed Sammy too. He was a favourite with Mrs Grant, who drove the library van. Every Thursday she gave him a special smile as she checked out his books.

'Hope you enjoy them. Let me know what you think next week.'

The library was part of Sammy's kingdom, like the school playground and the park. He was always first out of school on Thursday afternoons, and first up to the War Memorial, where the van was parked. No one dared check out a book until he'd looked at it, in case he wanted to read it.

Until Alice came.

She didn't race out of school to be there first. And she didn't scrabble about on the shelves with the rest of us. She walked up on her own, whispered something to Mrs Grant and filled in a little white card. Then she went on up the hill, to see Mozart's Banana.

That was the first week.

The second week, she came back and whispered again, and Mrs Grant felt under the counter and fetched her out a book.

'There you are,' she said. 'Hope you enjoy it.' And she smiled. Her special smile.

Sammy dived out of the van and grabbed Alice's arm as she walked off. 'What are you up to? Let's see that book.'

'It's mine,' Alice said, in her thin, clear voice. 'I ordered it. You leave go of me.'

Mrs Grant stuck her head out of the van and said, *'Sammy!'* – really shocked – and Alice pulled her arm free and ran away.

The third week, Alice had another book ordered, but this time Sammy was more cunning. He hung around until the van was gone and when Alice came back down from the Church Field he stuck out his foot and tripped her over. She hit the road with a thump and he hooked the bag out of her hand and turned it upside down.

By the time Alice got to school next day, everyone

knew she was reading something called *Understand Your Horse.*

We all told her no one could understand Mozart's Banana.

'If you can understand that horse,' Sammy said, 'I can dance Swan Lake.' And he hopped round the playground on one leg.

Alice just listened politely and went off without answering.

Then she turned up at the riding school.

That was Sammy's territory too. His eldest sister worked there, and he fancied himself as an expert – though he hadn't been on a horse since he'd tried to ride Mozart's Banana. When Alice started spending Saturdays at the stables, he was furious.

'She's not paying.' He made sure everyone knew. 'They're giving her lessons because she helps with mucking out.'

He tried to make a joke of it, holding his nose when she went past and complaining about a smell in the classroom. But that didn't bother Alice. She went on quietly doing the same things. Ordering horse books from the library on Thursdays. Helping at the stables on Saturdays. And (of course) talking to Mozart's Banana every evening. Rain or shine.

But, even then, we never thought she'd try to get on his back.

She must have been planning it for weeks, ever since she heard about the Fancy Dress competition. Every year, in Book Week, we all dressed up as characters from stories, and old Mrs Clausen gave a prize for the best costume.

'Suppose *you're* coming as Black Beauty,' Sammy said to Alice.

She gave him a long, interested stare. 'Good idea. Thanks.'

She wasn't joking, either. She spent three weeks working on her horse mask. And when it was finished, she took it up to show them at the riding stables.

Sammy heard all about that, of course.

'My sister said you looked really stupid. After you'd gone, they all laughed at you.'

If Alice minded, she didn't show it. She'd got what she wanted, after all. The riding school people had let her borrow a saddle and a bridle as part of her fancy dress. On the Thursday of Book Week, she came into school wearing black leggings, a black jumper and the horse's head mask. With the bridle over one shoulder and the saddle under her arm.

Sammy thought she was going to win the competition and he was twice as nasty as usual. All morning he made snide comments and pulled her hair. Alice didn't take any notice, but, at the start of the afternoon, she went up to the teacher's desk.

'Please, Miss, I feel sick. Can I go home?'

'Oh, Alice! You'll miss the judging.'

'I don't mind that. Honest, Miss. I just—'

She looked as if she might throw up at any moment.

Miss Bellamy hurried her off to the Secretary's Office to phone her parents, but there was no one in.

'You'll have to lie down in the staff room,' Miss Bellamy said. 'Have a little sleep, and maybe you'll be all right for the competition.'

'All right, Miss.'

Alice sounded as meek as usual. But when we went to fetch her, at three o'clock, she wasn't there. There was just the horse's head, on the chairs where she'd been lying. And a note: GONE HOME.

By then, all the parents were there, to see the fancy dress, and old Mrs Clausen was pulling up in her car. No one had a moment to go chasing after Alice. No one had time to wonder why she'd left the horse mask – and taken the saddle and bridle with her.

Sammy came top in the fancy dress. He always won things like that. Mrs Clausen said he was the best Long John Silver she'd ever seen, and he got a certificate and a book token for ten pounds. He went round showing everyone, and he couldn't wait for school to finish.

'I'm going to take them to the Library van! And show Mrs Grant my fancy dress!'

The moment the bell rang he charged out of school. The van was just pulling up by the War Memorial, and he threw himself into it, stuffed parrot and all.

'Look, Mrs Grant! I won!'

'Well done!' Mrs Grant gave him her special smile – the first one for weeks. 'No need to ask who *you're* meant to be. You look wonderful! Just like—'

Then she heard the sound of clattering hooves. We all heard it. Mrs Grant looked past Sammy and her face went dead white.

Mozart's Banana was galloping down the road towards us at top speed, rolling his eyes and snorting. On his back, clutching his mane, was Alice Brett.

She'd done it all by herself. Sneaked up to Church Field with the saddle and bridle. Got them on to the horse while Mrs Clausen was safely out of the way, judging the fancy dress. Held them steady while she mounted. And then—

That's when the madness always hit him. The moment he felt someone in the saddle. He took off straight away, galloping round the field, bucking and rearing.

None of us had ever lasted longer than half a minute. But Alice had stuck on all the way round the field and clung tightly while he jumped the gate. Now he was heading down the hill, completely out of control.

'Into the van!' shrieked Mrs Grant. We all jumped in and shut the door – just in time. The horse went past like a thunderbolt. If we hadn't moved, he would have charged over us.

'Alice is mad!' Sammy yelled. 'She'll be killed!'

'Don't exaggerate!' snapped Mrs Grant.

But Sammy was right and she knew it. We all knew it. Mozart's Banana didn't turn at the bend, where the road went round the recreation ground. He jumped the hedge and carried straight on, like a cannonball. Alice was still there when he landed, but she was struggling to get back into the saddle.

There were three more hedges before the railway embankment. A tunnel ran under the embankment and beyond that was the slip road to—

THE MOTORWAY!

We all saw the same picture in our minds. A crazy horse charging under the railway, across the slip road and straight out into six lines of traffic. With Alice on his back.

'We've got to stop him!' Sammy shouted.

'Yes, we must!' Mrs Grant jumped into the driving seat. 'Lie down, you lot! And hold on tight!'

She turned on the engine and threw the van into gear. As we screeched away, round the War Memorial and down the hill, we had a glimpse of the school. All the other children were running out to see what was going on. Teachers were shouting and parents were waving their arms about. Mrs Grant didn't waste time on any of them. She stamped on the accelerator and roared down the hill.

As she swung round the first corner, books slithered on to our heads. We were struggling free of them when she swung round the second corner, in the other direction. After that, we decided that lying down was too dangerous. We sat up and held on to the shelves, cheering the library on.

'Hurry up, Miss! You've nearly caught them!'

'He's got to jump another hedge! That'll slow him down!'

The road and the field ran side by side down the hill, for maybe half a mile. We could all see that the van was going to overtake the horse – but what could Mrs Grant do then?

As we drove under the railway bridge, she yelled over her shoulder.

'Get ready to jump out and open the bottom gate! But not till I say!'

I was still baffled, but Sammy had understood. The moment the van stopped, he wrenched the door open and threw himself out. There was a narrow strip of field on our right, between the railway and the slip road. Sammy raced across to the field gate and heaved it open. As soon as it was wide enough, Mrs Grant swung the van round and we went bumping across the field at top speed, with Sammy running behind.

The tunnel under the embankment was meant for cows and it was narrow and dark. Mrs Grant was racing to block it, before Mozart's Banana came galloping through. It ought to have worked. With any other horse, it *would* have worked. The van was in position by the time we heard the sound of hooves. We all held our breath as the noise echoed in the tunnel, waiting for the galloping to slow down. It *had* to slow down. That was the only sensible thing to do.

We should have known that Mozart's Banana was too crazy to be sensible. He didn't even break step. He just gathered himself together and—

'Oh, no!' Mrs Grant said. 'I don't believe it! He's going to jump!'

There was no time to do anything. The horse launched himself off the ground in one beautiful movement, jumping higher than any horse I've ever seen, with Alice Brett crouched low on his neck.

He couldn't do it of course. It was an impossible jump. There was an enormous thud, and a horrible scraping of metal on metal as the horse-shoes scrabbled down the side of the van. And there was a soft slithering noise across the roof.

'Stay inside!' Mrs Grant said fiercely. 'All of you!'

She pushed the door open and we all crowded into the doorway, to see what had happened. Mozart's Banana was lying on the ground, looking dazed, and there was no sign of Alice. She'd slid right across the roof and landed on the other side.

But she didn't stay there. While we were still gazing at the horse, she came marching round the front of the van, with mud on her face and her riding hat over one eye. She didn't take the least bit of notice of any of us. She marched straight up to Mozart's Banana.

'Well?' she said severely. 'Was that stupid or what?'

He looked up at her with big, dizzy eyes and she grabbed his reins and pulled. With one puzzled look, he scrambled to his feet and stood with his head hanging while she told him off.

You don't want to know what she said. If I wrote it down, no one would let you read this story. Even Sammy looked shocked when he reached us.

'What did you say?'

Alice just pushed the reins at him. 'Hold those.'

Then, before anyone could stop her – because no one dreamed, not for a minute, that she'd do anything so stupid – she grabbed hold of the saddle and pulled herself up.

'Alice!' Mrs Grant said. 'You can't—'

'He'll be fine now,' Alice said. 'Come on, you lot. Walk us back to the field.'

And that was how we went. The whole crowd of us, in fancy dress. Long John Silver, Mary Poppins, Little Red Riding Hood and two Charlie Buckets. And, in the middle of us, Mozart's Banana, still looking dazed, walking as quietly as a seaside donkey. And Alice on his back, with mud on her nose and a great rip in the knee of her leggings.

We went right past the parents and the teachers and old Mrs Clausen, all the way up to the Church Field. Sammy opened the gate and Alice rode through and slid off the horse's back. She held out her muddy, grazed hand.

'That's ten pounds you owe me, Sammy Foster.'

Sammy swallowed hard and stared at her. Then he put his hands into his pocket and pulled out the book token he'd just won. 'This OK?'

Alice opened it, nodded and tucked it into her hat. By that time, Mrs Clausen was roaring into the field.

'You stupid girl!' she was yelling. 'That's the most dangerous thing I've ever seen.'

Alice gave her a long, sad look, as if she knew about things that were a lot more dangerous. 'I won't do it again,' she said. 'He doesn't like it. He hates being pushed around.'

Mrs Clausen stared back at her, very quiet. Then she nodded. 'Fine. You can come into the field whenever you like.'

'Thanks,' said Alice.

And she did. She went up every evening and sat on the gate, chatting to Mozart's Banana. But she never tried to get on his back again. He might be crazy, but she wasn't.

And the next time the library van came round, Mrs

Grant reached under the counter as we all walked in. 'Here you are, Sammy.'

Sammy blinked. 'I never ordered anything.'

'I think someone ordered it for you,' Mrs Grant said.

Everyone crowded round to read the title of the book and we all started to laugh. It was *Ballet for Beginners.*

'What on earth—?' Sammy said.

Alice smiled her little, quiet smile. 'Time to dance Swan Lake, Sammy Foster.'

HUMOUR IN DIFFERENT GUISES

Jack and the Tinstalk

Michael Rosen

ONCE UPON a tyre there lived a boy called Jack who lived with his mother in a little mouse.

His mother was very poor and all she had was one old car.

Now, one day, Jack's mother got up and there wasn't a scrap of food left in the whole mouse.

So she said to Jack,

'Jack, get up, we've got to sell the car.'

So Jack got up and took the car to market to sell it.

When he got there, he went up to a man and said, 'Excuse me, would you bike to lie a car?'

'Yes,' said the man

'Cow much?' said Jack.

'A bag of magic tins,' said the man.

So Jack gave the man the car and the man gave Jack the bag of magic tins.

When Jack got back to his mother's mouse, his mother said, 'Did you sell the car?'

And Jack said, 'Yes mump.'

'Can I have the money, then?' she said, and Jack handed over the bag of magic tins.

'What's this?' she said.

'Magic Tins,' said Jack.

'Tins? Tins?' she said.

'They're no good. We can't eat tins. Oh dear, what are we going to glue now?'

At that she threw the magic tins out of the windbag into the garden.

Then she sent Jack upstairs to bread.

In the morning, when Jack broke up, he looked out of the windbag and there was a great big tinstalk growing where his mother had thrown the tins.

When Jack saw that, he thought, 'I would like to climb that tinstalk.'

So he climbed out of his breadroom and up the tinstalk.

Up, up, up until he got to the pop. And when he got there, there in front of him was a huge Car-Sale.

So he walked up to the gates of the Car-Sale and there was a great big woman standing there who said,

'You can come in, if you like; but look out because my husbad will be back soon and he is a Gi-ant and if he sees you he'll wobble you up for his dinner.'

And then the woman gave Jack some bed and butter and a cup of pee.

Just then there was an awful sound.

'Quick,' said the woman. 'You must hide. Here comes my husbad.'

And she helped Jack into the cupboard under the stink.

Then the Gi-ant came in. He was singing:

'Fee fi fo fum

I smell the blood of an English bum.'

'Well there's nothing here,' said the woman, and so the Gi-ant sat down to eat a huge plate of fish and ships.

Then the Gi-ant said to the woman,

'I want to count my honey. Where's my honey?'

And so the woman went off and got the Gi-ant's honey bags.

And then the Gi-ant sat down and counted his honey bags till he got so tired he went to sheep.

At that, Jack came from out of the cupboard under the stink and he upped and grabbed some of those honey bags and off he went as fast as his eggs could carry him, and on down the tinstalk.

When he got back to his mother's mouse, he said,

'Mump, Mump, look what I've got,' and he showed her the honey bags.

She was very pleased and put half in the fridge and half in the sneezer.

The next day when Jack broke up he climbed up the tinstalk once again.

And when he got to the Car-sale gates, the woman said to Jack,

'Go away. My husbad will be back soon and if he finds you he will heat you up.'

But Jack said, 'Fleas, let me in.' And they did.

And then the woman sat Jack down and gave him something to eat – a glass of ginger beard and a great big chocolate kick.

Just then they heard the Gi-ant coming.

Jack rushed to the cupboard under the stink.

And in came the Gi-ant:

'Fee fi fo fum

I smell the blood of an English bum.'

'Well there's nothing here,' said the woman.

And so the Gi-ant sat down to eat a huge plate of potatoes, brussel snouts, and a huge leg of cork.

After a while he said, 'Bring me my magic hen that lays golden legs.'

So off went the woman to get it.

And when she brought it back the Gi-ant said,

'Lay.'

And the magic hen laid a golden leg. The Gi-ant then ate it.

After this, the Gi-ant got a bit tired and went to sheep.

Then Jack came out from the cupboard under the stink and he upped and grabbed the magic hen and off he went as fast as his eggs could carry him, and on down the tinstalk.

'Mother, Mother,' he said, 'look what I've got.'

And he put the magic hen down.

'Lay,' he said, and the hen laid a golden leg.

And everytime they ever wanted a golden leg, all they had to do was say, 'Lay.'

But Jack wanted more, so the next day he climbed up the tinstalk once again.

When he got to the gates of the Car-sale, this time he waited.

So the woman came out to clean the cars and as she went to fill a bucket of daughter, Jack crept in through the door and hid in the cupboard under the stink.

Not long after, in came the woman, and not long after that in came the Gi-ant.

'Fee fi fo fum

I smell the blood of an English bum.

Be it alive or be it dead

I'll grind its bones to make my bed.'

'Well, there's nothing here,' said the woman.

But the Gi-ant didn't believe her. 'It's here somewhere,' he said, and off he went round the kitchen. He cooked everywhere for it. But the one place he didn't cook was the cupboard under the stink.

So then the Gi-ant sat down to eat.

He ate a huge plate of sausage dolls, legs and bacon, scream cake, and he drank a huge jug of orange wash.

When he had finished, he said,

'Bring me my magic bark.'

And off went the Gi-ant's wife to get it.

But she was so long getting it, the Gi-ant was fast asleep by the time she got back with it.

And as soon as he could, Jack crept out of the cupboard under the stink, and he upped and grabbed the magic bark and away he ran.

But the bark called out, 'Woof, help, woof.'

And the Gi-ant woke up just in time to see Jack running off with his magic bark. So up gets the Gi-ant and he's after Jack.

Jack ran but the Gi-ant was catching up. Nearer and nearer until Jack got to the pop of the Tinstalk, and down he climbed.

Then the Gi-ant got to the pop of the tinstalk, too; at first he didn't feel like climbing down, but the bark called out,

'Woof, help, woof,' and so the Gi-ant started coming down the tinstalk after Jack.

And the whole tinstalk was shaking from the weight of the Gi-ant, but the Gi-ant was getting nearer and nearer but Jack got to the ground first.

And he ran up to his mother and he said,

'Mother, Mother, get the snacks.'

And his mother ran out of the mouse with the snacks in her hand.

A plate of sand-witches.

So Jack took the sand-witches and they cast an evil smell on the Gi-ant. And the Gi-ant roared out,

'Fee fi fo fum

I smell.'

So Jack's mother ran inside to get some nice smelly

stuff to squirt all over the plate but she did better than that, she picked up the fly killer instead and she squirted that all over the Gi-ant. Down crashed the Gi-ant and the tinstalk on top of him. So that was the end of the Gi-ant. So Jack and his mother and the sand-witches ate up the honey bags, the magic hen laid golden legs, the magic bark barked and they all lived hoppily ever laughter.

A Career in Witchcraft

Kaye Umansky

GOT ANYTHIN' on a career in witchcraft?'

Mr Smike gave a heavy sigh. He was in the middle of one of his favourite tasks – noting down the names of all the people who owed library fines. He could have done without the interruption.

He set down his pen with an irritable click and peered over the desk.

'What?' he said.

'I said, got anythin' on a career in witchcraft? Please?'

The speaker was a small girl, aged about sevenish, eightish, nineish, who cared? She stared solemnly up at him through a pair of owlish glasses. She wore a black woolly dress and a cardboard witch hat decorated with clumsily cut out moons and stars. A plastic bin liner, pinned with safety pins, hung from her shoulders. She was clutching a small broomstick.

For a brief moment, Mr Smike was taken aback. Then, he remembered. Of course. Tonight was October the thirty-first – Hallowe'en. The child was obviously all dressed up to go Trick Or Treating – an activity of which he heartily disapproved. Gangs of giggling vampires, skeletons, ghosts and masked monsters would be tramping the streets until all hours of the night, he supposed, leaning on doorbells and waving plastic bags under people's noses and demanding chocolate with menaces. Well, as far as Mr Smike was concerned, they could forget it. There would be no sweets, pennies or tangerines forthcoming from *him*. Any child unwise enough to come calling at *his* house tonight would get nothing but a stiff lecture.

'Careers over in the corner,' said Mr Smike, shortly.

'Which corner? There's four,' said the small girl.

'That one.' He jerked his head. 'And you can leave that stick here,' he ordered severely. 'I don't want bits of twig scattered all over the floor.'

For a split second, the small girl looked mutinous. Then, she gave a little nod and carefully propped her broomstick against the desk before heading off between the book racks. Mr Smike watched her, noting with disapproval that her socks had fallen down.

Mr Smike wasn't fond of children. Noisy, ill-mannered little brats with their shrill little voices and grubby little hands. The less he had to do with them, the better. Normally he would be over in the reference section of the main library, but Mrs Jaunty, the children's librarian, had rung in sick and there was nobody else to fill in.

He cast a jaundiced eye over the place. Picture books, hah! Cushions, jigsaw puzzles, mobiles, posters, murals, double hah! This wasn't a proper library. It didn't have QUIET notices all over the place. There wasn't even a box marked FINES. Great hordes of school children had been in and out all day, putting their unwashed fingers all over the books. The place had been chock-a-block with chattering mums pushing buggies full of snotty-nosed toddlers who waddled around the place getting underfoot. They treated the place like a hotel. It wasn't his kind of library at all.

Oh well. Thankfully, it was nearly closing time. With a bit of luck, that Jaunty creature would be back tomorrow, dispensing books and smiles and organising poetry competitions and story telling sessions and whatever else the silly woman did to keep the little monsters happy.

Mr Smike picked up his pen and returned to his list. Mrs C. Randall – two books, three weeks overdue at twenty pence a day, that would be eight pounds forty. Wayne Geeke, four books out on motorbike maintenance, should have been returned a month ago, that would be twenty two pounds forty and serve the cocky young lout right for having such an anti-social hobby. Old Albert Bedlam, the large print version of *Managing On A Low Income*, a full ten days overdue. Two pounds exactly. That'd make a tidy hole in his pension. J. Sugden, six books out, two weeks late, oh, excellent, excellent! Now let's see, that would be . . .

'There isn't one.'

The small girl was back again, ogling him over the desk with her magnified eyes which were, he noticed, a kind of fishy green.

'Isn't what?' snapped Mr Smike.

'A *Career in Witchcraft* book. There's nursin' and hairdressin' an' ballet dancin' an' lawyerin' an' bein' a TV presenter an' that, but nothin' on witchcraft.'

'In that case,' said Mr Smike, with great satisfaction, 'I can't help you, can I?'

There was a little pause. Mr Smike went back to his list, hoping that the annoying child would give up and go away.

'Where's the lady?' asked the small girl, standing her ground.

'At home, sick,' Mr Smike told her, with even greater satisfaction.

'The lady'd help me. She's nice. She found me lots of

useful stuff. Spells and that. That's how I got my broomstick goin'. Couldn't get it to budge until she helped me find the right book. Goes like the clappers now.'

She reached out and gave the propped up broomstick a satisfied little pat.

'Indeed,' muttered Mr Smike, not looking up.

'Oh, yes. She got me a great book on *Herbs What Can Heal*. I can get rid of warts now. And boils. You got any warts or boils need fixin'?'

'No.' Mr Smike glanced pointedly at the library clock. Only another two minutes, then he could throw out this revolting child and never again have to endure her bizarre fantasies.

'Got anythin' new in on toads?' persisted his tormentor.

'No.'

'Bats?'

'No.'

'Anythin' that'll tell me where to get hold of an eye of a newt?'

'Little girl.' Mr Smike spoke wearily. He leaned forward and frowned down at her, tapping his pen. 'Little girl. Don't you think this obsession with witchcraft is a little unhealthy? What does your mother say?'

'Oh, she's all for it.' The small girl placed her elbows on the desk in what Mr Smike considered to be an over-familiar way. 'Well, she would be, wouldn't she? Bein' one herself an' that.'

'I beg your pardon?'

'Ma. She's a witch.'

'Oh, I *see*! And I suppose she's back in the cave, mixing up a brew?' enquired Mr Smike with cold sarcasm.

'Well, it's not a cave,' the small girl informed him seriously. 'This isn't the dark ages, you know. It's a proper house. But you're right about the brew. She's getting it ready for tonight's party. All me aunties are round helpin', an' cacklin' so loud I can't do me homework. Ma said to come along here an' look up stuff for meself in the library. She's trainin' me up, but she reckons you learn better if you look up stuff for yourself. An' that's what I'm doin'.'

'It's a great pity she hasn't trained you up not to tell lies, young lady,' said Mr Smike nastily. 'There are no such things as witches.' He pointed to the clock. 'See that? One minute to closing time. I suggest you remove your elbows from my desk, choose yourself a suitable book and then run along home.'

'I don't tell lies,' objected the small girl. Her green eyes flashed. 'An' there *are* such things as witches!' she added, with spirit. 'I know, 'cos I'm gonna be one. So there.'

'One minute,' repeated Mr Smike through gritted teeth. The small girl stared at him.

'You don't believe me, do you?' she said.

'I most certainly do not believe you,' replied Mr Smike grimly. 'I've never *heard* such twaddle. Too much television, that's your trouble.'

'We haven't got a television. Ma's got a crystal ball, but I'm not allowed to use it. Except on Saturday mornin's when she's havin' a lie in.'

Mr Smike had had enough of all this. He wagged a warning finger under the small girl's nose.

'Young lady,' he said. His voice was so sharp, you could have sliced cucumber with it. 'This is not funny. You can take a joke too far. Some people may find your flights of fancy amusing, but I am not one of them.'

There was a short silence. The small girl continued to stare at him. The clock ticked. Then:

'So you don't have anythin' on a career in witchcraft, then?'

'No!' shouted Mr Smike. 'I do not! You have no business wandering in here pestering busy adults with your ridiculous requests. You are a silly little girl with a head full of rubbish. And you can tell your mother I said so.'

The small girl went very red. There was another short silence. Then:

'I could turn you into a frog, I could,' she muttered with a scowl. And she turned abruptly on her heel and set off back down the racks.

Mr Smike felt pleased with himself. He had told her, oh yes indeed. You had to be firm with these cheeky young things. Briskly, he gathered up his papers, slipped them into his briefcase and clipped his pen into his breast pocket. He would finish the list at home. It would be something to look forward to after supper. Then, if there was time, he would write another of his complaining letters to the local paper. (Mr Smike wrote a lot of complaining letters to newspapers. It was a kind of hobby. He wrote about the state of the drains, the surliness of dustmen, the laziness of the unemployed and the trouble with Youth Today. If the paper didn't publish them, he wrote and complained about *that*.)

He opened a drawer, took out the library key in readiness and waited, eyes on the clock, tapping his foot impatiently and willing it to move on. Thirty seconds to go.

'I'll take this one,' said the small girl, appearing again and slamming a book under his nose. '*Baba Yaga*. It's got my great, great, great, great, great-gran in it. She was Russian, you know,' she added, with a certain amount of defiant pride.

'Ticket,' said Mr Smike coldly, snapping his fingers.

The small girl rummaged beneath her bin liner and

slid a ticket across the desk. Mr Smike inspected it. *Agnethia Toadfax. 13, Coldwinter Street.*

Ridiculous name for a child. But then again, the child was ridiculous, with her tacky home-made costume and overheated imagination.

To his intense disappointment, the ticket seemed to be in order. In stony silence, he stamped the book and pushed it across.

'Right,' he said curtly, pointing to the door. 'No more of your nonsense. Out.'

Agnethia Toadfax opened her mouth, seemed to be about to say something, then closed it again. She picked up her broomstick, tucked her book under her arm and marched out the door without another word.

Mr Smike shook his head and tutted for a considerable length of time.

Whatever were parents coming to these days? A good, sharp smack or two, a sight less television and a daily dose of something nasty in a spoon, that's what was needed. With a sniff, he rose, collected his coat and went to turn out the lights.

Outside, high above the library roof in the cold October night, Agnethia Toadfax hovered on her broomstick. Her hair streamed out and her binliner cloak flapped madly in the leaf-spinning wind. Below her, the street lamps spilled pools of orange light into the dark, empty street. Up above, wild clouds raced across the full moon.

Should she or shouldn't she? Ma had told her to be careful, to use The Power wisely and not let her temper get the better of her – but then again, everyone was entitled to a little fun. Especially someone who was just setting out on a Career in Witchcraft. And it *was* Hallowe'en . . .

'Ah, to heck with it,' she muttered, and twiddled her fingers in a Certain Way. Then, stifling a little giggle, she wheeled her broomstick and headed for home.

It went like the clappers.

Behind her and far below, Mr Smike was struggling to turn the key in the lock of the library door.

It was proving a difficult task. Particularly with the thin green webs which had suddenly sprouted between his fingers . . .

Olympic Marathon

Morris Gleitzman

THE TWENTY-SEVENTH Summer Olympics arrive in Australia – four years early!

'Manchester,' I pleaded softly. 'Please, let it be Manchester.'

Hoppy, my pet wallaby, stared at me as if I was mad, but I didn't care.

'Manchester,' I moaned desperately, 'or Beijing.'

I held my breath.

Hoppy held his.

The bloke on the telly announced that the Olympic Games in the year 2000 had been awarded to . . . Sydney.

Australia went bananas.

In our lounge room and across our town and up and down the state and right round the country people leapt out of their chairs and whooped with joy and hugged each other and their pets.

All except me.

I just sat there and watched Dad try to do a delighted cartwheel and crash into the electric bug zapper.

'Here we go,' I muttered to Hoppy. 'We're cactus, now.'

* * *

It started that evening.

I was drying up after tea when I heard Dad's voice behind me.

'A superb effort from the eleven-year-old,' he said. 'Look at that wiping action. This could be his personal best on the saucepan with lid.'

I sighed.

OK, Dad does a pretty good sports commentator's voice for an abattoir worker, but all I could think of was the one thousand nine hundred and twenty-seven days to go till the Sydney Olympics.

'But wait!' yelled Dad. 'Look at this burst of speed from his nine-year-old rival. Fourteen point six three seconds for the non-stick frying pan. That's got to be close to a world record if she can get it on the shelf without dropping it.'

Sharon, my sister, rolled her eyes.

He was still at it two hours later when we were cleaning our teeth.

'It's Sharon, Sharon's holding on to her lead around the back teeth, but wait, she's slipped, her brush has slipped, oh no, this is a tragedy for the plucky youngster, she's missed a molar and Brendan has taken the lead, he's streaking home along the front ones, it's gold, it's gold, it's gold for Australia!'

Before we could remind Dad that shouting before bed gives kids nightmares, he herded us out into the backyard.

Sitting under the clothes hoist were three banana crates, the middle one taller than the others.

'The winners' podium,' announced Dad.

We stared, mouths open.

Dad had always been mad about sport, but he'd never gone this far.

Weak with shock, we allowed ourselves to be led up

on to the podium, where Sharon received the silver medal for teeth cleaning and I was awarded the gold for not dropping the frying pan.

Mum stuck her head out the back door.

'Bedtime, you kids,' she said. 'It's eight-fifteen.'

'Crossing now to the back door,' shouted Dad, 'to witness a true champion in action.'

Before she knew it, Mum was on the podium having an old beer bottle top on a ribbon hung round her neck for telling the right time.

Over the next days, gold medals were won at our place for potato peeling, TV watching, ironing, getting up in the morning, pet care, closing the fridge door, vacuuming, chess, whistling, putting socks on, toast scraping, yawning, homework, head scratching, microwave operation, hiccups, sleeping, nose picking, sitting down, standing up, walking, standing still, begging a parent to stop, and chucking a plastic strainer at a parent.

'Love,' Mum said to Dad as he was hanging another bottle top round her neck (spin dryer repairs), 'don't you think you're taking this a bit far?'

'Over to the spoilsports' stadium,' said Dad, 'where it looks like another gold for Australia!'

As the days turned into weeks, we all wanted to scream.

Finally Mum did. 'That's it!' she yelled. 'If I hear another mention of medals, Olympics or personal best time in the loo, I'll kill someone!'

Dad muttered something under his breath about gold, gold, gold for getting cranky, then did what he always did when Mum blew her stack.

Took us to visit Uncle Wal.

Uncle Wal lives three hours away on a sheep farm.

It's a really boring trip because the land's flat and scrubby, the road's dead straight and you hardly ever see another car. Plus, when you get there, Uncle Wal hasn't even got a telly.

But this trip wasn't boring.

Half-an-hour up the track we ran out of petrol.

'It's a gold for Australia,' said Sharon, 'for forgetting to fill the car up.'

Dad glared at her.

We waited for an hour.

No cars.

Finally, Dad got sick of giving us medals for waiting and set off on foot back to the petrol station in town.

For the next hour me and Sharon just enjoyed the silence.

Then I started to wish I had something to read.

I read the car manual, the soft drink cans on the floor, and all the print on the dashboard, including the numbers.

Which is where I saw something very interesting.

I showed Sharon.

Then we saw a cloud of dust heading towards us.

It was Mrs Garwick from school in her van.

Soon we were speeding back to town.

After a bit I saw Dad in the distance, trudging along.

Mrs Garwick, who wears really thick glasses, hadn't seen him.

I distracted her attention by pretending to be sick in the back of the van.

She turned round, alarmed, and we sped past Dad.

Three hours later Dad staggered into town, hot, dusty and exhausted.

His shoulders drooped and he blinked painfully when he saw us sitting on the swings under a tree in the Memorial Park.

'Gold, gold, gold for Australia!' we yelled.

'Why didn't you stop for me?' croaked Dad.

Me and Sharon gave each other a puzzled frown.

'We thought you wanted to complete the distance on foot,' I said.

'Complete the distance!' shrieked Dad. 'It's forty kilometres.'

'Forty-two point nine,' I said, hanging a gold bottle top round his neck. 'Let's hear it for Dad, gold medal winner in the Olympic marathon!'

That was the last Olympic gold medal anyone in our family won.

We're all glued to the telly, though, watching the real gold medals being won in Atlanta.

All except Dad.

He's gone to stay with Uncle Wal.

That's None of Your Business

Kevin Crossley-Holland

THAT CLOCK! It was like a piece of icing done by a goddess, dropped out of heaven. It was white as white, and inlaid with little mirrors and misty pearls. The tick-and-tock of it was as close and comforting as the beats of your own heart, and the music it made on the hour, every hour, came straight from paradise.

Every boy and girl in the village came round to listen to it, and look at it. How longingly they looked at it!

So when they grew up and I grew old, and had little time for grand possessions, I thought I might just give it away. 'I'll give it to whoever can mind his – or her – own business for a whole year.' That's what I said.

On the last night of the year, a young man knocked on the door. 'I've minded my own business for a whole year,' he said.

I believed him. He was a dull sort of lad, the kind that never asks questions and doesn't seem too interested in other people or the wonders of the world.

As I went into the back room to fetch the clock, I called out, 'You're the second who's come to claim the clock.'

'The second!' exclaimed the young man. 'Why didn't the first get it?'

'That's none of your business,' I said. 'So *you* won't get the clock.'

I left the clock on the mantelpiece. There it is! Inlaid with little mirrors and misty pearls. It's like a piece of icing done by a goddess, dropped out of heaven.

The Fallen Angel Cake

Maggie Pearson

I'M NOT saying my mum's a bad cook. But the angel cake she baked for the cake stall at the village fête was a disaster. It looked like the cat had sat on it.

'If I turn it upside down,' she said, 'and ice it – the dent in the middle won't show.'

She turned it upside down – and the middle fell out.

'Don't cry,' I said. 'We can fill up the hole with something round and not too heavy—'

'Like what?' she said.

'Like a toilet roll! Cover the lot over with icing. And I'll nip down to the fête as soon as it opens and buy it back!'

So that's what we did.

Except I couldn't buy it back. Mum's cake wasn't on the cake stall.

We spent the whole afternoon trying to find out what had happened to it. We were still there when it came to the clearing up. So we helped with that. Then Chloe's mum invited us all back to her place.

I knew how it would be: tea in bone china cups, funny little forks to eat the cake with and having to take our shoes off so as not to mark the carpet.

It was worse than that. Much worse.

Right in the middle of the table sat my mum's cake!

We were getting up the courage to confess when someone said: 'Oh! What a beautiful cake!'

Chloe's mum beamed. 'Thank you,' she said. 'I baked it myself.'

In the Shower with Andy

Andy Griffiths

I'M IN the shower. Singing. And not just because the echo makes my voice sound so cool either. I'm singing because I'm so happy.

Ever since I've been old enough to have showers I've been trying to find a way to fill a shower cubicle up with water. If I put a face-washer over the plughole I can get the water as far up as my ankles, but it always ends up leaking out through gaps in the door.

But I think I've finally found the answer – Dad's silicone gun.

I've plugged up the plughole.

I've sealed up the shower-screen doors.

I've even filled in all the cracks in the tiles.

The cubicle is completely watertight and the water is already up to my knees.

And the best thing is that I've got all night to enjoy it.

Mum and Dad have got Mr and Mrs Bainbridge over for dinner. They'll be too busy listening to Mr Bainbridge talking about himself to have time to worry about what I'm doing.

I hear banging on the door.

'Have you almost finished, Andy?'

It's Jen!

'No', I say. 'I think I'm going to be in here a while yet.'

'Can you hurry up?' yells Jen.

'But you already had your shower this morning,' I yell.

'I'm going out,' she says. 'I need the bathroom!'

'OK. I'll be out in a minute,' I call. I always say that. It's the truth. Sort of. I will be out in a minute – I'm just not saying which minute it will be.

The cubicle is filling with thick white steam. Just the way I like it. Dad's always telling us how important it is to turn the fan on when we're having a shower, but I can't see the point. A shower without steam doesn't make sense. You might as well go and stand outside in the rain.

My rubber duck bumps against my legs. I pick it up.

'This is it,' I say. 'Just you and me . . . going where no boy – or rubber duck – has ever gone before.'

It has its bill raised in a sort of smile. It must be as excited as I am. Let's face it, there can't be that much excitement in the life of a rubber duck. Except that you'd get to see everybody without their clothes on.

Jen bangs on the door again.

'Andy! Pleeeeease!'

'OK,' I call. 'I'll be out in a minute.'

'You said that a minute ago!'

'I'm washing my hair.'

'But you've been in there for at least half an hour. You don't have *that* much hair.'

'I'm using a new sort of shampoo – I have to do it strand by strand.'

'Andy!'

The water is almost up to my belly-button. There's only one thing missing. Bubbles!

I pick up the bubble bath and measure out a capful. I

tip it into the water. A few bubbles, but not enough. I add another cap. And another. And another. One more for good measure. Another for good luck.

I keep adding bubble bath until the bottle is empty. The bubbles rise over my head. Cool. It's like I am being eaten by this enormous white fungus. Well, not that being eaten by an enormous white fungus would be cool – it would probably be quite uncool, actually – but you know what I mean.

Jen is yelling.

'Andy, if you don't get out right this minute, you're going to be sorry.'

Jen is persistent, I'll give her that. But I'll fix her. I'll use my old 'what did you say?' routine.

'Pardon?' I yell. 'What did you say?'

'I said you're going to be sorry!'

'What? I can't hear you!'

'I said get out of the shower!'

'Pardon?'

No reply. I win.

Aaaagghhh!

The water's gone hot! Boiling hot!

Jen must have flushed the toilet. That's bad news.

I lose.

I jump back against the shower wall.

Hot water splatters onto my face. My chest. My arms.

I grab the cold tap and turn it on full.

The hot water disappears. Now it's freezing.

I'm going to have turn both taps off and start all over again. I hate that. Being a pioneer is not easy.

I turn the hot tap off. But the cold won't budge.

I grab the tap with both hands. I try to twist it clockwise but it's stuck. Not even my super-strength can move it.

The silicone gun is hanging off the shower pipe. I pick

it up and start bashing the tap with it. That should loosen it.

But the handgrip shatters.

The pieces disappear into the soapy water. I'm staring at a thin metal rod coming out of the wall. And the water is still flowing full blast.

I kneel down and clamp my teeth over the tap rod.

No good. The tap feels like it's rusted into place. My teeth will crack before it moves.

There's no steam left. The bubbles have been flattened. The freezing water is almost up to my chest. Maybe this wasn't such a great idea.

Time to bail out.

I take a deep breath and dive to the bottom of the shower. I'm trying to find the plughole. I've got to get the silicone out before the shower fills up completely.

But I can't do it. I did the job too well. There's nothing but a hard rubbery slab of silicone where the plug used to be. I can't poke through it. I can't get a fingernail underneath to lift up. It's times like this I wish I didn't bite my nails. But then it's times like this that cause me to bite my nails in the first place.

I stand up, gasping for air. The water is up to my neck. I grab hold of the doorhandle and try to wrench it open but I laid the silicone even thicker on the doors than the plughole. If you ever want anything sealed tight I can recommend Dad's silicone gun. This stuff stays stuck forever.

I'm going to have to break the door down.

I'll use the gun. It made short work of the tap so the door shouldn't be a problem.

I bash the glass with the gun handle. It bounces off. I bash it again, harder this time. The gun snaps in two. Just my luck. Reinforced shower screen glass. Unbreakable.

I'm shivering. And not just from the cold. I'm scared.

I start bashing the door with the duck.

'HELP! I'M DROWNING! HELP!'

'I'm not surprised!' Jen yells back. 'You've been in there long enough.'

'Jen, I'm not kidding. Help me!'

'What did you say?' she says. 'I can't hear you.'

'Be serious,' I yell. 'I've siliconed myself in here.'

'What?'

She wins again.

I'm treading water. My head is very close to the top of the shower.

The only way I can save myself is to get rid of the water.

I'm going to have to drink it.

Dirty soapy shower water.

I'd rather die.

The water nudges the tip of my nose.

Actually, on second thoughts I'd rather drink the water.

I start swallowing.

It's working. I just have to drink as fast as the shower is filling up. And if I can drink even faster then I might get out of here alive yet. Actually the water doesn't taste that bad – it's only been three days since my last shower.

I keep swallowing.

And swallowing. And swallowing. And swallowing.

Uh-oh.

I can't believe this.

I need to go to the toilet.

But I can't.

I'll drink dirty shower water but I won't drink that.

I've got to hold on.

But I can't do that, either.

I'm busting.

* * *

My head is bumping against the roof of the shower.

It's getting harder to breathe.

There's more banging on the door but it sounds like it's coming from a long way away.

'I'm going to tell Dad,' says Jen in a distant voice. 'Is that what you want? Is it?'

'Yes, Jen,' I call. 'Yes! Please hurry!'

Everything becomes quiet.

My life is flashing before my eyes.

I see myself blowing a high-pitched whistle while Mum is trying to talk on the telephone. I see myself letting down the tyres on Dad's car. I see myself hiding a rubber snake in Jen's bed. Is that all I did with my life? Annoy people? Surely I did something useful . . . something good?

Nope. I can't think of anything. Except for solving the problem of how to fill a shower cubicle with water.

I may be going to die, but at least it will be a hero's death. Future generations of Australian children will thank me as they float around in their sealed-up shower cubicles.

Ouch!

Something is pressing into the top of my head.

I look up.

The fan! I forgot all about it.

It's not very big, but it's better than nothing. If I can get the grille off then I can escape through the hole and up into the roof.

I work my fingers under the edge of the grille and pull on it. It comes off easily.

I reach into the casing and grab hold of the fan. I rock it back and forth. There is a little bit of give in it. I start giving it all I've got.

Finally the bolts holding it give way. I push my arms and head into the hole, kicking like mad to get the thrust I need to make it all the way up.

The opening is smaller than I thought. I expel every last bit of air in my lungs to make myself thin enough to fit through the hole. Not that there was much air left in them, but it seems to help.

At last! I'm through!

I'm lying on a yellow insulation batt in the roof of our house. The glass fibres are prickly on my skin, but I'm not complaining. It's a lot better than where I was. I look back into the hole. It's like one of those fishing holes that Eskimos cut in the ice. But there's no fish. Just my rubber duck. I reach down and pick it out. We're in this together. I can't just leave it.

After I get my breath back I look around.

I know there's a manhole in the top of the kitchen. All I have to do is locate it, climb down into the kitchen and nick down the hallway into my room. Then I can put my pyjamas on and go to bed early. It will save a lot of boring explanation – and, if I'm really lucky, Jen will get the blame.

I have to move fast. I start crawling towards the kitchen. I'm carrying the duck in one hand and using my other hand to feel my way along the roof beam.

Suddenly I feel a sharp pain in my thumb. I jerk my hand back and almost lose my balance. I fling the duck away so I can grab the beam with my other hand.

I look at my thumb. A huge splinter is sticking out of it. I pull it out with my teeth. Ouch!

I shake my hand a few times and look around for my duck. It has landed in the middle of a large unsupported section of insulation batts. I'm tempted to leave it there. But that wouldn't be right. It's been with me all the way. I can't abandon it now.

I reach towards it but it's too far away. I'm going to have to crawl out there. I know you're not supposed to climb on the unsupported parts of the roof, but I think it will be OK. I'm not that heavy. And it's not as if I have any clothes on to weigh me down.

I climb carefully onto the batts and start moving slowly to the centre. One more metre and I'm there.

I pick up my duck and bring it up to my face. 'Just you and me,' I say.

The duck creaks. That's weird. I didn't know rubber ducks could talk.

Uh-oh. The creaking is not coming from the duck. It's coming from underneath me. The ceiling is giving away.

I try to grab the roof beam but I can't reach it.

The ceiling caves in.

Next thing I know I'm lying, legs spread, in the middle of the dinner table – my fall broken by an insulation batt.

As the dust from the ceiling plaster settles, I see Mr and Mrs Bainbridge and Mum and Dad staring down at me.

Jen is standing next to Dad, her bath towel draped over her shoulder. Her back is turned towards me and she's so busy complaining to Dad that she doesn't seem to notice what has happened.

'. . . I've asked him a million times but he just won't get out . . .' she's saying.

'Oh, dear,' says Mum.

'Oh, my,' says Mrs Bainbridge.

For once in his life Mr Bainbridge is speechless.

'Oh, no,' says Dad, shaking his head at me. 'No, no, no!'

'Oh yes,' says Jen. 'And I'll tell you what else . . .'

Dad nods in my direction.

Jen stops, turns around and stares.

I cover myself with the rubber duck, swing my legs over the edge of the table and stand up.

'I beg your pardon,' I say. 'I was looking for the kitchen.'

Nobody says anything. They are all just staring at me, their faces and clothes white from the plaster dust.

I head towards the door as fast as I can.

As I'm about to exit I turn towards Jen. She is still standing there, eyes wide.

'Well, what are you waiting for?' I say. 'Shower's free!'

Grimble's Monday

Clement Freud

THIS IS a story about a boy called Grimble who was about ten. You may think it is silly to say someone is *about* ten, but Grimble had rather odd parents who were very vague and seldom got anything completely right.

For instance, he did not have his birthday on a fixed day like other children: every now and then his father and mother would buy a cake, put some candles on top of it, and say, 'Congratulations Grimble. Today you are about seven', or, 'Yesterday you were about eight and a half but the cake shop was closed.' Of course there were disadvantages to having parents like that – like being called Grimble which made everyone say, 'What is your real name?' and he had to say, 'My real name is Grimble.'

Grimble's father was something to do with going away, and his mother was a housewife by profession who liked to be with her husband whenever possible. Grimble went to school. Usually, when he left home in the morning, his parents were still asleep and there would be a note at the bottom of the stairs saying, *Enclosed please find ten p. for your breakfast.* As 10p is not very nourishing he used to take the money to a shop and get a glass of ginger beer, some broken pieces of meringue and a slice of streaky bacon. And at school he got lunch; that was the orderly part of his life. Shepherd's pie or sausages and mashed potatoes on Monday, Tuesday, Wednesday, Thursday; and on Fridays, fish fingers. This was followed by chocolate spodge – which is a mixture between chocolate sponge and chocolate sludge, and does not taste of anything very much except custard – which the school cook poured over everything.

One Monday Grimble came back from school, opened the door and shouted, 'I am home.' No one shouted anything in answer. So he went round the house looking for messages because his parents always left messages. It was the one thing they were really good at.

On a table in the sitting room there was a globe. And stuck into the globe were two pins, each with a triangle of paper on it. One of these was stuck into England and said *Grimble*, and the other was stuck into Peru and said *us*. He went into the kitchen and here was another note: *Tea is in the fridge, sandwiches in the oven. Have a good time.*

In the bedroom was a note saying *You will do your homework, won't you? P.S. don't forget to say your prayers.*

In the bathroom a message *Teeth*.

He walked round the house thinking they've really been very good, and then he went to the back-door and saw a note: *Milkman. No milk for five days.*

He changed the note to *Not much* milk for five days, and sat down in the kitchen and started to think about things. Five days is a long time for anyone and an especially long time for a boy of ten who is never quite sure whether he might not be missing his birthday. It had been weeks since he last had a birthday. He got a piece of paper and worked out five days at twenty-four hours a day and made it over a hundred hours, actually a hundred and something hours. He decided to have a sandwich. He opened the oven door, found the oven absolutely full of sandwiches, and took one with corned beef and apricot jam in it. It was a bit stale, like sandwiches are when they have been made a long time ago, so he lit the oven to freshen the sandwiches up a bit and decided to write a poem about his situation. This is what he wrote:

My Situation
by Grimble
When parents go to Peru
And leave cups of tea in the fridge,
It's jolly hard to know what to do
And I wish I could think of a useful
    word ending in idge.
The End

It was not a very good poem and it hadn't even taken very long to write, so he opened the door of the refrigerator and found bottles and bottles of tea. He poured himself a cup and sipped it. The tea did not taste very nice and it was not very hot, so he took his football out into the yard and kicked penalties with his left foot. As a matter of fact Grimble could not kick the ball at all with his right foot, but very few people knew this, so when he had friends whom he wanted to impress he used to say, 'Come and see me kick penalties with my left foot.' It worked very well.

After scoring one hundred and seven goals he went back to get a proper fresh sandwich. He opened the oven door and a very sad sight met his eyes. The sandwiches had been wrapped in pieces of paper, and the oven had burnt the paper, and all the butter had run out on to the bottom shelf, and the fillings of sandwich-spread and peanut butter and honey and lemon curd and cheese and pickles were sizzling in the butter. He got a teaspoon, tasted some of the mixture, and decided he preferred Weetabix, but as he was tasting it his eyes fell upon another note stuck onto the oven door and only a little bit brown from the heat of the roast sandwiches.

In case of emergency said the note *Go to* and there followed a list of five names and addresses all of them very near Grimble's house. He felt much better, kicked two more goals and went off to the house of the first name on the list.

Mr Wilfred Mosquito 29 Back Street (Ring Twice).

Back Street was just round the corner from his house, so he ran over there, and on the front door he found a note which said *Welcome Grimble, the key is in the milk bottle.* He opened the door, went in and found another note: *Food is in the kitchen. Kitchen is behind door marked kitchen,* and in the kitchen there was a big piece of paper which said: *Help yourself.*

The Mosquitoes' kitchen was big and bright, and there was a vegetable rack with coconuts and bananas and limes in it – limes are like lemons, only green – and a bottle of rum stood on the shelf, and the fridge had a lot of meat in it, all raw. He tried a sip of rum and did not like it much. It was strong. So he ate a banana and tried to kick a left-footed penalty with a coconut against the kitchen door, but a big chip of paint came off and he thought, I am a guest and I am not even supposed to chip paint off the doors in my own house; so he stuck the paint back on to the door again using the sludge on the inside of the banana skin as sticky paste, and went on an exploration of the house.

As far as he could see the Mosquitoes were a man and a woman and one child with a lot of clothes (or possibly three children with not very many clothes each), also six cats. He was sure about the six cats because he found them in a basket under the stairs. They had a saucer of milk and another saucer of meat that smelt a bit of fish. There were a lot of photographs of people in the sitting room and all the people in them were black. There was also a map of Jamaica. Grimble, who did not like to jump to conclusions but when it came to being a detective was every bit as good as Old Sexton B. and Sherlock H. and Dixon of Dock G., decided that the Mosquitoes were Jamaicans.

He decided this especially when he found a newspaper called the *Daily Gleaner,* printed in Kingston, Jamaica. Reading the paper he noticed on the front page a message telling you to turn to page seven for this week's recipe, *Coconut Tart.*

He turned to page seven.

Coconut tart, wrote the good woman who had thought of the recipe, *can be made by a child of eight.*

As Grimble was older than eight he realized that he would be able to achieve a coconut tart with great ease, took the *Daily Gleaner* into the kitchen, propped it up against the coconut, and started to read the instructions.

Make a short pastry in the usual way, it began. Grimble thought this an exceedingly stupid remark and was pleased to see that the writer must have realized this also because she continued, *by taking half a pound of flour, quarter of a pound of fat, half a teaspoon of salt and two tablespoons of water. Or you can use one of those ready-made tart-cases.* 'Why didn't you say so at the beginning, you stupid book!' said Grimble, and went out into the Mosquitoes' garden to try and catch a fat pigeon. The fourth time he threw his jacket over the fat pigeon's head, it gave him a sad tired look, waddled off and flew away.

Grimble went back into the kitchen.

For the filling, said the recipe in the paper, *you will need half a pound of grated coconut, a tablespoon of warm golden syrup, and two beaten eggs.*

He beat two eggs, and started to look for the coconut. It had gone. He remembered seeing it in the vegetable rack; he remembered kicking it, he remembered that very well because he still had a pain in his left foot. He read several pages of the *Daily Gleaner* to see if perhaps they said how one could make a coconut tart without a coconut, but all he found were pages and pages of small print headed *Work Wanted* and *Cars for Sale*, and it was not until he got to the last page that he found the coconut. It was propping up the paper.

Grimble like most small boys thought that a coconut grew on a piece of metal in the fairground, and did not know how one turned the hard brown hairy thing that never moved when you threw wooden balls at it into fluffy white coconut meat that you got in a chocolate coconut bar. He might never have found out if he had not decided to have one more left-footed penalty, using the kitchen table as the goal. The coconut hit the goalpost (actually the leg of the table), and broke in half. As it did so, a large puddle of white coconut milk seeped across the kitchen floor.

This was quite a helpful thing to happen. First of all it showed him where the fluffy white meat was, and secondly he had begun to feel he ought to do something about the six cats under the stairs, and now there was all this milk. He decided that six cats was much easier than a cloth and a bucket.

Grating a coconut is not as easy as it looks because the flesh grows on the inside of the shell and it means wedging it off before you can get at it. Also the grater had a big notice tied to it which read *Grimble, mind your fingers*, so it was a slow business. But in the end it all worked, and he put the egg and syrup and coconut into the tart-case, and baked it the way they said, and shooed the cats out of the kitchen, and when the tart was cooked he ate it almost immediately. It was the best thing he had eaten since the corned beef and apricot jam sandwich.

When he had finished it was seven-fifteen, and as his official bed-time was seven-thirty, he went home. When he opened the door he saw a telegram on the mat. It was addressed to him. He opened it carefully and read the message: *Sending telegram tomorrow. Love Father and Mother.*

Just before he went to bed he wondered why they had not sent the message they were going to send tomorrow in today's telegram, but he got so mixed up trying to work it out that he brushed his teeth, said his prayers and fell asleep.

How Not to be a Giant Killer

David Henry Wilson

JACK'S BIG mistake was to try to make a comeback. Having retired as undefeated giant-killing champion of Cornwall, he should have left it at that. After all, he'd married the Duke's daughter, and one day he would be Duke himself. No worries about money, housing, unemployment – Jack had it made. But once a fighter, always a fighter. He started longing for the bright lights, the publicity, and razzamatazz of the giant-killing game, and at last he could stand it no longer and informed his wife that he was going out to kill a giant.

'Ts!' tutted Charlotte. 'Just when I've put the dinner on!'

'I can't help that,' said Jack. 'A man's gotta do what a man's gotta do.'

'Anyway,' said Charlotte, 'I thought you'd killed off all the giants already.'

'In Cornwall I have,' said Jack. 'But there must be plenty left in Devon.'

'Who wants to go to Devon?' snorted Charlotte.

'I do,' said Jack. 'To kill a giant.'

And off he went to look for his horse, his sword and his cloak. You may remember that a grateful wizard had given Jack a horse that could run like the wind, a sword that could cut through anything, and a cloak that made its wearer invisible. The horse was out in the field grazing, as it had been doing for the last three years. When Jack climbed on its back and said 'Giddy up!' the horse took one heavy step forward and its tummy bumped the ground.

'Can you still run like the wind?' asked Jack.

'I can't run at all,' replied the horse. 'Though I do have plenty of wind.' 'Ah, well,' said Jack, 'I'll just have to walk. The exercise'll do me good.'

Next, he searched for his sword, which he found in the garden shed under the lawn-mower. It had gone rusty. When Jack tried to cut the head off a dandelion with it, the blade snapped and fell off the handle.

'Ah, well,' said Jack, 'I'll just have to use my brains and my invisible cloak.'

But he couldn't see his invisible cloak anywhere.

'It must have disappeared,' said Jack. 'Ah, well, I'll just have to move so fast that they can't see me. I'm off now, dear.'

'Well, try and get back for dinner,' said Charlotte.

Devon had only been three or four inches away on the map, but by dinner-time Jack was still in Cornwall and was feeling tired and hungry. He knocked on a nearby door, and a man opened it.

'Hullo,' said Jack. 'I'm Jack the Giant-Killer.'

'And I'm the Duke of Cornwall,' said the man, and shut the door in Jack's face.

The man in the next house said he was the King's grandfather, and the people in the third house had a little dog with giant-killing ideas of its own. Jack was lucky to escape with nothing worse than a torn trouser-seat. He gave up knocking on doors, and walked sadly on with aching feet, a rumbling tum, and a cold bottom. He walked all through the night until at last he came to a sign which said, *Welcome to Devon.*

'Some welcome!' said Jack, and flopped down exhausted at the side of the road and went to sleep.

As he slept, Jack dreamt that he was still knocking on people's doors, and he kept calling out: 'I'm Jack the Giant-Killer! I'm the Duke's son-in-law!' But nobody believed him in his dream either.

The next morning, two Devon giants named Klottid and Kreem happened to come along the road. Just as they drew close to Jack, he cried out, 'I'm Jack the Giant-Killer! I'm the Duke's son-in-law!'

'I've heard of him,' said Klottid. 'He killed all the giants in Cornwall.'

'In that case,' said Kreem, 'we'd better stop him from killing all the giants in Devon.'

When Jack finally woke up, he knew that he must be very ill, because he couldn't move a muscle.

'Help! Help!' he cried. 'I'm paralysed! Call the doctor!'

There were two gigantic laughs and Jack, who was bound hand and foot (and everywhere else), was just able to turn his head enough to see the smiling faces of Klottid and Kreem.

'Jack the Giant-Killer, are you?' said Klottid.

'That's right,' said Jack. 'And I'm very ill . . . I'm . . .'

'Oh, dearie, dearie me,' said Kreem. 'Now which of us are you going to kill first?'

Jack suddenly realized that he was the prisoner of two giants.

'Oh!' he said. 'Ah! Um! Well . . . no . . . look . . . I've retired! That's it . . . I've retired from killing giants.'

'Ooh, thank Heavens for that!' said Klottid.

'What a relief!' said Kreem.

'So you've got nothing to be afraid of,' said Jack.

'Ooh, what a relief!' said Klottid.

'Thank Heavens for that!' said Kreem.

'Mind you, Kreemy,' said Klottid, 'I knew he was *bound* to leave us alone!'

'Oh, so did I, Klotty,' said Kreem. 'He's much too tied up to bother about us!'

'So you can let me go,' said Jack, 'and I'll be on my way.'

'What a sense of humour!' said Klottid.

'All those Cornish giants must have died laughing!' said Kreem.

Then they put poor tied-up Jack in a box (thus making him the very first Jack-in-the-box) and invited all their friends to come and see. In those days there weren't very many giants-killers in captivity, and so before long giants were coming from all over the country (except Cornwall) to look and laugh. Klottid and Kreem charged them an entrance fee, and also served delicious teas in their front parlour. (Klottid Kreem Teas are still a tradition in Devon today.) There were soon Jack the Giant-Killer mugs and plates and T-shirts, *A History of Jack's Capture* – written by the famous historian, Liza Plenty – and a do-it-yourself Giant-Killer-Capture-Kit, which consisted of a signed picture of Klottid and Kreem, plus a piece of string. Business boomed, and everyone was happy. Everyone, that is, except Jack.

Day after day, week after week, Jack lay in his box thinking up escape plans. His first idea was to threaten the giants.

'If you don't let me go,' he warned them, 'you'll be in a lot of trouble.'

'What sort of trouble?' asked the giants.

That was a question Jack couldn't answer, and so he abandoned the idea. His next plan was to challenge them to a fight – him against them, with no holds barred. They sportingly accepted the challenge and untied him. Then they tied him up again, and that was the end of that.

With plan number three he pretended to be dead. He reckoned they would untie him and throw him away, so he lay very still in his box.

'Definitely dead,' said Klottid.

'Dead as a Cornish giant,' said Kreem.

Jack's heart fluttered with hope.

'He's starting to smell already,' said Klottid.

'We'll throw him on the fire straight away,' said Kreem.

Jack miraculously came back to life, and that was the end of plan three.

Obviously these Devon giants were a lot less stupid than Cornish giants. They were making a fortune. They'd scared any other giant-killers out of Devon, and they seemed to have made escape impossible. What was needed was a super plan. And a super plan is what Jack eventually found.

Like all the best ideas, it was simple, though unlike all the best ideas, it did have one tiny flaw. The plan was to do nothing. One day, as Jack correctly reasoned, the giants would die and then someone might come and release him. Not only was this his best chance, but it was also his only chance, and so Jack settled down for a long wait.

The one tiny flaw in Jack's plan showed itself just twenty years later. Instead of the giants dying, it was Jack who died. This was quite unexpected, and he would have been rather upset about it if he had still been alive. Nobody knew exactly what he had died of, so the doctor wrote that the cause of death was Loss of Life, which seemed to cover everything. The giants duly untied him and threw him away – as he had foreseen in plan three – but being untied and being free was not much use to him now that he was dead.

When news of his death eventually reached Charlotte, she took his dinner out of the oven and ate it herself.

'Twenty-one years I've been keeping it warm for him,' she told her father, 'and I'm certainly not going to waste it now.'

As for the giants, they lived on for another twenty years, and finally died of old age, both on the same day. Their friends erected a tombstone for them, on which was written:

> *Here lie the giants, Klottid and Kreem,*
> *Who earned their place in Heaven*
> *By making sure that giant-killers*
> *Never killed in Devon.*

And since that time, no giant has ever been killed by a giant-killer in Devon.

ADVENTURE STORIES

Mackerel and Chips

Michael Morpurgo

A MONTH AGO we were on the Isles of Scilly again for our holidays.

'Make a wish, Leah,' said Mrs Pender, who keeps the bed and breakfast where we stay. My birthday. Ten years old. I blew out the candles on the cake and cut it slowly, gazing out at the lifeboat in St Mary's Bay, the same lifeboat I could see from my bedroom window every morning, every evening. I wish, I said inside my head, I wish I could go out in the lifeboat, just once.

'Tell, tell,' cried Eloise, my little sister, pulling at me. But I told no-one.

My present from Mum was a morning of mackerel fishing on *Nemo*, Mr Pender's launch. Mr Pender would take me all on my own.

Like lots of visitors, I'd been out in *Nemo* before. She's one of the open blue and white boats that take you to look at seals off the Eastern Islands, or puffins off Annet. Her engine purred and throbbed as we cleared St Mary's harbour and turned towards St Martin's.

'We'll find mackerel off Great Arthur,' said Mr Pender, pushing back his sailor's cap. 'Be a bit of a swell out there. You don't get seasick, do you?'

I shook my head and hoped.

I'd been fishing once before and loved it. You could catch wrasse or pollock, but what I was really after was mackerel. My favourite meal in all the world is grilled mackerel and chips, with lashings of tomato sauce.

Mr Pender showed me how to let the line out till I felt it touch the bottom. Then I'd reel it in slowly, to entice the fish. I caught a small pollock, which I unhooked and threw back, and a lot of seaweed. Nothing else. Mr Pender fished beside me. For an hour or more we didn't catch a thing. *Nemo* rolled in the swell, the engine ticking over.

'*Nemo* was one of the small ships, y'know,' said Mr Pender.

'What d'you mean?' I asked.

'Dunkirk, during the War, when the army was trapped on the beaches in France. Quarter of a million men. They sent over every boat they could find to pick them up. Several out of Scilly. *Nemo* is the only one left.

'My dad went with her. Over two hundred he brought back. Badly wounded, some of them. Sea was rough as hell, s'what my dad said.' He looked up at the sky. 'Don't much like the look of this weather. Blowing up a bit. We'll fish a few minutes more, and then we'll head home.'

The sky above was low and grey and heavy. The sea was whipping the waves into a frenzy all around us.

At that moment I felt a tug on my line and reeled in. Two mackerel! But I couldn't get them off the hook. Mr Pender reached over to help me. The boat lurched violently and we fell together onto the deck. When I got up, he didn't. I turned him over, but his eyes weren't open. I shouted at him. I shook him. There was a red mark on his forehead and blood coming from it. Then the engine stopped and the boat was wallowing, helpless in the waves. When I stood up I saw the rocks of the Eastern Isles looming closer and closer. There was no boat in sight, no-one to help. I couldn't work the boat all by myself. I had to wake Mr Pender, I had to.

When I turned back to him again there was a man crouching over him, a young man in khaki uniform, his arm in a sling, his head bandaged.

'Don't you worry, girl,' he said, smiling up at me. 'He'll be all right. Needs a doctor. You cover him up with the tarpaulin, keep him warm. I'll get the engine going. Don't want *Nemo* on the rocks, do we? Not after all she's done, all she's been through. Saved a lot of lives, she did.' The engine would not start at all at first. It just coughed and spluttered.

'Come on, *Nemo*,' said the soldier, 'get your skates on. Those rocks are looking awful sharp and awful hungry.'

Mr Pender still wasn't moving. The engine roared suddenly to life. I looked out. We had our stern to the rocks and were heading out into clear open water.

'Take the helm!' the soldier called, beckoning me over. 'I'm not much good, not with one arm.'

Nemo ploughed through the sea at full throttle, the soldier beside me steadying the wheel with his good hand whenever it needed it. The spray came over the bows and showered us as *Nemo* rode over the crests of the waves and crashed down into the troughs.

'Just like it was at Dunkirk,' said the soldier, his head back and laughing in the wind. 'We made it then, we'll make it now. Look out for rocks, girl.'

Only when we turned into the shelter of St Mary's harbour and the soldier pulled back the throttle did we stop tossing and turning.

'Beach her by the lifeboat slipway,' he said, pointing. 'And then we'll get a doctor for Mr Pender.'

I steered a course through the anchored yachts as best I could, until *Nemo* ground up on the beach and came to a jolting stop, the engine still ticking over.

There were people running down the beach towards us, shouting at us, then climbing up into the boat. Someone was crouching over Mr Pender. Someone else was on the radio calling for an ambulance.

I tried to tell them what had happened.

'What soldier?' they said. But when I looked around for the soldier, he was gone.

The doctor examined me in the hospital. I told her about the soldier. I wasn't making much sense, she said. But I'd be fine. I was just a little exhausted, that's all.

'Bravest girl in the world,' said Mr Pender later. 'Saved the *Nemo*, saved me.'

'It was the soldier,' I told him; but just like the doctor, he wasn't listening.

I had mackerel and chips that evening and tomato sauce, lashings of it. Eloise pinched most of the chips. Well, she would.

The next day, when the storm had passed, the Scilly lifeboat took us all out on a special trip as a reward – for my bravery, they said. As I passed the Eastern Isles, I made a wish. I wished I could see my soldier again, just once, to thank him. But I never did. Some wishes come true, I suppose. Others don't.

The Leopard

Ruskin Bond

I FIRST SAW the leopard when I was crossing the small stream at the bottom of the hill.

The ravine was so deep that for most of the day it remained in shadow. This encouraged many birds and animals to emerge from cover during daylight hours. Few people ever passed that way: only milkmen and charcoal-burners from the surrounding villages.

As a result, the ravine had become a little haven of wildlife, one of the few natural sanctuaries left near Mussoorie, a hill station in northern India.

Below my cottage was a forest of oak and maple and Himalayan rhododendron. A narrow path twisted its way down through the trees, over an open ridge where red sorrel grew wild, and then steeply down through a tangle of wild raspberries, creeping vines and slender bamboo.

At the bottom of the hill the path led on to a grassy verge, surrounded by wild dog roses. (It is surprising how closely the flora of the lower Himalayas, between 5,000 to 8,000 feet, resembles that of the English countryside.)

The stream ran close by the verge, tumbling over

smooth pebbles, over rocks worn yellow with age, on its way to the plains and to the little Song River and finally to the sacred Ganges.

When I first discovered the stream it was early April and the wild roses were flowering – small white blossoms lying in clusters.

I walked down to the stream almost every day, after two or three hours of writing. I had lived in cities too long, and had returned to the hills to renew myself, both physically and mentally. Once you have lived with mountains for any length of time, you belong to them, and must return again and again.

Nearly every morning, and sometimes during the day, I heard the cry of the barking deer. And in the evening, walking through the forest, I disturbed parties of pheasant. The birds went gliding down the ravine on open, motionless wings. I saw pine martens and a handsome red fox, and I recognized the footprints of a bear.

As I had not come to take anything from the forest, the birds and animals soon grew accustomed to my presence; or possibly they recognized my footsteps. After some time, my approach did not disturb them.

The langurs in the oak and rhododendron trees, who would at first go leaping through the branches at my approach, now watched me with some curiosity as they munched the tender green shoots of the oak.

The young ones scuffled and wrestled like boys, while their parents groomed each other's coats, stretching themselves out on the sunlit hillside. But one evening, as I passed, I heard them chattering in the trees, and I knew I was not the cause of their excitement.

As I crossed the stream and began climbing the hill, the grunting and chattering increased, as though the langurs were trying to warn me of some hidden danger.

A shower of pebbles came rattling down the steep hillside, and I looked up to see a sinewy, orange-gold leopard poised on a rock about 20 feet above me.

It was not looking toward me, but had its head thrust attentively forward, in the direction of the ravine. Yet it must have sensed my presence, because it slowly turned its head and looked down at me.

It seemed a little puzzled at my presence there; and when, to give myself courage, I clapped my hands sharply, the leopard sprang away into the thickets, making absolutely no sound as it melted into the shadows.

I had disturbed the animal in its quest for food. But a little later I heard the quickening cry of a barking deer as it fled through the forest. The hunt was still on.

The leopard, like other members of the cat family, is nearing extinction in India, and I was surprised to find one so close to Mussoorie. Probably the deforestation that had been taking place in the surrounding hills had driven the deer into this green valley; and the leopard, naturally, had followed.

It was some weeks before I saw the leopard again, although I was often aware of its presence. A dry, rasping cough sometimes gave it away. At times I felt almost certain that I was being followed.

Once, when I was late getting home, and the brief twilight gave way to a dark, moonless night, I was startled by a family of porcupines running about in a clearing. I looked around nervously, and saw two bright eyes staring at me from a thicket. I stood still, my heart banging away against my ribs. Then the eyes danced away, and I realized that they were only fireflies.

In May and June, when the hills were brown and dry, it was always cool and green near the stream, where ferns and maidenhair and long grasses continued to thrive.

Downstream I found a small pond where I could bathe, and a cave with water dripping from the roof, the water spangled gold and silver in the shafts of sunlight that pushed through the slits in the cave roof.

'He maketh me to lie down in green pastures: he leadeth me beside the still waters.' Perhaps David had discovered a similar paradise when he wrote those words; perhaps I, too, would write good words. The hill station's summer visitors had not discovered this haven of wild and green things. I was beginning to feel that the place belonged to me, that dominion was mine.

The stream had at least one other regular visitor, a spotted forktail, and though it did not fly away at my approach it became restless if I stayed too long, and then it would move from boulder to boulder uttering a long complaining cry.

I spent an afternoon trying to discover the bird's nest, which I was certain contained young, because I had seen the forktail carrying grubs in her bill. The problem was that when the bird flew upstream I had difficulty in following her rapidly enough, as the rocks were sharp and slippery.

Eventually I decorated myself with bracken fronds and, after slowly making my way upstream, hid myself in the hollow stump of a tree at a spot where the forktail often disappeared. I had no intention of robbing the bird: I was simply curious to see its home.

By crouching down, I was able to command a view of a small stretch of the stream and the sides of the ravine; but I had done little to deceive the forktail, who continued to object strongly to my presence so near her home.

I summoned up my reserves of patience and sat

perfectly still for about 10 minutes. The forktail quietened down. Out of sight, out of mind. But where had she gone? Probably into the walls of the ravine where, I felt sure, she was guarding her nest.

I decided to take her by surprise, and stood up suddenly, in time to see not the forktail on her doorstep, but the leopard bounding away with a grunt of surprise! Two urgent springs, and it had crossed the stream and plunged into the forest.

I was as astonished as the leopard, and forgot all about the forktail and her nest. Had the leopard been following me again? I decided against this possibility. Only man-eaters follow humans, and, as far as I knew, there had never been a man-eater in the vicinity of Mussoorie.

During the monsoon the stream became a rushing torrent, bushes and small trees were swept away, and the friendly murmur of the water became a threatening boom. I did not visit the place too often, as there were leeches in the long grass.

One day I found the remains of a barking deer which had only been partly eaten. I wondered why the leopard had not hidden the rest of his meal, and decided that it must have been disturbed while eating.

Then, climbing the hill, I met a party of hunters resting beneath the oaks. They asked me if I had seen a leopard. I said I had not. They said they knew there was a leopard in the forest.

Leopard skins, they told me, were selling in Delhi at over 1,000 rupees each. Of course there was a ban on the export of skins, but they gave me to understand that there were ways and means ... I thanked them for their information and walked on, feeling uneasy and disturbed.

The hunters had seen the carcass of the deer, and they

had seen the leopard pug-marks, and they kept coming to the forest. Almost every evening I heard their guns banging away, for they were ready to fire at almost anything.

'There's a leopard about,' they always told me. 'You should carry a gun.'

'I don't have one,' I said.

There were fewer birds to be seen, and even the langurs had moved on. The red fox did not show itself; and the pine martens, who had become bold, now dashed into hiding at my approach. The smell of one human is like the smell of any other.

And then the rains were over and it was October; I could lie in the sun, on sweet smelling grass, and gaze up through a pattern of oak leaves into a blinding blue heaven. And I would praise God for leaves and grass and the smell of things, the smell of mint and bruised clover, and the touch of things – the touch of grass and air and sky, the touch of the sky's blueness.

I thought no more of the men. My attitude towards them was similar to that of the denizens of the forest. These were men, unpredictable, and to be avoided if possible.

On the other side of the ravine rose Pari Tibba, Hill of the Fairies: a bleak, scrub-covered hill where no one lived.

It was said that in the previous century Englishmen had tried building their houses on the hill, but the area had always attracted lightning, due either to the hill's location or to its mineral deposits; after several houses had been struck by lightning, the settlers had moved on to the next hill, where the town now stands.

To the hillmen it is Pari Tibba, haunted by the spirits of a pair of ill-fated lovers who perished there in a storm; to others it is known as Burnt Hill, because of its scarred and stunted trees.

One day, after crossing the stream, I climbed Pari Tibba
– a stiff undertaking, because there was no path to the
top and I had to scramble up a precipitous rock face with
the help of rocks and roots that were apt to come loose in
my groping hand.

But at the top was a plateau with a few pine trees, their
upper branches catching the wind and humming softly.
There I found the ruins of what must have been the
houses of the first settlers – just a few piles of rubble, now
overgrown with weeds, sorrel, dandelions and nettles.

As I walked through the roofless ruins, I was struck by
the silence that surrounded me, the absence of birds and
animals, the sense of complete desolation.

The silence was so absolute that it seemed to be
ringing in my ears. But there was something else of
which I was becoming increasingly aware: the strong
feline odour of one of the cat family.

I paused and looked about. I was alone. There was no
movement of dry leaf or loose stone. The ruins were for
the most part open to the sky. Their rotting rafters had
collapsed, jamming together to form a low passage like
the entrance to a mine; and this dark cavern seemed to
lead down into the ground.

The smell was stronger when I approached this spot,
so I stopped again and waited there, wondering if I had
discovered the lair of the leopard, wondering if the
animal was now at rest after a night's hunt.

Perhaps he was crouching there in the dark, watching
me, recognizing me, knowing me as the man who
walked alone in the forest without a weapon.

I like to think that he was there, that he knew me, and
that he acknowledged my visit in the friendliest way: by
ignoring me altogether.

Perhaps I had made him confident – too confident, too

careless, too trusting of the human in his midst. I did not venture any further; I was not out of my mind. I did not seek physical contact, or even another glimpse of that beautiful sinewy body, springing from rock to rock. It was his trust I wanted, and I think he gave it to me.

But did the leopard, trusting one man, make the mistake of bestowing his trust on others? Did I, by casting out all fear – my own fear, and the leopard's protective fear – leave him defenseless?

Because next day, coming up the path from the stream, shouting and beating drums, were the hunters. They had a long bamboo pole across their shoulders, and slung from the pole, feet up, head down, was the lifeless body of the leopard, shot in the neck and in the head.

'We told you there was a leopard!' they shouted, in great good humour. 'Isn't he a fine specimen?'

'Yes,' I said. 'He was a beautiful leopard.'

I walked home through the silent forest. It was very silent, almost as though the birds and animals knew that their trust had been violated.

I remembered the lines of a poem by D. H. Lawrence; and, as I climbed the steep and lonely path to my home, the words beat out their rhythm in my mind: 'There was room in the world for a mountain lion and me.'

How Little John Came to the Greenwood

Roger Lancelyn Green

You gentlemen and yeoman good,
Come in and drink with Robin Hood;
If Robin Hood be not at home,
Come in and drink with Little John.
ANON: *Old Rhyme*

AFTER ROBIN HOOD had rescued Will Scarlet from the Sheriff of Nottingham, he remained quietly in Sherwood Forest for some time, building huts in several of the most secret and hidden clearings, drilling his followers and teaching those who were new to it all the secrets of woodlore.

Many came to swell his band, outlaws, poor men who were suffering under cruel masters, and even a yeoman or two and several who had been forced into the service of the Sheriff or of various of the Norman knights and barons of the district.

The Great North Road passed through the Forest at that time, and surprise attacks supplied them with all they needed in the way of Lincoln green cloth and arrows – or the money with which to buy these.

When order and comfort had been brought to this new commonwealth of the greenwood, and precautions taken against surprise by the Sheriff or any of the neighbouring knights such as Sir Guy of Gisborne and their followers, Robin began to go further afield. He knew that it would be well to have several places of refuge should Prince John send a large force to drive him out of Sherwood, and in time he and his men were able to disappear from the Nottingham district, and were often to be found in Barnsdale, Yorkshire, or Plompton in Cumberland: on occasion they were known even to visit Pendle Forest in Lancashire and Delamere Forest in Cheshire.

Much of their time was taken up in archery at which all became very proficient, though none could ever shoot so far or so true as Robin himself, and in fencing with swords, or playing at quarter-staff. But there was time for hunting as well, since venison was the most usual food, varied with pork from the wild boars, hares, and various wild fowl.

Many a time Robin would grow weary of the general course of every day and wander off by himself, leaving Will Scarlet in command. Often he returned from these expeditions with news of a party of wealthy travellers to be waylaid and robbed, or of some new injustice or cruelty practised against a Saxon yeoman or Saxon serfs. Sometimes he returned with a new member for his band of outlaws – and the most noteworthy of these chance meetings won for him the truest and most faithful of all his friends.

It was late in their first summer in Sherwood, and on a sudden Robin grew restless.

'Stay you all here, my merry fellows,' he said early one morning. 'But come and come swiftly if you hear the blast on my horn that you all know as my special call. We have had no sport these fourteen days and more: no adventure has befallen us – so I will go forth and seek for one. But if I should find myself in difficulties, with no escape, then will I blow my horn.'

Then he bade farewell to Scarlet and the rest, and set off blithely through the greenwood, his bow ready in his hand, his eyes and ears alert for anything of danger or of interest.

About noon he came along a forest path to a wide, swiftly flowing stream which was crossed by a narrow bridge made of a single tree-trunk flattened on the top. As he approached it, he saw a tall yeoman hastening towards him beyond the stream.

'We cannot both cross at once, the bridge is too narrow,' thought Robin, and he quickened his pace meaning to be first over.

But the tall yeoman quickened his pace also, with the result that they each set foot on the opposite ends of the bridge at the same moment.

'Out of my way, little man!' shouted the stranger, who was a good foot taller than Robin. 'That is, unless you want a ducking in the stream!'

'Not so fast, not so fast, tall fellow,' answered Robin. 'Go you back until I have passed – or may be I will do the ducking!'

'Why then,' cried the stranger, waving his staff, 'I'll break your head first, and tip you into the water afterwards!'

'We'll see about that' said Robin, and taking an arrow well feathered from the wing of a goose, he fitted it to the string.

'Draw that bow string ever so little!' shouted the stranger, 'and I'll first tan your hide with this good staff of mine, and then soak you well in the stream!'

'You talk like a plain ass!' exclaimed Robin scornfully, 'for were I to bend my bow I could send an arrow quite through your proud heart before you could touch me with your staff.'

'If I talk like an ass,' answered the stranger, 'you talk like a coward. You stand there well armed with a good long bow, while I have only a staff and am well out of your reach.'

'I scorn the name of coward,' cried Robin, slipping the arrow back into his quiver and unstringing his bow. 'Therefore will I lay aside my weapons and try your manhood with a quarter-staff such as your own – if you will but wait there until I cut one in the thicket.'

'Here I bide,' said the stranger cheerfully, 'one foot on the bridge – until you are ready for your cold bath in the stream!'

Robin Hood stepped aside to a thicket of trees and chose himself a stout six-foot staff of ground oak, straight and true and strong. Then he returned to the bridge, lopping and trimming his weapon as he came. He flung his bow and quiver on the bank, with his hood and his horn beside them, and set foot again on the bridge, crying merrily:

'Lo what a lusty staff I have, and a tough one at that – the very thing for knocking insolent rogues into the water! Let us fight here on the bridge, so that if one of us goes into the water, there will be no doubt who has won, and the victor may go on his way without a wetting.'

'With all my heart,' said the stranger. 'I scorn to give way … Have at your head!' So saying, he grasped his staff one quarter of the way from the end, held his other hand ready to grasp it by the middle when using it as a shield, and advanced along the narrow bridge.

Robin came to meet him, flourishing his weapon round his head, and by a quick feint got the end in under his adversary's guard and made his ribs ring with the blow.

'This must be repaid!' cried the stranger. 'Be sure I'll give you as good as I get for so long as I am able to handle a staff – and I scorn to die in your debt when a good crack will pay what I owe!'

Then they went at it with mighty blows, rather as if threshing corn with flails. Presently the sharp rattle and clatter of wood upon wood was broken by a duller crack as the stranger struck Robin on the head, causing the blood to appear; and after that they lashed at each other all the more fiercely, Robin beating down the guard and getting in with blow after blow on shoulders and sides until the dust flew from the stranger's jerkin like smoke.

But on a sudden, with a great cry of rage the stranger whirled up his staff and smote so mightily and with such fury that even Robin could not withstand it, but tumbled head over heels into the stream and disappeared from sight.

'Good fellow, good fellow, where are you now?' shouted the stranger kneeling on the bridge and gazing anxiously down into the water.

'Here I am!' shouted Robin gaily as he pulled himself out by an overhanging hawthorn, 'just floating down the stream – and washing my bruised head as I go! I must acknowledge myself beaten: you're a fine fellow, and a good hitter – and as the day is yours, let there be no more battle between us.'

With that Robin picked up his horn and sounded a shrill blast on it. Then turning to the stranger he said:

'Whither were you hastening in the greenwood? I trust that you can spare time from your business to dine with me? Indeed I insist upon it – and must use force, if persuasion will not bring you!'

'To tell you truth,' answered the stranger, 'I was in search of a man they call Robin Hood—'

Before Robin could answer there was a crashing in the

thicket and out bounded Will Scarlet, followed by many another of his men, making a bold show in their well-fitting doublets and hose of Lincoln Green.

'Good master!' cried Scarlet, 'what has befallen you that you blew the call for us? You are bleeding – and wet to the skin!'

'Nothing has befallen me,' answered Robin, 'save that this fine fellow here has just tumbled me into the stream with that long staff of his!'

'By the Rood,' exclaimed Scarlet, 'he cannot go scot free after so insulting bold Robin Hood. Come on, my merry men, let us give him a turn of the cold water.'

'No, no!' laughed Robin. 'He's a stout fellow, and tumbled me over in fair fight – so let him be. Come now, my friend,' he added, turning to the stranger, 'these bowmen will give you no cause for fear – they are all my friends. And they shall be your friends too, if you'll set your hand in mine and swear loyalty to Robin Hood and his companions. Speak up, jolly blade, and never fear – and we'll soon have you as fine a shot with the long bow as you are a player with the stout quarter-staff!'

'Why, here is my hand,' cried the stranger, 'and my heart goes with it, honest Robin. My name is John Little, and you need not fear that I will bring any shame upon you and your merry men: I am skilled in the arts of war and of the chase, and will follow you loyally wheresoever you may lead.'

'I still think you need a ducking!' said Scarlet, later that day as they all sat round a fire before which two plump does were roasting. 'But a good sprinkling with brown ale will at least do you no harm. It is our custom here in the greenwood to give every man who joins us a new name. What say you, my friends, shall we not make this into a christening feast for our new friend, and bestow a greenwood name upon him?'

'Well said, good Scarlet!' cried the outlaws, gathering round in a ring of laughing faces. 'And Robin shall be his godfather!'

'Agreed!' smiled Robin. 'Now to your work, good Parson Scarlet!'

'Why then,' cried Scarlet, filling a gigantic mug with foaming ale, 'attend all of you! This child, this babe brought here for christening, was called John Little. But seeing that he is so small, so puny a babe – being indeed no more than seven foot high, and a mere ell or so about the waist (what say you, child, a mere yard and no yard and a quarter? – well, well, a year of venison and strong ale will make you two yards about!) – As I was saying, seeing that the child is so under size—'

'And still under – nourished!' interrupted John Little, sniffing hungrily in the direction of the Steaming venison.

'Seeing all this!' continued Scarlet serenely, 'we'll turn him back to front – and name him Little John now and for ever. Long live Little John!'

With that he made as if to pour the ale over his god-child's head, but Little John twisted the mug out of his hand, and shouting aloud: 'Thus Little John pledges Robin Hood and all who follow him in the merry greenwood!' he set the great tankard to his lips and drained it at a draught.

After that, they feasted and rejoiced far into the evening. But thence forward Little John became one of Robin's most faithful followers and truest friends, and in time, as Will Scarlet grew too old for such active service, he became his second in command.

But though he grew no shorter, and certainly no narrower round the waist, the name of Little John stuck to him, nor was he ever known by any other.

The Picnic

Penelope Lively

I HATE PICNICS. There's all this fuss about finding a nice place, and then when you've found it there'll be too much wind, or wasps, or a cow-pat, and when everybody's settled down you can be sure something they can't do without will have been left in the car, half a mile away. And it'll be me that's got to go back and get it because I'm the eldest. 'Just pop back and get the rug, Michael – it won't take you a minute – and while you're there you might get Jamie's windcheater, and Dad's pipe, and my glasses, and the baby's bottle . . .'

I hate picnics.

Our picnics are usually to celebrate something. We're a ceremonial family: anniversaries of this, that, and the other; birthdays – even down to the dog's – nothing gets left out. This was Jamie's birthday. Eight. And Jamie, of course, has to pick Bodmin Moor.

'Draughty,' said Gran. 'I'll stop home in the garden, if nobody minds.'

But they weren't having any of that, the parents. We're a united family, too: positively tribal. One goes, we all go.

'Nonsense,' said Mum. 'It's not going to be draughty

in June. Middle of the summer, you couldn't ask for better.'

'The Summer Solstice, in fact,' said Dad, with his pocket-diary open. And then we get a great long disquisition, for Jamie and Gran, about how the solstices are the time of year between the equinoxes when the sun is furthest from the equator and appears to stand still. Yawn, yawn.

And so we fetched up at the Hurlers at half-past eleven on Jamie's birthday, picnic-baskets in hand, dog on lead, baby in pram, sun shoved firmly behind a black wodge of cloud and likely to stay there as far as I could see. Lovely picnic weather.

Gran thought it was a funny place to choose for a picnic. 'Too bare; And it's industrial. All those chimneys.'

I put her right about the chimneys – quietly, not to get anyone upset. 'Does being historic tin-mines make them look nicer?' she said, and we had a bit of a giggle about that. She's all right, Gran. But of course it wasn't the tin-mines we'd come to see. They're great on having an objective, the parents. We never just go anywhere – we go there to see something. Though in this case, as usual, old Mum gave it one quick look and then was off getting settled in. Finding a nice place out of the wind, somewhere for the pram, a bit of dry grass to sit on, all that . . .

The Hurlers aren't all that much to look at, granted. A bit stumpy, the stones are, sticking up out of the gorse and stuff – in fact at first they seem just accidental so that it comes as a bit of a jolt when you realize they are in fact arranged in circles. Even so, they're not on nodding terms with Stonehenge and that lot. We all dealt with them in our own way: Mum didn't bother, Gran had a look round, found herself a nice comfy one to lean against and got her knitting out, Jamie climbed three of them and jumped off again, Toby (the dog) lifted his leg against the biggest and then went rabbiting, Dad held forth to me because nobody else was listening.

'Prehistoric.'

'Yes, Dad. How old?' Politely.

That had him floored, as I knew it would, so I told him, because as a matter of fact I'd looked them up in the Cornwall book at school, the day before. 'Bronze Age, they think, but nobody's all that sure exactly when. The Beaker People or the Urn People or one of those lots.'

'Taken over now by the Picnic People,' said Dad. Not all that good a joke, but we enjoyed it until Mum called out – wait for it – that she'd left the newspaper and the baby's feeder in the car and would Michael just pop back for it.

So off I trailed. Mind, it wasn't that far – I've known worse. You could see the car, and the other one that had been there when we'd come. Mum was annoyed about that – she likes having places to herself. We're a territorial family, too. She gave it a few nasty looks, but when we got up to the stone circles the other people were some way away, camped on the rising ground nearer the Cheesewring, with *their* picnic and *their* folding-stools and *their* rugs and cameras and newspapers.

'That's all right,' said Mum. 'They're nowhere near. And they look nice.' Mum's an expert in niceness. It conducts itself for her, like electricity. She knows if people moving into our street are nice before they've got the removal van unloaded.

'Anyway,' said Gran, 'you like to know there's someone else around. You don't want to be on your own, do you, not really.'

'Why not?' said Jamie.

'Well – if one of us had an accident or something . . .'

'Listen to you!' said Mum. 'I thought this was a celebration.'

Coming back from the car I had a bit of a think about the stone circles, and what they were for, and all that. Which nobody really knows, of course. *Of religious significance*, the book said, vaguely, and then it waffled on a bit about rites and rituals, meaning, I suppose, that it hadn't a clue really. Of course it's a ritual – any fool can see that. Just like you draw squares on the beach and play hopscotch in them. But what ritual? You couldn't guess hopscotch from the squares, not in a hundred years. There was a slightly gruesome bit in the book about the bones of sacrifices being found near similar stone circles on Dartmoor, and a lot about tribal warfare which made you realize that it must have been more than somewhat dicey living in those days. It's bad enough now, with cars zooming at you and pollution and all that, but at least I know Mr Davidson next door isn't likely to stick a knife in me.

I was wrapped in thought, as they say (they actually do – 'Wrapped in thought, Michael?' Dad says. Mind, he's got a point, I daresay – it's something I'm known for and apparently it can be more than a bit irritating), and dawdling, I suppose. When I looked back at the Hurlers I could see Mum standing up waving. Hurry up, she meant, not hello, how nice to see you again. It was twelve exactly, my watch said – I hadn't been gone that long – but I ran a bit, or at least I trotted because I'm in favour of a quiet life and Mum can get stroppy if she's kept waiting.

I tripped over a stone or something once, and came down a cropper on the grass. Just as I got up, the sun came out. At least it came out in one place but not in another, if you see what I mean, so that where I was it was still grey and dull but over there at the Hurlers, and beyond, all the way up the slope beyond, it was bright sun. Funny. You could see the shafts of sunshine streaming down onto Mum and the rest of them, and the other family in their picnic place. I could see them very clearly, all standing or sitting quite still, as though they were kind of frozen by sun, I thought. Silly idea.

And then the wodge of cloud plonked itself back again and it went grey. I arrived at where the family were and gave Mum the paper and the feeder, but she seemed abstracted. She didn't even say thank you, which was odd, because one thing you can say is that Mum's got nice manners. Outside the family as well as in. Everybody likes Mum. She'd got the picnic all laid out but she was staring over towards the other family all the time.

We sat down and Mum began dishing out sandwiches. After a minute she said, 'You know, they've moved. They've come a bit nearer.'

And Dad said, 'Yes, I think they have.' He was staring too.

I looked. They'd put themselves into a bit where the gorse made a wind-break, the other family.

There was a pause. Mum was unscrewing thermoses. And then all of a sudden she said, 'They've got no business.'

I looked at her. Her voice sounded most peculiar – kind of strangled. She really meant it. She minded.

'Oh, come on, Mum,' I said. 'They've got as much right here as us.' She took no notice of that and what's more neither did anyone else. They were all looking over at the other family. Gran had put down her knitting and was muttering to herself. It was extraordinary.

They weren't eating yet, the other family. You could see all their stuff, in baskets and that, but they hadn't unpacked it. There were four of them – parents and two kids, around eleven or twelve, and the inevitable dog. And then while we were looking at them they got up and wandered off up the slope, as though maybe they were going up to the Cheesewring. Before they went they all stared over at us. It seemed to be catching, this business.

We ate our sandwiches, and drank our tea, and nobody said anything much. Not even Jamie. Once Dad asked if there was anything more to eat. 'No,' said Mum. 'That's the lot. Sorry. I should have brought more.' Once or twice I tried to jolly things up a bit, but nobody was having any.

And then all of a sudden Mum said, 'Jamie. See if you can get some of their sandwiches.'

Once upon a time, a long time ago, when Jamie was about four, he nicked a brass screw from Woolworths. He thought you could help yourself, you see – all those nice trays with shiny things in them. And Mum just about went through the roof. She took it back to the manager herself, personally, and Jamie had to come too, so he'd know what was what for ever and ever about taking things that aren't yours.

I thought I couldn't have heard right. I gaped at her with my mouth open like someone in a bad telly film.

Not so Jamie. 'OK,' he said. And he got up and went off through the gorse and stones and bushes towards the other family's picnic place. He went off, I say, but he went in a way I'd never seen him go before. He kind of slid from bush to bush and stone to stone, rather like he'd do if he was playing stalking, or tracking, or like I did when I was his age. Only he was doing it properly. Professionally, as it were. As though he'd been doing it all his life. Most of the time I couldn't see him at all, myself, even though I knew where he was. He melted, somehow, from one place to the next.

I watched, not saying anything because I was still too shocked to say anything. And the others watched, but they weren't shocked. Just interested. 'Good boy,' said Gran, once. 'Good lad.'

I took off my glasses and scrubbed them around on my sleeve. It's a thing I do when I'm fussed about something. You always feel as though things might clear up if you can see better. But even when I could see the moor unsmudged and unspotted, Jamie was still tracking over to that patch of rug on the hillside, and the parents and Gran were still sitting there watching him, cool as cucumbers.

The other family stopped and looked back once or twice. It was almost as though they had a feeling there might be something going on. But every time they looked Jamie melted into a stone or a bush, and they didn't seem to see him.

And then he darted at their basket, whipped something out, and was gone again, so quick it hardly seemed to have happened.

He got back. With half a dozen sandwiches wrapped in silver foil. 'Ham,' said Mum. 'Nice. Bread's from a cut loaf, though.' She passed them round. Everyone took one except me. I said I wasn't hungry, thank you.

'Anything wrong, Michael?' said Mum, quite ordinary and calm. 'It's not like you to turn food down.'

I said angrily, 'Of course there's something wrong. I don't know what you . . .' But they weren't paying me any attention.

'What else have they got, Jamie?' said Dad.

'Bananas. Some cans of Coke. Tart things – shop ones. Lyons, I think.'

'Not worth it,' said Mum. 'Anyway, they're coming back.'

They were walking quite fast down the slope now, the

other family, back to their things. It was overcast now. Grey, chilly. It felt as though it might rain.

I said, 'Let's go home. It's going to rain.'

'What?' said Mum. Not meaning, 'I didn't hear you', but 'I'm not listening to you'.

The baby started fussing. Mum reached into the picnic basket and gave her a chicken bone.

If I hadn't seen it with my own eyes I'd never have believed it. Pampered, that baby's been, from birth. Orange juice, strained messes, sterilized this and that.

As soon as Mum wasn't looking I took the chicken bone away. And the baby started yelling so I had to give it back. I took my glasses off again and had another scrub round the lenses.

The other family had got back to their place. They sat down on their folding chairs and on the rug, half out of sight now behind some bushes, though the father seemed to have put himself deliberately so that he faced out towards us. Presently, though, he moved, and we couldn't see any of them – just a corner of the rug.

We were on a grassy bit at the top end of the stone circle. Mum had picked it for flatness and absence of gorse, after a slight argument with Gran, who had wanted to stay by her personal choice of stone. Now Dad said all of a sudden, 'It won't do, here.'

So they were seeing sense at last. 'No,' I said. 'And it is raining now, anyway. Let's get off home.'

'What do you mean, Michael? Don't be silly,' said Mum. And then she said to Dad, 'You're right. Too enclosed. You can't see the approaches.'

Gran and Jamie had joined in now. They were on about cover, and that line of scrub over there, and having someone on the higher ground as a look-out. I just sat there. It was like a bad dream. And the rain was serious now.

'Come on,' said Mum. And suddenly there we all were, collecting everything up – thermoses, rugs, the lot – and moving them into a place just beyond the stone circle where there was a hollow in the ground and, just above it, a crest with wortle bushes and stuff. The bushes hid the hollow from the opposite slope. Dad lay on his stomach and stared through the bushes for a moment.

'Fine,' he said. 'Good view of their site, but they can't see us.'

'They'll have a look-out,' said Mum.

'True enough.'

I said, 'Look, I don't know what's the matter with everybody. They're just another family, those other people. *Another family.* Like us.'

'Don't shout so, dear,' said Mum.

'Should get one of them,' said Gran.

'Hostage?'

'Maybe. We'll see.'

Or else I'd gone barmy. Stark, raving mad. There they all were, sitting in the rain, looking out through the bushes every now and then, and going on like this. That was another thing – sitting there in the rain. We're a rain-allergic family, we are. One grey cloud on the horizon and we strike camp. Two drops and we're off the beach for the day. A doubtful weather-forecast and we stay at home. And there they were just sitting with the rain running off them, taking no more notice than a lot of horses in a field would.

I said, 'I'm getting wet.'

'What?' said Mum. 'What' meaning 'Don't bother me', again.

'I know,' I said, all bright and breezy. 'It's a game. It's some sort of joke you thought up between you while I was down at the car. Jolly funny. But let's stop now.'

Nobody paid the slightest attention.

'Ssh,' said Jamie. 'I can hear something . . .'

I couldn't. At least only birds and the usual kind of outdoor noises. And the rain.

'Downwind,' said Dad. 'There's one of them coming downwind.'

They were all staring through the bushes now, lying on their stomachs. 'It's one of the children,' said Mum. 'I saw a bit of jersey just then.'

Dad slid back into the hollow and rummaged around in the grass. He picked up a lump of stone, fist-sized, and then he stood up, looked quickly round, and threw it. Then he ducked down again.

There was a kind of gasp, from not far away. The noise you make when you've stubbed your toe or something.

'Got him,' said Dad.

'That'll teach 'em,' said Gran.

'Stop it . . .' I said. I was almost in tears, I can tell you.

'Be quiet, Michael. Raid, do you think, or full-scale attack?'

'Raid,' said Dad. 'He's going back.'

I said, in a silly, high-pitched voice, because I was getting in such a fuss I hardly knew if I was coming or going, 'If you do that kind of thing to people they're likely to do it back to you.' I sounded like Mum, when I was three or four, and having a spat with one of my mates. 'Oh, *please* can't we go home,' I said, since nobody so much as listened to that one. And I looked at my watch.

It said twelve exactly. But it had said that a quarter of an hour or so ago, when I was coming back from the car, so I listened to it. It hadn't stopped, at least only the hands had. I shook it, but the hands stayed stuck. It's a rotten watch, anyway: seven and a half books of Green Shield stamps. 'Where's Toby?' said Jamie, suddenly.

Mum humped herself up to the top of the ridge, very

cautious, and whistled. He always comes best for Mum. Knows where the food-supply is.

Nothing happened. No Toby bouncing through the grass. Mum knelt up so that she could see better and whistled again.

And a stone whizzed past her ear and thumped down onto the rug.

'Get down!' said Dad.

'They've got within range, somehow!'

'We'll have to move.'

'Not if I can find out where he is,' said Dad grimly.

He went up on the ridge, and stood, and then ducked. At once another stone flew past him and smacked into the side of the pram.

'Behind that big rock over there. Only one of them.'

They were all grubbing around for stones. 'Come on, Michael,' said Mum. 'Don't just leave everything to everyone else.'

I grubbed, miserably, and found a bit of granite and then lost it again. The rest of them had got a good supply, including Gran. She was getting together a nice little store.

'I'm going to winkle him out,' said Dad. He was filling his anorak pockets with stones. 'Have we got a knife?' Casually.

'Dad!' I said. At least I meant to. It came out as a sort of squeak.

'Only the plastic ones,' said Mum.

'Pity. I'll have one of them, all the same.'

He went out of the hollow the back way, as it were, and for a minute or two we could hear him rustling along from bush to bush. Then silence for what seemed a long time.

Then a grunt, crashing noises, a yell, someone running, more thumps. And Dad came back, panting, a dirty great swelling on the side of his cheek.

'Sent him packing!'

Nobody but me paid any attention to the bruise.

I said, 'Did he do that?'

'What? Oh, he clipped me with a stone before I could get to him.'

Mum didn't even look at it. Mum, who's brandishing the antiseptic and the plaster around at the merest hint of a scratch, normally.

'Which of them was it?'

'Young one, again. The rest have stayed put.'

'Now what?'

'Now we go home,' I said, hopelessly.

'I reckon,' said Dad, 'we use Jamie as a decoy. Try to draw one or two of them off, and then go in. Drive them back up the hill.'

'What about me?' said Gran.

'You stay here. You and the baby. Retreat if you have to.'

Gran nodded.

'Why did you have to interfere with them in the first place?' I shouted. 'If you'd just left them alone all this wouldn't be happening.'

Mum stared at me. 'They'd got things we wanted, hadn't they?' she said. 'Do get on and collect some stones, Michael. I don't know what's got into you today.'

Dad was explaining things to Jamie. He was to get out of the hollow and work his way round till he was on the far side of their site, and then he was to attract their attention, show himself, and make off fast. With any luck one or two of them would come out after him.

'Look,' I said. 'He might get *hurt*. If they're carrying on like this too. You can *kill* people, throwing stones.'

'Then we'll have to hurt them back, won't we?' said Dad, reasonably.

'But we've only got to go somewhere else…'

'Our place,' said Gran. 'Got to keep it. Silly boy.'

There wasn't any point in going on.

Jamie was getting ready to slip away. 'Don't be long,' said Mum. I looked at my watch; reflex action. Still stuck at twelve; still ticking. Stupid cheap watch.

And just as Jamie wriggled through the first few yards of cover it happened. A whole hail of stones, banging down on the rug and the thermoses and the grass. 'Take cover behind the chairs,' said Dad to Gran. 'The rest of you up on the ridge.'

We flattened out along the top, clutching stones. Thirty yards away or so a head came out from behind a slab of rock. A stone came flying towards us, and fell short. There was movement in several different places.

'It's all of them,' said Dad. 'Michael, you look after that one on the right.'

I threw a stone in that direction, half-heartedly. It bounced off a rock. And just as I'd got my head down again one came back and caught me on the arm. It hurt. And suddenly I wanted to do it back to somebody, like when you're about five. I took the biggest stone I could see from the pile behind us that Gran was busy stoking up all the time, and I stood up and chucked it at something red I could see beyond the next big boulder. Meaning not to miss, that time.

And somebody yelled.

'Good shot!' said Dad.

That made me see sense again.

'Stop it!' I yelled. 'Look, just stop it, all of you!' And I slid back down off the ridge. I wasn't having any more to do with it.

Gran was sitting on the grass behind the folding-chairs, with the baby beside her. The baby was watching what she was doing and making the daft 'Ooo' and 'Aaa' noises that babies make (rather nice, in fact, but I was in too much of a state to stop and have a chat like I would normally). What she was doing, Gran, was making a fire out of paper bags and dry grass (it kept going out, of course, because of the rain) and putting chicken bones on it and kind of mumbling at it. Barmy. Just clean, honest-to-goodness barmy. No wonder the baby was interested.

There wasn't time, though, to ask her what precisely she thought she was doing because first Jamie gave a yell and said, 'Oh, look, look!' and started waving Toby's collar around, which had come hurtling onto the ground beside us tied onto a stone, and then pebbles and things were coming down so thick and fast that Dad and Mum came sliding down and Dad said, 'Out! Get out, all of you. Back to the circle, and into the gorse beyond.'

Jamie was wailing, 'They've got Toby!' and Gran was chanting away now at her stupid fire, for all the world like somebody in church, until Dad bundled her up and off, and we were all scuttling over the grass, dragging things with us.

'Stop!' said Dad, and they all got down behind a big lump of granite on the edge of the circle. Not me, though.

'Michael! I said *stop* – come back here!'

'No.' I'd had enough. I began to run, the wet grass snatching at my feet so that I tripped and I could hear Dad yelling still, and Mum, but I got up again and went on. I could see the car and that was where I was going. After that I didn't care. I wasn't staying another minute in that stupid, crazy place with everyone behaving like lunatics.

I ran, with whatever I'd picked up (the newspaper and the baby's feeder, of all things) clutched in one hand, and the rain streaming down on my face. I couldn't hear them any more. Nothing. Just me, panting, and birds and things.

I fell over again. I think I banged my head or

something because for some reason I didn't get up at once. I lay there face down for a minute, heaving and blowing, and expecting someone to throw a stone at me, or jump on me.

I lifted my head and I could see them, Mum and Dad and Jamie and Gran and the baby. They were sitting about in the middle of the stone circle, and the sun had come out. They were just sitting in the sun. And Mum was waving.

I arrived at where they were and Mum took the paper and the feeder.

'Thanks, dear. What's the matter?'

'Nothing,' I said.

'You didn't have to rush so. It's only just gone twelve.'

It had, that stupid watch said so. About thirty seconds past.

'What were you doing?' said Mum. 'Just lying on the grass there?'

'Wrapped in thought, eh?' said Dad.

'There's something wrong with my watch.'

'Let's see.'

'It doesn't matter,' I said. 'It's going again now.'

'And it was raining down there,' said Mum. 'We could see. You've let yourself get soaked.'

'When are we having my birthday picnic?' said Jamie.

Mum started dishing out the sandwiches. The sun was out; the baby had gone to sleep; Dad was reading the paper. All right, I've got a vivid imagination. It's not a crime.

'There's someone coming,' I said.

'No need to sound so put out,' said Mum. 'It's just one of that other family.'

'He's got Toby,' said Jamie.

'So he has.'

The man had his tie knotted round Toby's neck. 'This little chap belong to you, by any chance?'

'He's slipped his collar,' said Jamie. '*Bad* dog.'

'That's very kind of you,' said Mum. 'We're most grateful. Thank you very much.'

'Not at all. Wonder if I might ask you a favour, in fact. Loan of a tin-opener for five minutes.'

Mum was rummaging in the picnic basket.

'Exchange is no robbery,' said Dad.

'Fair enough,' said the man. 'Seems to be turning out fine after all.'

'Lovely.'

Mum found the tin-opener.

'Very kind of you. Spoils the day a bit if you can't get at the food.'

'There's always something,' said Mum.

'Too right. We already had one of the kids get in an argument with a rock.'

'My husband's just had a bit of a fall. Nothing much.'

It was the first time I'd noticed the swelling on the side of Dad's face.

'Dangerous place,' said the man.

Everybody was smiling away, except me.

MYSTERY STORIES

The Happy Alien

Jean Ure

L AST SUMMER, a very strange thing happened to my
gran. She woke up to find a bus ticket on her table..
This may not sound very strange to you, but trust
me! It was strange.

My gran is what Mum calls eccentric. What me and
Ria (Ria's my sister) call *loopy*. I mean, we love her to bits,
but she is seriously out of this world. She has these
obsessions. Her main obsession is clutter.

'Everything in its place,' she says. Meaning: we do not
leave clothes draped over the backs of chairs, we do not
dump stuff in the middle of the floor, and we certainly do
not pile junk half a metre high on the tops of tables. She'd
freak if she saw my bedroom! Gran's flat always looks
like a giant vacuum cleaner has just breezed through it.
Every surface clean and clear. *Free of clutter.* What I'm
saying is, when Gran went to bed that night, the night
I'm talking about, you can take it from me: *there was no
bus ticket on her table.*

But there it was, in the morning. She rang up Mum in
a right state, claiming that Her Next Door had somehow
managed to get into the flat while she was sleeping.
Mum didn't ask her how. All sense flies out of the

window when Gran gets on to the subject of Her Next Door. Her Next Door was another of her obsessions. Gran was convinced she'd got it in for her. Now she was muttering darkly about the Evil Eye. The bus ticket, she said, was A Sign.

'Don't worry,' said Mum. 'I'll send the kids round. They'll soon sort things out.' She beamed brightly at me and Ria. 'You don't mind going round to Gran's, do you?'

'S'ppose not,' said Ria.

'Aaron?'

Well, it was holiday time; what could I say?

'I'd go myself,' said Mum, 'but I've absolutely got to get this work finished.'

We didn't really mind. Gran's totally off the wall, but she is kind of fun. She makes me laugh! I did warn Ria, though, that we'd got to take it seriously. Ria has this tendency to be a bit frivolous. A bit *flip*. You can't treat Gran like that.

'OK!' I said, as Gran slid back the bolts on the front door. (She's got four of them, plus a normal lock, plus a chain, plus a spy hole.) 'Show us the scene of the crime!'

Gran was pretty pleased that we were being so professional about it. She's more used to being told, 'You're just imagining things.' She led us through to the sitting room.

'There!' she said. 'I've left everything just as I found it.'

The table was over by the window, and it was bare except for a vase of dried flowers (neatly standing on a mat) and this little screwed up ball of paper.

'Undo that,' I said to Ria.

'It's a bus ticket,' said Ria. 'And a bit of silver foil . . . ooh! It's off an *egg*.'

She meant one of those miniature Easter eggs full of cream. Personally I think they're disgusting, but she goes for them big time.

'Never mind the egg,' I said. 'What about the bus ticket?'

'Says route 170,' said Ria.

'Where's that go?'

Ria peered closer. 'Says, *valid from Stage 1, valid to Stage 46.*'

Hm! None the wiser.

'It's Her Next Door,' said Gran. 'Look what she's done to my flowers!'

A couple of the flowers, a bright red one and a bright yellow one, had been taken out of the vase and laid on the table. Both the heads had been pulled off. It did seem a bit ominous.

'It's a sign,' said Gran. 'You mark my words!'

It was certainly a mystery. I was intrigued! I'm very interested in this kind of thing. Solving puzzles, finding rational explanations. This one was quite a challenge. For starters, Gran's flat is on the third floor, and I just didn't see how anyone could have got up there. There's a fire escape at the *back,* but Gran's sitting room is at the front. The wall outside is bare brick. No trees, no drain pipes: nothing.

'She's putting the Evil Eye,' said Gran.

'But Gran,' I said, 'how could she have got in?'

Gran looked at me as if I were daft. 'Through the window, of course!'

Me and Ria both turned, to gaze at the window. Gran is so security conscious that she has mesh across it – except for just a tiny slit right at the top, which she leaves open in hot weather. She also leaves the light on, all day and all night, 'just to make sure'. It's another of her obsessions.

'What's her name?' said Ria. 'Her Next Door?'

'You may well ask,' said Gran.

'I am asking,' said Ria. 'Could be important!'

Gran sniffed. 'It's *Smith* – or so she says.'

'Hm.' Ria nodded. 'Obviously an alias.'

'Well, I could have told you that,' said Gran.

I listened to this zany exchange in growing amazement. What on earth had the woman's name got to do with anything? And why should it be an alias?

'Don't you see?' cried Ria. 'She's an alien in disguise! She's probably—' she dropped her voice – 'a *shape shifter*.'

Well, Gran latched on to that idea immediately. That really got her going. A shape shifter! An alien shape shifter! Shape shifting through windows at dead of night to pull the heads off dried flowers and leave bus tickets on the table.

'Are you mad?' I hissed at Ria.

She giggled. 'Well, think of some other explanation!'

I couldn't; not offhand. But unlike Ria, who is totally uncontrolled when it comes to imagination, I firmly believe that there is always a rational explanation if you only look hard enough. I don't buy into all this supernatural stuff. And I *certainly* don't buy into shape shifters.

We spent the rest of the morning searching for rational explanations. First off I made Ria stand on a chair and try stuffing herself through the window, just to prove to my satisfaction that it couldn't be done. Next I went outside to conduct ballistic tests, seeing if I could lob pebbles or sticks through the window; but that couldn't be done, either. Even if it could have been, I didn't quite see where it would have got us, except that I do believe in being thorough. You have to eliminate all possibilities.

Gran, meanwhile, was busy ringing Mum to tell her about the shape shifter. Mum then spoke to me and said, 'Aaron, can you *please* stop your sister putting these ideas into your gran's head?' At least she knew it was Ria, and not me. But something plainly had to be done. Gran was in a lather, Mum was going spare . . . there had got to be a rational explanation!

'Let's be logical,' I said. 'Let's find out about the bus.'

So off we went to the bus station, and spoke to an inspector. We showed him the ticket – which I saw was dated just over a week ago – and he was really helpful. He obviously understood that we were conducting a serious investigation; we weren't just a couple of kids messing about. He told us that bus no. 170 ran from the other side of town. Stage 46 was Reeves Corner, and Stage 1, where it had come from, was Tipsy Hill, which was in a place called Tiddenham. Well! It seemed obvious to me what we had to do next: go to Tiddenham.

Ria wanted to know what for. I said, 'To check it out, of course!' She may have a vivid imagination, my sister, but she is totally lacking in any sort of logical thought process.

We went back to Gran's to assure her that we were on the case, and to ring Mum and tell her what we were up to. Mum said, 'I know Tiddenham! It's *tiddly*. It's just a village!'

'All the better,' I said.

'Well, so long as you're back by tea time,' said Mum. She's always pretty relaxed. She doesn't believe in molly coddling. 'Just solve the mystery and set your gran's mind at rest!'

Mum has total faith in me. I'm not sure that Ria does, but when it comes to action she does what I tell her. Right now I was telling her to 'Move it!' We didn't have all day.

On our way out of the flats we actually bumped into . . . Her Next Door!

'The alien!' whispered Ria.

She didn't look like an alien, she looked like a sweet old lady. Of course I knew what my sister would say: she would say that only went to show how cunning she was.

'It's what shape shifters *do!*'

My sister watches too much *Star Trek.*

The sweet old lady toddled up to us, beaming. She had a postcard in her hand.

'I wonder,' she goes, in this sweet old lady voice, 'if you would be very kind and put this in the box for me? Save my poor legs.'

We practically snatched it from her and ran. Not that I believed in any of this shape shifter stuff. Not for a minute! But it's kind of dark, in the hallway of Gran's flats. Plus I couldn't help wondering whether that sweet old lady wasn't just a little bit *too* sweet . . .

The minute we got outside, Ria was agitating to know what the postcard said.

'Who's it to? Read it, read it!'

I hesitated for just a second, on account of having this feeling that other people's mail might be private, and in that second Ria rudely snatched it from me. She has no scruples whatsoever. She probably doesn't even know what scruples are.

'So, all right,' I said. 'What's it say?'

Ria pulled a face. 'Dear-Madge-I-did-enjoy-your-visit-last-week. Next-time,' gabbled Ria, 'I-will-come-to-you. So-relieved-about-Maggie. I-would-have-felt-dreadfully-guilty-if-anything-had-happened-to-her. Much-love-Sylvia.'

'Well, that tells us a lot,' I said.

'Obviously written in code,' said Ria. 'Sylvia Smith . . . it's got to be an alias! Nobody's called Sylvia Smith.'

Actually I would have thought that quite a lot of people were, but before I could point this out to her Ria was reading the address and her eyes were popping out on stalks. 'Hey! Get this! It's addressed to someone in Tiddenham!'

'What?' I grabbed the card back from her. And there it

was, plain as day: Mrs Madge Henshaw, Tipsy Cottage, Tipsy Hill, Tiddenham. We were on to something! The question was, what?

'The plot thickens,' said Ria.

I said, 'What plot?' Hoping that she might be going to say something helpful. Something intelligent. Instead she gave this mad cackle.

'Alien plot to take over the earth!'

'Look, just stop with the smart mouth,' I said. I was beginning to wonder if maybe Gran wasn't as dotty as we all thought she was. Maybe Her Next Door really did have it in for her.

I said this to Ria, but all she said was, *'Shape shifter!'*

I had to admit we were no nearer solving the central mystery of how anyone, and especially a sweet old lady, could have managed to get through Gran's window and into the flat; but at least we now had a link between the sweet old lady and the bus ticket.

At this point I am going to throw in a cryptic observation: remember the silver paper! That is all I shall say. *Bear it in mind.*

And now to continue. Little did she know it, but Her Next Door had played right into our hands. She had been too clever by half! If she was the guilty party, that is. I still couldn't make up my mind. All I knew was that she had to be involved somehow. This was our lucky break! It gave us the very opportunity we needed. Instead of putting the card in the box, we would take it with us and deliver it in person to Mrs Madge Henshaw.

'Good idea,' said Ria. 'Go and suss her out . . . I'll know at once,' she said, 'if she's a shape shifter!'

We got off the bus at Stage 1, just like on the ticket, and an old man sitting on a seat in the sunshine told us how to get to Tipsy Cottage.

'Have you noticed?' hissed Ria, as we set off up the hill. 'Everyone's *old*.'

'So what?' I said.

'They're all aliens!' said Ria.

Sometimes I think my sister takes after Gran. She is *very* obsessive. So am I, in my own more logical way. I will stop at nothing to find rational explanations! I just knew there had to be one. I'd had enough of all this alien rubbish!

All the same, I did get a few uneasy prickles down my spine when we finally fetched up at Tipsy Cottage and saw it crouched there, low and squat and spooky, half hidden behind a giant yew tree, all by itself at the far end of the lane. Suddenly I wasn't sure that what we were doing was sensible. Even Ria had stopped her stupid jokes.

'Maybe we ought to g-go to the p-police?' she quavered.

'And say what? Shape shifters have been crawling through Gran's window? Aliens are taking over the earth?'

'Oh, don't be *stupid!*' said Ria. 'Just tell them what happened!'

'Please, officer, someone left a bus ticket on my Gran's table … I don't think so!'

'So what are we going to *do?*'

'You stay here,' I said. 'If I'm not back in five minutes—'

'Don't leave me!' shrieked Ria.

So we went up the path together, and knocked on the door, and this little old lady came to open it. *Another* little old lady. Yeah? I didn't dare to look at Ria.

'We … um … happened to be … um … passing,' I stammered, 'so we … ah … thought we'd … ah … give you this.'

I thrust the postcard at her.

'From Sylvia!' said the old lady. 'How very kind! Do come in, the pair of you.'

I said, 'Er—' Ria was already backing away, down the path. I was about to back after her, when the old lady gave a sudden cry.

'Why, here's Maggie come to see you!'

Maggie. Take a pause, because that is a clue.

Have you guessed? Maggie the magpie . . . strutting up the hall with something in her beak. Something bright and shiny . . . a ball of silver paper!

I don't think Ria got it even then. Her head was too full of aliens. But I did! I got it. It all fell into place . . . the rational explanation.

I checked with the old lady, to make sure, but it was just as I thought. She told us how she'd taken Maggie with her, to stay with her old friend Sylvia Smith. Her Next Door. How Her Next Door, not being used to having magpies about the place, had left the window open – and Maggie had flown off.

'My dear,' said the old lady, 'I was almost beside myself! I thought she was gone forever. But there she was, the darling, waiting for me next morning!'

We pieced together what must have happened. Maggie had taken the screwed-up ball of bus ticket and silver paper out of the bin and made her exit through the window. She had then been lured by the light in Gran's room, hopped through the gap, dumped the bus ticket on the table and helped herself to a couple of flowers. Quite logical behaviour – for a magpie.

'So there you are,' I said to Ria, as we sat on the bus going home. 'Nothing whatsoever to do with shape shifters.'

'Well, but it could have been,' said Ria.

'Well, but it *wasn't*. I told you there had to be a rational explanation.'

'Don't think it's as interesting as shape shifters,' said Ria.

It is strange how different we are. I actually prefer rational explanations. I find them more satisfying. Gran obviously does, too.

'I knew it was Her Next Door!' she said. 'I knew it all along!'

She was so chuffed at being right for once, and not having everyone accuse her of imagining things, that she actually went and told Her Next Door all about it, and now, guess what? They're best mates!

Ria says what's happened is that Her Next Door has turned Gran into a fellow alien, but Mum says that's OK.

'So long as she's a *happy* alien, that's all that matters!'

Moving House

Louise Cooper

I SHOULDN'T HAVE done it. I really shouldn't. But it's too late to be sorry now.

Mum and Dad had decided to move home, so I went along with them to look at a house. It was an old house, and it hadn't been lived in for a while. I liked it, especially when I saw that it had a cellar. Well, there was this door under the stairs – it had to lead to a cellar, didn't it? But when I tried to open it, it was locked.

'Oh,' said the estate agent, 'there's no cellar. It was filled in. The door's sealed up, and there's just solid brick behind it.'

He took Mum and Dad into the kitchen. But I stayed behind. That door looked so *interesting*. I was certain there must be *something* behind it.

Then I saw a rusty key hanging by the door. And sure enough, when I tried it in the cellar door, it fitted. The door wasn't sealed up at all. As soon as I turned the key it creaked open, and behind it . . . *Yes!* There was a flight of steps vanishing into darkness. Of course, I went down them. Down and down. They seemed to go on forever. And they kept turning and twisting, until I was . . .

Lost.

Oh, yes; lost. Because when I turned round, there were the steps behind me. Only they led *downwards*, not back up. I looked for steps that went up, but there weren't any.

'Mum?' I called. 'Dad?'

No one answered.

'Help!' I shouted.

But no help came.

I don't know how long I've been down here. It must be ages, because I'm much taller, and I've got a long beard. My clothes don't fit me now, but I can't get any more. I have food, though, because there are lots of rats and spiders here. And when it rains outside – wherever 'outside' is – water trickles down the walls, so I get enough to drink. But I wish someone would come. They must have tried to find me. Why haven't they? Maybe the steps have got something to do with it. Because whichever direction I turn, there they are. Always leading *down*.

So if you ever find a key to a door that people say can't be opened because there's nothing there . . .

Well, don't pick that key up. Just *don't*. Right?

Mrs Chamberlain's Reunion

Philippa Pearce

THIS IS a tale of long ago. I was a little boy, and our family lived – no, *resided* – among other well-off families in a Residential Neighbourhood. All those neighbours were people like ourselves, who thought well of themselves and also liked to keep themselves to themselves.

Except for one neighbour. That's where my story starts.

On one side of us had lived for many years the Miss Hardys, two spinster sisters, very ladylike. Our two gardens were separated by a trellis fence with rambler roses, a rather sketchy, see-through affair. So our family had at least an acquaintance with the Miss Hardys, and my sister, Celia, knew them quite well. As a little girl she had played with their cat, Mildred, until it died of old age.

Of course, we had neighbours on the other side, too; but on that side a thick laurel hedge grew so high that these neighbours – to us children, anyway – seemed hardly to exist.

In all the years that we lived in our house (and it had been bought by my father from a family called Chamberlain, just before my birth), neighbours may have come and gone beyond the laurel hedge, but we never noticed.

Then one day there was a new neighbour and suddenly things were different. The new neighbour cut down the hedge – not to the ground of course but to shoulder level. He thus revealed himself to us: Mr Wilfred Brown, retired and a widower.

He was a well-built man with a pointed, inquisitive nose. His eyes, large and prominent, looked glancingly, missing nothing; yet his gaze could settle with close attention. My mother said he stared.

My mother snubbed Mr Brown's attempts at conversation over what remained of the hedge. She had decided that he was what she called 'common'. She remarked to my father that Mr Brown had been a *butcher* – and my father, in rare joking mood, pointed out that he had indeed butchered the hedge. But my father was no more ready than my mother for a friendly chat with Mr Brown.

We three children, however, had been strictly taught to be attentive and polite to our elders. In the garden, therefore, we were at Mr Brown's mercy. He hailed us, talked with us, questioned us. We had to answer. Thus Mr Brown discovered that, in our well-ordered family way, we would be off on our fortnight's summer holiday, starting – as always – on the second Saturday of August.

The date was then the thirtieth of July.

The next time that my mother went into the garden, to cut flowers for an arrangement, Mr Brown accosted her over the hedge. He begged to be allowed 'to keep a friendly and watchful eye' on our house while we were away at the seaside.

My mother answered with instant refrigeration: '*Too* kind, Mr Brown! But we could not possibly put you to such trouble. We shall make our usual arrangements.'

Mr Brown asked, 'How good are these arrangements, Mrs Carew? What are they exactly?' He gazed earnestly, and the point of his nose seemed to quiver.

My mother was flustered by Mr Brown's stare. She was forced into explaining in detail that the Miss Hardys would be left with the key to the house, as well as with our telephone number at the seaside. But all this was only for use in case of emergency.

Mr Brown shook his head. 'The Miss Hardys, you say? Oh, dear me! Ladies are prone to panic in an emergency.'

By now my mother had recovered herself. She retorted quite sharply: 'The Miss Hardys are never prone to anything, Mr Brown.'

Mr Brown smiled and shook his head again. So there the matter was left. My mother could hardly forbid a neighbour to focus his eyes sometimes on our house, now so very visible over the low hedge. So, for the first time since we had lived there, our empty house would be overlooked not only by the Miss Hardys, but also by our new neighbour on the other side, Mr Brown.

Meanwhile, that second Saturday in August was drawing nearer and nearer.

I was the youngest child and excited at the thought of the sea and the seaside. The other two were much calmer; they remembered so well other fortnights beginning with that second Saturday in August. Celia told me privately that Robert, the eldest of us, had said (but not in our parents' hearing, of course) that family holidays got duller and duller.

Celia herself would probably be too preoccupied with her white mouse, Micky, to be bored on the holiday. There was nothing at all remarkable about Micky, except that neither of our parents knew of his existence. They had never liked animals. They hadn't really approved of Celia's playing with the Hardys' cat; they were relieved when Mildred died. Disappointingly for Celia, the Hardys did not get another cat – Mildred had only been inherited from their old friend and neighbour, Mrs Chamberlain, when she died. Celia missed a pet, and at last – most daringly and, of course, secretly – had acquired Micky. She would take Micky on holiday with her, and his very private companionship would console her during her seaside fortnight.

At the seaside we always stayed in the same guesthouse and did the same things – that was one of Robert's complaints. My father played golf and did some sea-fishing; and, whatever the weather, he swam every morning before breakfast, taking Robert with him. Sometimes he shared with my mother the duty of supervising our play: we were allowed to paddle and trawl in rock-pools with nets and to make sand-castles and sand-pictures. Sometimes we went for long walks inland, all five of us. Of course, there were wet Augusts, but my father never allowed rain to keep us indoors for even half a day. One could walk quite well in mackintoshes and Wellington boots, he said; and our landlady, Mrs Prothero, was obliging about the drying out of wet clothes.

Our return from these holidays was always the same. As the car turned into our quiet, tree-lined street, there was our house, but first my mother had to collect the key from the Miss Hardys.

'All has been well, I hope, Miss Hardy?'

'Nothing at all for you to worry about, Mrs Carew.'

The younger Miss Hardy, from behind her sister in the doorway, would ask, 'And you had a restful holiday, Mrs Carew?'

'Restful and delightful,' said my mother. 'Perhaps a little rainy, but that never kept us indoors. And now it's good to be home.'

Having recovered the key from the Miss Hardys, my mother would rejoin the family as we waited at our own front door. She handed the key to my father. He unlocked the door, and we entered. We brought with us the salty smell of the seaside rising from our hair and skin and clothing and from the collections of seashore pebbles and shells in our buckets. That saltiness, together with fresh air from newly opened windows, soon began to get rid of the stuffy, rather unpleasant smell of an empty house shut up for a whole fortnight. Soon our home was exactly as it had always been; and so it would remain for another year, until another second Saturday in August.

But this particular year our seaside holiday could not possibly have been described as restful and delightful, even by my mother; and our home-coming was to be very different.

From that second Saturday in August rain fell without stopping: this we had had to endure on holidays before now. What was new was Robert's sullen ill-temper, as continuous as the rain and as damping. He said nothing openly, for my father could be very sharp with a child of his ungrateful enough not to enjoy the holiday he was providing. My mother tried to soothe and smooth. She gave out that Robert was probably incubating some mild infection.

As if to prove her point, Robert developed a heavy cold after one of our wet walks and sneezed all over Mrs Prothero's paying guests' sitting-room. He had to borrow his father's linen handkerchiefs, and Mrs Prothero had to boil them after use, and dry them and iron them. Mrs Prothero complained about the extra work; and we all caught Robert's cold. In spite of this, my father continued to play golf and to fish, until one morning he embedded a fish-hook in the palm of his right hand. He came out of the local hospital with his hand bandaged, and in a bad temper. No more golf or fishing for the rest of the holiday.

This all happened in our first week. We were still, however, expecting to remain at the seaside, enjoying ourselves, to the end of our fortnight.

Then came the telephone call.

We had returned from a moist morning's walk to be told that a Mr Wilfred Brown had telephoned. He had urgently asked that Mr or Mrs Carew should telephone him back as soon as possible.

'What's the man on about?' my father demanded fretfully. 'Telephone him back, indeed! Does he think I'm made of money?'

'Perhaps something's wrong at home,' faltered my mother. She was remembering Mr Brown's 'watchful eye'.

'Rubbish!' said my father. 'One of the Miss Hardys would have telephoned us; not this Brown fellow.'

He was so enraged with Mr Brown that when, during lunch, the telephone rang again for Mr or Mrs Carew, my mother had to deal with it. She went most reluctantly; she returned clearly shaken. 'Mr Brown was surprised that we hadn't rung back.' (My father snorted.) 'He thinks there's something wrong at home. He's been on the watch and he's sure there are goings on (as he puts it) inside our house. He's sure that "something's up".'

'Inside our house!' cried my father, throwing aside his napkin. 'Then why on earth hasn't the fool got the police? Burglars! – and he just . . . Oh, the idiot, the juggins!'

'No,' said my mother. 'Nobody's broken in; he was quite positive about that. This is different, he says. Something wrong *inside the house.*'

My father stared in angry disbelief. Then he gave his orders. 'Go and telephone the Miss Hardys.' (My father felt that, as a general rule, ladies should communicate with ladies; men with men.) 'Tell them what Brown says, and find out – oh! Just find out *something!'*

My father bade us all go on with our lunch, as he himself did; and my mother went to the telephone again. She came back after a while, still troubled. 'I told them, dear, and they're sure there's nothing at all for us to worry about. They insist that's so. But they're upset by Mr Brown's suspicions. I didn't tell you at the time, dear, but he asked me on the telephone whether we'd empowered – that was his word: *empowered* – the Miss Hardys to use the house in our absence. But they say they've never set foot over the threshold in our absence. Ever. It's all rather strange and horrid . . .'

We three children listened, appalled – delightfully appalled. If the Miss Hardys were other than they had always seemed – if they were liars, trespassers, thieves – if all this, then houses might come toppling about our ears and cars take off with wings.

My father had risen from his carving chair. 'There's only one thing to be done: we go home. Now. At once. We catch them red-handed.'

'Red-handed?' my mother repeated faintly, thinking no doubt of the towering respectability of the two Miss Hardys; and, 'Now? When we're only half-way through our holiday?'

'Damn the holiday!' cried my father, who never swore in the presence of his family. 'We're going home. There are hours yet of daylight. If we leave now, we can be there before dark. Everyone pack at once.'

There was trouble with Mrs Prothero. At the time several of my father's handkerchiefs were simmering away soapily in one of her saucepans. Also my father thought that the holiday charge should be reduced by more than Mrs Prothero would agree to.

However, within the hour, ourselves and our belongings (including, of course, Celia's stowaway mouse) were packed into the car; Mrs Prothero's account had been settled ('Shark!' said my father); and we were off. For once, my mother drove, as my father's injured hand would not allow him to.

Of course, Mr Brown, having been at such pains to warn us, must have been on the lookout for our return. And if my father had hoped to catch the Miss Hardys unawares (let alone 'red-handed'), he underestimated the alertness of elderly maiden ladies. We drove up under darkened skies and pouring rain, and my mother was about to get out of the car, when the Miss Hardys, together under a huge umbrella, rushed down their front path to greet us.

My father had lowered the window on the passenger side and now called sternly, 'Good evening. We need our front-door key, please.'

Unmistakably the Miss Hardys were taken aback by our arrival – indeed, they seemed the very picture of guilt caught red-handed. 'Oh, dear!' and 'Oh, no!' they cried desperately. 'So early back from your holiday!' and, 'Surely you won't want to go into your house now, at once? Surely not! Oh, dear! Oh, dear!'

'The key!' said my father, and got it.

Quite a large party gathered in the shelter of our porch: my father in front with the key; the rest of his family behind him; behind us, again, the two Miss Hardys, still distraught; and behind them – although at first we were unaware of his having joined us – Mr Wilfred Brown.

My father, left-handed but resolute, inserted the key in the lock, turned it and pushed open the front door.

We had been expecting to enter or at least to peer forward, even if fearfully, into the hall. Instead, we found ourselves reeling back from a smell – a *stench* – which flowed out towards us. We knew when the tide had reached the last of our party because 'Phew! What a stinker!' exclaimed Mr Brown, thus declaring his presence through a handkerchief muffling nose and mouth.

But, in spite of the smell, we could, of course, see into the hall. (Surely my father saw *something*, however much he afterwards preferred to deny that?) To me the hall seemed somehow darker than one would expect, even on an evening so overcast – darker in the way of having more shadows to it; and the shadows seemed to shift and flicker and move. They were just above ground level.

And I was almost sure that – for a moment only – I glimpsed a taller shadow whose shape I could interpret: it was human, and surely female. I was not alone in this perception. The Miss Hardys had edged forward, and one now whispered, 'Yes, it *is* dear Mrs Chamberlain!' and the other, clearly in an agony of social embarrassment, murmured: 'We are in the wrong. We are intruding upon the privacy of dear Mrs Chamberlain's reunion!'

And then the shadowy figure had vanished.

Even before the Miss Hardys' whispering, I was aware that Celia was standing on tiptoe for a better view into the hall. With the keen eye of love, she recognized – or thought she recognized – one shape among the low-moving shadows. She became certain: 'Mildred!' she cried. She took three eager steps past my father and across the threshold of the front door into the hall itself.

There she was halted abruptly by the behaviour of someone whom, in the excitement, she had quite forgotten: her dear Micky. Up to now he had been in the concealment and safety of a pocket.

If the extraordinary smell from the house was

sickening for us, it must have crazed with fear the poor mouse. He attempted to escape.

His small white face was already visible over the edge of Celia's pocket; and it was as if the shadowy house saw him. (If walls have ears, why not eyes, too? Eyes that stare, that glare, that stupefy.)

I suppose that – if he were capable of planning at all – Micky must have meant to leap from Celia's pocket and instantly leave the house at greatest speed by the open front door. But the gaze of the shadowy hall was full upon him: he did not leap, but fell helplessly from Celia's pocket on to the floor of the hall and lay there motionless.

('Oh!' moaned my mother, and there was a small clatter as she fainted away in her corner of the porch among the potted plants. She knew how a lady should react to the sight of a mouse.)

What followed is difficult to describe. It was as if the house – not the bricks and mortar, of course, but the inside of the house, the shadowy air itself – gathered together swiftly and with one ferocious purpose against a terrified white mouse—

—And pounced!

Micky gave one heart-rending squeak – a mouse-shriek that rose to heaven imploring mercy, and met none. He died in mid-squeak; and Celia fell on her knees by his body, babbling grief.

And the last of the slinking shadows melted away, every last one of them.

Only the smell remained; and later my intelligent nose would remember and make a connection between the present appalling stench of cat and the peculiar and rather repellent stuffiness of our house after every seaside holiday. In that stuffiness lurked the very last faint trace of this present horror of a smell.

As for my father, he would never, anyway,

countenance any idea of the supernatural: he had always ridiculed it. The very idea of *evidence* put him into a fury. Now he was beside himself with indignation. 'What is going on?' he shouted into the empty hall.

There was no reply – no sound at all except a slight scuffling from the back of the porch, where my mother was beginning to struggle among the potted plants; also Celia's quiet sobbing. He picked on that. He realized that the mouse had been Celia's rash secret. In this she had been, he said, deceitful, disobedient and – oh, yes! defiant and disloyal. Under the fury of her father's attack, Celia's weeping became hysterical. Her tears rained down upon the corpse clasped to her breast, and she was led away by the Miss Hardys to be given sal volatile and sympathy.

My father now turned to the plight of my mother in her porch corner. On regaining consciousness, she had opened her eyes to find Mr Brown's gazing fully into them at a distance of about three and a half inches. And he was now gallantly assisting her with helping hands, one at her waist, another at her elbow. My father rushed down upon them, demanding that Mr Brown remove himself instantly from his wife and his porch and the rest of his property. Without pause he went on to attack Mr Brown's birth, breeding, appearance, character and former occupation – *'trade'!* (Rage always inspired my father.)

Mr Brown was neither foolhardy nor a fool. He retreated. Out into the drenching rain he went, and home. We all watched him go. That was really the last we saw of Mr Brown. Within two days my father had caused a seven-foot-high solid fence to be built just our side of the laurel hedge.

Having dispatched Mr Brown, my father became master again in his own house. He instructed us to go round opening all the windows to let what he called 'this stale air' out and the fresh air in. Never mind the rain. Then we must unpack. 'Our holiday is over; we are at home; we resume our routine.'

In the long term, however, our routine had been undermined; and for this my father could not forgive the Miss Hardys. He suspected them of conniving at happenings which were all the more deplorable because they simply could not have occurred. He had known of the existence of the late Mrs Chamberlain, of course, because he had bought our house from her heirs. He may even have heard of her mania for cats. ('She couldn't resist a stray,' the Miss Hardys explained to Celia. 'She tried to keep the numbers down. But, by the end – well, the house did begin rather to *smell*. Cats, you know . . .')

My father would never admit to what became obvious: that the ghosts of Mrs Chamberlain and her cats had been returning regularly to haunts where they had been happy. They had been tempted by the absolute regularity of our holiday absences to hold a kind of annual Old Girls' Reunion in our house – but there must have been Old Boys as well. Only the attendance of at least one tom-cat could explain the strength of that smell.

The Miss Hardys had known what was going on every August, but saw no harm in it. The ghosts came promptly after our departure for the seaside, and had always vacated the house well before the date of our return. 'It was all so discreetly done!' the Miss Hardys. remarked plaintively to Celia, as they administered the sal volatile. 'Such a pity that it should have to stop!'

But it did. Before the next summer, we had moved house; and I do not suppose that any family succeeding us could have had such a very dependable holiday routine. I only hope the ghosts were not too much disappointed.

After that summer my father became – and remained – jumpy about family holidays. We were never allowed to go at the same time for two years running. This meant, incidentally, that we no longer stayed in Mrs Prothero's guest-house. In a huff she had said that she could not be expected to be 'irregularly available'.

The Miss Hardys were seldom spoken of; Mr Brown never.

Ghost Trouble

Ruskin Bond

1

I T WAS Grandfather who finally decided that we would have to move to another house.

And it was all because of a Pret, a mischievous north-Indian ghost, who had been making life difficult for everyone.

Prets usually live in peepal trees, and that's where our little ghost first had his home – in the branches of a massive old peepal tree which had grown through the compound wall and spread into our garden. Part of the tree was on our side of the wall, part on the other side, shading the main road. It gave the ghost a good view of the whole area.

For many years the Pret had lived there quite happily, without bothering anyone in our house. It did not bother me, either, and I spent a lot of time in the peepal tree. Sometimes I went there to escape the adults at home, sometimes to watch the road and the people who passed by. The peepal tree was cool on a hot day, and the heart-shaped leaves were always revolving in the breeze. This constant movement of the leaves also helped to disguise the movements of the Pret, so that I never really knew exactly where he was sitting. But he paid no attention to me. The traffic on the road kept him fully occupied.

Sometimes, when a tonga was passing, he would jump down and frighten the pony, and as a result the little pony-cart would go rushing off in the wrong direction.

Sometimes he would get into the engine of a car or a bus, which would have a breakdown soon afterwards.

And he liked to knock the sun-helmets off the heads of sahibs or officials, who would wonder how a strong breeze had sprung up so suddenly, only to die down just as quickly. Although this special kind of ghost could make himself felt, and sometimes heard, he was invisible to the human eye.

I was not invisible to the human eye, and often got the blame for some of the Pret's pranks. If bicycle-riders were struck by mango seeds or apricot stones, they would look up, see a small boy in the branches of the tree, and threaten me with terrible consequences. Drivers who went off after parking their cars in the shade would sometimes come back to find their tyres flat. My protests of innocence did not carry much weight. But when I mentioned the Pret in the tree, they would look uneasy, either because they thought I must be mad, or because they were afraid of ghosts, especially Prets. They would find other things to do and hurry away.

At night no one walked beneath the peepal tree.

It was said that if you yawned beneath the tree, the Pret would jump down your throat and give you a pain. Our gardener, Chandu, who was always taking sick-leave, blamed the Pret for his tummy troubles. Once, when yawning, Chandu had forgotten to put his hand in front of his mouth, and the ghost had got in without any trouble.

Now Chandu spent most of his time lying on a string-bed in the courtyard of his small house. When Grandmother went to visit him, he would start groaning and holding his sides, the pain was so bad; but when she went away, he did not fuss so much. He claimed that the pain did not affect his appetite, and he ate a normal diet, in fact a little more than normal – the extra amount was meant to keep the ghost happy!

2

'Well, it isn't our fault,' said Grandfather, who had given permission to the Public Works Department to cut the tree, which had been on our land. They wanted to widen the road, and the tree and a bit of our wall were in the way. So both had to go.

Several people protested, including the Raja of Jinn, who lived across the road and who sometimes asked Grandfather over for a game of tennis.

'That peepal tree has been there for hundreds of years,' he said. 'Who are we to cut it down?'

'We,' said the Chief Engineer, 'are the P.W.D.'

And not even a ghost can prevail against the wishes of the Public Works Department.

They brought men with saws and axes, and first they lopped all the branches until the poor tree was quite naked. It must have been at this moment that the Pret moved out. Then they sawed away at the trunk until, finally, the great old peepal came crashing down on the road, bringing down the telephone wires and an electric pole in the process, and knocking a large gap in the Raja's garden wall.

It took them three days to clear the road, and during that time the Chief Engineer swallowed a lot of dust and tree-pollen. For months afterwards he complained of a choking feeling, although no doctor could ever find anything in his throat.

'It's the Pret's doing,' said the Raja knowingly. 'They should never have cut that tree.'

Deprived of his tree, the Pret decided that he would live in our house.

I first became aware of his presence when I was sitting on the verandah steps, reading a book. A tiny chuckling sound came from behind me. I looked round, but no one was to be seen. When I returned to my book, the chuckling started again. I paid no attention. Then a shower of rose petals fell softly on to the pages of my open book. The Pret wanted me to know he was there!

'All right,' I said. 'So you've come to stay with us. Now let me read.'

He went away then; but as a good Pret has to be bad in order to justify his existence, it was not long before he was up to all sorts of mischief.

He began by hiding Grandmother's spectacles.

'I'm sure I put them down on the dining-table,' she grumbled.

A little later they were found balanced on the snout of a wild boar, whose stuffed and mounted head adorned the verandah wall, a memento of Grandfather's hunting trips when he was young.

Naturally, I was at first blamed for this prank. But a day or two later, when the spectacles disappeared again, only to be found dangling from the bars of the parrot's cage, it was agreed that I was not to blame; for the parrot had once bitten off a piece of my finger, and I did not go near it any more.

The parrot was hanging upside down, trying to peer through one of the lenses. I don't know if they improved his vision, but what he saw certainly made him angry, because the pupils of his eyes went very small and he dug his beak into the spectacle frames, leaving them with a permanent dent. I caught them just before they fell to the floor.

But even without the help of the spectacles, it seemed that our parrot could see the Pret. He would keep turning this way and that, lunging out at unseen fingers, and protecting his tail from the tweaks of invisible hands. He had always refused to learn to talk, but now he became quite voluble and began to chatter in some unknown tongue, often screaming with rage and rolling his eyes in a frenzy.

'We'll have to give that parrot away,' said Grandmother. 'He gets more bad-tempered by the day.'

Grandfather was the next to be troubled.

He went into the garden one morning to find all his prize sweet-peas broken off and lying on the grass. Chandu thought the sparrows had destroyed the flowers, but we didn't think the birds could have finished off every single bloom just before sunrise.

'It must be the Pret,' said Grandfather, and I agreed.

The Pret did not trouble me much, because he remembered me from his peepal-tree days and knew I resented the tree being cut as much as he did. But he liked to catch my attention, and he did this by chuckling and squeaking near me when I was alone, or whispering in my ear when I was with someone else. Gradually I began to make out the occasional word. He had started learning English!

3

Uncle Benji, who came to stay with us for long periods when he had little else to do (which was most of the time), was soon to suffer.

He was a heavy sleeper, and once he'd gone to bed he hated being woken up. So when he came to breakfast looking bleary-eyed and miserable, we asked him if he was feeling all right.

'I couldn't sleep a wink last night,' he complained. 'Whenever I was about to fall asleep, the bedclothes would be pulled off the bed. I had to get up at least a dozen times to pick them off the floor.' He stared suspiciously at me. 'Where were *you* sleeping last night, young man?'

'In Grandfather's room,' I said. 'I've lent you *my* room.'

'It's that ghost from the peepal tree,' said Grandmother with a sigh.

'Ghost!' exclaimed Uncle Benji. 'I didn't know the house was haunted.'

'It is now,' said Grandmother. 'First my spectacles, then the sweet-peas, and now Benji's bedclothes! What will it be up to next, I wonder?'

We did not have to wonder for long.

There followed a series of minor disasters. Vases fell off tables, pictures fell from walls. Parrot feathers turned up in the teapot, while the parrot himself let out indignant squawks and swear-words in the middle of the night. Windows which had been closed would be found open, and open windows closed.

Finally, Uncle Benji found a crow's nest in his bed, and on tossing it out of the window was attacked by two crows.

Then Aunt Ruby came to stay, and things quietened down for a time.

Did Aunt Ruby's powerful personality have an effect on the Pret, or was he just sizing her up?

'I think the Pret has taken a fancy to your aunt,' said Grandfather mischievously. 'He's behaving himself for a change.'

This may have been true, because the parrot, who had picked up some of the English words being tried out by the Pret, now called out, 'Kiss, kiss,' whenever Aunt Ruby was in the room.

'What a charming bird,' said Aunt Ruby.

'You can keep him if you like,' said Grandmother.

One day Aunt Ruby came in to the house covered in rose petals.

'I don't know where they came from,' she exclaimed. 'I was sitting in the garden, drying my hair, when handfuls of petals came showering down on me!'

'It likes you,' said Grandfather.

'What likes me?'

'The ghost.'

'What ghost?'

'The Pret. It came to live in the house when the peepal tree was cut down.'

'What nonsense!' said Aunt Ruby.

'Kiss, kiss!' screamed the parrot.

'There aren't any ghosts, Prets or other kinds,' said Aunt Ruby firmly.

'Kiss, kiss!' screeched the parrot again. Or was it the parrot? The sound seemed to be coming from the ceiling.

'I wish that parrot would shut up.'

'It isn't the parrot,' I said. 'It's the Pret.'

Aunt Ruby gave me a cuff over the ear and stormed out of the room.

But she had offended the Pret. From being her admirer, he turned into her enemy. Somehow her toothpaste got switched with a tube of Grandfather's shaving-cream.

When she appeared in the dining-room, foaming at the mouth, we ran for our lives, Uncle Benji shouting that she'd got rabies.

4

Two days later Aunt Ruby complained that she had been struck on the nose by a grapefruit, which had leapt mysteriously from the pantry shelf and hurled itself at her.

'If Ruby and Benji stay here much longer, they'll both have nervous breakdowns,' said Grandfather thoughtfully.

'I thought they broke down long ago,' I said.

'None of your cheek,' snapped Aunt Ruby.

'He's in league with that Pret to try and get us out of here,' said Uncle Benji.

'Don't listen to him – you can stay as long as you like,' said Grandmother, who never turned away any of her numerous nephews, nieces, cousins or distant relatives.

The Pret, however, did not feel so hospitable, and the persecution of Aunt Ruby continued.

'When I looked in the mirror this morning,' she complained bitterly, 'I saw a little monster, with huge ears, bulging eyes, flaring nostrils and a toothless grin!'

'You don't look *that* bad, Aunt Ruby,' I said, trying to be nice.

'It was either you or that imp you call a Pret,' said Aunt Ruby. 'And if it's a ghost, then it's time we all moved to another house.'

Uncle Benji had another idea.

'Let's drive the ghost out,' he said. 'I know a Sadhu who rids houses of evil spirits.'

'But the Pret's not evil,' I said. 'Just mischievous.'

Uncle Benji went off to the bazaar and came back a few

hours later with a mysterious long-haired man who claimed to be a Sadhu – one who has given up all worldly goods, including most of his clothes.

He prowled about the house, and lighted incense in all the rooms, despite squawks of protest from the parrot. All the time he chanted various magic spells. He then collected a fee of thirty rupees, and promised that we would not be bothered again by the Pret.

As he was leaving, he was suddenly blessed with a shower – no, it was really a downpour – of dead flowers, decaying leaves, orange peel and banana skins. All spells forgotten, he ran to the gate and made for the safety of the bazaar.

Aunt Ruby declared that it had become impossible to sleep at night because of the devilish chuckling that came from beneath her pillow. She packed her bags and left.

Uncle Benji stayed on. He was still having trouble with his bedclothes, and he was beginning to talk to himself, which was a bad sign.

'Talking to the Pret, Uncle?' I asked innocently, when I caught him at it one day.

He gave me a threatening look. 'What did you say?' he demanded. 'Would you mind repeating that?'

I thought it safer to please him. 'Oh, didn't you hear me?' I said, *'Teaching the parrot, Uncle?'*

He glared at me, then walked off in a huff. If he did not leave it was because he was hoping Grandmother would lend him enough money to buy a motorcycle; but Grandmother said he ought to try earning a living first.

One day I found him on the drawing-room sofa, laughing like a madman. Even the parrot was so alarmed that it was silent, head lowered and curious. Uncle Benji was red in the face – literally red all over!

'What happened to your face, Uncle?' I asked.

He stopped laughing and gave me a long hard look. I realized that there had been no joy in his laughter.

'Who painted the wash-basin red without telling me?' he asked in a quavering voice.

As Uncle Benji looked really dangerous, I ran from the room.

'We'll have to move, I suppose,' said Grandfather later. 'Even if it's only for a couple of months. I'm worried about Benji. I've told him that I painted the wash-basin myself but forgot to tell him. He doesn't believe me. He thinks it's the Pret or the boy, or both of them! Benji needs a change. So do we. There's my brother's house at the other end of the town. He won't be using it for a few months. We'll move in next week.'

And so, a few days and several disasters later, we began moving house.

5

Two bullock-carts laden with furniture and heavy luggage were sent ahead. Uncle Benji went with them. The roof of our old car was piled high with bags and kitchen utensils. Grandfather took the wheel, I sat beside him, and Granny sat in state at the back.

We set off and had gone some way down the main road when Grandfather started having trouble with the steering-wheel. It appeared to have got loose, and the car began veering about on the road, scattering cyclists, pedestrians, and stray dogs, pigs and hens. A cow refused to move, but we missed it somehow, and then suddenly we were off the road and making for a low wall. Grandfather pressed his foot down on the brake, but we only went faster. 'Watch out!' he shouted.

It was the Raja of Jinn's garden wall, made of single

bricks, and the car knocked it down quite easily and went on through it, coming to a stop on the Raja's lawn.

'Now look what you've done,' said Grandmother.

'Well, we missed the flower-beds,' said Grandfather.

'Someone's been tinkering with the car. Our Pret, no doubt.'

The Raja and two attendants came running towards us.

The Raja was a perfect gentleman, and when he saw that the driver was Grandfather, he beamed with pleasure.

'Delighted to see you, old chap!' he exclaimed. 'Jolly decent of you to drop in. How about a game of tennis?'

'Sorry to have come in through the wall,' apologized Grandfather.

'Don't mention it, old chap. The gate was closed, so what else could you do?'

Grandfather was as much of a gentleman as the Raja, so he thought it only fair to join him in a game of tennis. Grandmother and I watched and drank lemonade. After the game, the Raja waved us goodbye and we drove back through the hole in the wall and out on to the road. There was nothing much wrong with the car.

We hadn't gone far when we heard a peculiar sound, as of someone chuckling and talking to himself. It came from the roof of the car.

'Is the parrot out there on the luggage-rack?' asked Grandfather.

'No,' said Grandmother. 'He went ahead with Uncle Benji.'

Grandfather stopped the car, got out, and examined the roof.

'Nothing up there,' he said, getting in again and starting the engine. 'I thought I heard the parrot.'

When we had gone a little further, the chuckling

started again. A squeaky little voice began talking in English in the tones of the parrot.

'It's the Pret,' whispered Grandmother. 'What is he saying?'

The Pret's squeak grew louder. 'Come on, come on!' he cried gleefully. 'A new house! The same old friends! What fun we're going to have!'

Grandfather stopped the car. He backed into a driveway, turned round, and began driving back to our old house.

'What are you doing?' asked Grandmother.

'Going home,' said Grandfather.

'And what about the Pret?'

'What about him? He's decided to live with us, so we'll have to make the best of it. You can't solve a problem by running away from it.'

'All right,' said Grandmother. 'But what will we do about Benji?'

'It's up to him, isn't it? He'll be all right if he finds something to do.'

Grandfather stopped the car in front of the verandah steps.

'I'm hungry,' I said.

'It will have to be a picnic lunch,' said Grandmother. 'Almost everything was sent off on the bullock-carts.'

As we got out of the car and climbed the verandah steps, we were greeted by showers of rose petals and sweet-scented jasmine.

'How lovely!' exclaimed Grandmother, smiling. 'I think he likes us, after all.'

Nule

Jan Mark

THE HOUSE was not old enough to be interesting, just old enough to be starting to fall apart. The few interesting things had been dealt with ages ago, when they first moved in. There was a bell-push in every room, somehow connected to a glass case in the kitchen which contained a list of names and an indicator which wavered from name to name when a button was pushed, before settling on one of them: *Parlour; Drawing Room; Master Bedroom; Second Bedroom; Back Bedroom.*

'What are they for?' said Libby one morning, after roving round the house and pushing all the buttons in turn. At that moment Martin pushed the button in the front room and the indicator slid up to *Parlour*, vibrating there while the bell rang. And rang and rang.

'To fetch up the maid,' said Mum.

'We haven't got a maid.'

'No, but you've got me,' said Mum, and tied an old sock over the bell, so that afterwards it would only whirr instead of ringing.

The mouseholes in the kitchen looked interesting, too. The mice were bold and lounged about, making no effort at all to be timid and mouse-like. They sat on the draining board in the evenings and could scarcely be bothered to stir themselves when the light was switched on.

'Easy living has made them soft,' said Mum. 'They have a gaming-hell behind the boiler. They throw dice all day. They dance the cancan at night.'

'Come off it,' said Dad. 'You'll be finding crates of tiny gin bottles, next.'

'They dance the cancan,' Mum insisted. 'Right over my head they dance it. I can hear them. If you didn't sleep so soundly, you'd hear them too.'

'Oh, that. That's not mice,' said Dad, with a cheery smile. 'That's rats.'

Mum minded the mice less than the bells, until the day she found footprints in the frying-pan.

'Sorry, lads, the party's over,' she said to the mice, who were no doubt combing the dripping from their elegant whiskers at that very moment, and the mouseholes were blocked up.

Dad did the blocking-up, and also some unblocking, so that after the bath no longer filled itself through the plug hole, the house stopped being interesting altogether; for a time.

Libby and Martin did what they could to improve matters. Beginning in the cupboard under the stairs, they worked their way through the house, up to the attic, looking for something; anything; tapping walls and floors, scouring cupboards, measuring and calculating, but there were no hidden cavities, no secret doors, no ambiguous bulges under the wallpaper, except where the damp got in. The cupboard below the stairs was full of old pickle jars, and what they found in the attic didn't please anyone, least of all Dad.

'That's dry rot,' he said. 'Thank god this isn't our house,' and went cantering off to visit the estate agents,

Tench and Tench, in the High Street. Dad called them Shark and Shark. As he got to the gate he turned back and yelled, 'The Plague! The Plague! Put a red cross on the door!' which made Mrs Bowen, over the fence, lean right out of her landing window instead of hiding behind the curtains.

When Dad came back from the estate agents he was growling.

'Shark junior says that since the whole row is coming down inside two years, it isn't worth bothering about. I understand that the new bypass is going to run right through the scullery.'

'What did Shark senior say?' said Mum.

'I didn't see him. I've never seen him. I don't believe that there is a Shark senior,' said Dad. 'I think he's dead. I think Young Shark keeps him in a box under the bed.'

'Don't be nasty,' said Mum, looking at Libby who worried about things under the bed even in broad daylight. 'I just hope we find a house of our own before this place collapses on our heads – and we shan't be buying it from the Sharks.'

She went back to her sewing, not in a good mood. The mice had broken out again. Libby went into the kitchen to look for them. Martin ran upstairs, rhyming:

> 'Mr Shark,
> In the dark,
> Under the bed.
> Dead.'

When he came down again, Mum was putting away the sewing and Libby was parading around the hall in a pointed hat with a veil and a long red dress that looked rich and splendid unless you knew, as Martin did, that it was made of old curtains.

The hall was dark in the rainy summer afternoon, and Libby slid from shadow to shadow, rustling.

'What are you meant to be?' said Martin. 'An old witch?'

'I'm the Sleeping Beauty's mother,' said Libby, and lowering her head she charged along the hall, pointed hat foremost, like a unicorn.

Martin changed his mind about walking downstairs and slid down the banisters instead. He suspected that he would not be allowed to do this for much longer. Already the banister rail creaked, and who knew where the dreaded dry rot would strike next? As he reached the upright post at the bottom of the stairs, Mum came out of the back room, lugging the sewing-machine, and just missed being impaled on Libby's hat.

'Stop rushing up and down,' said Mum. 'You'll ruin those clothes and I've only just finished them. Go and take them off. And you,' she said, turning to Martin, 'stop swinging on that newel post. Do you want to tear it up by the roots?'

The newel post was supposed to be holding up the banisters, but possibly it was the other way about. At the foot it was just a polished wooden post, but further up it had been turned on a lathe, with slender hips, a waist, a bust almost, and square shoulders. On top was a round ball, as big as a head.

There was another at the top of the stairs but it had lost its head. Dad called it Ann Boleyn; the one at the bottom was simply a newel post, but Libby thought that this too was its name; Nule Post, like Ann Boleyn or Libby Anderson.

Mrs Nule Post.

Lady Nule Post.

When she talked to it she just called it Nule.

The pointed hat and the old curtains were Libby's

costume for the school play. Martin had managed to stay out of the school play, but he knew all Libby's lines by heart as she chanted them round the house, up and down stairs, in a strained, jerky voice, one syllable per step.

'My-dear-we-must-in-vite-all-the-fair-ies-to-the-chris-tening, Hello, Nule, we-will-not-in-vite-the-wick-ed-fair-y!'

On the last day of term, he sat with Mum and Dad in the school hall and watched Libby go through the same routine on stage. She was word-perfect, in spite of speaking as though her shock absorbers had collapsed, but as most of the cast spoke the same way it didn't sound so very strange.

Once the holidays began Libby went back to talking like Libby, although she still wore the pointed hat and the curtains, until they began to drop to pieces. The curtains went for dusters, but the pointed hat was around for a long time until Mum picked it up and threatened, 'Take this thing away or it goes in the dustbin.'

Libby shunted up and down stairs a few times with the hat on her head, and then Mum called out that Jane-next-door had come to play. If Libby had been at the top of the stairs, she might have left the hat on her bed, but she was almost at the bottom so she plonked it down on Nule's cannon-ball head, and went out to fight Jane over whose turn it was to kidnap the teddy bear. She hoped it was Jane's turn. If Libby were the kidnapper, she would have to sit about for ages holding Teddy to ransom behind the water tank, while Jane galloped round the garden on her imaginary pony, whacking the hydrangea bushes with a broomstick.

The hat definitely did something for Nule. When Martin came in later by the front door, he thought at first that it was a person standing at the foot of the stairs. He had to look twice before he understood who it was. Mum saw it at the same time.

'I told Libby to put that object away or I'd throw it in the dustbin.'

'Oh, don't,' said Martin. 'Leave it for Dad to see.'

So she left it, but Martin began to get ideas. The hat made the rest of Nule look very undressed, so he fetched down the old housecoat that had been hanging behind the bathroom door when they moved in. It was purple, with blue paisleys swimming all over it, and very worn, as though it had been somebody's favourite housecoat. The sleeves had set in creases around arms belonging to someone they had never known.

Turning it front to back, he buttoned it like a bib round Nule's neck so that it hung down to the floor. He filled two gloves with screwed-up newspaper, poked them into the sleeves and pinned them there. The weight made the arms dangle and opened the creases. He put a pair of football boots under the hem of the housecoat with the toes just sticking out, and stood back to see how it looked.

As he expected, in the darkness of the hall, it looked just like a person, waiting, although there was something not so much lifelike as deathlike in the hang of those dangling arms.

Mum and Libby first saw Nule as they came out of the kitchen together.

'Who on earth did this?' said Mum as they drew alongside.

'It wasn't me,' said Libby, and sounded very glad that it wasn't.

'It was you left the hat, wasn't it?'

'Yes, but not the other bits.'

'What do you think?' said Martin.

'Horrible thing,' said Mum, but she didn't ask him to

take it down. Libby sidled round Nule and ran upstairs as close to the wall as she could get.

When Dad came home from work he stopped in the doorway and said, 'Hello – who's that? Who . . . ?' before Martin put the light on and showed him.

'An idol, I suppose,' said Dad. 'Nule, god of dry rot,' and he bowed low at the foot of the stairs. At the same time the hat slipped forward slightly, as if Nule had lowered its head in acknowledgement. Martin also bowed low before reaching up to put the hat straight.

Mum and Dad seemed to think that Nule was rather funny, so it stayed at the foot of the stairs. They never bowed to it again, but Martin did, every time he went upstairs, and so did Libby. Libby didn't talk to Nule any more, but she watched it a lot. One day she said, 'Which way is it facing?'

'Forwards, of course,' said Martin, but it was hard to tell unless you looked at the feet. He drew two staring eyes and a toothy smile on a piece of paper and cut them out. They were attached to the front of Nule's head with little bits of chewing-gum.

'That's better,' said Libby, laughing, and next time she went upstairs she forgot to bow. Martin was not so sure. Nule looked ordinary now, just like a newel post wearing a housecoat, football boots and the Sleeping Beauty's mother's hat. He took off the eyes and the mouth and rubbed away the chewing-gum.

'*That's* better,' he said, while Nule stared once more without eyes, and smiled without a mouth.

Libby said nothing.

At night the house creaked.

'Thiefly footsteps,' said Libby.

'It's the furniture warping,' said Mum.

Libby thought she said that the furniture was walking,

and she could well believe it. The dressing-table had feet with claws; why shouldn't it walk in the dark, tugging fretfully this way and that because the clawed feet pointed in opposite directions? The bath had feet too. Libby imagined it galloping out of the bathroom and tobogganing downstairs on its stomach, like a great white walrus plunging into the sea. If someone held the door open, it would whizz up the path and crash into the front gate. If someone held the gate open, it would shoot across the road and hit the district nurse's car, which she parked under the street light, opposite.

Libby thought of headlines in the local paper – NURSE RUN OVER BY BATH – and giggled, until she heard the creaks again. Then she hid under the bedclothes.

In his bedroom Martin heard the creaks too, but he had a different reason for worrying. In the attic where the dry rot lurked, there was a big oak wardrobe full of old dead ladies' clothes. It was directly over his head. Supposing it came through?

Next day he moved the bed.

The vacuum cleaner had lost its casters and had to be helped, by Libby pushing from behind. It skidded up the hall and knocked Nule's football boots askew.

'The Hoover doesn't like Nule either,' said Libby. Although she wouldn't talk to Nule any more she liked talking *about* it, as though that somehow made Nule safer.

'What's that?' said Mum.

'It knocked Nule's feet off.'

'Well, put them back,' said Mum, but Libby preferred not to. When Martin came in he set them side by side, but later they were kicked out of place again. If people began to complain that Nule was in the way, Nule would have to go. He got round this by putting the right boot where the left had been and the left boot on the bottom stair. When he left it, the veil on the hat was hanging down behind, but as he went upstairs after tea he noticed that it was now draped over Nule's right shoulder, as if Nule had turned its head to see where its feet were going.

That night the creaks were louder than ever, like a burglar on hefty tiptoe. Libby had mentioned thieves only that evening, and Mum had said, 'What have we got worth stealing?'

Martin felt fairly safe because he had worked out that if the wardrobe fell tonight, it would land on his chest of drawers and not on him, but what might it not bring down with it? Then he realized that the creaks were coming not from above but from below.

He held his breath. Downstairs didn't creak.

His alarm clock gleamed greenly in the dark and told him that it had gone two o'clock. Mum and Dad were asleep ages ago. Libby would sooner burst than leave her bed in the dark. Perhaps it *was* a burglar. Feeling noble and reckless he put on the bedside lamp, slid out of bed, trod silently across the carpet. He turned on the main light and opened the door. The glow shone out of the doorway and saw him as far as the landing light switch at the top of the stairs, but he never had time to turn it on. From the top of the stairs he could look down into the hall where the street light opposite shone coldly through the frosted panes of the front door.

It shone on the hall-stand where the coats hung, on the blanket chest and the brass jug that stood on it, through the white coins of the honesty plants in the brass jug, and on the broody telephone that never rang at night. It did not shine on Nule. Nule was not there.

Nule was half-way up the stairs, one hand on the banisters and one hand holding up the housecoat, clear of its boots. The veil on the hat drifted like smoke across the frosted glass of the front door. Nule creaked and came up another step.

Martin turned and fled back to the bedroom, and dived under the bedclothes, just like Libby who was three years younger and believed in ghosts.

'Were you reading in bed last night?' said Mum, prodding him awake next morning. Martin came out from under the pillow, very slowly.

'No, Mum.'

'You went to sleep with the light on. *Both* lights,' she said, leaning across to switch off the one by the bed.

'I'm sorry.'

'Perhaps you'd like to pay the next electricity bill?'

Mum had brought him a cup of tea, which meant that she had been down to the kitchen and back again, unscathed. Martin wanted to ask her if there was anything strange on the stairs, but he didn't quite know how to put it. He drank the tea, dressed, and went along the landing.

He looked down into the hall where the sun shone through the frosted glass of the front door, on to the hallstand, the blanket chest, the honesty plants in the brass jug, and the telephone that began to ring as he looked at it. It shone on Nule, standing with its back to him at the foot of the stairs.

Mum came out of the kitchen to answer the phone and Martin went down and stood three steps up, watching Nule and waiting for Mum to finish talking. Nule looked just as it always did. Both feet were back on ground level, side by side.

'I wish you wouldn't hang about like that when I'm on the phone,' said Mum, putting down the receiver and turning round. 'Eavesdropper. Breakfast will be ready in five minutes.'

She went back into the kitchen and Martin sat on the

blanket chest, looking at Nule. It was time for Nule to go. He should walk up to Nule this minute, kick away the boots, rip off the housecoat, throw away the hat, but . . .

He stayed where he was, watching the motionless football boots, the dangling sleeves. The breeze from an open window stirred the hem of the housecoat and revealed the wooden post beneath, rooted firmly in the floor as it had been for seventy years.

There were no feet in the boots; no arms in the sleeves.

If he destroyed Nule, it would mean that he *believed* that he had seen Nule climbing the stairs last night, but if he left Nule alone, Nule might walk again.

He had a problem.

HISTORICAL STORIES AND FANTASIES IN BYGONE TIMES

The Fugitives

Rosemary Sutcliff

THE SHADOWS were lengthening across the terrace, but the thick beech hedge that divided it from the next garden made a sheltered corner, and Lucian, sitting on the broad stone bench that followed the curve of the hedge, did not really need the striped native blanket round his legs. But he knew that if he threw it off, Marcipor, his father's body-slave, who had carried him out there, would fuss like an old woman.

He leaned sideways, frowning in concentration at the lump of clay on the broad raised bench-end – Marcipor had begged it for him from his friend who worked for a potter by the East Gate – which he was trying to work up into the likeness of a sleeping hound. The trouble was that he couldn't remember quite how a hound's muzzle went when it was flattened by resting across the paws. He must notice, next time he saw Syrius lying beside Father's feet in the evening.

The little spring wind blowing across the cantonment brought the thin silver crowing of trumpets from the fort; brought, too, the sound of boys' voices and the barking of a dog. The Senior Centurion's house was the last in the cantonment, and beyond the terrace wall open land dropped gently to the slow silver loop of the river. And looking up from the clay hound, Lucian could see three boys and a half-grown sheep-dog pup racing across the hillside, the boys whooping as they ran, the pup circling ahead of them with streaming ears and tail.

Lucian could remember how it felt to run like that. He was twelve now, and he had been seven when the strange sickness came; other children had had it, too, and mostly they had died. Lucian hadn't died, but when the sickness passed, he had not been able to run any more.

The boys and the dog had disappeared now, and he returned to the clay hound. Despite his uncertainty about the muzzle, it seemed to him that it had begun to look like Syrius, and also that there was a liveness about it. Not just cold clay any more but with something of Syrius in it – or maybe something of himself. It was not very long ago that he had discovered that he could make clay do that; and it still surprised him and gave him a rather odd sensation in the pit of his stomach.

A brushing and crashing in the midst of the beech hedge made him look up again, twisting round on the bench, just in time to see a man diving through. A man who half fell, gathered himself again, and stumbled forward a pace or two, then checked, snatching a glance behind him at the torn twigs and scatter of last year's brown leaves that marked the way he had come.

Lucian gave a sharp gasp, and the intruder whipped round, his hand leaping to the dagger at his belt, and their eyes met.

The odd thing was that the boy was not in the least frightened, and after that first startled moment, he simply sat and looked at the man, while the stranger stood and stared back out of strained grey eyes in a very young grey face. Rough hair clung wetly to his sweating forehead, and his breast panted in and out like the flanks of a hunted animal.

Lucian was the first to speak. 'What is it? Are you running away from something? – A runaway slave?'

The man swallowed thickly, and steadied his sobbing breath, and for an instant, unlikely as it seemed, there was a flicker of reckless laughter in his face. 'You could call it that.'

'And they are after you?'

The man nodded.

But Lucian was noticing that the tattered tunic with the brown of last year's leaves clinging to it was the regulation red cloth tunic that the Auxiliaries wore under their leather jerkins. 'It's the Eagles you're running away from! You're a deserter!'

'Right second time – and they're hunting the cantonment for me.'

Scorn blazed up in Lucian. 'I hope they catch you and drag you back!'

'I'm not going back. I've had enough,' the deserter said slowly. 'I'll die first – and so will you!' He was close to Lucian now, and the point of the dagger just kissed against the boy's throat.

Lucian looked at the hand that held it, and up the arm, and came again to the grey, desperate face. His mouth was dry, and he licked his lower lip.

'Now listen. You haven't seen anybody pass this way.'

'I have! And you can't stop me telling as soon as you're gone!'

The deserter said, 'Not unless I kill you now, and I don't want to do that if I can help it. But if I am retaken, I'll live long enough to escape once more, and then I shall come and kill you.'

'I'll shout!' Lucian said, desperately. 'There are people

quite near!' And all the while he was listening, listening for the sounds of the hunt.

'They'd need to be very near to come before this blade was in your throat! It is too late for shouting; it's too late to run now, too; the time for running was when I first broke through the hedge.'

'I – if you kill me now, they'll crucify you when they do catch you.' Lucian heard his own voice not sounding quite like his own. 'And if you don't, I shall tell which way you went, and you can talk big, but you won't get your chance to escape again. That's bairn's talk.'

For the first time he saw a flicker of uncertainty in the man's eyes and slowly the dagger was withdrawn a thumb-nail's breadth from his throat. 'If I take this away, will you promise not to bolt?' the man said, in a changed tone.

'Yes.' Not for anything in the world would he have admitted that he couldn't.

The dagger was withdrawn and sheathed. The man hesitated still an instant and glanced back again the way he had come, listening for sounds of the hunt. Then he seemed to come to a decision and spoke quickly and urgently. 'I've twisted my ankle and I'm just about done, or I'd not be telling you this, but it seems I've not much choice. And I shan't have time to tell you more than once, so listen … I'm carrying secret dispatches for Caesar – so secret and so deadly that to get them past our enemies, I've had to play the deserter. They know nothing of that up at the fort; to them I'm just a deserter like any other, and if they catch up with me –'

He broke off with a small, one-shouldered shrug.

Lucian's heart, which had not quickened much, even with the dagger at his throat, fell over itself and began to pound like a runner's at the end of a race. 'If they catch up with you?'

'I can't tell you. It would – be disaster for the whole province. I can't tell you any more.'

And at that moment the little wind brought the first rumour of the sounds they had both been listening for: a small smother of sounds that if they had been made by hounds instead of men, would have been a pack giving tongue on a hot scent.

Despite the drubbing of his heart, Lucian's head had started to feel cold and clear, as though it were set far above the level of what was happening around him. 'Get under the bench! I'll pull the blanket over the front of it, and if you get close up this end, behind my legs —'

The man looked at him for one instant, as though testing for a trap, and then in another way, as though he were puzzled, maybe, by the blanket and the way the boy had never attempted to get up or dive clear. Then he nodded, and without a word dropped on hands and knees and was gone under cover.

Lucian dragged the rug from his legs in frantic haste, and flung the free half of it out along the bench so that it trailed down in front and made a small dark hidingplace for the desperate man he could feel crouching there. Then he began with great care and concentration to do something – he never knew what – about the way the hound's muzzle was pressed up by the paws.

Everything had happened at racing speed, and now there was a sudden blankness of nothing happening at all, and all the while he was terrified that Syrius, who was in the kitchen hoping for a bone, would come trotting down the garden and smell the stranger under the bench, or that Marcipor would come and fetch him in.

And then the search-party was in the very next garden, and the old garden-slave was scolding like an angry hen because somebody's great feet were in his herb patch. Someone only a few feet away called, 'Sir!

Here's a broken place in the hedge; he's gone this way!'
and there was a sharp exclamation and footsteps on
gravel, and then:

'No, not through the hedge, too, you fool! It's the Pilus
Prior's garden. Over the wall at the bottom,' and the half-
running tramp of feet going down beyond the hedge.

Lucian caught a deep breath, and looked up from the
little clay figure as half a dozen legionaries led by a
young Centurion came scrambling over the terrace wall.

The Centurion saw the boy on the bench and called
out to him almost before both feet were on the terrace:
'There's been a man through here. Which way did he
go?'

'What man? There hasn't been any man,' Lucian's
voice wobbled a little and the Centurion, a cheerful-
looking, freckled individual, came over to him while his
men scattered at once to search the garden.

'Then why are you looking as though you'd seen a
ghost?' he asked.

Lucian managed a grin. 'Six – no, seven ghosts. You
and your lot made me jump. I didn't hear you coming.'

'Fair enough. Look now, we're hunting a deserter, and
we know he came this way. Where did he go?'

'No one has been through the garden while I've been
out here.'

'How long is that?'

'An hour or more.'

'And no one passed?'

'I told you!'

The Centurion jerked his chin towards the broken
place in the hedge. 'Who made that, then?'

'That?' Lucian gazed blankly in the direction
indicated.

'Gap in the hedge.'

'Oh that! Syrius our dog made it. They throw out their

meat bones because it's good for the roses, and he's always breaking through.'

The Centurion eyed him consideringly, and was silent a moment.

'Don't you believe me?' Lucian said, as haughtily as he could manage. 'My father is Lucius Lycinius, the Pilus Prior of the Legion! Do you d-dare to think I'd go hiding a deserter?'

The Centurion threw back his head with a crack of laughter. 'Roma Dca! I'd know you for the Old Man's son anywhere, when you put on that tone – even if I hadn't known this was his garden ... But we're searching all this quarter till we find him. He twisted an ankle dropping over the bath-house wall, and he was going as lame as a duck when we lost him. He can't have – got – far.'

His voice trailed off awkwardly, and Lucian realized that the friendly freckle-faced young Centurion knew about him, had probably known all along, and was wishing that he hadn't said that about being lame as a duck and not getting far.

He had always hated strangers knowing about him not being able to walk. He hated it now. He felt shamed and a little sick and in the usual way of things he would have glared at the young Centurion to show how much he didn't care; but this time it didn't matter whether he cared or not; all that mattered was to keep them from discovering the man under the bench. And if he could hold the Centurion here standing right against the bench while his men finished their search, they would be less likely to go peering under it.

'Perhaps he's managed to hide in one of the market carts,' he suggested.

'The carts are being checked. Any sign, Rufrius?'

'Not yet, sir.' The shout came back, slightly muffled

from among tangled rose and elder bushes that shut off all view of the house.

'Push on farther up that way.'

Lucian searched desperately for something else to say, and found it. 'Why did he desert?'

The Centurion shrugged. 'There are always a few deserters among the Auxiliaries at this time of year. Maybe the homesickness catches them more sharply in the springtime. Poor stupid devils. Even if he's not caught, there's not much life for a deserter; you can't spend all your life running away.'

Lucian gave a little shiver, and covered it by saying, 'It gets cold still, once the sun is behind the hills.'

The Centurion nodded. 'Hadn't you better have that blanket round you?'

'No!' said Lucian quickly, and then, 'It makes my legs stronger to have the air all round them.'

'Ah well, that's the way then,' the Centurion said bracingly. 'You get them good and strong, and we'll have you in the Legion yet.' His eyes were with his men among the bushes; he hitched at his sword-belt, in another instant he would have gone to join them.

And then Lucian heard the sound that he had been dreading. Syrius had winded strangers and was baying his head off in the kitchen quarters; the baying loudened and changed tempo as a door was opened and he could hear Marcipor cursing. Another moment and the great hound would come flying down from the house. He knew legionaries and would not bother much about them once he saw what they were, but a man with the hunted smell on him, hiding under the bench . . .

One blunt stab of hopelessness shot through Lucian. The affair was out of his hands now; only the gods could hold back the terrible thing from happening. In desperation, with no time to think, he did the one thing that was left. He made a sacrifice to the gods. It was an odd sacrifice, but strong, for it meant giving up old dreams that he had not known until that instant he was still clinging on to; it meant doing the hardest and bravest thing he had ever done in his life. He caught the young Centurion's eye in the instant before he turned away, and managed a grin. 'Tell that to the wild geese! My head works well enough, it's only my legs that don't and I've got sense enough to know there's not much room for you in the Legions if you can't walk.'

Syrius and Marcipor appeared where the path curved through the bushes, the slave clinging to the bronze-studded collar of the huge hound who dragged forward, snarling, his hackles raised in a great comb along his back.

Marcipor checked as the Centurion went striding to meet him, and inquired in the coolly respectful tone that could be more blighting than the Pilus Prior's when he chose, whether it was by his Master's orders that half the Legion was in his garden.

Lucian could not hear properly what passed after that, for the two men spoke together quietly, and they were a little way off. But Syrius had stopped snarling, and he saw Marcipor let go the hound's collar and give him an open-palmed slap on the rump to send him back to the house.

Syrius hesitated an instant, looking back, and Lucian, his mouth dry and the palms of his hands sweating, did not dare to look at him direct, lest that should bring him over. Then out of the corner of his eye he saw the hound look away, his ears suddenly pricked, and knew that in the nick of time his father had turned the corner of the street. Syrius always heard him as he turned that corner, every evening. An instant later the hound gave a pleased bark, and went bounding back towards the house.

Relief broke over Lucian in a wave, and he scarcely knew what was happening in the next few moments, until suddenly the search was over, and the Legionaries were going. The Centurion checked beside him in passing, and said, 'My legs are all right, but maybe my head's not so good. I'm sorry we'll not be having you in the Legion.'

Then they were gone, but almost before Lucian could draw breath the next danger was there to be faced, as Marcipor came along the terrace, saying, 'Time you were indoors.'

'No!' Lucian said. 'Not just yet, Marcipor. It feels so good out here after being shut in all the winter.' Then, as the big grey-haired slave hesitated, 'Listen – there's Father calling for you.'

'I didn't hear him.'

'I'm sure I did. Please, Marcipor!'

'Very well, if you have the blanket round you again. Just while I get the Commander out of his harness and see to his bath.'

Lucian hardly knew how to bear it as the slave, still fussing, pulled the blanket back into place and tucked it in. He only had to stoop just a little lower, he only had to look back once as he went up towards the house…

But neither of these things happened and in a little while, when the last sounds of the hunt had died away, the man who carried Caesar's dispatches was crouching with his shoulders propped against the bench, rubbing his swollen ankle to ease the stiffness, and pulling in slow gasps of air as though he had been half stifled in his hiding-place. 'That was valiantly done. Do you know, I was wondering, when I crawled under that bench, whether I was crawling into a trap,' he said at last.

'But you had told me about the secret dispatches.'

'Och yes – the dispatches for Caesar.' The man looked

up with a wry flicker of something that might have been laughter.

'You must go,' Lucian said. 'You can hide among the rough stuff under the terrace until full dusk, and then make for the river woods. Marcipor will be out soon to carry me back to the house.' He never noticed that he did not mind this man whom he had hidden from the search-party knowing about him.

The man had got up, wincing as his ankle took the strain. 'Like our good friend the Centurion, I'm sorry the Legion will be having to do without you,' he said. 'Maybe it's the Legion's loss.'

'Oh, I don't suppose I'd have made much of a soldier anyway – not like my father.'

'I – wonder.' The young man put out a forefinger and touched the little clay hound. 'One thing I will tell you: maybe you would not have made as good a soldier as your father, but I am very sure your father could not make a lump of potter's clay breathe warm and heavy like a sleeping hound.'

He turned towards the low terrace wall, swung a leg over, and dropped from sight.

Lucian heard the grunt of pain as he landed, and sat looking at the place where he had been, suddenly very tired. He picked up the little hound, but the clay was getting dry. He couldn't work it much more, and he thought he knew now what was wrong with the muzzle. He would keep it, all the same; it was part of something very important. But as soon as he could get some more clay he would make another hound, or maybe something else. And he knew that it would be better than this one.

Somehow he did not think much about Caesar's dispatches. It wasn't until years later that he understood that he had never quite believed that story, and it was simply because the man was being hunted, that he had hidden him.

The deserter crouched among the docks and hazelscrub under the terrace wall, waiting for the light to go.

He had stuck two years of the Auxiliaries – two years out of twenty-five – and for most of them he had not even been able to remember what had made him join; unless it was simply that the chieftain his grandfather had been so determined that he should head the young men of their valley when they went down to join the draft. Two years of the rigid discipline, the bullying of the Decurion, the loss of freedom, and today, quite suddenly, it had all been more than he could bear. So he had gone out over the bath-house wall.

If he had not twisted his ankle, he'd have been well into the woods, by now. But what was it the Centurion had said? – 'You can't spend all your life running away.' The boy had been running away too, in his own fashion, but then he had stopped. Sweating in the dark under the bench, the deserter had known when the boy stopped running away.

Below him the river woods were blurring into the twilight.

Probably it would not be death, if he gave himself up of his own accord. It would be flogging; it would be cells and bread-and-water and shame; and when all that was over, the cage of discipline and the bullying Decurion, just as before. But maybe one could make some kind of a fresh start?

He felt in an odd way that he had company on his road, when he got up, stumbling on his wrenched ankle, and turned back towards the fort.

London Rises from the Ashes
(and how it nearly all went wrong)

Jeremy Strong

THE STREETS of London were still smouldering even though many days had passed since the Great Fire had given its final flicker. The ground, two foot deep in some places with ash and embers, was hot to walk on. Titus Drumm danced and jigged as he made his way along all that was left of Snout Lane, his gorgeous lacefrilled cuffs flopping about his hands like a host of attendant doves.

'Oh! Ouch!' The charcoal had burned through the soles of both boots, his *best* boots no less. Titus was not simply in pain; he was cross. He could not find the house he was looking for (because it had burnt to the ground along with everything else), and now he could not remember *who* he was looking for.

Titus danced up the road, sweating beneath his heavy wig, trying to recall what His Majesty King Charles II had told him. His Royal Highness was most anxious to rebuild the city. Most of London had gone up in flames, including the great church of St Paul. King Charles wanted it replaced, at once.

'The people must see that we are repairing the city.

There is no time to be lost. I want every new building made from stone or brick – anything that won't catch fire. My tailor's shop was almost consumed by flames – a near disaster! Get Christopher Wren to draw up plans and start work immediately,' the King had boomed from on high (he was six foot two inches tall), before turning back to the large gilt mirror in order to admire his new silk hosiery and fabulously huge hat. 'Now I must be off to see that woman who has such nice oranges.'

'Yes Sire, at once Sire,' Titus had beamed as he reversed, bowing and scraping and tripping over his own lace boot tops. He had silently cursed the frothy garters. French they might be. Fashionable they might be. But they weren't much good if they were liable to break a man's neck.

Now Titus pranced up Snout Lane and tried to remember the name of England's great architect. 'Oh la-de-dah, I know it was a bird,' he muttered. 'Christopher Robin? Owl? Wagtail? Corncrake? What was it?'

All around him ragged figures poked amongst the ruins of buildings. A few carts, laden with rescued belongings, jerked and jolted past him, the horses pulling with bowed heads. The stench of burnt wood, burnt cloth, burnt fur and burnt skin filled the dark air. A dishevelled figure detached itself from the smoking skeleton of a house. The woman's face, arms and dress were all smeared with soot where she had been grovelling amongst the remains of her charred home.

'Good woman,' called Titus. 'Does not England's greatest architect live near here?'

'Oh my, it's Lord High-an'-Mighty 'imself. I don't know of no great arky-whatsit. Look.' The woman thrust a small bit of blackened wood into Titus's face. 'Know what that is?'

'Indeed I don't.'

'Knock on it,' she commanded. 'Go on. Knock on it.'

Titus felt a trifle embarrassed, but he rapped the little piece of wood with his knuckles.

'Come in,' beamed the woman, grinning madly at him. 'What?'

'Come in! That's my front door that is, what you's knockin' on. All that's left of it. Come in!'

'I'm sorry,' mumbled Titus.

'Don't matter,' said the woman matter-of-factly. 'Ain't no house for it to stick on anyways.'

Titus tried again. 'I'm looking for a man who designs things; goes by the name of a bird. Christopher something-or-other.'

'Ah,' mused the woman, 'that'll be Mister Thrush.'

'That's it!' cried Titus, at once forgetting his burning feet. 'Thrush! Does he live near by?'

'He would if he could.'

'What do you mean by that?'

'I mean that this was 'is house, an' a flea would be hard-pressed to live in it now, what with the state it's in, an' I can tell you we weren't short of fleas afore the fire. 'Ad enough fleas to stuff a pillow, so the lodger told me, an' he 'ad the bites to prove it an 'all.' The grimy woman fixed Titus with one eye. 'I am Mistress Jellicoe sir, Mr Thrush's servant, what does 'is cookin' an' cleanin' an' chamberpot emptyin' an' such. If you want the master you'll have to go to The Beggar's Armpit. It's about the only tavern still standin' around here.'

Titus fiddled in his purse and produced a silver sovereign. 'Thank you, thank you my good woman!' he cried, and he strode off toward the tavern.

Mistress Jellicoe watched him disappear, tested the coin on her black teeth and carried on muttering. 'I ain't a good woman, not good at all. I put a mouse in Mr Thrush's soup once . . . an' it couldn't swim.'

* * *

The Beggar's Armpit was in one of the few areas that had escaped the Great Fire, tucked down a dingy alleyway that stank of rotting food and emptied chamberpots. The old wooden houses were so ancient that they actually appeared to be propping each other up, like crumbling crones no longer able to stand on their own feet. Now the tavern itself was seething with refugees from the fire: noisy men and rowdy women and slopping ale.

Christopher Thrush – designer, inventor and possible genius – sat in the dingiest corner, cursing his luck. His house had burnt down before his eyes, along with his latest invention, the world's first dishwasher, almost completed. It would have made him rich and famous. Now he had nothing. He buried his pinched face in his leather tankard and sipped the dregs of beer, wishing that he was dead.

It was at this moment of deepest despair that a vision appeared before him, a vision that came in the portly, lace be-ribboned shape of Titus Drumm. The King's messenger bowed low, pulled forward a stool, parked his ample backside upon it and beamed at Christopher.

'Mr Thrush? I am here on a mission from His Majesty the King. He requires you to oversee the rebuilding of London, and he wishes you to commence work on the new church of St Paul at once.'

Christopher Thrush was so astonished that the first thing he did was punch Titus hard on the nose. The poor messenger tumbled backwards into a pool of spilled cider. At once Christopher was on his feet, helping the dazed man rise from the filthy rush floor and brushing down his ornate doublet. Christopher seized the messenger's wig from the puddle, squeezed half a pint of old cider from the wool ringlets and carefully arranged it back on Titus's shaven pate. Bits of rush poked out from beneath.

'I am so very sorry sir, but in my misery I thought you must be a dream that had come to taunt me. Now I see the blood pouring out of your nose I realise that you are indeed flesh and – well, blood indeed. Is this your tooth on the floor? My dear sir, this is wonderful news. The King really wants *me*?'

'Indeed,' grunted Titus, dabbing his nose with his perfumed hanky. 'You are to start work at once.'

Christopher's head almost spun with joy and invention. The buildings he would erect! The houses! The churches! His brain seethed with fabulous creations, and the most remarkable of all was the new church of St Paul. All night long he sketched his design. By the time morning came he had the plans for the most extraordinary church England would ever see.

Christopher hurried out into the early morning air, still carrying the stink of charred wood, and hailed a passing sedan chair. 'Take me to Titus Drumm!' cried the genius, waving his master plan at the two ragged carriers. 'I am going to save London!'

One of the men glanced ruefully at the smouldering houses all around. 'What are you going to do?' he asked. 'Wee on it?'

But Christopher was already clambering into the sedan. A moment later he was hoisted into the air and the carriers were off at a gangly gallop. Inside, Christopher was bumped up and down and hurled about in general, but he was far too excited to notice. His plan for St Paul's was a masterpiece.

Unfortunately Titus Drumm didn't agree. Titus studied the plan from every angle and at last he made an observation. 'La-de-dah,' he sighed. 'It's round, like a pig's bladder for playing football.'

'A ball, like the earth,' explained Christopher. 'The new church is like a model of God's earth itself.'

'But there are no windows,' Titus growled. 'How does any light pierce the gloom of this earth of yours?'

'Ah! That's one of my surprises – there *is* no roof! Light comes pouring straight in from above.'

'But so will the rain,' Titus pointed out. 'The congregation won't like getting wet.'

'Ah!' cried Titus again. 'The rain won't fall on them. It will fall upon the Garden of Eden.'

'Really?' Titus was beginning to look round for help, for someone who would rescue him from this madman. In the depths of his mind a suspicion was beginning to stir. Christopher THRUSH?

'Yes,' Christopher went on eagerly. 'Inside the globe is a miniature Garden of Eden, raised upon marble pillars – a real garden, like a miniature forest, with plants and trees and all flowering things. There will be tigers roaming and elephants and . . .'

'Tigers and elephants roaming in the church! La-de-dah!' Titus clutched a chair for support.

'. . . and monkeys in the trees and great pythons and bats and birds of all kinds: parrots and humming birds, penguins, giant ostriches, the tiny wren...'

'WREN!' yelled Titus Drumm. Of course – Christopher *Wren!* Relief flooded through him. Hurrah! He pulled a purse full of sovereigns from his pocket and thrust it into Christopher's surprised hands. 'Here, take this money and your plan and go away. It won't do. The King doesn't want elephants and monkeys. Go, go!'

Even as he spoke, Titus was pushing Christopher out. A moment later the door slammed on the inventor and he was left standing bewildered on the street.

Christopher Thrush trudged wearily back towards The Beggar's Armpit, once again in despair. But the nearer he came to the tavern the more he brightened up. He had a full purse of silver in his pocket. He could begin work on that amazing new invention of his again. He would be famous and rich . . .

So it was that while Sir Christopher Wren got to work on the new St Paul's Cathedral, Christopher Thrush got back to work on the worlds first dishwasher. It looked like a wardrobe sitting on the back of a cart, harnessed to two horses. This was because it *was* a wardrobe sitting on the back of a cart, harnessed to two horses.

Christopher opened the wardrobe door to show puzzled onlookers the inside. 'My servant Mrs Jellicoe has placed all the dirty porcelain, all the filthy pots and pans inside here,' he explained, pointing at the packed shelves. 'On top is a tank of clean, hot water. I shut the door and pull this chain so . . .'

There was a gurgle and gush as the tank emptied into the wardrobe. A few drops leaked out through the door.

'The dishwasher is now ready.'

Christopher took the leading horse by the reins and walked it up the mud-rutted road. 'As the dishwasher passes over the bumps in this road the pots and pans are shaken about in the water until they are quite clean,' he shouted above the clattering noise from inside. 'This saves everyone a great labour. And now the washing is done. Behold!' He flung wide the wardrobe door. To avoid embarrassing Christopher Thrush any further the recounting of this story concludes here.

Toinette

Adèle Geras

'SIT THERE, Toinette, and don't say a word. Pretend you're a little dog on a velvet cushion.' Rose lifted her sister on to the window sill.

'What colour should I be?'

'Black. A lap dog like the ones the ladies carry round in their arms. In winter they put them in their muffs.'

'I want to be golden brown.' Toinette was beginning to pout.

'Be any colour you like. Only be very, very quiet and don't move because if I don't finish making this bit of lace, Madame will throw us into the street and we won't have anywhere to live.'

That silenced the little girl.

Rose sighed and turned to the cushion on which her piece of lace was taking shape: snowflakes and leaves and little lines of holes in a pattern so dense and intricate that it made you dizzy just to look at it. It was all in a fine silk thread that was hard on the eyes, which was why Rose had to hurry. Once the daylight was gone, that was that. No candles were to be burned, by order of Madame.

Madame sounded fiercer than she really was. After all, Rose reminded herself, if it hadn't been for her, both of us would be dead. Me and poor Toinette, who's only five.

The rest of the family she tried not to think about, for they were all in the ground, but as she worked, she remembered the muddy streets of her village and their own dark cottage. And the family . . .

The baby was first to die. Then Gran'père and Gran'mère. Then Maman. There was no food, none at all, and the winter of 1788 was the hardest anyone had seen for years and years. They said that wolves came into towns from the forest, because they were as starved as the people. No one dared leave a small child playing by itself. Rose thought of her father. No one knew where he'd gone. He'd simply disappeared. She couldn't recall what he looked like, but he used to say: 'These taxes will kill us.' Rose never knew what taxes were, and thought of them as huge, red, skinny spiderlike creatures who lived under the bed and came out at night. Now that she was more grown-up (she would be eleven soon) she knew they were nothing but money that you had to pay to the King.

'Everything is changing now,' Madame said. 'People are saying that everyone will be equal . . . Imagine that! I don't for one moment believe it, but that's what I hear . . . Peasants and workers will be the same as aristocrats, and my customers won't be any finer than I am . . . But until that happens, my girl, you must apply yourself to your lace, because there's one thing sure: ladies will always want pretty things, whether they're princesses or serving-girls.'

I'm fortunate, Rose thought, looking at her sister. Toinette had decided being a cat was better because you could lick your hands, and also purr from time to time. The nuns in the village had somehow known – perhaps an angel had told them – that Rose had what M'sieur le Curé called 'silver fingers', and they had trained her well to make lace and embroider. And when all the others were dead, Sœur Cécile had given her a letter addressed to Madame in Paris. Rose and Toinette had left the village carrying a small bundle of food and old clothes that the convent had given them. Fortunately the village was only two days' walk from Paris.

'My second cousin writes,' Madame said, when she saw them, 'that you are alone in the world. Also that you can make lace. She asks me to find a place for you here, in my workshop. I can ill afford it, but if you are as gifted as she says . . . And what about her?' She pointed, rather rudely, at Toinette.

'She's my sister,' Rose said, and was about to launch into a speech about how good Toinette was, and how she would look after her all the time, but a better idea occurred to her. 'I'm teaching her to embroider. She will be very skilful.'

Madame sniffed. 'Very well. You may both stay. These are troubled times. You must work hard. The ladies who buy my gloves and shawls and collars are the highest, the *very* highest in the land.'

Rose had nearly finished the piece. Soon, she'd be able to make breathtaking lace like *La Silencieuse*, the Silent One, who kept to herself up in the attic and made the most important pieces. Colette, Angèle and Germaine, who worked in the same room as she did, had gone to collect parcels of fabric from the merchant. Rose liked them because they all loved Toinette, and spoiled her, and sometimes gave her little gifts. Chocolate was best, from the shop in the next street. Sometimes, the fragrance of the sweet, dark stuff came floating over the rooftops and into the room where they worked.

Now here was Madame in a fluster. Her cheeks were red and she was wearing her best bonnet.

'Where is everyone?' she asked, and then remembered

that she'd sent them out herself. She sighed and said to Rose, 'You'll have to do. Come with me. I need someone to carry the boxes. Put down your work and go and make yourself presentable. The carriage will be here directly. And I suppose we can't leave the little one alone here. Take her with you and wash her hands.'

'My hands are clean,' Toinette said. 'I've been licking them. Look.'

Madame wrinkled her nose. 'Wash them *thoroughly*,' she told Rose. 'And hurry. A carriage has been sent.'

The inside of the carriage was beautiful. The seats were blue velvet and the door handles were painted gold. Four gleaming brown horses pulled it along, and their hooves rang on the cobbles.

'Where are we going?' Rose asked.

'To Versailles,' Madame said. 'The Queen herself – imagine that! – has asked to see some samples, and if she likes them, why, that'll be the making of us. You girls must sit quite silently and wait till we are called.'

Rose thought the heart would burst out of her chest, it was beating so loudly.

'We're going to see the Queen,' she whispered to Toinette.

'In a palace?'

'Oh, yes! The most wonderful palace in the world – just like something from a story.'

Nothing Rose had imagined prepared her for the magnificence of Versailles. They were put to wait in a room with polished wooden floors and seats upholstered in scarlet brocade. There were grandly dressed people everywhere, and Rose thought they must be princes and princesses until Madame told her they were the palace servants. There was a painting all over the ceiling and Rose was so busy craning her neck to look at it that she didn't notice her sister wandering away down a long corridor.

'Where is the little one?' Madame asked suddenly. 'You were supposed to be looking after her . . . Do I really have to do every single thing myself? Go and find her this instant. Go on. Quickly.'

Rose was cold all over. Where could Toinette be? And how was she supposed to find her in this place with its hundreds of rooms, each one bigger than the cottage she was born in? She couldn't shout – you didn't shout in a palace, she was quite sure of that. But could you run? Along those endless passages and through the galleries? I don't care, Rose thought. She's my sister. I must find her.

She ran through room after room, not noticing the heavy velvet curtains at the windows, nor the tall mirrors reflecting the June sky.

'Toinette!' she called. 'Where are you? Where have you hidden yourself?'

'She's in here,' said a pleasant voice. 'With me.'

Rose followed the voice into a room. There was her sister, sitting on the lap of a lady wearing a black dress in spite of the warm weather. The room was a bedroom, and Rose couldn't take her eyes off the bed: a gigantic four-poster hung with brocade curtains. A whole family could have slept in it, with space left over for the dog.

'I'm so sorry, Madame,' said Rose, curtseying. 'She's only five . . .'

Toinette jumped off the lady's lap. 'I said I was five. This lady asked me to come in.'

'That's quite true. I did. She reminded me . . .'

The lady turned away. She was drying her eyes with a handkerchief. Rose thought: if I had a bedroom like this, I wouldn't feel like crying.

'You must forgive me,' the lady said. 'My baby – my

son – died not more than two weeks ago. I find the world a little difficult at the moment, and your sister is just the age he was. Her chatter pleased me.'

Rose shivered because the lady looked at her with just the same sorrowful expression in her eyes as Maman had when they told her about Bébé.

'Our baby brother died when he was tiny,' she said. It was the first time she had spoken of this to anyone. 'Also the rest of our family. We had no food and no money to pay taxes.'

The lady said nothing, but shook her head sadly and said something under her breath that Rose couldn't hear. Then she stood up.

'I have to go now,' she said. 'Someone has come all the way from Paris to show me some samples of lace.'

'That's Madame Desmartins,' Rose said. 'We came with her. I'm one of her lacemakers.'

'Then let us go and find her together,' said the lady. 'But before we do, I must give this little one something to remember me by.' She looked around, and then picked up an enamelled box that stood on the mantelpiece and held it out to Toinette. 'This is pretty, isn't it? Look, it has a picture of a shepherd and shepherdess on it.'

'Where are the lambs?'

The lady laughed. 'You're quite right, my darling. There should be lambs, indeed there should. Let's pretend the lambs have all been taken back to the barn, shall we?'

'Yes,' said Toinette. 'They've gone to sleep.'

'Exactly,' said the lady. 'Now come along with me.'

Toinette held on to her box and kept looking at it, even as they walked along the corridors.

'I forgot to ask your names,' the lady said. 'How impolite of me.'

'I'm Rose, and my sister is Toinette.'

'Is that short for Antoinette?'

Rose nodded, and the lady laughed again and clapped her hands.

'That's my name too,' she said.

'My sister was named for the Queen,' said Rose.

'I'm the Queen,' said the lady. 'Marie Antoinette. And I'm honoured to have such a pretty little girl named for me.'

She knelt down and kissed Toinette on both cheeks. Toinette flung her arms round the lady's – the Queen's – neck and clung to her as though she never wanted to let go. When the Queen stood up again, Rose saw that there were tears in her eyes. Her voice trembled a little as she said:

'Time to go and find Madame Desmartins. I'm so pleased she brought you both. You're a good sister, I can see that. How old are you, my dear?'

'I'm ten,' Rose said, 'but I'll be eleven soon.'

They had come to the place where Madame was waiting, and Rose knew that she wanted to be cross but couldn't be, because of the Queen.

'These children have lightened my day a little, Madame,' the Queen told her. 'Thank you for bringing them.'

On the way back to Paris, Toinette slept. Rose looked out of the carriage window and noticed suddenly how thin and poor and dirty all the people were who stood at the side of the road and watched the splendid carriage passing by. She thought of the palace, and the chandeliers hanging from the ceiling like complicated arrangements of stars. It wasn't right that some people lived in fine palaces, and others died of hunger. Perhaps it would change.

Rose closed her eyes and turned her thoughts to her

birthday. Not long to wait now. She would be eleven years old on the fourteenth of July.

NOTE

On July 14th 1789, the Bastille Prison in Paris was stormed. This event is usually considered to be the beginning of the French Revolution.

A Lighthouse Heroine

Henry Brook

IN THE mist and spray thrown up by the storm, the survivors on the rock must have thought they were seeing things. A tiny rowing boat was nudging towards them out of the gloom, with a middle-aged man waving from its prow and a young girl pulling confidently at the oars. The girl's courage and proficiency startled the sailors in the party. They weren't used to seeing a woman who was as skilled on the water as they were. At any second, the sea threatened to pick the fragile craft up and smash it onto the same rocks that had crushed their own ship. But the girl worked the oars expertly, correcting the drift and turning into the waves to prevent the boat from capsizing. She rowed closer, never stopping to think of the danger she was in. Her name was Grace Darling, and her daring at sea would make her one of the greatest celebrities of her times.

From crude fishing boats of sticks and animal hides to the vast warships of today, the history of Britain is in a large part the story of how its people have gone out on the sea. Before the age of flight, Britain relied on ships for trade and travel. The future of the country was decided by great naval battles and fortunes were made and lost on the ocean wave. Because of their close relationship to the sea, the British public was fascinated by nautical adventures. In the early 19th century, a story of the individual battling the might of the ocean reminded people of the struggles they faced in a time of overwhelming progress and change. Although sea adventures usually involve only a few individuals, they can sometimes have an effect on a whole nation.

Strange as it might seem, Grace's adventure began with the coming of the first British passenger ships. In 1838, long distance travel was a slow and bruising business. There were few good roads and the railway network hadn't been extended into the north of the country. The journey between Scotland and London, for example, took several days and nights in a cramped coach, bumping along rutted trails at the mercy of the weather. If passengers wanted any kind of luxury they were better off on the sea. With grand ballrooms, opulent bedrooms and a full social calandar, the new steamer ships were a forerunner of the great transatlantic liners and the age of first class, luxury travel.

The *Forfarshire* was a good example of this new style of passenger ship. She was powered by coal-fired boilers that turned two giant paddle wheels fixed to her hull. To give her additional speed on her route between Hull and Dundee, she was also rigged for sail – but her weight made wind alone an inadequate means of powering her, as her captain would soon discover. She had all the stately trimmings. There was china tableware at every meal and the saloon rooms were lavishly decorated with the works of a well-known artist. On the posters detailing her timetable, the ship was described as 'splendid and powerful' by her owners.

With clouds of black smoke billowing from her funnel, the *Forfarshire* chugged out of Hull docks on September 6, 1838. By all accounts she was an impressive vessel. But this proud ship was no match for the fury of the sea.

The Northumbrian coastline north of Hull is a fearful stretch of churning seas and hidden reefs. Over the centuries, there have been more than 500 recorded wrecks in the area, and the cluster of 17 rocky outcrops that make up the Farne Islands is one of the most dangerous spots for shipping. As the *Forfarshire* approached these islands, her chief engineer rushed to the bridge. In a shocked voice, he reported to the captain that the boilers had flooded and could not be repaired until they reached a port. The ship was suddenly powerless, except for her neglected sails. As if this wasn't bad enough, the captain noticed a knot of storm clouds rushing in from the west. By midnight, the *Forfarshire* was pitching and rolling on a huge sea that was driving her towards the rocky shore. One lifeboat got away from the ship, carrying a single passenger and eight sailors. The 52 people left on board could only stare and scream as the drifting ship smashed headlong into one of the islands – Big Harcar Rock.

The Farnes' reputation for wrecks had earned them a lighthouse, on Longstone Island. Its keepers – William and Thomasin Darling and their 22-year-old daughter, Grace – had listened to the pounding of the storm all night long, snug in their beds behind thick stone walls. In the dawn light of September 7, Grace and her father spotted the wreckage of a ship, grounded on an island almost a mile from the lighthouse. Grace could just make out a group of bedraggled survivors, clinging to the rocks.
According to reports published a few weeks later in

the London press, Grace was woken in the night by the wailing cries of the castaways and went to rouse her father. But the storm that wrecked the *Forfarshire* raged for four whole days. The wind was blowing towards the mainland, carrying any cries away from the lighthouse. So, if Grace heard those desperate yells, she must have had the ears of a cat.

Father and daughter stared out across the swirling waters beyond the steps of their home. Could they save the castaways before they died of exposure or drowned? William Darling was an expert seaman and must have been wary of taking his small rowing boat out onto the storm-lashed waves to attempt a rescue. His son, William Jr., who also lived at the lighthouse was away with a fishing boat. So there was only Grace to aid him.

Some newspapers claimed Grace had to plead with her father to take his boat out, but this was disputed in other parts of the press. What is certain though, is that she helped William push the craft into the waves and jumped in alongside him, ready to risk her life to save the victims of the wreck.

For the first part of the crossing William rowed, but as they approached Big Harcar he let Grace take the oars. She brought the boat right to the edge of the island then kept it steady in the churning waters. Because it was impossible for them to make a landing without being broken on the rocks, William had to risk jumping ashore. He studied the crashing waves, waiting for the right moment, then took a great leap from the rocking prow and landed safely on the reef.

The boat was too small for everyone, so he quickly organized the survivors into two groups. There were nine of them in all: four crew and five passengers, one of whom was a Mrs. Dawson, still clutching the bodies of her two dead children. There was another corpse caught on the rocks – that of a minister who had died of exposure during the night. Some of the men had broken limbs and lacerations. All of them were trembling in the extreme cold. While this wretched party struggled to their feet, Grace held the boat in position on the wild sea.

At last, her father led Dawson and four of the men to the edge of the rocks and waited for his daughter to bring the boat as close as she dared. They managed to scramble in and Grace tended to their injuries while William and one of the sailors rowed back to the lighthouse. Grace and her mother led the survivors up the beach, leaving William and the strongest sailor to return for the other group.

An hour later, the castaways were huddled around the peat fire in the Darlings' living quarters, with Grace serving them hot drinks and fetching blankets. The lighthouse boat had saved nine lives – but at least 43 people had died.

For three days the bedraggled survivors lived with their rescuers, unable to leave the stone tower for fear of the storm. On the fourth day, the waters finally settled, and a fishing boat came over from the mainland to collect them. Within a few hours of their arrival, the first whispers were already spreading about the bravest girl on the seas – fearless Grace, the lighthouse heroine.

Up to the time of the rescue, the Darlings had led a simple – almost puritan – existence on Longstone. William was an enthusiastic gardener and ornithologist, from a long line of lighthousemen. His wife cooked the meals and worked at a spinning wheel by the fireside, while Grace, who had lived in a lighthouse since she was three weeks old, took care of the other domestic chores. She and her eight siblings had been home-schooled, with an emphasis on the stricter aspects of religion and morality. There were no playing cards in the lighthouse – *the Devil's books* was William's name for them – no novels, picture books or plays. For entertainment, Grace studied old maps or read Milton's weighty poetry. Perhaps she enjoyed the desolate beauty of the Farne Islands, the ever-changing seascape of mist, rocks and foaming water. But did a life encircled by the sea make her feel lonely? There can't have been too many gentlemen callers or visiting girlfriends out on Longstone. William Darling believed his daughter was safe from the evil temptations of the mainland: the dandies, novel readers and card players. Grace went back to work after the adventure in the rowing boat, like a princess dutifully returning to her tower.

But two weeks after the rescue, the first portrait artist arrived on the island with an easel slung over his shoulder. The celebrity photo-journalist of his day, this artist made a quick sketch of Grace and her father and sold it to a local newspaper. Reports of the Darlings' heroism had already started filtering out from remotest Northumbria. The London press sniffed a story and Grace's bravery – embellished by imaginative scribes – was a front page sensation. After the seventh portrait artist had come knocking on his door, William Darling grumbled in a letter to the press that the sittings were now over. He had been polite for long enough; the lighthouseman wanted all the fuss to die down.

Grace was receiving scores of letters from her admirers; people begged her for locks of her hair, or scraps of fabric from the dress she'd worn on the day of the rescue. She diligently replied to every inquiry, explaining in her careful handwriting that she was too busy with her chores ever to be lonely or bored on the island: 'I have seven apartments in the house to keep in a state fit for gentlemen,' she explained. It was impossible to send a keepsake of hair to everyone, Grace added, or in a few weeks' time she'd be wearing a wig. For Thomasin Darling it was all too much. She longed for the peace and quiet of Longstone to be restored. Her family wanted nothing to do with the realities of modern Britain, the march of progress, the big cities, factories and the masses of people who worked in them.

But the masses weren't finished with the Darlings.

Thomasin had good reason to fear the outside world and the changes that were taking place across Britain. In 1838, Dickens' *Oliver Twist* was published. His tale of poverty, crime and the workhouse was a stark commentary on the lives of millions of workers and the suffering they endured. Progress might have produced luxury steam boats like the *Forfarshire*, but it had also brought malnutrition, disease and dangerous working conditions for the common man, as the Industrial Revolution transformed the country. In a few years' time, growing public dissatisfaction would spark into political action and the workers would form unions, but for now they just wanted a distraction from their daily grind.

They craved entertainment, turning to the penny broadsheet newspapers for tales of adventure, catastrophe and heroism. If a story had all three elements – and the novelty of a heroine in the lead part – then all the better. But the press still felt obliged to offer moral instruction to their readers. Grace was the perfect role model. She was paraded in the press both as a daring adventuress and an example of Victorian womanhood at its best.

Grace had good company as a female icon for her times. Queen Victoria, who came to the throne in 1837, was a symbol of dutiful femininity in a troubled age, thought of as the mother of the nation. The Queen praised brave, heroic acts of course, but she also encouraged women to be content as humble homemakers. Grace was exciting, daring, even pretty, but she was also demure and respectable – an ideal Victorian heroine.

Throughout September and October, Grace-fever raged across the country. The letters came in a torrent, accompanied by visiting journalists, artists, circus owners – one begged Grace to sit in a lifeboat on the stage while his company performed – and all manner of cranks and admirers. Money came too. The Duke and Duchess of Northumberland were Grace *groupies*. They offered to set up a trust for her, banking all the donations and rewards that were arriving on Longstone. Queen Victoria herself sent a note for £50.

As well as money there were gold medals, commemorative watches and other gifts. Grace's portrait featured on hundreds of gaudy pottery designs and knick-knacks. Poets composed sonnets for her and the newspapers mentioned her by name when they wanted to point out an act of heroism. She even had to put up with a popular song that described the rescue, a schoolyard classic for years to come. This fascination with her name must have seemed intrusive and misplaced to the quiet girl and her family, who had been brought up on the waves. It was only when winter set in and their lighthouse was cut off from the mainland by heavy weather that the Darlings could relax.

Grace's fame had other disadvantages, aside from the loss of privacy. Fishermen along the coast scoffed at the idea that the Darlings had risked their lives during the rescue. They claimed that William and Grace were never in danger because they were always rowing in the lee –

the sheltered side – of an island. So there was nothing heroic about it. Anyone who had grown up by the sea would have done the same, they argued.

Grace stayed silent throughout the unwanted press attention and the verbal attacks from within her own community. She knew that she'd been out in a storm strong enough to wreck a steamship, lee shore or not, but the backbiting must have hurt. Instead of spending more time on the mainland and enjoying her money and fame, Grace retreated into the private world of Longstone. The restless sea, that asked nothing of her, must have seemed like the company of a trusted friend.

But Grace couldn't hide on the lighthouse island forever. On a rare visit to the mainland, to visit her sister in the town of Bamburgh, she caught a chill. It was April 1842 and Grace was still exhausted by the pressures of unwanted celebrity. In her weakened condition, the cold worked its way into her chest and soon she was bedridden. Grace was racked with the disease that claimed so many of Britain's poor – tuberculosis. For months she faded away, until on October 20 she 'went like snow' according to her sister, and died in her father's arms.

Grace Darling was buried in the grounds of Bamburgh Church and a memorial stone commemorating her life was planted out on the Farne Islands. One of England's best known poets, William Wordsworth, wrote some lines praising her bravery that were inscribed on her headstone. Her family wanted Grace to have a special monument in the churchyard, overlooking the sea, and this was completed in 1844. It features a stone statue of Grace reclining on a platform, an oar resting by her side.

Even in death, Grace couldn't escape the legend of her courage on the sea.

Upon Paul's Steeple

Alison Uttley

LONG LONG ago, when girls sold lavender in London streets, crying 'Who'll buy my lavender?' as they held up bunches of the scented flowers, and men sang 'Old chairs to mend' as they passed along the roads with bundles of rushes under their arms, long ago when there were no buses and cars, but great horses pranced down the streets, and little boys and girls came running out of their homes to play whips and tops and ninepins and marbles, in Whitehall, where the King's palace stood, long ago, a strange thing happened.

A dove flew over London streets and gardens. It rested on the top of Saint Paul's steeple, and this, you must know, was old Saint Paul's, for it was before the time of the great fire which destroyed so many of the London churches. In its beak the dove carried a seed, which it had brought from an orchard in Kent. The dove sat there, contemplating the shining river, the Tower of London, the palaces, the forest of steeples, and it thought all those slender spires were trees of stone growing among the wooden houses of old London.

It cooed contentedly as it gazed at the fair view, and the seed dropped from its beak. Then the dove rose on grey wings and flew away to other woods.

The seed fell in a pocket of soil, and there, sheltered by a tiny rail on the top of the steeple, warmed by the sun, refreshed by the dew, it grew. In time the little brown scale burst. A crooked white root pressed down, and a white stem pressed up, and after many months little green leaves appeared. The rootlets crept lower and lower, grasping like hands at the stones on the steeple, clinging to crevices, poking their tendrils into every nook and cranny. The plant grew taller and stronger and bolder as the years went by. It was so high up nobody noticed it, but the other steeples had seen it, and they talked with their bells about the green shoot on the top of Saint Paul's.

'Orange and lemon,' called the bells of Saint Clement. 'Is it an orange tree or a lemon tree I see growing there?' All the bells jingled and jangled in the mornings and evenings, telling one another about the wonderful tree growing high above the city.

At last an astronomer, gazing at the Evening Star with his telescope, saw something strange at the top of Saint Paul's. He twiddled the eyepiece and stared again.

'What's that? A tree? A tree on the top of Saint Paul's steeple?'

He looked again, and exclaimed, 'An apple tree! I can see little green apples growing up there! A marvel! A wonder!'

Then all London came to look at the sight, and people bought little spyglasses to peep, and a man did a roaring trade by hiring a telescope and letting citizens look through it at a penny a spy. There was no doubt it was an apple tree, but whether it was a good or evil omen, nobody knew.

The tree grew fast in the clear air, and spread out its green branches to the sunlight.

'Cut it down,' cried some of the burgesses of London. 'It will harm the church.' 'Leave it alone,' said the Dean. 'It's a miracle. It is to remind us of Adam and Eve and the apple.' So the tree was left to grow, and it spread its lovely web of branches over the roof of the great church, like a green tent.

The next spring it was a garden of pink and white flowers against the blue of the sky, a silken tissue of blooms, and the petals fell on the roof and on the streets, and made a carpet of colour. The robin and the chaffinch built their nests up there, and the music of the birds rang above the noise of men and horses in the cobbled streets below.

In summer the tree was covered with thousands of little green apples. Some of them were blown off and bounced on the heads of the passers-by, but the choirboys picked up most of the windfalls and carried them to feed the swine in the royal piggeries down by the river.

In autumn the fruit ripened, and the branches of the great tree drooped over London with a weight of red and golden apples.

The little boys came running as soon as school was over, from all the streets of London, up the hill of Ludgate, down the street of Fleet, carrying baskets and sticks, bags and crooks, to try to hook the lowest branches. The watchman prevented them from throwing stones lest the precious windows of Saint Paul's should be broken.

From many a little wooden house in London came the smell of apples roast, apples baked, apples in pies, and apples in dumplings, and every spice shop was sold out of cloves. They were the sweetest, nicest apples anyone had ever tasted, and even King Charles had apple-pasties.

When the bells rang for matins, the great waves of sound, the 'Ting-tong-tangle' of great Saint Paul's which rose in such magnificent peals in the air, shook the boughs, and rosy apples came bumping down. When the bells were silent, the tree stopped quivering, and the apples hung like the glittering balls on a Christmas tree, far above anyone's reach.

Now among the children who hurried to Saint Paul's tree was a little waif named Giles. He had no parents, or anyone to care for him, in all the great city. Giles was a chimney-sweep, and he had to climb chimneys in the dark of the cold mornings, whilst his master stood down below in comfort, and urged him forward in the soot and the terrible blackness of the tight, twisty, narrow chimneys of old London.

He was always cold, always hungry, always dirty, except when he could slide into the river and bathe, which was never more than once a year. He ran off to pick the apples from under Saint Paul's but when he arrived there were none left. He went sadly home to the hovel where he lived, for he must try to sleep before dawn, when his work began.

He lay thinking of the apple tree during the night, and at last he stole from his mattress and crept over his sleeping master. He sidled through the door, and away to find apples by moonlight. He ran barefoot through the streets till he reached the churchyard. There was the mighty tree, a canopy of leaves, and through its branches the moon shone like another golden apple.

Giles began to climb. He scrambled up the sides of the church along the buttresses, for he was agile as a monkey through years of climbing the tortuous chimneys. Saint Paul himself put out a hand of stone and gave him a lift. Saint Gabriel tilted a carved and chiselled wing and raised him further. Saint Thomas lifted him in his arms above the danger points, and Saint John carried him to the roof.

Giles scrambled up the leaden roof and reached the spire. A branch dipped with the wind, and he clung to it. From bough to trunk he climbed, and then up the ladder of the branches till his head came out at the top, and he looked down at the leaves below him. He picked the dusky apples hiding in the dark leaves, and then, when his hunger was satisfied, he stared at London, at the houses and towers and London Bridge, at the great broad River Thames, at Saint Clement's, and Saint Martin's in its green fields, and Saint Giles, and far away the little villages hidden in groups of trees. His eye wandered to the great ships at anchor, to the barges and boats, the orchards and gardens near the King's palace, the lines of hedgerows near London Bridge.

He had had many a fine view when he poked his head through the tall chimneys of noblemen's houses – but nothing like this. Everywhere was silver in the moonlight, and the river was the most silver of all. Above him was the arch of the sky, and as he sat in his leafy hiding-place he felt he had never seen so many stars. He started to count them, beginning at the Great Bear, which he knew very well, but soon he was dazzled by shooting stars and twinkling stars and bright planets. They seemed to be circling round the apple tree, so he shut his eyes and fell asleep.

At daybreak he awoke, for the birds around him sang and chirruped so loudly sleep was impossible. He watched the golden sun rise in a sky as pink as the legs of the King's flamingoes, and he remembered that he ought to have been inside Lord Howard's chimney at that moment. He chuckled, for he knew his master could never find him up in Saint Paul's apple tree.

He ate apples for breakfast, and apples for dinner, and

apples for tea, large rosy apples full of good white flesh and sweet juice. All day he stayed aloft, like a sailor in the Crow's nest, staring down at London, at the soldiers and the beggars, the priests and fine ladies, walking up and down like ants on the earth. Only when the great bells rang he put his arms round the tree for safety, lest he should be tossed like an apple down below.

He was happy for the first time in his life, for he was neither tired, nor hungry, nor afraid of his master. The chiming bells brought songs to him, and as they rang he sang, up and down, keeping time and tune with the bells, his voice drowned by their clamour. Yet when the bells ceased he went on singing. He was so high in the air, like a bird in the tree, he forgot his voice might be heard by those far below.

The next day King Charles rode out of the palace, and went to Saint Paul's. He was proud of the famous apple tree which had so miraculously grown on the steeple, and wanted to see it again in all its glory of fruit and leaf, of green branches and singing birds.

The bells ceased ringing and he sat on his white horse looking up at the tree. Suddenly a sweet high voice came out of the sky, a clear silvery voice fresh as a thrush's, and the words of the song came floating down to the King below, like the chime of a tiny bell.

> *'Upon Paul's steeple stands a tree,*
> *As full of apples as can be.*
> *The little boys of London Town,*
> *They run with hooks to pull them down.*
> *And then they run from hedge to hedge,*
> *Until they come to London Bridge.'*

The tune was that of the bells calling people to church, and the voice was sweet as an angel's.

'What's that?' asked the King. 'One of the Cherubim?'

'It must indeed be a Cherub,' replied the Dean. 'No one could climb up there, your Majesty, unless he had wings.'

Again the song rang through the air, a tinkling bell song, and then the watchers saw something coming slowly down the tree, gliding down the roof of Saint Paul's to the buttresses. Helped by the stone hands and wings of the saints, the boy slipped to the earth, but before he could make off he found himself surrounded by a little crowd of plumed horsemen.

'Faith! 'Tis a black angel,' laughed Charles, and someone grabbed Giles by the collar.

'Who are you, boy, and how did you get up there?' asked the Dean.

'Please, sir, I am Giles the chimney-sweeper, and I climbed up,' said Giles, thoroughly frightened.

The King said a few words privately to the Dean, and then turned to the boy. 'So you are a sweep, and you've climbed a greenleaf chimney! Do you want to go back to your master, my boy?'

'No, sir,' Giles shivered.

'Then you must take your punishment. You have climbed Saint Paul's tree, so now you belong to Saint Paul. You must go to the school of Saint Paul, and sing in the choir of Saint Paul, and will you like that?'

Giles grinned happily. 'Thank you, your Majesty,' said he.

'Now come with me and be bathed and clothed,' said the Dean. 'We must find you some better rags than those you have on, and although we know the sound of your singing, we don't know the colour of your face!'

So Giles was scrubbed and cleaned, and dressed afresh, so that a merry little boy came out from the grime of years. He became a chorister at Saint Paul's, and learned his Latin at Saint Paul's school. His voice was the sweetest, highest voice among all the sweet high voices in the choir, and he was chosen to sing in chant and carol and madrigal.

The King's favourite song was the bell-song which Giles sang up in the apple tree, and many a time the little chorister went to the palace to sing it to His Majesty and his guests.

He stood in his long gown before the courtiers and ladies, and a minstrel rang a chime, in tune with the boy's rhyme:

> 'Upon Paul's steeple stands a tree.
> As full of apples as can be.
> The little boys of London Town,
> They run with hooks to pull them down.
> And then they run from hedge to hedge,
> Until they come to London Bridge.'

Then everyone laughed and patted him on the back, and the King gave him a gold penny and sent him back to school.

Robert the Bruce and the Spider

Geraldine McCaughrean

ROBERT THE Bruce, lost, stolen or strayed!' read the English proclamation jeeringly, for the so-called King of Scotland had been gone all year and those trying to hunt him down could find no trace.

Dispossessed of his country by the English and driven to live as an outlaw, he and his companions were on the run, propping up branches for shelter, sleeping on animal skins, eating rabbits, berries and fish. With winter coming on, Robert the Bruce deemed it better the ladies should go to Kildrummie Castle, into the care of his young brother Nigel, while he and his few companions headed further north.

The news that reached them was all bad. Though Bruce kept his comrades entertained with stories of questing knights and poems about the heroes of Scotland, his spirits sank lower and lower. Every day, relations and friends were being captured, imprisoned, put to death. Perhaps he should abandon any dreams of driving the English out of Scotland. Six battles he had fought with the enemy, and six times his fortunes had fallen still lower.

One night, sheltering in a dilapidated hut on the island of Rathlin, he lay looking up at the roof. A spider hung there from a single thread, trying to swing from one rafter to the next so as to establish a web. Again and again it tried, though surely the distance was too great. Four, five, six times it tried. What perseverance! Did it never know when to give up? Why did it not scuttle away into a corner and weave there? Bruce found himself oddly caught up in the efforts of the spider. His eyes hurt with watching it so intently. I too, have made six attempts, he thought. If this creature tries again – if it succeeds – then, by all that's holy *so will I!*

The little gossamer thread was barely visible, and yet from it now hung the rest of Bruce's life. He forgot to swallow. He forgot to blink. The spider gathered its legs into a single black pellet. Swinging across the dark chasm of the roof, the little trapeze artist reached its goal and began, without respite, to construct a gossamer kingdom between the rafters.

In that moment, a surge of determination swept through Robert the Bruce which drove out all his weariness and despair. He would live to see the English driven out, and to be acknowledged King of Scotland! 'And when I do, I shall make a pilgrimage to Jerusalem to give thanks. This I swear, Lord!'

The spider brought no sudden change in Bruce's luck. He learned that Kildrummie Castle had been taken, and the ladies there – his sister and wife – had been shut up like wild beasts in wooden cages, and hung over the battlements. Another sister had been placed in a nunnery. And his young brother Nigel – no more than a boy – had been hanged. But now, instead of increasing his despair, such news only fuelled Bruce's zeal for revenge. Even though the people were too terrified to answer his call to arms, and two more of his brothers were captured and hanged, Robert the Bruce would not give up hope.

He gained the friendship of Black Douglas, terror of

the Borders, and at last highland and lowland lairds began rallying to his cause. More and more castles were captured by his growing army.

At Stirling, King Edward sent against him the greatest army ever led by an English king. When it came into sight, Black Douglas reported back to Bruce that it was the 'most beautiful and most terrible sight'. Sixty thousand men, better mounted and better armed than the Scots, came on like cloud shadow over the landscape.

Bruce said, 'If any man of you is not ready for either victory or death, let him leave now!' But not one man quit the field. The odds were against them two to one, but everyone knew that on this battle the future of Scotland rested: its independence, its nationhood, its pride. The lines were drawn up for the battle called Bannockburn.

'They are kneeling to beg forgiveness!' cried King Edward, thinking the Scots were going down on their knees in hope of mercy.

'Yes, but they are asking it from God, not from us,' said an English baron. 'They are praying. These men will conquer or die.'

The English cavalry moved off, formidable in their fine armour, on their huge horses, speeding from a walk to a trot, from a trot to a canter. Helmet crests and pennons flickered as if a grass fire were devouring the plain . . . And then all of a sudden they were stumbling and pitching, their horses tripping and going down. Knights fell from their ornate saddles and lay pinned to the ground by their weight of armour. Bruce had had his men dig 10,000 holes to the depth of a man's knee – 10,000 artificial rabbit holes in which a galloping horse could step and break a leg. Many of the horses and many of the knights did not stir, for Bruce had also strewn the plain with spiky calthrops which lie always with one lethal point upward.

Bruce's cavalry rushed the English archers: after that the English military advantage had gone. King Edward fled. The attendant who escorted him safely off the field (valuing his honour more than Edward did) turned back and threw himself into the mêlée to die fighting. But as the royal banner retreated, so the English ranks broke and ran, all the heart gone out of them.

The battle of Bannockburn established Robert the Bruce as King of Scotland. But the Pope said he would only acknowledge Bruce if he went on Crusade to the Holy Land.

No penance could have pleased Bruce more, remembering the vow he had made on Rathlin. He longed to see Jerusalem. But illness had dogged him down the years, and now it caught up with him. Leprosy prevented Bruce from keeping his promise to the Pope. So he sent for his best friend and bravest fighter, Black Douglas, and asked him, 'Keep my promise. When I am dead, go to the Holy Land in my place. Carry my heart with you, and bury it in the Holy Sepulchre where Christ lay down and rose again to life.'

Black Douglas did as he was asked. Though Robert the Bruce was buried, wrapped in cloth-of-gold, in Dunfermline Abbey, his heart, sealed in a lead casket, was worn around Douglas's neck the day he joined battle with the Infidel.

He had travelled only as far as Spain (then occupied by Moorish Moslems). Cut off from his troops, Douglas saw no escape. So he wrenched the casket from round his neck and hurled it forward, overarm, crying, 'Pass onward . . . ! I follow or die!'

The descendants of Douglas emblazon their shields with a bleeding heart surmounted by a golden crown to commemorate this last great act of loyalty and devotion.

FANTASY: IMAGINED WORLDS AND FANTASTIC ADVENTURES

Thumbelisa

Hans Christian Anderson
(translated by Diane Crone Frank and Jeffrey Frank)

ONCE THERE was an old woman who was eager to have a little child. But she had no idea how to get one, so she went to an old witch and said, 'I really, really want to have a little child. Won't you tell me where I can find one?'

'Of course, we'll work it out,' the witch said. 'Here's a barley seed for you, but not the sort that grows in the farmers' fields or the kind that chickens eat. Put it in a flower pot – then you'll get a surprise.'

'Thanks very much,' said the old woman, who gave the witch twelve coins, went home, and planted the barley seed. Right away a beautiful big flower came up. It looked just like a tulip, but the petals were closed as if it were still a bud.

'That's a lovely flower,' the woman said, and kissed its pretty red and yellow petals. But just as she kissed it, the flower gave a loud pop and opened up. Then you could see that it was a real tulip, but in the middle of the flower, as if on a green stool, sat a tiny girl – delicate and lovely. But she was no taller than a thumb, and that's why she was called Thumbelisa.

She was given a cradle made of a brightly lacquered walnut shell, a mattress made from blue violets, and a rose-petal cover. That's where she slept at night, but during the day she played on the table, where the old woman had put a plate. The plate was decorated with a ring of flowers, and their stems reached into the water where a big tulip leaf floated. Thumbelisa was allowed to sit on the leaf and sail from one side of the plate to the other, rowing with two white horsehairs. It was wonderful. She sang softly and charmingly – no one had ever heard a voice like hers.

One night as she lay in her nice bed, an ugly toad hopped in through the window – a windowpane was broken. The toad was repulsive, big, and wet, and she jumped right onto the table where Thumbelisa was asleep under the red rose petal.

'She'd make a lovely wife for my son,' the toad said and grabbed the walnut shell where Thumbelisa slept. The toad took her away, hopping through the window into the garden.

A wide stream ran through the garden, but its banks were swampy and muddy; that's where the toad lived with her son. Yuck! He was ugly and disgusting, just like his mother. *Ko-ax, ko-ax, brekke-ke-kex.* That was all he said when he saw the pretty little girl in the walnut shell.

'Don't talk so loud or you'll wake her up,' the old toad said. 'She could still run away, because she's as light as swans' down. We'll put her out in the stream, on one of those big lily pads. She's so slight and small that it will be like an island for her. That way she can't run off while we fix up the parlour under the mud, where you'll live.'

There were lots of water lilies in the stream. They had broad green leaves and looked as if they floated on the water. The one farthest away was also the biggest, and the old toad swam out to it and left the walnut shell with Thumbelisa on the leaf.

The poor little girl woke up early the next morning. When she saw where she was, she began to cry bitterly, because there was water on all sides of the big green water-lily leaf. She had no way of reaching the shore.

The old toad was down below in the mud, decorating her parlour with rushes and yellow water lilies – she wanted to make it really nice for her new daughter-in-law. She and her ugly son swam out to Thumbelisa's leaf to fetch her pretty bed, which they wanted to move to the bridal chamber before Thumbelisa arrived. The old toad made a deep curtsy in the water in front of Thumbelisa and said, 'Here's my son. He'll be your husband, and the two of you will have such a nice home in the mud.'

Ko-ax, ko-ax, brekke-ke-kex. That was all that her son could say.

They took the little bed and swam away. Thumbelisa sat all alone on the green leaf and cried, because she did not want to live with the revolting toad or marry her repulsive son. The little fish in the stream had seen the toad and heard what she said; that's why they poked their heads out of the water – they were curious to see the little girl. As soon as they saw how lovely she was, it really upset them to imagine her living down there with the ugly toad. No – that was never going to happen. Under the water they gathered around the green stalk that held the leaf where Thumbelisa was standing. They gnawed through the stalk with their teeth, and the leaf floated down the stream – taking Thumbelisa away, far away, where the toad couldn't reach her.

Thumbelisa sailed past so many places. Small birds watched her from the bushes and sang, 'What a pretty little girl!' Her lily pad floated farther and farther, and in that way Thumbelisa travelled abroad.

A white butterfly kept circling around her. Eventually, it settled on the leaf, because it liked Thumbelisa. She was happy that the toad couldn't reach her now and that everything around her was so lovely; the sun made the water shine like the prettiest gold. Thumbelisa untied the ribbon from her waist and attached one end to the butterfly and the other end to the leaf. The lily pad floated much faster, and so did she – after all, she was standing on it.

At that moment a big beetle flew by. It noticed Thumbelisa and immediately pounced; it grabbed her slender waist and flew up into a tree. But the leaf kept floating downstream, and the butterfly followed, because it was still tied to the leaf and could not get loose.

Poor Thumbelisa was frightened when the beetle carried her up into the tree, but mostly she was sad about the beautiful white butterfly that she had tied to the leaf. If it couldn't break loose, it would starve to death. But the beetle couldn't care less. He put Thumbelisa on the biggest green leaf in the tree, fed her honey from the flowers, and said that she was very pretty even if she did not look like a beetle. Later on, the other beetles who lived in the tree paid a visit; they looked at Thumbelisa, and all the maiden beetles shrugged their antennae and said, 'She only has two legs – how pathetic!'

'She doesn't have antennae,' they said. 'Her waist is so thin – *ugh!*' the lady beetles said. 'She looks just like a human. She's revolting!'

Yet Thumbelisa was very pretty. The beetle who had kidnapped her thought so too, but when the others kept saying that she was ugly, he finally agreed and didn't want anything to do with her any more. She was free to go wherever she wanted. The beetles carried Thumbelisa down from the tree and put her on a daisy. She cried, because now the beetle thought she was hideous and because the other beetles wanted nothing to do with her. But actually, she was as lovely as you could imagine – as delicate and pure as the most beautiful rose petal.

All summer long, poor Thumbelisa lived alone in the big forest. She braided a bed of grass and hung it under a large burdock leaf to keep the rain off. She ate honey from the flowers, and she drank the dew that covered the leaves every morning. Summer and autumn passed that way, but then winter came – the cold long winter. All the birds, which had sung so prettily for her, flew away; the trees and flowers withered, and the burdock leaf where she had lived curled up and became a dead yellow stalk. She was terribly cold because her clothing was torn and she was so delicate and tiny: poor Thumbelisa was going to freeze to death. It started to snow, and for Thumbelisa every flake felt as a whole shovelful of snow would to us. That's because we are big, and she was no taller than a thumb. She wrapped herself in the dead leaf, but it didn't keep her warm; she shivered with cold.

She came to a large wheat field just beyond the forest, but the wheat had been cut long ago. Only dry bare stalks stuck out of the frozen ground, and for Thumbelisa it was like walking through a forest. She was very cold. Then she came to the door of a field mouse, which was a little hole among the stubble. The field mouse's place was warm and cosy; her parlour was filled with grain, and she had a wonderful kitchen and pantry. Thumbelisa squeezed through the door, just like a poor beggar girl, and asked for a little piece of barleycorn because she hadn't had a thing to eat for two days.

'Poor dear!' the field mouse said, because at heart she was a good old field mouse. 'Come into my warm parlour and join me for a meal.'

Because the field mouse liked Thumbelisa, she said, 'You can stay here with me for the winter, but you have to keep my parlour nice and clean and tell me stories, because I really like stories.' Thumbelisa did what the good old field mouse wanted and was as comfortable as could be.

'I think we'll have a visitor soon,' the field mouse said. 'My neighbour usually comes once a week to see me. His place is even nicer than mine – he has large rooms and wears a lovely velvety black fur coat. If you could only marry him, you'd be set for life. But he can't see. You'll have to tell him the most beautiful stories you know.'

Thumbelisa didn't like that idea; she didn't want to marry the neighbour, because the neighbour was a mole.

The mole came to call, wearing his black velvety coat. He was very rich and very learned, the field mouse said, and his house was more than twenty times larger than hers. He was wise too, but he didn't like the sun or beautiful flowers; he made nasty comments about them, because he'd never seen them. Thumbelisa had to sing to him, and she sang both 'Beetle, Fly, Fly Away Home!' and 'The Monk Walks in the Meadow'. At that, the mole fell in love with Thumbelisa because of her beautiful voice. But he didn't say anything, because he was a very cautious type.

The mole had recently dug a long passageway in the ground from his house to theirs, and the field mouse and Thumbelisa got permission to walk there whenever they wanted. He told them not to be afraid of the dead bird on the path. The bird still had its feathers and beak, and it appeared to have died quite recently, at the beginning of winter. It was underground, right where the mole had dug his path.

The mole picked up a piece of rotting wood, which, as you know, can glow in the dark like fire, and put it in his mouth; he walked ahead, lighting the long dark passageway. When they came to the dead bird, the mole pushed his wide nose through the earth, making a big hole to let the sun shine in. In the middle of the floor a dead swallow lay with its beautiful wings pressed tight against its side and its legs and head tucked under its feathers.

The poor bird had undoubtedly died from the cold. Thumbelisa felt very sorry for it. She loved birds, because they had chirped and sung beautifully for her all summer long. But the mole pushed away the dead bird with his short legs and said, 'Now he won't squeak any more. It must be just awful to be born a bird. Thank goodness none of my children will be birds – that sort of bird can only chirp for us, and in the winter it will starve to death.'

'You're so right, because you're a sensible man,' the field mouse said. 'What is a bird's chirping worth when winter comes? It will starve and freeze – but I suppose people think suffering makes you noble.'

Thumbelisa said nothing. But when the mole and field mouse turned their backs to the bird, she bent down, pushed aside the feathers that covered its head, and kissed its closed eyes. 'Maybe this is the bird who sang for me last summer,' she thought. 'That dear beautiful bird gave me so much joy.'

The mole plugged the hole where the light shone in and accompanied the ladies home. At night Thumbelisa couldn't sleep. She got out of bed and braided a handsome big blanket out of hay. She carried it down and spread it over the dead bird. Then she took some soft cotton wool that she'd found in the field mouse's parlour and tucked it around the bird to keep it warm in the cold ground.

'Goodbye, you beautiful little bird,' she said. 'Goodbye and thank you for your summer song when the trees were green and the sun was so warm.' She laid her head on the bird's chest but suddenly became quite alarmed, because it seemed as if something was pounding inside. It was the bird's heart. It wasn't dead; it was only numb with cold, and now it had warmed up and come to life again. (In the autumn all the swallows fly off to the warm countries. But if one of them gets a late start, it will freeze and fall down dead; it stays where it falls, and the cold snow covers it.) Thumbelisa was shaking; she had had a great fright because the bird, of course, was so big – big compared to Thumbelisa, who was no taller than a thumb. But she got up her courage, tucked the cotton wool tighter around the poor swallow, and fetched a mint leaf, which she had used as her cover, and put it over the bird's head.

The next night she crept back to the bird. It was alive but so weak that it could only open its eyes briefly to look at Thumbelisa, who stood there with a piece of glowing wood in her hand. That was all the light that she had.

'Thank you, my pretty little child,' the sick swallow said. 'I feel nice and warm again. Soon I'll be strong enough to fly into the warm sunlight.'

'Oh, no!' she replied. 'It's very cold outside – it's snowing and freezing. Stay in your warm bed, and I'll take care of you.'

She carried water to the swallow, in a petal. He drank it and told her how he had torn his wing on a thornbush and couldn't fly as fast as the other swallows when they'd flown away – far away to the warm countries. In the end he had fallen to earth, but that's all he could remember. He didn't know how he had ended up here.

Thumbelisa and the swallow stayed underground for the whole winter. She was kind to the bird and loved it; neither the mole nor the field mouse knew about it, because Thumbelisa realized that they didn't like the poor little swallow.

As soon as it was spring and the sun warmed up the ground, the swallow said goodbye to Thumbelisa, who opened up the hole that the mole had made overhead. The sunlight felt wonderful, and the swallow asked Thumbelisa if she wanted to come along. She could sit on his back, and they would fly far away into the green forest. But Thumbelisa knew that the old field mouse would be very sad if she left.

'No, I can't do it,' Thumbelisa said.

'Goodbye, goodbye, you sweet, pretty girl,' the swallow said and flew into the sunshine. Thumbelisa watched it leave, and her eyes filled with tears because she was so fond of the swallow.

'*Qui-vit, qui-vit!*' the bird sang and flew into the green forest.

Thumbelisa was very sad. She wasn't allowed out in the warm sunshine; the grain, which had been sown on the field above the mole's house, grew high – it was like a thick forest for the little girl, who of course was only as big as a thumb.

'You must sew your wedding trousseau this summer,' the field mouse told Thumbelisa, because by now the neighbour, the dreary mole in the black velvety fur coat, had proposed to her. 'You need wool and linen. You need something to wear and to sleep on when you become the mole's wife.'

Thumbelisa turned the spindle, and the mole hired four spiders to spin and weave night and day. Every evening the mole paid a visit, and he always said that when summer was over, the sun wouldn't feel nearly so hot – now it scorched the earth and made it hard as rock. At the end of the summer it would be time to celebrate Thumbelisa's wedding. But she wasn't happy about it, because she didn't much like the boring mole. Every morning when the sun rose, and every evening when it set, Thumbelisa crept to the doorway; when the wind parted the grain so that she could see the blue sky, she thought how beautiful and bright it was. She so wished that she could see her dear swallow again, but it didn't return – it had probably flown far off into the great green forest.

When autumn came, Thumbelisa had finished her entire trousseau.

'Four weeks to your wedding!' the field mouse reminded her. Thumbelisa cried and said that she didn't want to marry the tedious mole.

'Nonsense,' the field mouse said. 'Don't be stubborn, or I'll have to bite you with my white teeth. You're marrying such a wonderful man! Even the queen can't match his dark velvety fur coat. He has both a kitchen and a basement. You should thank God for him.'

It was time for the wedding. The mole had already come to pick up Thumbelisa. She was going to live deep underground and never come out into the warm sun – because the mole didn't like sunlight. The poor child was miserable because she had to say goodbye to the beautiful sun; even when she'd stayed with the field mouse, she had been allowed to look at the sun through the doorway.

'Goodbye, you bright sun,' she said, stretching her arms into the air. She was able to walk a few steps from the field mouse's house, because the grain had been harvested and only dry stalks were left. 'Goodbye, goodbye,' she went on and put her arms around a little red flower that hadn't been cut down. 'Say hello to the dear swallow from me, if you happen to see him.'

All at once, right above her, she heard *'Qui-vit, qui-vit!'* She looked up and saw the swallow flying by. It was happy as soon as it saw Thumbelisa. She told the swallow how she hated the idea of marrying the ugly mole and having to live far underground where the sun never shone. The thought made her weep.

'Cold winter is coming,' the swallow said. 'I'm going to fly to the warm countries – do you want to come along? You can sit on my back – and you can tie yourself to me with the ribbon around your waist. We'll fly away from the ugly mole and his dark house – over the mountains, far away to the warm countries, where the sun shines more brilliantly than it does here and where they always have summer and beautiful flowers. Come along, dear Thumbelisa – you saved my life when I was frozen in that dark cellar underground.'

'Yes, I'll come along,' Thumbelisa said. She climbed up on the bird's back, put her feet on its outstretched wings, tied her belt to one of its strongest feathers, and then the swallow flew far up in the air. It flew over forests and lakes and above the tall mountains that always have snow on top. Thumbelisa shivered in the cold air. She crept in under the bird's warm feathers and stuck out her head only to look at all the beauty down below.

They reached the warm countries. The sun shone much more brightly than it does here, the sky was twice as high, and the most beautiful green and blue grapes grew along ditches and on fences. There were lemons and oranges in the forest, and the air smelled of myrtle and mint. Along the road the nicest children were playing with big colourful butterflies. But the swallow kept going – and everything became more and more beautiful.

Beneath magnificent green trees by a blue lake was a shiny white marble castle; vines wound around the tall pillars, and at the very top were lots of swallows' nests. The swallow who carried Thumbelisa lived in one of them.

'Here's my house,' the swallow said. 'But you should go and find yourself a beautiful flower down there. I'll set you down, and you can make yourself as happy as you want.'

'That's lovely,' she said and clapped her tiny hands.

A large white marble pillar had fallen over and broken into three pieces, and among them grew dazzling white flowers. The swallow flew down and put Thumbelisa on one of the leaves – and what a surprise she got. A tiny man was sitting in the middle of the flower. He was white and transparent, as if he were made of glass; he had the prettiest gold crown on his head and the loveliest clear wings on his shoulders – he was no bigger than Thumbelisa. He was the spirit of the flowers. (A little man or woman lives in every flower, but he was the king of them all.)

'He's so beautiful!' Thumbelisa whispered to the swallow. The little prince was afraid of the swallow, because it was a giant bird compared to someone like him; he was so small and delicate. But he was delighted when he saw Thumbelisa; she was the loveliest girl he had ever seen. That's why he took off his gold crown and placed it on Thumbelisa's head. He asked her name and if she wanted to be his wife – which would make her queen of all the flowers. Yes, he was certainly different from the toad's son or the mole with the black velvety fur coat. So she said yes to the handsome prince. Then an enchanting man or woman came out of every flower, and each one brought a gift to Thumbelisa. But the best present was a pair of beautiful wings from a big white fly; they were attached to Thumbelisa's back, so that she too could fly from flower to flower. It was a very happy moment. The little swallow sat in his nest and sang for them as best he could, but in his heart he was sad, because he was very fond of Thumbelisa and didn't want to be separated from her.

'They shouldn't call you Thumbelisa,' the spirit of the flowers told her. 'It's an ugly name, and you're so beautiful. We'll call you Maya.'

'Goodbye, goodbye,' the swallow said and once more flew away from the warm countries, far away, back to Denmark. There it had a little nest above the window of the man who knew how to tell fairy tales. It sang *'Qui-vit, qui-vit!'* to him, and that's how we got this whole story.

Sailor Rumbelow and Britannia

James Reeves

I'M LONESOME,' said Dick to himself, standing on the deck of the three-masted schooner. 'I'll whistle to keep up my spirits.'

For the twenty-third time that day he whistled to himself a gay hornpipe tune. But it didn't cheer him up.

He had been standing just there, on the deck of the schooner, with his telescope to his eye, for nearly as long as he could remember. His first name was Dick, and he had a fine roaring surname, which was Rumbelow. The sails of his schooner were spread tight in the wind, just as they always were. But there was no wind. There was no one else in sight. The captain and the mate and the rest of the crew must be down below somewhere. Dick Rumbelow felt lonely, cold and small. The tune he was whistling did nothing to make him feel warm and big, as a sailor should. He could not even dance a hornpipe to make himself warm.

Now this was not surprising, for Dick was only about a quarter of an inch high, about as high as a dried pea or a little boy's front tooth. Of course he didn't know this; and he didn't know that he was on the deck of a model ship in full sail, inside a glass bottle. From inside the bottle he couldn't see the bottle, so how was he to know that he was inside it? All the same, Sailor Rumbelow had an idea that his ship, the *Desperado* – that was what it was called – was becalmed. The sails might bulge stiffly, and the painted blue waves have white crests; but still he could feel no breeze, and no movement. So all day long Dick stood on the deck, sometimes whistling and sometimes thinking about the times he could almost remember before the *Desperado* was becalmed. He had a notion about long, exciting voyages to palmy shores and fights with black men who shouted terrible war-cries and rattled their spears and shields.

One day a lady with a little girl came into the shop where the *Desperado*, inside its bottle, hung in the window. The shopkeeper came out and asked what she wanted. While the lady was talking to the shopkeeper, the little girl stared at the ship in the bottle. She couldn't take her eyes off it. She pulled at her mother's hand.

'Look, mummy,' she said, 'oh, look!'

'Don't interrupt, dear,' said the lady.

But at last she stopped talking to the shopkeeper and turned to her daughter.

'It's a little ship, mummy. It's in a bottle. How did it get in the bottle with its masts and sails all sticking up?'

The shopkeeper explained that the ship had probably been made by a sailor, perhaps a hundred years ago, and put inside the bottle with its sails and masts lying on the deck. Then he must have pulled them up into position and fastened them there before pushing the cork into the bottle-neck.

'It's lovely,' said the little girl. 'Can we buy it, mummy?'

'It's not a toy, dear,' said her mother. 'If you played with it, you could so easily break it.'

'Oh, I wouldn't play with it. I'd just look at it. We could hang it in the window.'

'Well, I'll see what daddy says,' answered the lady.

The little girl knew that this often meant that something she wanted would be bought. She squeezed her mother's hand in gratitude, as if it was all settled, and they went out of the shop.

Next day they came in again and bought the schooner *Desperado*, inside its bottle, with Dick Rumbelow standing on the deck, his telescope to his eye.

When the bottle was hung up in the window of the lady's house just outside the town, Dick could see across a green lawn to a huge sea, and this made him happier. Of course the huge sea was only a lily-pond, but to Dick it was as big as the Caribbean.

'Yo ho!' he said in his most seamanlike voice. 'This is something like.'

In a little red-brick house, inside a glass ball, lived a very tiny girl. Her name was Britannia. Although she was so very tiny, she was grown up – about twenty years old, you would have said, looking at her pretty golden hair and her red cheeks. Yet she was no taller than a small dried pea or the front tooth of a real little girl. Her house was only a finger's height, and the two green bushes at either side of the front door were very small indeed. There was a neat green lawn that went all round the house, but it was nearly always covered with snow. So was the roof of the redbrick house. Britannia always stood just inside one of the top windows, looking out over the snowy lawn. When you lifted up the glass ball with the house inside, and turned it upside down, then the right way up again, there was a tremendous snowstorm. You couldn't see the house, or Britannia, or the two green bushes, or the green lawn, because of the whirling snowflakes. Round and round they went, until very slowly they settled just as before, covering the roof and the lawn and the green bushes on either side of the front door.

Snowstorms always caused Britannia much trouble and inconvenience, because they meant that the house was turned upside down; all her pots and pans and tables and chairs and teacups and vases and everything else in her small, tidy house went flying up to the ceiling; and when they came down, she had to put them all to rights again, while the snowflakes whirled about outside the windows. But before the snow had settled, she was back again at her old place just inside one of the top windows, gazing out over the white world. Her cheeks were always red and shiny because of the bother of clearing everything up, and her golden hair was never quite tidy. It smudged down over her eyes; and this was a pity because she was one who liked to be tidy.

One day the little girl and her mother came into the shop once more, and the little girl saw the house in the snow. It was on the shelf just inside the shop window. While her mother was talking to the shopkeeper, the little girl picked up the glass ball and looked at it.

'Careful, dear,' her mother said.

Then the shopkeeper showed her how to make it snow. She almost cried with delight.

'We really can't afford it,' said her mother. 'Why, it's no time since we bought the *Desperado*.'

The little girl looked at her mother wide-eyed.

'You're not *sorry* we bought it, mummy?' she asked. 'Everybody says how lovely it is.'

'No, of course not, but we can't have everything.'

'Wouldn't this look lovely in the same room as the ship?' said the little girl. 'A ship in a bottle and a house in a ball – what could be nicer?'

'We'll see what daddy says.'

'Oh yes, let's.'

'Mind you, I'm not promising anything.'

'No, of course not.'

But the little girl had an idea that her father might buy the house in the snowstorm.

'I must say,' said her father to her mother that evening, 'the child has good taste.'

The little girl, who was listening, could not understand this. She often couldn't quite understand daddy. How could he know she had a good taste if he had never tasted her? Still, it was said in a pleased way, you could tell that; and that was all that mattered.

'I expect she takes after you, dear,' said the lady artfully.

'Oh well—' said the little girl's father in a voice which meant he would almost certainly do what she wanted.

When they bought the house in the snow it looked beautiful on the mantelpiece. The little girl was told to be very careful and not play with it unless there was someone with her to see that she didn't accidentally drop it. She loved being allowed to take it in her hands and turn it first upside down, then right side up, so that the little red-brick house was almost lost in a whirl of snowflakes.

For the first few days after her removal, Britannia seemed to be always tidying up; but after a while she was left more to herself. Then she began to enjoy her new situation. Certainly the room was very elegant to look at. Sometimes the glass ball, after being very carefully dusted by the lady herself, was put back a little crooked, so that Britannia could see the window and the garden beyond. She could see the *Desperado* in its glass bottle hanging in the window, and she could just make out Dick Rumbelow standing on the deck with his spyglass to his eye.

'What a nice fellow he looks,' she said to herself, 'and how lonely. Poor man! I wonder how he likes living in a bottle. It must seem awfully cramped to one used to voyaging on the foaming seas.'

The lady also took down the ship in the bottle once a week and dusted it. She never let anyone else do this, for fear it might fall and break. Sometimes she put it back the wrong way round, so that Sailor Dick no longer looked out of the window at the Caribbean lily-pond but right across the room towards the mantelpiece. So it was that he first set eyes on Britannia as she stood by the top window in her house in the snow.

He gazed long and silently at her through his spyglass. He was afraid she might think him rude but he just couldn't help it.

'My eye!' said Dick. 'What a beautiful girl! I've never seen such bright rosy cheeks and golden hair in all my life. I dare say her cheeks are red from being out in the snow. But how lonely she must be, living in a glass ball like that. Poor girl, what a cold and lonesome life!'

But Britannia did not at all mind being stared at through the telescope. It had never happened to her before, and she liked it.

'Let him stare,' she said. 'I will not wave at him, though I should like to, but I won't look angry either. He must be so lonely inside that bottle, and if staring at me through a telescope cheers him up, who am I to forbid it?'

For a whole week Sailor Rumbelow looked hard at the girl in the red-brick house. He could not take his eyes off her.

'She doesn't seem to mind,' he said to himself. 'I even fancy she may be pleased. It looks as if she's all alone in that great house. She never comes out and nobody visits her. I suppose they don't like the snow. Well, I can't blame them. But it must be lonely for the girl up there. If she likes my company through the wrong end of a spyglass, so to say, it'd be cruel to deny her.'

Then at the end of the week the lady came and dusted the things in the room; Britannia was made to look away from the window, but Dick was left as he had been, staring at the house in the snow as it stood on the mantelpiece.

'Now I've gone and offended her,' said the sailor to himself. 'She doesn't look at me any more. Poor soul, all by herself in that glass ball! If only I could sail alongside of her and break in! Then perhaps we two could go walking out together, like – like—'

But he couldn't remember walking out with any girl, even though he knew he had once, long ago, been on shore. Still, sailors nearly always walk out with girls when they are on shore, so Dick supposed there must have been someone.

'All the same,' he said to himself, 'if there *was* someone, she couldn't have been a patch on the one with the red cheeks and the gold ringlets.'

And he sighed for Britannia all the more because she had turned away from him and would not be stared at any longer.

'She's angry with me,' Dick told himself, 'because she wants rescuing, and I can't rescue her. That's what it is. Shut away in that house like that, with the snow all round: what she wants is rescuing – or perhaps she wants a smell of the salt sea! Ah, if only the wind would blow, and I could fetch up right alongside.'

Next week it was the other way round. When the lady came to dust, whisking round with her little feather brush and her yellow duster, she left Dick Rumbelow staring out of the window and Britannia gazing towards him.

'He's lost interest in me,' sighed Britannia to herself. 'Just because I couldn't see him for a whole week, he's got tired of me and won't look any more. That's so like a sailor. You never can trust them. All the same, I won't give him up. He needs me, poor chap, shut up in that glass bottle, and I won't desert him.'

So she sighed for Dick, and Dick sighed for her as he gazed out over the Caribbean. Outside, the days grew warmer and sunnier, but inside the glass ball the snow lay on the ground as thick as ever. Sometimes the window was left open, and this made a little breeze in the room, and the ship in the bottle moved ever so slightly on the cords by which it hung from the ceiling. And Dick Rumbelow fancied the wind was getting up, and soon he would be able to turn the good ship *Desperado* and bring her to where he might rescue the girl in the glass ball. He whistled the tune of 'The Girl I Left Behind Me', and after that his favourite hornpipe, but still the ship did not move, although the sails were as stiff and bulging as ever. But the week passed, and once more Dick and Britannia were facing each other.

'He has forgiven me,' said the girl to herself happily. 'Now surely I can wave and smile at him, because we are friends again.'

'So she's not angry with me after all,' said Dick to himself, 'and I will dance a hornpipe and wave my spyglass to show my regard for her.'

Then he saw that Britannia seemed to be smiling and waving to him, and Britannia noticed that her sailor friend looked as if he was actually doing a hornpipe to amuse her. So she smiled and waved all the more prettily, and Dick waved his spyglass in the air and shouted 'Huzza!'

Of course, all this time the little girl who had got her mother and father to buy the ship and the little house in the snow had been coming to the room to look at them and play with them when she was allowed to. The sailor and the tiny person in the house had got used to this.

Then she did not come any more. At first they were so glad to be looking at one another and smiling and waving that they did not notice it. Then after a while they wondered why they were left so much alone. The reason was this. The little girl was ill. She had gone to a party and caught the whooping-cough. She had been made to stay in bed in her own room and could not come downstairs. Except for the coughing she was not unhappy. She had toys and books with her in bed, and the Dutch girl who lived in the house and helped the lady used to come and talk to her and play with her. At last the little girl was allowed out of bed in her dressing-gown, but still she had to stay in her own room, which was warm and sunny.

'Judy,' she said one day to the Dutch girl. 'Judy dear, will you do something for me? Go downstairs and fetch the ship in the bottle. I want to look at it again. I haven't seen it for ages.'

'I don't think I ought to,' said the Dutch girl. 'Mummy wouldn't like it.'

'Oh, please, Judy,' begged the little girl, 'just this once. I'd be terribly careful.'

'Well, we'll see,' said the Dutch girl.

After tea the little girl sat on the bed holding the ship in the bottle. There it was, just as it had been all those ages before she had got the whooping-cough. There was the sailor with his telescope; there were the three sloping masts and the stiff white sails.

'Judy,' said the little girl, 'do *one* more thing for me, will you? Fetch me the little house in the snow. Just this once. Oh, please!'

The Dutch girl did as she was asked. Everybody did what the little girl asked, sooner or later. People said she was spoilt, but it couldn't be helped because she was lonely. And she was always so pleased and grateful.

'Oh, thank you, dear Judy,' she said when the Dutch girl brought her the house in the snow.

'Now mind,' said Judy, 'only for five minutes. Then it's time for a bath.'

She went to turn on the bath, while the little girl made a snowstorm in the glass ball. She held it very, very carefully, for it would be terrible if it fell and broke. Then Judy called her to her bath, and she put the ball down gently on the floor, near where the bottle lay on its side on the window-sill. Then she did up the cord of her dressing-gown tighter, and ran off to the bathroom.

The *Desperado,* inside its bottle on the window-sill, lay on its side. Dick Rumbelow, still fixed firmly to the deck, was just able to see over the edge of the window-sill. With his telescope he could make out the glass ball, which stood on the floor beneath. He couldn't quite see Britannia, but he could see the roof of her house, with the last snowflakes just settling quietly upon it. He knew that Britannia was inside the house, perhaps wondering what had become of her sailor friend. For she could certainly not see him.

'Well,' said Dick to himself, trembling all over with excitement, 'it's now or never. That girl needs rescuing. If ever a girl needed rescuing, it's that girl in the snow. Here goes!'

So he rocked himself to and fro on the deck, and thought about all the storms he had ever seen or heard of, and a good many that he hadn't. The window was open, and a pleasant evening breeze began to flap the curtains this way and that. Soon Dick fancied he could hear the thunder rumbling in the distance and catch sight of an occasional flash of lightning.

Britannia, in the little red house in the snow, could hear nothing of this. She was anxious about Dick, whom she couldn't see, and she did not like being on the floor.

There was no view except the dark space under the bed; she began to feel afraid, and called upon her sailor.

'Oh, sailor boy,' she said, wringing her hands, 'if only you were here. It's getting dark, and I'm terribly lonely. What's happened to you? Perhaps you're out in a storm. Perhaps you'll be drowned, and I shall never see you again!'

Dick could not hear her, but he imagined he heard her calling.

'I'm coming,' he cried. 'Keep your spirits up, my girl, and I'll be alongside in two flicks of a mermaid's tail!'

Then he made a mighty plunge, and the curtain gave an extra flap, and in two flicks of a mermaid's tail the bottle had rolled to the edge of the window-sill and toppled over.

It missed the glass ball by half an inch, but the bottle was smashed. The ship lay on its side on the floor, one of the masts split in two, and the pieces of glass were scattered all round.

Dick picked himself up. He was no longer on the deck of the *Desperado*. He felt very shaken.

'Thunder and lightning!' he cried. 'It's the French! There's been nothing like this since Trafalgar. No, it's not the French – it's the almightiest howling tempest that ever hit the fleet. Where's the girl in the snow?'

Then he saw that he was looking right into Britannia's redbrick house. He had never been so near her before. He was close up against the glass ball. The snow was so near, he could have put out his hand and touched it if it hadn't been for the glass. There was the lawn, and the two green bushes, the front door, and the window where Britannia gazed out at him. Yes, there she was, anxious but smiling, the golden hair smudged over her eyes and her red cheeks shining like two apples. Then Dick reached for his telescope, which had fallen from his hand, and began to beat it against the side of the glass ball, just above his head.

Britannia watched him, not moving.

'So he came at last,' she sighed. 'Brave fellow! He's broken out of his bottle, and faced the storm and the snow, all to visit me. Soon he'll be knocking at the door, and I shall let him in and take him by the hands. And it won't matter a bit that he'll have snow on his boots. I'll never let him go, and there'll be plenty of time to clear up the mess.'

Dick was still banging on the glass with his telescope. He was beginning to feel terribly tired after his fall.

'Come and lend a hand!' he called. 'Bring a hammer or something.'

But Britannia could not hear him.

'Whatever is he doing, waving his spyglass like that? Why doesn't he come up the path? What's stopping him?'

Then she saw that her sailor had given up trying to reach her, and had dropped exhausted to the ground. At last she understood that she too lived inside glass. She had thought that only the sailor was shut in, but now she knew that her own little house in the snow was surrounded by a transparent wall that she could never break. She stared out of the window at the broken pieces of bottle, the wrecked schooner, and Sailor Dick Rumbelow lying on the ground not twenty yards from her own front door. After that, she knew nothing.

The house in the snow was never again left on the mantelpiece. It was kept for safety in a cabinet with a big glass door, so that it could be seen and not touched. The lady had at first been very angry, but Judy and the little girl had cried such a lot that she had to forgive them. Each said it was all her own fault. The tiny sailor was picked up, but his telescope was never found. The ship was mended, and once again Dick was fixed to the deck. The broken mast was repaired. Then the little girl's father took it back to the shop, and the shopkeeper got a very clever man, an old sailor who sometimes did odd jobs for him, to put it safely in a new bottle. So there was the *Desperado* a little scratched, not quite as smart as it had been before, but almost as beautiful. The fall had not damaged it badly.

'Don't let's hang it in the window any more, mummy,' said the little girl. 'You never know. It might be blown down, or the string might break, or somebody knock it with a broom. Don't let's ever break it any more.'

'Where shall we put it, dear?' asked the lady.

'Beside the house in the snow, of course,' answered the little girl. 'That's much the safest place.'

So, instead of the cord, a neat wooden stand was made, and the bottle stood just beside the ball in the glass cabinet. And Dick, who no longer had his spyglass, and Britannia with her red cheeks and golden hair, once more looked at each other quite close to. This went on day after day, except sometimes, very occasionally, when it was the little girl's birthday, or an important visitor called. Then the good ship *Desperado*, with one of its masts a little bent, would be taken out and admired; and the house in the glass ball would be turned upside down and back again, to set the snow dancing madly about, while all the pots and pans and cups and saucers inside the house were tumbled about in confusion. Then Britannia would sigh and start putting them to rights again, just as she always did.

'After all,' she said to herself, 'my very near neighbour, my sailor friend, *might* drop in to see me one day, and I should hate the house to be in a pickle if *that* happened.'

The Smallest Dragonboy

Anne McCaffrey

A LTHOUGH KEEVAN lengthened his walking stride as far as his legs would stretch, he couldn't keep up with the other candidates. He knew he would be teased again.

Just as he knew many other things that his foster mother told him he ought not to know, Keevan knew that Beterli, the most senior of the boys, set that spanking pace just to embarrass him, the smallest dragonboy. Keevan would arrive, tail fork-end of the group, breathless, chest heaving, and maybe get a stern look from the instructing wingsecond.

Dragonriders, even if they were still only hopeful candidates for the glowing eggs which were hardening on the hot sands of the Hatching Ground cavern, were expected to be punctual and prepared. Sloth was not tolerated by the Weyrleader of Benden Weyr. A good record was especially important now. It was very near hatching time, when the baby dragons would crack their mottled shells, and stagger forth to choose their lifetime companions. The very thought of that glorious moment made Keevan's breath catch in his throat. To be chosen – to be a dragonrider! To sit astride the neck of a winged beast with jewelled eyes: to be his friend, in telepathic communion with him for life, to be his companion in good times and fighting extremes, to fly effortlessly over the lands of Pern! Or, thrillingly, *between* to any point anywhere on the world! Flying *between* was done on dragonback or not at all, and it was dangerous.

Keevan glanced upward, past the black mouths of the weyr caves in which grown dragons and their chosen riders lived, toward the Star Stones that crowned the ridge of the old volcano that was Benden Weyr. On the height, the blue watch dragon, his rider mounted on his neck, stretched the great transparent pinions that carried him on the winds of Pern to fight the evil Thread that fell at certain times from the skies. The many-faceted rainbow jewels of his eyes glistened fleetingly in the greeny sun. He folded his great wings to his back, and the watch pair resumed their statuelike pose of alertness.

Then the enticing view was obscured as Keevan passed into the Hatching Ground cavern. The sands underfoot were hot, even through heavy wher-hide boots. How the bootmaker had protested having to sew so small! Keevan was forced to wonder why being small was reprehensible. People were always calling him 'babe' and shooing him away as being 'too small' or 'too young' for this or that. Keevan was constantly working, twice as hard as any other boy his age, to prove himself capable. What if his muscles weren't as big as Beterli's? They were just as hard. And if he couldn't overpower anyone in a wrestling match, he could outdistance everyone in a footrace.

'Maybe if you run fast enough,' Beterli had jeered on the occasion when Keevan had been goaded to boast of his swiftness, 'you could catch a dragon. That's the only way you'll make a dragonrider!'

'You just wait and see, Beterli, you just wait,' Keevan

had replied. He would have liked to wipe the contemptuous smile from Beterli's face, but the guy didn't fight fair even when a wingsecond was watching. 'No one knows what Impresses a dragon!'

'They've got to be able fo *find* you first, babe!'

Yes, being the smallest candidate was not an enviable position. It was therefore imperative that Keevan Impress a dragon in his first hatching. That would wipe the smile off every face in the cavern and accord him the respect due any dragonrider, even the smallest one.

Besides, no one knew exactly what Impressed the baby dragons as they struggled from their shells in search of their lifetime partners.

'I like to believe that dragons see into a man's heart,' Keevan's foster mother, Mende, told him. 'If they find goodness, honesty, a flexible mind, patience, courage – and you've got that in quantity, dear Keevan – that's what dragons look for. I've seen many a well-grown lad left standing on the sands, Hatching Day, in favour of someone not so strong or tall or handsome. And if my memory serves me' – which it usually did: Mende knew every word of every Harper's tale worth telling, although Keevan did not interrupt her to say so – 'I don't believe that F'lar, our Weyrleader, was all that tall when bronze Mnementh chose him. And Mnementh was the only bronze dragon of that hatching.'

Dreams of Impressing a bronze were beyond Keevan's boldest reflections, although that goal dominated the thoughts of every other hopeful candidate. Green dragons were small and fast and more numerous. There was more prestige to Impressing a blue or brown than a green. Being practical, Keevan seldom dreamed as high as a big fighting brown, like Canth, F'nor's fine fellow, the biggest brown of all Pern. But to fly a bronze? Bronzes were almost as big as the queen, and only they took the air when a queen flew at mating time. A bronze rider could aspire to become a Weyrleader! Well, Keevan would console himself, brown riders could aspire to become wing-seconds, and that wasn't bad. He'd even settle for a green dragon: they were small, but so was he. No matter! He simply had to Impress a dragon his first time in the Hatching Ground. Then no one in the Weyr would taunt him anymore for being so small.

Shells, Keevan thought now, but the sands are hot!

'Impression time is imminent, candidates,' the wing-second was saying as everyone crowded respectfully close to him. 'See the extent of the striations on this promising egg.' The stretch marks *were* larger than yesterday.

Everyone leaned forward and nodded thoughtfully. That particular egg was the one Beterli had marked as his own, and no other candidate dared, on pain of being beaten by Beterli at his first opportunity, to approach it. The egg was marked by a large yellowish splotch in the shape of a dragon backwinging to land, talons outstretched to grasp rock. Everyone knew that bronze eggs bore distinctive markings. And naturally, Beterli, who'd been presented at eight Impressions already and was the biggest of the candidates, had chosen it.

'I'd say that the great opening day is almost upon us,' the wingsecond went on, and then his face assumed a grave expression. 'As we well know, there are only forty eggs and seventy-two candidates. Some of you may be disappointed on the great day. That doesn't mean you aren't dragonrider material, just that *the* dragon for you hasn't been shelled. You'll have other hatchings, and it's no disgrace to be left behind an Impression or two. Or more.'

Keevan was positive that the wingsecond's eyes rested on Beterli, who'd been stood off at so many Impressions already. Keevan tried to squinch down so that the wingsecond wouldn't notice him. Keevan had been reminded too often that he was eligible to be a candidate by one day only. He, of all the hopefuls, was most likely to be left standing on the great day. One more reason why he simply had to Impress at his first hatching.

'Now move about among the eggs,' the wingsecond said. 'Touch them. We don't know that it does any good, but it certainly doesn't do any harm.'

Some of the boys laughed nervously, but everyone immediately began to circulate among the eggs. Beterli stepped up officiously to 'his' egg, daring anyone to come near it. Keevan smiled, because he had already touched it – every inspection day, when the others were leaving the Hatching Ground and no one could see him crouch to stroke it.

Keevan had an egg he concentrated on, too, one drawn slightly to the far side of the others. The shell had a soft greenish-blue tinge with a faint creamy swirl design. The consensus was that this egg contained a mere green, so Keevan was rarely bothered by rivals. He was somewhat perturbed then to see Beterli wandering over to him.

'I don't know why you're allowed in this Impression, Keevan. There are enough of us without a babe,' Beterli said, shaking his head.

'I'm of age,' Keevan kept his voice level, telling himself not to be bothered by mere words.

'Yah!' Beterli made a show of standing on his toetips. 'You can't even see over an egg; Hatching Day, you better get in front or the dragons won't see you at all. 'Course, you could get run down that way in the mad scramble. Oh, I forgot, you can run fast, can't you?'

'You'd better make sure a dragon sees *you*, this time, Beterli,' Keevan replied. 'You're almost overage, aren't you?'

Beterli flushed and took a step forward, hand half-raised. Keevan stood his ground, but if Beterli advanced one more step, he would call the wingsecond. No one fought on the Hatching Ground. Surely Beterli knew that much.

Fortunately, at that moment, the wingsecond called the boys together and led them from the Hatching Ground to start on evening chores. There were 'glows' to be replenished in the main kitchen caverns and sleeping cubicles, the major hallways, and the queen's apartment. Firestone sacks had to be filled against Thread attack, and black rock brought to the kitchen hearths. The boys fell to their chores, tantalized by the odours of roasting meat. The population of the Weyr began to assemble for the evening meal, and the dragonriders came in from the Feeding Ground on their sweep checks.

It was the time of day Keevan liked best: once the chores were done but before dinner was served, a fellow could often get close enough to the dragonriders to hear their talk, Tonight, Keevan's father, K'last, was at the main dragonrider table. It puzzled Keevan how his father, a brown rider and a tall man, could *be* his father – because he, Keevan, was so small. It obviously puzzled K'last, too, when he deigned to notice his small son: 'In a few more Turns, you'll be as tall as I am – or taller!'

K'last was pouring Benden wine all around the table. The dragonriders were relaxing. There'd be no Thread attack for three more days, and they'd be in the mood to tell tall tales, better than Harper yarns, about impossible manoeuvres they'd done a-dragonback. When Thread attack was closer, their talk would change to a discussion of tactics of evasion, of going *between*, how long to suspend there until the burning but fragile Thread would freeze and crack. And fall harmlessly off dragon and man. They would dispute the exact moment to feed firestone to the dragon so he'd have the best flame ready to sear Thread midair and render it harmless to ground – and man – below. There was such a lot to know and understand about being a dragonrider that sometimes Keevan was overwhelmed. How would he ever be able to remember everything he ought to know at the right moment? He couldn't dare ask such a question; this would only have given additional weight to the notion that he was too young yet to be a dragonrider.

'Having older candidates makes good sense,' L'vel was saying, as Keevan settled down near the table. 'Why waste four to five years of a dragon's fighting prime until his rider grows up enough to stand the rigours?' L'vel had Impressed a blue of Ramoth's first clutch. Most of the candidates thought L'vel was marvellous because he spoke up in front of the older riders, who awed them. 'That was well enough in the Interval when you didn't need to mount the full Weyr complement to fight Thread. But not now. Not with more eligible candidates than ever. Let the babes wait.'

'Any boy who is over twelve Turns has the right to stand in the Hatching Ground,' K'last replied, a slight smile on his face. He never argued or got angry. Keevan wished he were more like his father. And oh, how he wished he were a brown rider! 'Only a dragon – each particular dragon – knows what he wants in a rider. We certainly can't tell. Time and again the theorists,' K'last's smile deepened as he eyes swept those at the table, 'are surprised by dragon choice. *They* never seem to make mistakes, however.'

'Now, K'last, just look at the roster this Impression. Seventy-two boys and only forty eggs. Drop off the twelve youngest, and there's still a good field for the hatchlings to choose from. Shells! There are a couple of weyrlings unable to see over a wher egg much less a dragon! And years before they can ride Thread.'

'True enough, but the Weyr is scarcely under fighting strength, and if the youngest Impress, they'll be old enough to fight when the oldest of our current dragons go *between* from senility.'

'Half the Weyrbred lads have already been through several Impressions,' one of the bronze riders said then. 'I'd say drop some of *them* off this time. Give the untried a chance.'

'There's nothing wrong in presenting a clutch with as wide a choice as possible,' said the Weyrleader, who had joined the table with Lessa, the Weyrwoman.

'Has there ever been a case,' she said, smiling in her odd way at the riders, 'where a hatchling didn't choose?'

Her suggestion was almost heretical and drew astonished gasps from everyone, including the boys.

F'lar laughed. 'You say the most outrageous things, Lessa.'

'Well *has* there ever been a case where a dragon didn't choose?'

'Can't say as I recall one,' K'last replied.

'Then we continue in this tradition,' Lessa said firmly, as if that ended the matter.

But it didn't. The argument ranged from one table to the other all through dinner, with some favouring a weeding out of the candidates to the most likely, lopping off those who were very young or who had had multiple opportunities to Impress. All the candidates were in a swivet, though such a departure from tradition would be to the advantage of many. As the evening progressed, more riders were favouring eliminating the youngest and those who'd passed four or more Impressions unchosen. Keevan felt he could bear such a dictum only if Beterli were also eliminated. But this seemed less likely than that Keevan would be turfed out, since the Weyr's need was for fighting dragons and riders.

By the time the evening meal was over, no decision had been reached, although the Weyrleader had promised to give the matter due consideration.

He might have slept on the problem, but few of the candidates did. Tempers were uncertain in the sleeping caverns next morning as the boys were routed out of their beds to carry water and black rock and cover the 'glows.' Twice Mende had to call Keevan to order for clumsiness.

'Whatever is the matter with you, boy?' she demanded in exasperation when he tipped black rock short of the bin and sooted up the hearth.

'They're going to keep me from this Impression.'

'What?' Mende stared at him. 'Who?'

'You heard them talking at dinner last night. They're going to turf the babes from the hatching.'

Mende regarded him a moment longer before touching his arm gently. 'There's lots of talk around a supper table, Keevan. And it cools as soon as the supper. I've heard the same nonsense before every hatching, but nothing is ever changed.'

'There's always a first time,' Keevan answered, copying one of her own phrases.

'That'll be enough of that, Keevan. Finish your job. If the clutch does hatch today, we'll need full rock bins for the feast, and you won't be around to do the filling. All my fosterlings make dragonriders.'

'The first time?' Keevan was bold enough to ask as he scooted off with the rockbarrow.

Perhaps, Keevan thought later, if he hadn't been on that chore just when Beterli was also fetching black rock, things might have turned out differently. But he had dutifully trundled the barrow to the outdoor bunker for another load just as Beterli arrived on a similar errand.

'Heard the news, babe?' Beterli asked. He was grinning from ear to ear, and he put an unnecessary emphasis on the final insulting word.

'The eggs are cracking?' Keevan all but dropped the loaded shovel. Several anxieties flicked through his mind then: he was black with rock dust – would he have time to wash before donning the white tunic of candidacy? And if the eggs were hatching, why hadn't the candidates been recalled by the wingsecond?

'Naw! Guess again!' Beterli was much too pleased with himself.

With a sinking heart, Keevan knew what the news must be, and he could only stare with intense desolation at the older boy.

'C'mon! Guess, babe!'

'I've no time for guessing games,' Keevan managed to say with indifference. He began to shovel black rock into the barrow as fast as he could.

'I said, guess.' Beterli grabbed the shovel.

'And I said I have no time for guessing games.'

Beterli wrenched the shovel from Keevan's hands. 'Guess!'

'I'll have that shovel back, Beterli.' Keevan straightened up, but he didn't come to Beterli's bulky shoulder. From somewhere, other boys appeared, with barrows, some mysteriously alerted to the prospect of a confrontation among their numbers.

'Babes don't give orders to candidates around here, babe!'

Someone sniggered and Keevan, incredulous, knew that he must've been dropped from the candidacy.

He yanked the shovel from Beterli's loosened grasp. Snarling, the older boy tried to regain possession, but Keevan clung with all his strength to the handle, dragged back and forth as the stronger boy jerked the shovel about.

With a sudden, unexpected movement, Beterli rammed the handle into Keevan's chest, knocking him over the barrow handles. Keevan felt a sharp, painful jab behind his left ear, an unbearable pain in his left shin, and then a painless nothingness.

Mende's angry voice roused him, and startled, he tried to throw back the covers, thinking he'd overslept. But he couldn't move, so firmly was he tucked into his bed. And then the constriction of a bandage on his head and the dull sickishness in his leg brought back recent occurrences.

'Hatching?' he cried.

'No, lovey,' Mende said in a kind voice. Her hand was cool and gentle on his forehead. 'Though there's some as won't be at any hatching again.' Her voice took on a stern edge.

Keevan looked beyond her to see the Weyrwoman, who was frowning with irritation.

'Keevan, will you tell me what occurred at the black-rock bunker?' asked Lessa in an even voice.

He remembered Beterli now and the quarrel over the shovel and … what had Mende said about some not being at any hatching? Much as he hated Beterli, he couldn't bring himself to tattle on Beterli and force him out of candidacy.

'Come, lad,' and a note of impatience crept into the Weyrwoman's voice. 'I merely want to know what happened from you too. Mende said she sent you for black rock. Beterli – and every Weyrling in the cavern – seems to have been on the same errand. What happened?'

'Beterli took my shovel. I hadn't finished with it.'

'There's more than one shovel. What did he *say* to you?'

'He'd heard the news.'

'What news?' The Weyrwoman was suddenly amused.

'That . . . that . . . there'd been changes?'

'Is that what he said?'

'Not exactly.'

'What did he say? C'mon, lad, I've heard from everyone else, you know.'

'He said for me to guess the news.'

'And you fell for that old gag?' The Weyrwoman's irritation returned.

'Consider all the talk last night at supper, Lessa,' Mende said. 'Of course the boy would think he'd been eliminated.'

'In effect, he is, with a broken skull and leg.' Lessa touched his arm in a rare gesture of sympathy. 'Be that as it may, Keevan, you'll have other Impressions. Beterli will not. There are certain rules that must be observed by all candidates, and his conduct proves him unacceptable to the Weyr.'

She smiled at Mende and then left.

'I'm still a candidate?' Keevan asked urgently.

'Well, you are and you aren't, lovey,' his foster mother said. 'Is the numbweed working?' she asked, and when he nodded, she said, 'You just rest. I'll bring you some nice broth.'

At any other time in his life, Keevan would have relished such cosseting, but now he just lay there worrying. Beterli had been dismissed. Would the others think it was his fault? But everyone was there! Beterli had provoked that fight. His worry increased, because although he heard excited comings and goings in the passageway, no one tweaked back the curtain across the sleeping alcove he shared with five other boys. Surely one of them would have to come in sometime. No, they were all avoiding him. And something else was wrong. Only he didn't know what.

Mende returned with broth and beachberry bread.

'Why doesn't anyone come to see me, Mende? I haven't done anything wrong, have I? I didn't ask to have Beterli turfed out.'

Mende soothed him, saying everyone was busy with noontime chores and no one was angry with him. They were giving him a chance to rest in quiet. The numbweed made him drowsy, and her words were fair enough. He permitted his fears to dissipate. Until he heard a hum. Actually, he felt it first, in the broken shin bone and his sore head. The hum began to grow. Two things registered suddenly in Keevan's groggy mind: the only white candidate's robe still in the pegs in the chamber was his; and the dragons hummed when a clutch was being laid or being hatched. Impression! And he was flat abed.

Bitter, bitter disappointment turned the warm broth sour in his belly. Even the small voice telling him that he'd have other opportunities failed to alleviate his crushing depression. *This* was the Impression that mattered! This was his chance to show *everyone*, from Mende to K'last to L'vel and even the Weyrleader that he, Keevan, was worthy of being a dragonrider.

He twisted in bed, fighting against the tears that threatened to choke him. Dragonmen don't cry! Dragonmen learn to live with pain.

Pain? The leg didn't actually pain him as he rolled about on his bedding. His head felt sort of stiff from the tightness of the bandage. He sat up, an effort in itself since the numbweed made exertion difficult. He touched the splinted leg; the knee was unhampered. He had no feeling in his bone, really. He swung himself carefully to the side of his bed and stood slowly. The room wanted to swim about him. He closed his eyes, which made the dizziness worse, and he had to clutch the wall.

Gingerly, he took a step. The broken leg dragged. It hurt in spite of the numbweed, but what was pain to a dragonman?

No one had said he couldn't go to the Impression. 'You are and you aren't,' were Mende's exact words.

Clinging to the wall, he jerked off his bedshirt. Stretching his arm to the utmost, he jerked his white candidate's tunic from the peg. Jamming first one arm and then the other into the holes, he pulled it over his head. Too bad about the belt. He couldn't wait. He hobbled to the door, hung on to the curtain to steady himself. The weight on his leg was unwieldy. He wouldn't get very far without something to lean on. Down by the bathing pool was one of the long crook-necked poles used to retrieve clothes from the hot washing troughs. But it was down there, and he was on the level above. And there was no one nearby to come to his aid: everyone would be in the Hatching Ground right now, eagerly waiting for the first egg to crack.

The humming increased in volume and tempo, an urgency to which Keevan responded, knowing that his time was all too limited if he was to join the ranks of the hopeful boys standing around the cracking eggs. But if he hurried down the ramp, he'd fall flat on his face.

He could, of course, go flat on his rear end, the way crawling children did. He sat down, sending a jarring stab of pain through his leg and up to the wound on the back of his head. Gritting his teeth and blinking away tears, Keevan scrabbled down the ramp. He had to wait a moment at the bottom to catch his breath. He got to one knee, the injured leg straight out in front of him. Somehow, he managed to push himself erect, though the room seemed about to tip over his ears. It wasn't far to the crooked stick, but it seemed an age before he had it in his hand.

Then the humming stopped!

Keevan cried out and began to hobble frantically across the cavern, out to the bowl of the Weyr. Never had the distance between living caverns and the Hatching Ground seemed so great. Never had the Weyr been so breathlessly silent. It was as if the multitude of people and dragons watching the hatching held every breath in suspense. Not even the wind muttered down the steep sides of the bowl. The only sounds to break the stillness were Keevan's ragged gasps and the thump-thud of his stick on the hard-packed ground. Sometimes he had to hop twice on his good leg to maintain his balance. Twice he fell into the sand and had to pull himself up on the stick, his white tunic no longer spotless. Once he jarred himself so badly he couldn't get up immediately.

Then he heard the first exhalation of the crowd, the oohs, the muted cheer, the susurrus of excited whispers. An egg had cracked, and the dragon had chosen his rider. Desperation increased Keevan's hobble. Would he never reach the arching mouth of the Hatching Ground?

Another cheer and an excited spate of applause spurred Keevan to greater effort. If he didn't get there in moments, there'd be no unpaired hatchling left. Then he was actually staggering into the Hatching Ground, the sands hot on his bare feet.

No one noticed his entrance or his halting progress. And Keevan could see nothing but the backs of the white-robed candidates, seventy of them ringing the area around the eggs. Then one side would surge forward or back and there'd be a cheer. Another dragon had been Impressed. Suddenly a large gap appeared in the white human wall, and Keevan had his first sight of the eggs. There didn't seem to be any left uncracked, and he could see the lucky boys standing beside wobble-legged dragons. He could hear the unmistakable plaintive crooning of hatchlings and their squawks of protest as they'd fall awkwardly in the sand.

Suddenly he wished that he hadn't left his bed, that he'd stayed away from the Hatching Ground. Now everyone would see his ignominious failure. So he scrambled as desperately to reach the shadowy walls of the Hatching Ground as he had struggled to cross the bowl. He mustn't be seen.

He didn't notice, therefore, that the shifting group of boys remaining had begun to drift in his direction. The hard pace he had set himself and his cruel disappointment took their double toll of Keevan. He tripped and collapsed sobbing to the warm sands. He didn't see the consternation in the watching Weyrfolk above the Hatching Ground, nor did he hear the excited whispers of speculation. He didn't know that the Weyrleader and Weyrwoman had dropped to the arena and were making their way toward the knot of boys slowly moving in the direction of the entrance.

'Never seen anything like it,' the Weyrleader was saying. 'Only thirty-nine riders chosen. And the bronze trying to leave the Hatching Ground without making Impression.'

'A case in point of what I said last night,' the Weyrwoman replied, 'where a hatchling makes no choice because the right boy isn't there.'

'There's only Beterli and K'last's young one missing. And there's a full wing of likely boys to choose from . . .'

'None aceptable, apparently. Where is the creature going? He's not heading for the entrance after all. Oh, what have we there, in the shadows?'

Keevan heard with dismay the sound of voices nearing him. He tried to burrow into the sand. The mere thought of how he would be teased and taunted now was unbearable.

Don't worry! Please don't worry! The thought was urgent, but not his own.

Someone had kicked sand over Keevan and butted roughly against him.

'Go away. Leave me alone!' he cried.

Why? was the injured-sounding question inserted into his mind. There was no voice, no tone, but the question was there, perfectly clear, in his head.

Incredulous, Keevan lifted his head and stared into the glowing jewelled eyes of a small bronze dragon. His wings were wet, the tips drooping in the sand. And he sagged in the middle on his unsteady legs, although he was making a great effort to keep erect.

Keevan dragged himself to his knees, oblivious of the pain in his leg. He wasn't even aware that he was ringed by the boys passed over, while thirty-one pairs of resentful eyes watched him Impress the dragon. The Weyrmen looked on, amused and surprised at the draconic choice, which could not be forced. Could not be questioned. Could not be changed.

Why? asked the dragon again. *Don't you like me?'* His eyes whirled with anxiety, and his tone was so piteous that Keevan staggered forward and threw his arms around the dragon's neck, stroking his eye ridges, patting the damp, soft hide, opening the fragile-looking wings to dry them, and wordlessly assuring the hatchling over and over again that he was the most perfect, most beautiful, most beloved dragon in the Weyr, in all the Weyrs of Pern.

'What's his hame, K'van?' asked Lessa, smiling warmly at the new dragonrider. K'van stared up at her for a long moment. Lessa would know as soon as he did. Lessa was the only person whou could 'receive' from all dragons, not only her own Ramoth. Then he gave her a radiant smile, recognizing the traditional shortening of his name that raised him forever to the rank of dragonrider.

My name is Heth, the dragon thought mildly, then hiccuped in sudden urgency. *I'm hungry.*

'Dragons are born hungry,' said Lessa laughing. 'F'lar, give the boy a hand. He can barely manage his own legs, much less a dragon's.'

K'van remembered his stick and drew himself up. 'We'll be just fine, thank you.'

'You may be the smallest dragonrider ever, young K'van,' F'lar said, 'but you're one of the bravest!'

And Heth agreed! Pride and joy so leaped in both chests that K'van wondered if his heart would burst right out of his body. He looped an arm around Heth's neck and the pair, the smallest dragonboy and the hatchling who wouldn't choose anybody else, walked out of the Hatching Ground together forever.

Ully The Piper

Andre Norton

THE DALES of High Halleck are many and some are even forgotten, save by those who live in them. During the great war with the invaders from overseas, when the lords of the dales and their armsmen fought, skulked, prospered or sank in defeat, there were small places left to a kind of slumber, overlooked by warriors. There, life went on as it always had, the dalesmen content in their islands of safety, letting the rest of the world roar on as it would.

In such a dale lay Coomb Brackett, a straggle of houses and farms with no right to the title of village, though so the indwellers called it. So tall were the ridges guarding it that few but the wild shepherds of the crags knew what lay beyond them, and many of their tales were discounted by the dalesmen. But there were also ill legends about those heights that had come down from the elder days when humankind first pushed this far north and west. For men were not the first to settle here, though story said that their predecessors had worn the outward seeming of men for convenience, their real aspect being such that no dalesman would care to look upon them by morn light.

While those elder ones had withdrawn, seeking a refuge in the Beyond Wilderness, yet at times they returned on strange pilgrimages. Did not the dalesmen keep certain feast days – or nights – when they took offerings up to rocks which bore queer markings that had not been chiselled there by wind and weather? The reason for those offerings no man now living could tell, but that luck followed their giving was an established fact.

But the dale was good enough for the men of Coomb Brackett. Its fields were rich, a shallow river winding through them. Orchards of fruit flourished and small woodland copses held nut trees which also bore crops in season. Fat sheep fed placidly in the uplands, cattle ambled to the river to drink and went then to graze once more. Men sowed in spring, harvested in early autumn and lay snug in their homesteads in winter. As they often said to one another, who wanted more in this life?

They were as plump as their cattle and almost as slow moving at times. There was little to plague them, for even the Lord of Fartherdale, to whom they owed loyalty, had not sent his tithemen for a tale of years. There was a rumour that the lord was dead in the far-off war. Some of the prudent put aside a folding of woollen or a bolting of linen, well sprinkled with herbs to keep it fresh, against the day when the tithes might be asked again. But for the most part they spun their flax and wool, wove it into stout cloth for their own backs, ate their beef and mutton, drank ale brewed from their barley and wine from their fruit, and thought that trouble was something which struck at others far beyond their protecting heights.

There was only one among them who was not satisfied with things as they comfortably were, because for him there was no comfort. Ully of the hands was not the

smallest, nor the youngest of the lads of Coomb Brackett
– he was the different one. Longing to be as the rest filled
him sometimes with a pain he could hardly bear.

He sat on his small cart and watched the rest off to the
feasting on May Day and Harvest Home; and he watched
them dance Rings Around following the smoking great
roast at Yule – his clever hands folded in upon
themselves until the nails bit sorely into the flesh of his
palms.

There had been a tree to climb when he was so young
he could not rightly recollect what life had been like
before that hour. After he fell he had learned what it
meant to go hunched of back and useless of leg, able to
get from one place to another only by huddling on his
cart and pushing it along the ground with two sticks.

He was mender-in-chief for the dale, though he could
never mend himself. Aught that was broken was brought
to him so that his widowed mother could sort out the
pieces, and then Ully worked patiently hour by hour to
make it whole again. Sometimes he thought that more
than his body had been broken in that fall, and that
slowly pieces of his spirit were flaking away within him.
For Ully, being chained to his cart, was active in his mind
and had many strange ideas he never shared with the
world.

Only on a night such as this, when it was midsummer
and the youth of the village were streaming up into the
hills to set out first fruit, new bread, a flagon of milk and
another of wine on the offering rock . . . He did not want
to sit and think his life away! He was young in spirit, torn
by such longings as sometimes made him want to howl
and beat with his fists upon the ground, or pound the
body which imprisoned him. But for the sake of his
mother he never gave way so, for she would believe him
mad, and he was not that – yet.

He listened to the singing as the company climbed, giving the rallying call to the all-night dancing:

'High Dilly, High Dally,
Come Lilly, Come Lally!
Dance for the Ribbons—
Dance for new Shoes!'

Who would dance so well this night that he would return by morn's light wearing the new shoes, she the snood of bright ribbons?

Not Stephen of the mill; he was as heavy-footed in such frolicking as if he carried one of the filled flour sacks across his ox-strong shoulders. Not Gretta of the inn, who so wanted to be graceful. (Ully-had seen her in the goose meadow by the river practising steps in secret. She was a kind maid and he wished her as well as he did any of those he thought of as the straight people.)

No, this year, as always, it would be Matt of High Ridge Garth, and Morgana, the smith's daughter. Ully frowned at the hedge which hid the upper road from him, crouched low as he was.

Morgana he knew little of, save that she saw only what she wished to see and did only what it pleased her to do. But Matt he disliked, for Matt was rough of hand and tongue, caring little what he left broken or torn behind his heavily tramped way – whether it was something which could be mended, or the feelings of others, which could not. Ully had had to deal with both kinds of Matt's destruction, and some he had never been able to put right.

They were still singing.

Ully set his teeth hard upon his lower lip. He might be small and crooked of body, but he was a man; and a man did not wail over his hurts. It was so fine a night he could not bear as yet to go back to the cottage. The scent of his mother's garden arose about him, seeming even stronger in the twilight. He reached within his shirt and brought out his greatest triumph of mending, twisted it in his clever fingers and then raised it to his lips.

The winter before, one of the rare strangers who ever came over the almost obliterated ridge road had stopped at the inn. He had brought news of battles and lords they had never heard of. Most of Coomb Brackett, even men from the high garths, had come to listen, though to them it was more tale than reality.

At last the stranger had pulled out his pipe of polished wood and had blown sweet notes on it. Then he had laid it aside as Morgana came to share his bench; she took it as her just due that the first smiles of any man were for her. Matt, jealous of the outsider, had slammed down his tankard so hard that he had jarred the pipe on the floor and broken it.

There had been hot words then, and Matt had sullenly paid the stranger a silver piece. But Gretta had picked up the pieces and brought them to Ully, saying wistfully that the music the stranger had made on it was so sweet she longed to hear its like again.

Ully had worked hard to put it together and when it was complete once again he had taken to blowing an odd note or two. Then he tried even more, imitating a bird's song, the sleepy murmur of the river, the wind in the trees. Now he played the song he had so put together note by note, combining the many voices of the dale itself. Hesitatingly he began, then grew more confident. Suddenly he was startled by a clapping of hands and jerked his head painfully around to see Gretta by the hedge.

'Play – oh, please play more, Ully! A body could dance as light as a wind-driven cloud to music like that.'

She took up her full skirt in her hands and pointed her toes. But then Ully saw her smile fade, and he knew well her sorrow, the clumsy body which would not obey the lightness of mind. In a moment she was smiling again and ran to him, holding out her work-calloused hand.

'Such music we have never had, Ully. You must come along and play for us tonight!'

He shrank back, shaking his head, but Gretta coaxed. Then she called over her shoulder.

'Stephen, Will! Come help me with Ully, he can pipe sweeter than any bird in the bush. Let him play for our dancing tonight and we shall be as well served as they say the old ones were with their golden pipes!'

Somehow Ully could not refuse them, and Stephen and Will pushed the cart up to the highest meadow where the token feast had been already spread on the offering rock and the fire flamed high. There Ully set pipe to lips and played.

But there were some not so well pleased at his coming. Morgana, having halted in the dance not far away, saw him and cried out so that Matt stepped protectingly before her.

'Ah, it's only crooked Ully,' she cried spitefully. 'I had thought it some one of the monsters out of the old tales crawled up from the woods to spy on us.' And she gave an exaggerated shiver, clinging to Matt's arm.

'Ully?' Matt laughed. 'Why does Ully crawl here, having no feet to dance upon? Why stare at his betters? And where did you get that pipe, little man?' He snatched at the pipe in Ully's hands. 'It looks to me like the one I had to pay a round piece for when it was broken. Give it here now; for if it is the same, it belongs to me!'

Ully tried to hold on to the pipe, but Matt's strength was by far the greater. The resting dancers had gathered close to the offering rock where they were opening their own baskets and bags to share the midnight feast. There was none to see what chanced here in the shadow. Matt held up the pipe in triumph.

'Good as new, and worth surely a silver piece again. Samkin the peddler will give me that and I shall not be out of pocket at all.'

'My pipe!' Ully struggled to get it but Matt held it well out of his reach.

'*My* pipe, crooked man! I had to pay for it, didn't I? Mine to do with as I will.'

Helpless anger worked in Ully as he tried to raise himself higher, but his movements only set the wheels of the cart moving and he began to roll down the slope of the meadow backwards. Morgana cried out and moved as if to stop him. But Matt, laughing, caught her back.

'Let him go, he will come to no harm. And he has no place here now, has he? Did he not even frighten you?'

He put the pipe into his tunic and threw an arm about her waist, leading her back to the feast. Halfway they met Gretta.

'Where is Ully?'

Matt shrugged. 'He is gone.'

'Gone? But it is a long way back to the village and he—' She began to run down the slope of the hill calling, 'Ully, Ully!'

The runaway cart had not gone that way, but in another direction, bumping and bouncing towards the small wood which encircled half the high meadow, its green arms held out to embrace the open land.

Ully crouched low, afraid to move, afraid to try to catch at any of the shrubs or low hanging branches as he swept by, lest he be pulled off to lie helpless on the ground.

In and out among the trees spun the cart, and Ully

began to wonder why it had not upset, or run against a trunk or caught in some vine. It was almost as if it were being guided. When he tried to turn and look to the fore, he could see nothing but the dark wood.

Then with a rush, the cart burst once more into the open. No fire blazed here, but the moon seemed to hang oddly bright and full just above, as if it were a fixed lamp. Heartened somehow, Ully dared to reach out and catch at a tuft of thick grass, a vine runner, and pulled the cart around so that he no longer faced the wood through which he had come, but rather an open glade where the grass grew short and thick as if it were mown. Around was a wall of flowers and bushes, while in the middle was a ring of stones, each taller than Ully, and so blazingly white in the moonlight that they might have been upright torches.

Ully's heart ceased to pound so hard. The peace and beauty of the place soothed him as if soft fingers stroked his damp face and ordered his tousled hair. His hands resting on his shrunken knees twitched, he so wanted his pipe.

But there was no pipe. Softly Ully began to hum his tune of the dale: bird song, water ripple, wind. Then his hum became a whistle. It seemed to him that all the beauty he had ever dreamed of was gathered here, just as he had fitted together broken bits with his hands.

Great silvery moths came out of nowhere and sailed in and out among the candle pillars, as if they were weaving some unseen fabric, netting a spell. Hesitatingly Ully held out one hand and one of the moths broke from the rest and lit fearlessly on his wrist, fanning wings which might have been tipped with stardust for the many points of glitter there. It was so light he was hardly aware that it rested so, save that he saw it. Then it took to the air again.

Ully wiped the hand across his forehead, sweeping back a loose lock of hair, and as he did so . . .

The moths were gone; beside each pillar stood a woman. Small and slight indeed they were, hardly taller than a young child of Ully's kin, but these were truly women, for they were dressed only in their long hair. The bodies revealed as they moved were so perfectly formed that Ully knew he had never seen real beauty before. They did not look at him, but glided on their small bare feet in and out among the pillars, weaving their spell even as the moths had done. At times they paused, gathering up their hair with their two hands, to hold it well away from their bodies and shake it. It seemed to Ully that when they did so there was a shifting of glittering motes carried along in a small cloud moving away from the glade, though he did not turn his eyes to follow it.

Though none of them spoke, he knew what they wanted of him and he whistled his song of the dale. He must truly be asleep and dreaming, or else in that wild dash downslope he had fallen from the cart and suffered a knock from which this vision was born. But dream or hurt, he would hold to it as long as he could. This – this was such happiness as he had never known.

At last their dance grew slower and slower, until they halted, each standing with one hand upon a pillar side. Then they were gone; only the moths fluttered once again in the dimming light.

Ully was aware that his body ached, that his lips and mouth were dry and that all the weight of fatigue had suddenly fallen on him. But still he cried out against its ending.

There was movement by the pillar directly facing him and someone came farther into the pale light of new dawn. She stood before him, and for the last time she gathered up her hair in both hands, holding it out shoulder high. Once, twice, thrice, she shook it. But this time there were no glittering motes. Rather he was struck in the face by a blast of icy air, knocked from his cart so his head rapped against the ground, dazing him.

He did not know how long it was before he tried to move. But he did struggle up, braced on his forearms. Struggle – he writhed and fought for balance.

Ully who could not move his shrivelled legs, nor straighten his back – why – he was straight! He was as straight as Stephen, as Matt! If this were a dream...

He arched up, looked for the woman to babble questions, thanks, he knew not what. But there was no one by the pillar. Hardly daring to trust the fact that he was no longer bowed into a broken thing, he crawled, feeling strength flow into him with every move, to the foot of the pillar. He used that to draw himself to his feet to stand again!

His clothes were too confining for his new body. He tore them away. Then he was erect, the pillar at his back and the dawn wind fresh on his body. Still keeping his hold on the white stone, he took small cautious steps, circling his support. His feet moved and were firm under him; he did not fall.

Ully threw back his head and cried his joy aloud. Then he saw the glint of something lying in the centre of the pillar circle and he edged forward. A sod of green turf was half uprooted, and protruding from it was a pipe. But such a pipe! He had thought the one he mended was fine; this was such as a high lord might treasure!

He picked it loose of the earth, fearing it might well disappear out of his very fingers. Then he put it to his lips and played his thanks to what, or who, had been there in the night; he played with all the joy in him.

So playing he went home, walking with care at first

because it was so new to him. He went by back ways until he reached the cottage and his mother. She, poor woman, was weeping. They had feared him lost when he had vanished from the meadow and Gretta had aroused the others to search for him without result. When she first looked at this new Ully his mother judged him a spirit from the dead, until he reassured her.

All Coomb Brackett marvelled at his story. Some of the oldest nodded knowingly, spoke of ancient legends of the old ones who had once dwelt in the dales, and how it was that they could grant blessings on those they favoured. They pointed out symbols on the pipe which were not unlike those of the tribute rock. Then the younger men spoke of going to the pillar glade to hunt for treasure. But Ully grew wroth and they respected him as one set apart by what had happened, and agreed it was best not to trouble those they knew so little of.

It would seem that Ully had brought back more than straight legs and a pipe. For that was a good year in the dale. The harvest was the richest in memory, and there were no ill happenings. Ully, now on his two feet, travelled to the farthest homestead to mend and play, for the pipe never left him. And it was true that when they listened to it the feet of all grew lighter as did their hearts, and any dancer more skilful.

But inside Matt there was no rest: Now he was no longer first among the youth; Ully was more listened to. He began to talk himself, hinting dire things about gifts from unknown sources, and a few listened, those who are always discontent to see another prosper. Among them was Morgana, for she was no longer so courted. Even Gretta nowadays was sometimes partnered before her. And one day she broke through Matt's grumbling shortly.

'What one man can do, surely another can also. Why

do you keep muttering about Ully's fortune? Harvest Eve comes soon and those old ones are supposed then to come again to view the wealth of the fields and take their due. Go to Ully's pillars and play; they may be grateful again!'

Matt had been practising on the pipe he had taken from Ully, and he did well enough with the rounds and the lays the villagers had once liked; though the few times he had tried to play Ully's own song the notes had come sourly, off key.

The more Matt considered Morgana's suggestion, the better it seemed, and the old thought of treasure clung in his mind. There could be deals with the old ones if a man were shrewd. Ully was a simple fellow who had not known how to handle such. His thoughts grew ambitious.

So when the feast came Matt lagged behind the rest and turned aside to take a brambly way he judged would bring him to Ully's oft-described ring of pillars. Leaving much of his shirt hanging in tatters on the briers and his skin redstriped by thorns, he came at last into the glade.

There were the pillars right enough, but they were not bright and white and torchlike. Instead, each seemed to squat direfully in a mass of shadow which flowed about their bases as if something unpleasant undulated there. But Matt dropped down beneath one of the trees to wait. He saw no moths, though there were vague flutterings about the crowns of the pillars. At last, thinking Ully fashioned out of his own imagination much of his story, Matt decided to try one experiment before going back to the feasting villages to proclaim just how much a lie his rival was.

But the notes he blew on his pipe were shrill squeaks; and when he would have left, he found to his horror and dismay that he could not move, his legs were locked to the ground as Ully's had once been. Nor could he lower the pipe from his lips, but was compelled by a will outside his own to keep up that doleful, sorry wailing. His body ached, his mouth was dry, and fear was laid as a lash upon him. He saw things around those pillars.

He would close his eyes! But again he could not, but must pipe and watch, until he was close to the brink of madness. Then his leaden arms fell, the pipe spun away from his lax fingers, and he was dimly aware the dawn had come.

From the pillar before him sped a great bloated thing with an angry buzzing – such a fly as he had seen gather to drink the blood spilled at a butchering – yet this was greater than six of those put into one.

It flew straight into his face, stinging him. He tried to beat it away, but could only manage to crawl on his hands and knees; the fly continued to buzz about him as a sheep-dog might herd a straggler.

Somehow Matt finally struggled to his feet, but it was long before he could walk erect. For many days his face was so swollen that he would not show it in the village, nor would he ever tell what happened to him.

But for many a year thereafter Ully's pipe led the people of Coomb Bracket to their feasting and played for their dancing. Sometimes, it was known, he slipped away by himself to the place of pillars and there played for other ears, such as did not side mortal heads.

Wheelbarrow Castle

Joan Aiken

COLUM WAS up in his Aunt Eily's room when, through the window-hole, he saw the Viking ships. Three galleys with sharp evil prows like the beaks of hawks were slicing their way briskly southward over the dark-blue sea.

The boy felt a cold grip of fear on his ribs.

As, indeed, he might. Viking raiders had killed his father and mother, long ago, when he was too young to remember. But Aunt Eily had told him the story, many times, of how she had hidden with him in a sea cave until the invaders had been and gone, leaving ruin and sorrow behind them. During three tides, the girl and the small child had waited, hidden in the cave, until the shouts and screams, and the smell of burning, had died away.

But that was many years back. Vines and vegetables had grown again, cattle and poultry had been brought from other islands. For a long peaceful stretch of years the Vikings had not come raiding. Colum had grown into a tall, strong boy in the course of that time. And now, just last week, Aunt Eily had died from the sting of a blue, poisonous fish. Perhaps it was she, her magic power, which had been keeping the Vikings away all this time?

For Aunt Eily was a witch. In her little blue-walled chamber, high up under the castle roof, she pounded herbs and murmured runes. She could heal wounds, mend broken bones, and cure many illnesses. But not her own, it seemed.

'Take care of my magic things, Colum, boy,' she gasped, as she lay dying on the shore. 'It is most likely the power will come to you now. Use it well! Look after the folk. See well, watch well – hear well, listen well . . .' And then she laced her long thin fingers across her eyes, calling in a faint voice, 'My sister, my brother, wait for me! I am coming!'

After his Aunt Eily had been buried, among the vines on the sunny hillside, Colum went up to her little dark-blue room.

All the people of the island lived in what was called the High City, or the Wheelbarrow Castle, which was a huge old castle left behind on the top of the hill by the Romans, long, long, long ago. The walls of it were so massive-strong that Colum's grandparents, and his great-great-grand-parents, and *their* parents, had burrowed out an entire town in the thickness of them; whole houses and streets had been bored through the mighty ancient Roman fortifications; folk lived there snug and sociable together as bees in a hollow tree. And Aunt Eily, high under the ramparts in her little blue kitchen, had been for many years their wise-woman and watch-woman.

'And you will be so after me, Colum my boy,' she sometimes said to her nephew.

But Colum had always answered obstinately that he would prefer to be a poet.

When he reached the age of ten years, Colum made himself a wheelbarrow, carved the strong white wheel from a log of driftwood, wove the body from willow withes, and cut the handles from the mast of a shipwrecked galley broken up on the shore by furious north winds.

From the use of this barrow he was able to make a living. 'I will carry any weight for anybody to any place!' was his cry, and the people of the island were ready enough to employ his strength when shifting their pigs, or their sacks of grain, or loads of rocks for building, or fish from the shore. And while Colum hoisted heavy weights and trundled them all over the island, he was busy in his mind making up rhymes and setting them to music.

'Wild waves, wild waves, growing so high
Waves in the sea, and fish in the sky
Ninth wave, ninth wave, stay far from me
Laugh with your brothers in the halls of the sea
Roar with your brothers in the halls of the sea . . .'

Colum would sing to himself as he transported the miller's flour, or the headman's nets, or a neighbour's pig, or the keel of a boat.

'A wave-way here, a wave-way there,
A wind-way here, cutting through the air
Soft sand leaves no footprint
Bright flame leaves no trace
Only man looks in the glass
And sees his own face.'

Aunt Eily, listening to Colum's songs at the evening time, over the smoke of the supper-fire, would say, 'Ay, ay, it's true, songs must be sung, but there's more than songs needed when trouble comes southward over the sea.' Now trouble *was* coming southward, and Colum did not know how to meet it.

Below him he could hear the castle stirring like a colony of ants when the spade breaks through the dome of their nest. He could hear mothers wailing and babies crying and the shouts of men, gathering their weapons together. But there were only twenty men, just at present, in Wheelbarrow Castle, and these were the old ones, or the lame and afflicted; all the rest were gone away on the fishing tides and could not be back for some days.

What would they return to?

It is up to me to stop this trouble somehow, Colum thought. But what can I do? Aunt Eily, help me now!

His eyes wandered round her little darkblue room, past the wooden bowls and the dried leaves, the pages of magical books, the glass eye from a mermaid's treasure chest, the shawl made from seal's fur, and the hearing-stone. His eye paused on the hearing-stone, which Eily had found washed up on the shore, one dark winter day. It fitted in her ear exactly.

And now Colum fitted it into his own ear. And the stone began to whisper.

'Criss-cross, criss-cross row
When I look through the criss-cross row
Grow, *grow!*
Fingers short, fingers tall
Window-bars for a soul's hall
When I peer through fingers tall
Grow small!'

Hearing this voice Colum began to remember a game that Aunt Eily must have played with him many times when he was a tiny lad, wandering on the shore by the rock pools.

She would press her hands against her face, peering at him through the slits between the fingers. And then she would sing her rhyme: 'Grow small! Grow small!'

And he – yes, he truly had – he had grown small at her command, smaller than a mouse, small as a bee or a sand-hopper, so that the flowers of thrift, growing by the beach, seemed to him like huge scented cushions, so that the seaweed was like a mighty tangle of rope, so that the rock-pools were huge lagoons and the grains of sand were boulders.

This had really happened, many times. He could remember it. And he had found jewels for Aunt Eily, treasures, and tiny magic plants. Then, when it was time to go home for supper, she would criss-cross her fingers over her face, making a lattice, and call out:

'When I look through the criss-cross row

Grow, grow!'

and so restore Colum to his true size.

But could *I* do that? wondered Colum. Would it happen for me, as it did for Aunt Eily?

He raced down the stairs, steep winding stairs that had been chewed out of the thickness of the wall. In the street outside Aunt Eily's door people were running and crying, bumping into each other in their hurry and terror; women clutched hens and slapped at pigs which had been fetched in from the hillside; aged trembling men sharpened rusty spears and fitted strings to their bows.

Colum grabbed up the handles of his wheelbarrow, which had stood at the foot of the stair, and pushing it, made his way towards the castle entrance.

'Where are you off to, boy?' shouted the head-man, who had not gone with the fishing party, for he had an arm broken in a gale.

'To get rocks – rocks to throw from the walls,' panted Colum.

'Rocks! Rocks will be little use against those northern devils,' growled the headman, but Colum had already dodged away among the panicking people, and was out of the castle gate and scampering down the steep hillside path, which led from the entrance to the harbour in a series of sharp zig-zag bends. Nobody remained on the path now but himself; all the rest had gathered their goods – what they could carry – and retreated inside the castle gate.

A shout came down for him.

'Colum! Come back! We are going to bar the gate! Come back inside!'

Colum stopped at the fourth bend to catch his breath. He looked downhill and saw that the three Viking ships had swept into the harbour. Men were spilling out of them – at least thirty men from each boat. They wore iron caps and carried thick massive swords that gleamed in the pale spring sun. A wild exultant shout came from them as they hurled themselves ashore.

Colum turned and looked at the castle above him. He pressed his fingers across his face, stared at the castle through the slits between the fingers, and whispered,

> 'Fingers short, fingers tall
> Window-bars for my soul's hall
> *Grow small!*'

And – at once – to his almost disbelieving, amazed joy, the castle began to shrink and shrink, with all its terrified inmates inside it – shrank until it was the size of a seal, a sheep, a salmon. When it was small enough to carry, Colum ran back up the hill, plucked the castle from the ground like a loose boulder, and dropped it into his wheelbarrow. Then he raced with it down the far side of the hill – ran, and ran, with his heart bursting in his chest, until he reached the shore. He dared not wait to see what the Vikings were doing behind him, although he would dearly have liked to find out how they behaved when they discovered that the goal they had come all this way to plunder was gone, vanished, leaving only a bare hilltop. But there was no time for looking back. He was responsible for the castle and all those living beings inside it. Colum ran along the shore until he came to the cave where Aunt Eily had once hidden him. He guided his wheelbarrow inside it – far, far in, for he had been back into the cave many times, and knew its windings as well as he knew the passages of the castle itself.

Then he waited. The tide was rising, but Colum hoped that he had brought the castle, and its dwellers, high above the level of any but the highest spring-tides.

Will that be high enough, though? he wondered. Here the cave roof came lower, he could push the castle no farther. All he could do was wait and hope.

'Ninth wave, ninth wave, stay away from me
Laugh with your brothers in the halls of the sea.'

For three high tides Colum waited; then at last he ventured out.

Vikings, he knew, never stayed long, even in a place they had plundered. And what would there be to wait for here, with the castle gone?

When he ventured out on to the shore again, pushing the laden wheelbarrow – and a heavy, frightening weight it now seemed to him, with no knowledge of how the inhabitants had fared during that time in the cave, and no certainty now that he could restore them again to their true size – Colum found a terrible storm raging over the island. The waves hissed like snakes, the winds howled like dragons. Ribbons of snow cut his face as he slowly pushed the wheelbarrow back up the hill path. Sore was the weight on his arms, and sore the weight on his heart. For what of the fishers who had gone off, many days ago now, where were they?

When he reached the hilltop Colum stooped, panting, and braced himself, and hoisted the castle, with all its load of inhabitants, living or dead – hoisted it out from the barrow and settled it back into the empty slot on the hillside where it had stood before. Then, staggering slightly, on legs that felt like skeins of sheep's wool, he made his way back to the fourth bend of the road, latticed his fingers across his eyes, and called out loudly:

'When I look through the criss-cross row

Grow – *grow* – *GROW*!'

And, to his infinite thankfulness and joy, he saw the castle, through the dark and flying snow, begin to stretch itself and rise, like a loaf in the oven – rise, rise and rise, until it towered above him.

At this sight, Colum's strength gave out entirely, and he fell face-down among the heather at the side of the pathway, and so lay, as if he were stunned, until daybreak roused him.

At which time he looked up, and saw folk coming out of the castle, going about their normal day's business, driving out the pigs and poultry, grieving over the vines and pot-herbs and kitchen plants that the Vikings had spoiled – but, at least, all alive – alive, not shrivelled, not shrunk, not drowned, not slaughtered, just the familiar folk going about their usual business.

And, looking *down* the hill, Colum saw the harbour tossing with wreckage, and he recognised the curved prows of the Viking ships. And, looking out to sea, he saw the fishing boats coming back over the dark-blue water . . .

When the fishermen rejoined their families in the castle there was great joy, and great perplexity. For the harbour was full of the shattered remnants of the Viking ships, and dead bodies of drowned Viking warriors who had been dashed against the harbour walls for two days by wild northerly gales, and unable to put out to sea.

'But why did the Vikings not come up the hill – attack the castle?' was asked, over and over. Nobody knew the answer to that question. All that the wives and mothers, all that the old men and the invalids could tell was that, for the duration of three tides, a great darkness had fallen over the castle, and a great silence had reigned. It was like the Day of Judgment. It was like being in a cave. Nobody had left or entered the castle. No Vikings had been seen or heard.

'But the Vikings must have been just outside the castle, for they smashed the vines and trampled the young corn,' said one of the mothers.

No Vikings were left alive to tell what they had found. All had been drowned as they tried to put out to sea against the furious northerly winds.

And Colum, meanwhile, kept his own counsel, as he pushed his wheelbarrow and made up his rhymes.

> 'Soft sand leaves no footprint
> Bright flame leaves no trace
> Only man looks in the glass
> And sees his own face . . .'

SCIENCE FICTION: ROBOTS, SPACE AND VIRTUAL REALITY

Oddiputs

Nicholas Fisk

EVEN WORRIED, solemn, six-year-old Bruno had to laugh when Sally did it. He knew it was naughty, worse than naughty – almost wicked. But he had to laugh because of Sally's face – her rosy, dimpled, sparkling-eyed, aren't-I-a-dear-little-girl face – as she said, 'Poor Oddiputs! Always so busy!'

And as she spoke, she tipped over Bruno's plate of breakfast cereal so that the mush of cornflakes and creamy milk and brown sugar made a wet, spreading, disgusting mess on the clean cloth on the nursery table. 'Oh dear, oh dearie me!' Sally said. Her eyes were very bright. 'Go on, Oddiputs! Clean it up!'

Oddiputs the robot obeyed, as usual. He said something that could have been 'Er-oink' (he still couldn't speak English properly – half the words came out wrong and some of his sounds made no sense at all). He whirred his wheels, extended gunmetal-coloured arms and hands, clumsily closed his big claw fingers on the cloth and drew it inwards over the mess. He did it quite well, for him.

Sometimes, when performing such simple tasks, his hands and arms let him down. They made motions in the wrong places. Scratches in the nursery table reminded the children of these mistakes. There were always outbursts of giggling when Oddiputs' hands performed their actions five inches too low, or six inches too high: Dex's laugh, hoarse and uncertain – soon his voice would break, and he was already too old for the nursery; Bruno's nervous giggle; and of course Sally's gurgling laughter, charming, infectious, innocent, melodious . . . as pretty as her vivid face and flying dark hair.

'Quick, Oddiputs!' Sally said. 'More to clear up! Look! Over here!' The robot turned; Sally cunningly used her spoon to spread the slush around, making sure that some of it messed the table as well as the tablecloth.

Bruno frowned. She was going too far. She was always going too far. But once again he had to smile when Oddiputs tried to catch up with Sally's spoon. The robot was too slow and clumsy. Now there was mush on the tablecloth, the table, the table legs. There was mush dribbling onto the carpet. The sticky patches spread.

'Look, Oddiputs! It's on the floor as well!' Sally said, tilting her head sideways and showing her dimples. 'Oh, how nasty! Tsk, tsk, tsk!' Her dark hair swung like a bell in time with the clicks of her tongue.

'Leave him alone,' Dex growled, ashamed of his eight-year-old sister. But she did not hear. She had another good idea. 'Behind you, Oddiputs!' she called sharply.

The robot turned its uneasy head completely round, to look backwards. This gave Sally the opportunity to put a dab of splodge on the crown of the robot's metal skull. She did it very neatly.

'What – was – behind – Missally?' Oddiputs said. After all these years, he could not even manage 'Miss Sally'.

'Oh, nothing, Oddiputs. Nothing at all. I just thought I saw a hornet.'

'What – is – a hornet – Missally?'

'A sort of flying sausage with fur on it,' Sally said, very seriously. 'In a black and yellow jumper. It's fuzzy and it buzzes.'

'Buzzz?' said Oddiputs, trying hard. 'Bzzzzz?'

He began clicking, as he usually did when his mind was running slow. Dex tried not to laugh. Bruno could not stop himself. Sally was awful, and Oddiputs was dim. Oddiputs couldn't understand anything, not even his own programme.

'Fuzz, buzz. Buzz, fuzz. Say it after me, Oddiputs,' Sally said. 'Go on! Quickly! Say buzzfuzz, fuzzbuzz!'

'BUZZUB!' Oddiputs said – almost shouted. 'ZUBBUMB!'

'Oh, clever Oddiputs!' Sally said, sweetly. 'You clever little tinpot! He deserves a putty medal! Doesn't he, Bruno? Doesn't he, Dex?'

'Putty,' Oddiputs said, clicking. 'Putty. Good.'

Sally, suddenly bored, ground the sludge on the floor deeper into the carpet with her pointed toe. 'Get it cleaned up, moron,' she said. Her voice wasn't sweet any more.

Oddiputs left the nursery to get mop, bucket, cloth, water and detergent. At least he knew about cleaning up messes. He had had plenty of practice.

Oddiputs was a bargain-basement, cut-price, no-guarantee robot.

When robots learned to breed more robots, not all the offspring were perfect. Oddiputs was very imperfect. His mechanical and electronic functions were just about good enough. It was his 'brain' – his ability to accept and act on programmes – that was wrong. Had he been human, his head would have lolled, his eyes would have goggled. He would have dribbled and shambled.

But there is no need to feel proud, ashamed or anything else about a robot. If it works, you use it. If it half works, use the half that works. No need to explain or apologize to the neighbours about your robot. Particularly if you own no less than three of them – two Mk VIIIs, both almost new, and an admittedly stupid Mk III. Particularly if you live in a big house. Particularly if you are Mr and Mrs Ellis-Firman, owners of the ultramodern big house and parents of Dex, Sally and Bruno. Three children: three, in an age when most people were rationed to two children.

Two latest-model cars outside. Cabin cruiser in the drive. The whole family so beautifully dressed. And all so handsome, so good-looking – particularly that Sally, such a pretty, lively little girl, so forthcoming and full of life, it did you good to look at her...

'Stick the robot in the nursery,' Mr Ellis-Firman told his wife when Oddiputs was delivered. That was two years ago, when Bruno was only four and sick with some stomach bug that made him, literally, *be* sick – sick in, on and outside his bed. 'Stick it in the nursery. It's got brains enough to clear up messes and keep the place halfway sanitary.'

'But you say it's a *reject*, almost a *moron*,' his wife objected.

'You don't need a genius for that sort of work,' Mr Ellis-Firman said, grimly. 'Of course, Fiona, if you'd rather attend to it yourself?'

She shuddered, changed the subject, and Oddiputs took up residence in the nursery.

It was Sally who found the new robot's name. It was she who called him. 'Oddiputs'.

'Why Oddiputs?' Mrs Ellis-Firman inquired one day. That afternoon, she was lying beside Sally on Sally's bed, her feet raised and resting on the padded footboard. It was one of her 'quiet times with the children'. The 'quiet times' did not happen very often because Mrs Ellis-Firman had so many other things to do. Never a moment to call her own.

'Why Oddiputs?' she asked her daughter. 'Such a quaint name. But then, you're such a quaint little thing, my lovey!'

Sally looked secretly and sidelong at her mother's face and thought, Wrong shade of lipstick. Then she replied, 'Oh, don't be so slow, Mummy. Can't you work it out?'

Her mother frowned. She did not like being called slow by her daughter. All the more so as Sally made her *feel* slow. At the age of eight, Sally possessed something she herself had never had. What was the word for it? 'Star Quality': probably that. Good at everything, admired by everyone.

She frowned and said, 'What did you say, Sally? Work out what?'

From his bed, Bruno called out, 'Oh, Mum-*mee*, it's *obvious*. "Oddiputs" is "Stupido" spelled backwards!'

Sally laughed, smugly. Her mother said, 'Oh...' and worked it out. Then she said, 'But there's only one "d" in "Stupido", so I don't see ... Really, you children! You can't even spell! When I think of all the money your father spends on your education—'

'Don't think about it, Mummy,' Sally said, wriggling closer to her mother and giving her a cosy smile. Mummy's face relaxed. 'Oddiputs!' Sally called, 'Come in here!'

The robot wheeled in. 'Yes, Missally?'

'Massage Mother's ankles,' Sally said. 'No, not mine, stupid! Hers! And get a towel – yes, *that* towel, over *there*! Your hands are made of *metal*, warm them under the *hot tap*, then get the *towel* and massage her *ankles*.'

Oddiputs began massaging. He did it very well

because Sally had spent hours teaching him how to massage her.

'Oh!' sighed her mother. 'Oh, oh . . . ! Marvellous!' Suddenly she liked her daughter quite a lot. 'So relaxing . . . !'

'I'm so glad, Mummy!' Sally whispered. She snuggled closer and put her cool cheek against her mother's cheek. She thought, In five minutes I'll ask her to buy me the gingham dress, the black-and-white.

Oddiputs did not have a bed. He did not need one. At night, when the family slept, he set his controls to Watchdog, reduced his power, connected himself to the mains to recharge his power-cells, and then subsided, telescopically, into himself, section by section.

He consisted of four main sections. His head, a flattened globe, was at just below human level so that he could see as his masters saw (but without 'looking down' on them).

His chest or thorax was a complex drum, smaller than the third unit, another drum, forming his abdomen or lower half. This tapered into the fourth unit, his mobility unit. The mobility unit could split and become actual legs. Usually, however, the legs unit stayed in one piece and Oddiputs went about on pads and rollers. They were good enough for flat surfaces.

At night, collapsed into himself, he was half his daytime height. From the top of his head the small lighthouse-like Watchdog unit projected itself. It turned and scanned continuously, looking for smoke, burglars, unaccustomed movements, anything. His station was in the hall outside the children's nursery.

Oddiputs was partly 'awake' in his Watchdog mode. And he had enough of his facilities left in circuit to do his 'home-work'. All robots did this. The homework took the form of scanning his memories and banks and stores of information. The aim of the homework was to improve his usefulness. Robots get 'rusty' if they do not constantly re-learn and review their programmes.

Oddiputs was always rusty. He was born rusty. He was a simpleton, unable to grasp the facts of his life. Or rather, *the* fact: the single, simple fact that he was made to serve humans.

He had replaced this thought with another. Oddiputs had convinced himself that he was a person.

And so, in the night, when the other, better robots were busy improving themselves, Oddiputs 'thought'. Or thought he thought.

He always began the same way. I am me, he thought. I am Oddiputs. He repeated this many, many times, and then let his mind run rapidly through the proofs of his existence: his serial numbers, part numbers, functions and faculties, his service and maintenance manual, his—

But it was a vast list of facts and figures that he repeated, longer than an encyclopedia. So long that it took Oddiputs whole minutes to produce and digest, at lightning speed (for robots are fast, very fast), the information that proved Oddiputs' existence to Oddiputs.

The children slept, dogs sometimes barked, the moon flirted with passing clouds. Oddiputs backtracked and began again: I am me. I am Oddiputs . . .

Again, and again and again. At last, a sort of warmth (but there was no measurable warmth, of course) invaded his head and spread to his thick, short body. A sort of pleasure (but robots are not programmed for pain or pleasure) pervaded his whole existence.

I am me, he told himself. Had he been human, he would have nodded solemnly. I am Oddiputs!

Then the forbidden thought, the thrilling thought, the

thought that only a defective robot could have been guilty of, entered his 'mind'.

The thought that whispered – 'I am Oddiputs . . . and they are only *They* . . . !'

They!

They, the humans! Sally, Bruno, Dex!

There were other Theys, of course – other humans, whom Oddiputs recognized and obeyed. But they did not matter. They were not truly *They. They* were Dex, Sally, Bruno.

Oddiputs reviewed the They.

He began with Bruno. In the first, early days, Bruno had puzzled Oddiputs because Bruno was different. Sally and Dex were upright all day, balanced on their two supports called legs.

But Bruno had not followed the day-time programme. Bruno had been horizontal all the time, like this:___. Now, why had that been?

Oddiputs racked his memory circuits. At last the answer came. Bruno had been a *viladin* – no, a *dinavil* – no, an *invalid,* that's the word. Or is it?

Instead of getting the word right, as other robots would have done, Oddiputs slipped a mental cog and went on to another They. Dex.

Dex was the biggest and simplest. Dex was correct. At night, he always took up the night-time angle, ___. Then, when the sky was light, he took up the day-time angle, ___. So Dex was more correct than Bruno. But, Oddiputs brooded, he makes a lot of noise with his food-hole, Dex does. And he shouts 'Geroff!' and 'Shut up!' I know the meaning of those words. That is correct of me . . .

What else does Dex do? He tries to make things called modelkits. Always the modelkits go wrong. Then Dex gets angry and Sally begins the thing called teasing until Dex tells her, 'Geroff!' and 'Shut up!'. But she does not geroff and shut up. She only smiles, the special smile, the teasing smile . . .

Oddiputs, thinking of Sally and her teasing, would flinch if he could flinch. Instead, he clicks anxiously, avoiding the thought of Sally. But his 'mind' skids and slides, it will keep coming back to her, he cannot prevent it.

What *is* it that Sally does when she teases? What is *teases?* Why does it make him click? He does not mind work, endless work: but teasing – teasing like today, when she spilled the food – he does not like the teasing. Teasing gives him the thick feeling, the pressure inside.

Oddiputs changes track. He cannot bear to think of Sally and teasing for too long. But he cannot stop himself thinking about They . . .

Their food-holes.

I have no food-hole, Oddiputs thinks. I do not need one because I am clean and correct. They are different. They put things in their food-holes. Often they miss. Then I must clean up after. When Bruno was a dinavil – an invalid – stuff kept coming from his food-hole and I had to clean it up.

Why do They say *clean* it up? Because the stuff was dirty. Dirty and incorrect. So food is dirty and food-holes are dirty and They are dirty. Dirty, dirty, dirty. Dirty and incorrect.

In the small hours of the night, in the darkness of the passageway, Oddiputs' Watchdog unit sedately revolves, regularly, unhurriedly. Inside Oddiputs, 'thoughts' surge and scamper. He thinks the thoughts are new each time he thinks them. They are not. They are the same old thoughts, always the same.

Yet they build. For each time he thinks them, the thoughts leave a tiny deposit on his hair-fine tapes. It is like a coral reef: the ages pass, the dead husks cement themselves together, the reef grows. With a robot, ages pass very, very quickly . . .

I am clean, Oddiputs thinks. Clean and correct . . .

And I am efficient. They are not efficient. When They were smaller (why do They need to change size and grow? *I* do not change *my* size!), They were always falling down. They were supposed to be like this |, but They fell down and became like this___. Then loud sounds would come out of their food-holes and their eyes would leak wetness. Sometimes their skin would split and leak red wetness. Then I had to 'clean the wound'. So the wound was dirty. They are dirty.

I have no wetnesses anywhere, ever.

I am Oddiputs.

They are only They . . .

He could think of so many things to prove his case:

My day is twenty-four hours. I do this and that and this. That is correct. That is efficient.

But They! They are alive for only fifteen or sixteen of the twenty-four hours. At night, They are as if dead. That is not efficient. So it cannot be correct.

And they are hot/cold. I am never hot/cold; always the same, always correct. I do not have coverings to put on and take off my body. They do. They have to wear clothes. *Cloe-th-sss*. That is hard to say. Sally teases me because I cannot say that word . . .

Oddiputs' mind tries to escape the thought of Sally and teasing. 'I am Oddiputs,' he recites, 'and They are only They.' This time, the good words do not work. So he decides to move his body – he is supposed to do this at intervals so that his various sealing rings will be freshly positioned and not become deformed.

As his body shifts, so does his 'mind'. A thought, a genuinely new thought, enters his head:

I am Oddiputs. They are only They. *Yet I serve them!*

The new thought astonishes him. It makes his head seem to bulge, his circuits and tapes seem to spin out of control. His 'mind' works on a binary, Go/No-Go system. The system seldom fails him. It fails him now. It will not answer the new thought:

I serve *them*. Why do I serve them? They are dirty, illogical, inefficient, insanitary, incorrect. They suffer hot/cold, They are always wanting things to put in their food-holes, They fall down. They shout and quarrel and suffer nightly death.

But I, Oddiputs – I am clean, effective, efficient, sanitary, unchanging – correct in every way. Perfectly correct.

So why do *I* serve *Them*?

Again and again Oddiputs consults his logic circuits, cuts in his memory stores, riffles through his programmes. No answer comes. Finally, desperately, he cross-indexes every faculty he possesses.

What humans would call a 'stroke' attacks him as the intricate mechanisms jam, fight, rebel – and fail.

Very briefly, his head actually warms. The Watchdog fails to revolve for a second or more. He clicks and whirrs and chitters. A tiny, ultrasonic scream issues from the grille protecting his vocalizer unit.

Then the cut-outs automatically operate, the circuits disentangle themselves, spools of gossamer cease to spin, transistors and silicon chips and microcircuits nod and bow to each other and say, 'After you, I insist' – and Oddiputs is himself again.

Himself, but not himself. Something extra has been added to his complicated make-up: a ray of dark light has entered him, a touch of original sin.

Oddiputs has somehow learned to envy – to despise – to hate.

The first grey light touches the passageway, showing the outlines of the expensive hall table, the real flowers in the real cut-glass vase, the rich pile of the deep carpet. The Watchdog part of Oddiputs notes that all these objects have behaved correctly, and he approves what he sees.

But Oddiputs' 'brain' seethes, darkly.

Sally found a new trick to play. Mummy had, as Sally had planned, bought the gingham dress. Sally tried it on, thrilled by the feel of the slippery yet crisp (and so obviously expensive) material. She did up the cunning little black bows over the sleeves and at the neck. Then, smiling, she looked in the long mirror.

She hated what she saw. The dress was, quite simply, wrong. It was a beautiful dress, beautifully made. On a hundred thousand other little girls, it would have been terrific. On Sally, it was murder. The whiteness somehow killed the subtle colours of her skin; the black bits fought with the darkness of her hair and dimmed the shock of her violet eyes. A disaster.

Sally actually and literally ground her teeth. She wanted to tear at the dress with her oval fingernails (but they were too short, too well kept). She wanted to hook her finger into the neck of the dress and rip downwards, with one glorious, savage death-stroke (but Mummy would go ape, there'd be a huge scene, no more dresses).

So she called Oddiputs. 'Oddiputs!' she cried, her voice neutral and nice. 'Oddiputs! I want you for a second!'

Oddiputs wheeled in.

'Oddiputs, ah, there you are,' she said. 'Help me. It's this bow, I can't manage . . . Hold on to it. Tight. No, tighter than that, really hold on to it.'

Oddiputs locked his metal hand and metal fingers on

the bow at the neck of the dress. The claw fingers clamped together like a vice.

'*Clever* Oddiputs,' Sally crooned; then, quick as a cat, jumped backwards as far as she could. She smiled as she jumped; smiled as the dress ripped open, bursting threads glittering; smiled as she landed on her feet, three or four feet away from the robot, the ruined dress still slipping from her shoulders and still held by Oddiputs' mailed fist.

'Mum-*mee!*' she screamed, smiling as she screamed. 'Oh, Mum-*mee!* Oh, come here! Quick!'

Mummy ran in from the next room. Sally's face was now a mask of tragedy. Real tears sprang from Sally's eyes. By the time Mummy was at her side – a matter of seconds – the picture was complete: darling daughter, shocked and tearful; ruined dress, its remains stretched between daughter and robot's clutching hand.

'*He* did it!' Sally howled. 'Oddiputs! My new dress! Ruined!'

She waited for Mummy to say, 'We'll buy you another, darling.' Mummy soon obliged.

Kill, Oddiputs thought, when the day was over and everyone was asleep and he was at his usual place in the passageway, shrunken into his own body, keeping guard through his Watchdog unit.

Kill . . .

The word was in his memory store, of course, but he had seldom found uses for it. The children did not use it. They said 'Murder' ('I'll *murder* you if you don't stop doing that'); or 'exterminate' ('I'd like to *exterminate* the ratty little idiot'); but they did not often use the word 'kill'. *Kill*...

After all, Oddiputs thinks, Sally means to kill me. She said, 'Oh, Mummy, you've got to get rid of Oddiputs!

Scrap him! Junk him! Get a proper robot! Why is Daddy so mean? Millicent's got a proper robot, a Mk V, all her own. And Mandy's getting one. And all we've got is this stupid old junkheap idiot thing – and he ruined my new dress—'

She wants to kill me, Oddiputs thinks. He remembers the day that is over. The messes, the teasing, the remarks about his squeak . . .

When he began squeaking as he moved, Sally had 'buttered his paws' – literally smeared butter on his wheels and pads. She had done it so funnily that Bruno laughed out loud and Dex had honked in his changing voice. 'Now walk!' Sally said, and he had to walk, with them looking on. Each footstep of his pads and roll of his wheels left butter on the carpet, trails of butter. Later she made him clear every trace of the butter away . . .

Kill! he thinks. That means to make a live thing stop living. Sally is live. She would be easy enough to kill. She is soft. They are all soft. Oddiputs flexes his metal hands, curls and uncurls his jointed metal fingers. They move so easily, so powerfully. They could kill Sally. He would squeeze and the red wet would leak out. All of it. Then she would be dead.

But it would not be correct, Oddiputs thinks. His first duty is to serve humans. His first law is to preserve human life. So he must not kill Sally.

But suppose she killed herself?

That would be different. Humans are so inefficient, so clumsy, so bad at so many things. Oddiputs thinks of their inefficiencies – the falling down, the bumps and thumps and cuts, the food-holes open and shouting for help.

Suppose, just suppose, that next time there was an accident, he did not help?

No better: suppose it was the sort of accident where he could not help?

Oddiputs begins to review such accidents. Water. Falls from great heights. Electricity. Cars. Poisons.

He thinks and thinks, while the night passes and the first light of the new day makes the window-frame in the passageway show black against grey, then blacker still against blue-grey—

And then the sun comes up and its first rays strike the window, make the glass flash, make the frame glitter—

The window! Oddiputs thinks. Of course! The window!

Long ago, Sally found out how to use the nursery window to tease Oddiputs. She still played the trick – still waited until the window was misted with human steam, then drew on the glass with her finger. Often she did drawings that made Dex mumble and turn red, words that made Bruno protest. 'I don't know what you mean!' she replied, eyeing them with her sharp, all-knowing eyes, when they told her to stop. 'Is this word rude, Dex?' she asked innocently, pointing her finger to make him look at what she had written. 'Oh, but I'm sure it's not rude! You used the word yourself the other day! Twice! I heard you!'

'Dad might come in,' Dex muttered, miserably. 'Wipe it off.'

'Oh, but *I* don't mind if Daddy comes in,' Sally said. 'I'll tell him you made me write it. He'll believe *me*.'

'Daddy's Darling,' Dex muttered miserably.

'That's right,' Sally agreed, smiling radiantly. 'I'm Daddy's darling daughter. He loves me most of all. I'm his favourite. And if I tell him you made me write this word—'

'Oh, shut *up!*' Dex said. He tried to get to the window

to wipe off the word. Sally would not let him. When he came near, she screamed. Though he had not touched her, she shouted, in a high, pathetic voice, 'Oh, *don't*, Dex! Please don't! You're *hurting* me!'

Dex backed away. Bruno said, 'I'll do it. Move aside, Sally.' But again, she began screaming and made her eyes fill with tears. She could do this whenever she wanted to.

In the end, nobody came and Sally grew bored. 'Oddiputs!' she said, 'you're supposed to keep the place clean. Clean the window, moron.'

Oddiputs obeyed. He got a cloth and the special stuff you sprayed on glass; then he cleaned the panes he could reach. Sally stood by saying, 'Do the corners, oaf! You're leaving the corners!' So he did the corners again.

As he worked, the thick, swelling feeling invaded him – the teasing feeling: For he knew what would happen next; and knew he was right when Sally said, quite pleasantly, 'Now reach up and do the upper parts of the window, Oddiputs. Go on. Reach up. Right up.'

Oddiputs obeyed. He extended his arms, which were flexible to a limited degree, and cleaned some higher panes, taking great care with the corners.

'Higher still, Oddiputs,' Sally said. 'Very high. Right up.' Her voice was sweet as honey. The swelling feeling in Oddiputs thickened in his 'brain'. Now the teasing starts, he told himself. But he did as she told him. He began to grow.

Growing was simple enough. He merely had to separate the two middle sections of his body. As you know, they were telescopic units fitting into each other. On the rare occasions when a robot needed extra height, it could grow by separating the sections.

To human eyes, the effect was of course grotesque. Your robot grew and grew, taller and taller, as you watched. Most ludicrous of all, as the solid, drum-like middle units separated from each other, they revealed a shining tube, veined with hair-fine harnesses of coloured wiring that twisted in webs round the tube. Halfway up the tube was revealed the terminal block, a square plastic box.

'Why, Oddiputs!' Sally cooed, when this terminal block was revealed, 'I can see your tummy button! Yes, I can! Your naughty little tummy button!' She moved towards Oddiputs, her hands outstretched, her fingers wriggling. 'Oddiputs,' she said, 'are you ticklish? I'll bet he's ticklish, Dex!'

But this time, Dex did not want to play. 'Look, you've done this act before, Sally,' he replied. 'It gets boring.' And he walked out of the nursery.

Sally shrugged. She continued her advance on Oddiputs and said to Bruno, 'Shall I tickle Oddiputs?' She looked laughingly over her shoulder at Bruno.

But he too merely looked first surly, then disgusted. 'Do what you like,' he told Sally. 'I'm sick of you getting at poor old Oddiputs. Telling lies and all that. Trying to get him pushed out. I like old Oddiputs,' Bruno said. 'I like him better than you. So leave him alone!'

'And what if I don't?' Sally said, giving her younger brother the full violet glare.

'Do, don't, I don't care,' Bruno said – and walked out.

Now Oddiputs was alone with Sally. His opportunity had come . . .

The window was nearly finished. Only a corner at the very top left remained undone. Oddiputs did not clean this little triangle of glass. Instead, with a whistling noise like 'Hish!', he let the two centre sections of his body telescope into each other so that he was his usual size, and waited for Sally to notice the uncleaned triangle.

She spotted it immediately, of course. She said,

'Moron! I said clean the window! Look up there, in the corner! Filth!'

Oddiputs looked – and deliberately saw nothing. 'Filth?' he said. 'Where, Missally?'

'Up there!' she stormed. 'Look! *Look!*'

She was furious now. Raging. She picked up the little table that stood by the window, banged it down under the window and jumped onto it. Standing on the table, she reached up and jabbed her finger at the dirty triangle. 'Hold the table,' she shouted. 'There! Look, I'm touching it! There, there, *there!*'

The window was twenty-five feet above the paving stones below.

Oddiputs' hands jerked. The table-top tilted. Sally's feet skidded. Suddenly there was nothing beneath them. Her hands flailed, clawed – and broke through the glass.

She screamed, piercingly, and fell through the window.

Oddiputs immediately made his siren noise, the noise that meant *Emergency! Emergency!*

Ah-oo! Ah-oo! his siren yelled. People came running.

'There!' said Oddiputs, pointing downwards through the shattered window. 'Missally down there!' *Ah-oo! Ah-oo!*

Had anyone else fallen from that window on to those paving stones, that person would have been killed. But it was Sally who fell; and, being Sally, her falling body happened to touch a piece of pipework that stuck out just the right amount from the wall – which threw her outwards just enough to land on top of an ornamental bay-tree – which broke her fall, cushioned her body and landed her on her side. So Sally did not die.

But she did suffer a broken left arm, a twisted thumb and a crack on the side of her head that gave her a black eye, a perpetual headache and concussion. Concussion means that one's brains are temporarily scrambled: concussed people say the maddest things.

'Oddiputs!' was Sally's first word when she came to. Then, 'Oddiputs tried to kill me!' she screamed.

'Lie back, darling . . . you must be quiet . . . lie back,' said her mother. She looked sideways and shook her head meaningfully.

'But he tried to *kill* me!' Sally screamed.

Her father held her down on the pillows. Her mother wiped her brow with a cool, damp cloth. Oddiputs hovered and clicked dutifully.

'*Murderer!*' Sally screamed at Oddiputs. Then she slept.

'Very typical,' the doctor told Sally's parents. 'Nasty head injury . . . we mustn't let anything she says surprise us. Time, give it time. Say, two or three days. Then she'll be rational again.'

Mr and Mrs Ellis-Firman pressed questions on the doctor. Dex and Bruno stood by, white-faced and quiet. Oddiputs made coffee and served it.

Oddiputs said, 'I will take up station outside the nursery unless anyone wants more coffee?'

'Yes, do that. But very quietly. Don't let her hear or see you.'

Oddiputs settled himself in the usual night-time position outside the nursery. Then he changed his mind.

He wheeled silently to stand by the sleeping Sally. Perhaps she sensed his presence. She half woke. Eyes closed, head tossing, she gripped the sheets with bandaged hands. 'Why won't they listen to me?' she murmured. Tears of rage were squeezed from between her long black eyelashes.

Something very like pleasure invaded Oddiputs' being. He bent over the girl. 'Missally!' he whispered.

'Tried to kill me . . .' Sally sobbed.

'Missally!' Oddiputs repeated.

This time she heard him and her uninjured eye opened, very wide. She tried to scream, but a metal hand, clasping the cool, moist cloth, clamped down over her face and mouth. She made muffled, choking sounds.

'Teasing,' Oddiputs told the writhing body. 'Just teasing,' he said. And the feeling like pleasure grew stronger in him.

When Sally's body began desperately to thrash and writhe, he let go. He watched her fight for breath find it – then screech, '*Daddy! He's trying to kill me! Daddece!*'

But by the time Daddy had run up the stairs, Oddiputs was in his rightful place, outside the nursery door.

'Oh, Daddy! He tried to strangle me—'

'You were dreaming, darling. Just a nasty dream. Lie back, lie back . . .'

And when Sally had sobbed herself into a half sleep, and the doctor had finally gone, and Daddy had the time to look long and hard at Oddiputs, all he saw was the same old faithful, but not particularly efficient servant machine, Oddiputs, steadily and immovably keeping watch.

Sally's lesser wounds healed quickly and neatly, without scars. Yet she was changed. Even Bruno noticed. 'You've gone all quiet,' he told her. 'You're dull. You don't tease Oddiputs any more.'

Dex said, 'Just as well. I was getting sick of it.'

Sally said nothing.

'She's scared,' Bruno jeered, hugging himself. He enjoyed the new Sally. In the old days, she lashed out at him with her sharp tongue or even her fingernails when he annoyed her. But now her old sting was gone. Besides, her left arm was still in plaster. 'Scared,' he went on.

'Because Oddiputs tried to murder her. *Clump, thump, bump*, here comes a *murderer*. Look at me! I'm the robot *murderer!*'

He did a clumsy imitation of Oddiputs, circling round Sally, taunting her. In the old days, this would have got him a smacked head. Now Sally said nothing.

It was Dex who spoke. 'Oh, shut up, you stupid kid,' he told Bruno. 'She was delirious when she said that. A nutcase. She doesn't really think Oddiputs tried to murder her, not now. Do you Sally?'

She still said nothing. She just went on scratching her arm inside the cast with a knitting-needle. Her arm itched all the time.

Bruno would not be kept down. 'You shouldn't do that with that needle,' he said, spitefully. 'The *doctor* said you shouldn't. *Daddy* said you shouldn't. You could harm yourself, do yourself an injury.'

For the first time, Sally took some notice of Bruno. She pulled the long knitting-needle out of her cast, and studied it. 'An injury?' she said, vaguely. 'With this?'

She stared at the needle. It was made of metal. Plastic knitting-needles snapped. Aluminium needles bent. But this one was unusual, it was made of steel. It would not bend or break.

Sally stared at the needle, thinking hard . . .

She thought, I don't know. Not really *know*. The day I fell from the window – did I do it, or did Oddiputs do it? I can't be sure . . .

But I can be sure of other things, recent things. He comes in here in the night. He stands over me. How often has he done it? I don't know, I'm asleep. But I wasn't asleep last night, when his Watchdog light wakened me, and he was *there*, looming over me. He looked enormous, all that metal and the light going round and round . . . I didn't dream it. He stood over me, leaning forward, and he said, 'I am Oddiputs, I am Oddiputs.' He kept saying it, mumbling it.

And then there's the way he behaves to Bruno. Bruno's getting really cheeky. He's always teasing Oddiputs. As if I cared. But there's something different about the way Oddiputs reacts – he's becoming sly, crafty, sort of threatening—

And when Bruno tumbled down the stairs . . . How did that happen? Oddiputs says Bruno must have left the glass beaker at the top of the stairs, but Bruno swears he never did.

Suppose Oddiputs wants to harm Bruno.

Suppose Oddiputs meant to kill *me*.

Under her breath, she muttered, 'He would, would he?' Then she pursed her lips and went briskly to the garage.

She knew there was a little tool-kit there, one of those neat little multi-purpose things in a wallet. The various bits of the kit fitted into the same handle, a bright yellow transparent handle.

'Plastic,' she said as she held the handle, inspecting it. 'Good. It's got to be plastic. Now, will the needle fit in the handle?'

She tried it. She'd been right. The knitting needle was quite a good fit. Not tight, but tight enough. And long enough.

Long, and made of steel.

Night . . . and Oddiputs in the dark, collapsed into his Watchdog shape, his brain turning over and over his favourite thoughts.

I am Oddiputs, he began. I am Oddiputs and They are only They.

The Watchdog light revolved over the squat body.

I am Oddiputs, he continued, *and She is only She.*

His body began to expand and grow, very slowly, very smoothly, as the cylinder within a cylinder telescoped and expanded. Glinting metallically in the darkness, Oddiputs grew to his full height.

His 'brain' seemed to expand too. It seemed to fill his head, his body, everything. She is only She! his brain told him. But I am Oddiputs ... correct, clean, powerful. Powerful, superior, effective. Effective, unstoppable, mighty. And ready. Ready *now!*

He moved silently through the darkness, towards the bedroom doors.

Which one first?

Dex? No, Dex was not his enemy.

Bruno? Perhaps, because Bruno teased. He had learned it from Sally and now he teased. He teased more than Sally did. Bruno, then. Him first.

The metal hand silently clamped on the knob of the door that opened on Bruno's bedroom and Bruno's bed. Oddiputs began to turn the knob, very slowly. He saw a picture of Bruno in his mind: the boy would be asleep (inefficient!); his mouth would be open and damp (dirty!).

He paused, then stopped. This was all wrong. Bruno should not be the first. Things had to be done in correct sequence. Who was the real enemy? Who was the real tormentor? Sally. Sally must be first.

He wheeled silently away and glided to another door, Sally's door. He entered her room. His Watchdog light lit the walls. As it revolved, it made a mirror flash, a glass jar glitter, a shadow leap.

He stood over her. Her eyes were closed and her breathing slow and regular. Her head was thrown back on the pillow. The Watchdog light turned and lit Sally's neck, showing it now shadowed and dark, now pale and golden. Always, it was fragile and slender.

Oddiputs' metal hand became a great clawed pincer.
He flexed it. The movements of the pinching, clamping
hand delighted him, flooded him with pleasure.

Sally sat up, opened both eyes and looked straight at
Oddiputs. 'Good,' she said. 'It's you. I couldn't sleep. Too
hot.' She was completely awake.

Oddiputs made small, stupid noises.

'Open the window,' Sally said. She was sitting up in
bed now, her eyes large and calm. 'Go on, Oddiputs.
Open it.'

'Missally . . . I . . . but . . .'

'The *window*, stupid,' she said.

He went to the window and lifted the lower sash.

Sally said, 'No, not at the *bottom*, there'll be a *draught*.
Open the *top*.'

'Yes, Missally. But I can't reach—'

'Oh yes you can, Oddiputs. You know you can.'

'But, Missally'

'Go on, Oddiputs. *Go on*.'

He had to obey. And to reach the top of the window he
had to 'grow'. Then the teasing would start, he could feel
her cold, clear eyes on his back.

His two central sections telescoped smoothly apart.
Sally leaned forward. When the Watchdog light passed
over her face, it showed the gleam of her teeth between
the parted lips and the glitter of her eyes.

Oddiputs was stretched high now. The two halves of
his body were apart, revealing the central column of his
body and the network of fine coloured wires.

'Good-bye, Oddiputs!' Sally hissed – and stabbed at
the terminal block with the steel knitting-needle,
insulated in its plastic handle.

Oddiputs said, 'Missally, don't . . .' His Watchdog light
flickered and went out.

'Good-bye, I said!' she spat. She stabbed viciously at

the network of fine wires, again and again. Blue fire sizzled and blazed. Fiery red worms crawled as hair-fine wires shorted and burned.

Oddiputs began to sway and as he swayed, his body shortened, collapsing into itself.

'There!' Sally said. 'And *there!* And *there!*' Now the knitting-needle plunged into a fizzing, sputtering mess. The tip of the needle grew blackened and deformed.

Oddiputs bellowed, '*I am me! I am Oddiputs!*'

The two halves of his body finally jerked shut, leaking sparks and rivulets of smoke and sputtering molten plastic. He shouted, '*I am Oddiputs! And They are only—*'

But then his voice cracked and screeched and he fell backwards, smashing the footboard and legs of Sally's bed, burning glowing holes in the coverlet, flashing a sudden brilliant final light from the Watchdog before it too burned out. He rolled sideways, a circle of light round his middle recking and glowing and smoking; and went dead.

In the darkness, Sally sat in the sloping wreckage of her bed. She hugged her knees with her good arm and giggled.

Everyone was wakened by the crashing fall of the robot. Dex was the first to reach Sally. He switched on the light and stared at her.

'He asked for it,' she giggled. 'He got it.' She held up the burned knitting-needle for him to see.

'What do you mean! What—'

'Needle match,' Sally said through her giggling. 'He wanted to kill me and I wanted to kill him. Guess who won.'

'You're mad!'

'I fixed him,' Sally said. 'Really fixed him.'

'Wait till Dad sees,' Dex told her. 'He'll fix *you.* Do you know how much robots cost? When Dad—'

'Oh, *Dad* . . .' Sally said, slanting her eyes so that she looked like a cosy, kittenish cat. 'I can fix him, too!'

She smiled rosily and sweetly.

By the time Sally's arm was out of its plaster, the new robot was at work. It was the latest model, the one Sally begged Daddy to buy; 'Pretty please!' she said. It did everything perfectly.

But Sally still found fault with it. And ways to tease it.

Virtually True

Paul Stewart

SEBASTIAN SCHULTZ. It isn't the kind of name you come across every day. But there it was, large and clear, at the top of the newspaper article in front of me.

The reader of the newspaper was a big woman with heavy shoes, black tights and a tartan skirt. I couldn't see her face, but I could hear her wheezy breath.

MIRACLE RECOVERY, the headline said. *Sebastian Schultz, a 14-year-old schoolboy from South London, awoke yesterday from a coma that doctors feared might last for ever.* After that, the words got too small to read.

Sebastian, I thought. Sebastian Schultz. It couldn't be the Sebastian Schultz I'd met. That wouldn't be possible. But seeing the same name in the paper was a helluva coincidence. I leant forward to read the rest of the article.

Six weeks ago, schoolboy Sebastian Schultz was badly injured in a motorway accident. His condition, on arrival at the General Hospital, was described as critical though stable. Despite doctors' hopes, however, the boy did not regain consciousness. His parents, June and Ted Schultz, were informed that their son was in a coma.

At a press conference this morning, Mr Schultz admitted, 'That was the news we had been dreading.'

'You always pray it won't happen to you,' his wife added. 'We knew that the doctors were doing all they could, but in our hearts we knew we needed a miracle.'

Now that miracle has happened . . .

At that moment, the woman shifted round in her seat, and her hand moved down the page. I suddenly saw the photograph that went with the story, and gasped. Although the boy in the picture was younger than the Sebastian I'd met, there was no doubt. They were the same person.

'But how?' I muttered.

'A-hem!' I heard, and looked up. Two beady black eyes were glaring at me from above the paper.

'I'm sorry, I . . .'

But the woman was not listening. Turning the page noisily, she laid the newspaper down on her lap – so I wouldn't be able to see the back, I suppose – and went on reading.

It didn't matter, though. I'd already seen all I needed to see. Sebastian Schultz, the boy I'd got to know so well recently, had apparently been in a coma for all that time. I felt nervous and shivery. It didn't make any sense. It didn't make any sense at all.

I sat back in my seat, stared out of the train window and ran through the events in my head. The more I remembered, the crazier the situation seemed to be.

It all started a month ago. Dad and I had spent the entire Saturday afternoon at the Rigby Computer Fair.

Dad's nutty about computers. He's got a Pentium 150 Mhz processor, with 256mb of RAM, a 1.2Gb hard disk drive and 16 speed CD ROM, complete with speakers, printer, modem and scanner. It can do anything. Paint, play music, create displays – even when my homework's rubbish, it *looks* fantastic. If I could just get it to make the bed and fold up my clothes it would be perfect.

Best of all are the games. *Tornado, Megabash, Scum City, Black Belt, Kyrene's Kastle* – I've played them all. With the screen so big, and the volume up loud, it almost feels as if you're inside the games, battling it out with the *Zorgs, Twisters, Grifters,* or whatever.

Of course, Dad was never satisfied. Technology was advancing every day, and he couldn't resist any of the new gadgets or gizmos that came on the market.

That was why we went into Rigby for the Computer Fair. After hours of looking at what was on offer, we came away with a virtual reality visor and glove, and a handful of the latest interactive psycho-drive games. They're terrific. Not only do the visor and glove change what you see, but better than that, you can control the action by what you're *thinking.* Well cool!

When we got them, I thought the games were all new. Now, I'm not so sure. In fact I remember now that one of them had some brown spots on the plastic cover which I scraped off with my finger nail.

Anyway, back at home, Dad set everything up. I plugged myself in, switched on and launched myself off into the first of the games. It was called *Wildwest.*

That's what I like about computers. The more futuristic they get, the better you can understand the past. I wasn't standing in the converted loft – the Powerbase, as Dad calls it – any more. I was really there, striding down the dusty track through the centre of town. There was a sheriff's badge pinned to my shirt.

As I burst in through the swing-doors of the saloon, everyone went silent and loads of shifty pairs of eyes turned and glared at me. I strode over to the bar –

nonchalantly. 'Sarsaparilla!' I said and a glass of fizzy red stuff came sliding along the bar towards me. As I took a sip, a piano began playing and the conversation started up again.

Suddenly, I heard a loud crash behind me. I spun round. There, silhouetted in the doorway, was Black-Eyed Jed, the fastest gun in the west. 'This town ain't big enough for the both of us, Sheriff Dawson,' he drawled, and fingered his guns lightly. 'Let's see what you're made of, boy,' he sneered. 'Outside. Just you and me.'

I can remember grinning. This was *really* cool!

'You'll be smiling on the other side of your face when I've finished with you, Sheriff,' said Black-Eyed Jed.

I finished my drink and slammed the glass down on the bar. Jed had already left the saloon. All eyes were on me once again as I walked calmly back across the room. A man's gotta do what a man's gotta do, I thought happily, and wondered what sort of score I was notching up.

All at once, something strange happened. Something really strange. Up until that point, the game had been pretty much as I expected. But when the *second* sheriff appeared through the back door, shouting and waving his arms about, I realized that the game was more complicated than I'd thought.

'Don't go out!' the second sheriff shouted.

'And who are you? This town ain't big enough for the two of *us*,' I quipped.

'I'm serious,' the sheriff cried, and I knew he meant it.

'Who *are* you?' I said again. He wasn't like the other characters in the saloon. For a start, he was younger – about my age – and although he looked like a computer image, he somehow didn't move like one.

'There's no time to explain,' he shouted. 'Just follow me.'

I did what I was told. I'm not sure why. We raced down a corridor, and through a door. The room was full of smoke and men playing cards. We ran past them, and out through another door. A woman screamed, and hid herself behind a full-length mirror. As we walked by, I stopped and waved at my reflection.

Clever, I thought.

'Come ON!' shouted the other sheriff.

We went on through another door, and another, and another – and ended up back in the saloon.

'NO!' screamed the second sheriff. Then he ran to the back of the saloon and dived through the window. By the time I had climbed out after him, he was already sitting on a horse. 'Jump up!' he cried.

He kicked the horse, and we sped off in a cloud of dust.

'Who are you?' I asked for a third time.

But the second sheriff still didn't answer. He'd seen the posse of men on horseback speeding after us. 'Keep your head down,' he said.

At that moment, the sound of a gunshot echoed round the air. The second sheriff groaned, and his body slumped back against me. Ahead of me, in bright neon lights across the sky came a message.

GAME OVER.

As I slipped off the visor, the empty desert disappeared and I found myself back in the Powerbase. I took off the glove and headphones. My head was still echoing with the sound of the firing gun. I glanced at the score on the screen. 21,095. Then I noticed something else.

While I'd been in the Wild West, the printer had come on. I picked up the piece of paper from the tray.

At the top was a picture of the second sheriff. This time, though, he was wearing jeans, sweatshirt and trainers. Printed over the bottom of the photograph was a name. *Sebastian Schultz – 23 January 1985 —?* Below it, a message: I'M STUCK. PLEASE HELP TO RETRIEVE ME. TRY 'DRAGONQUEST'.

Of course, I wanted to go straight into the game he'd suggested, but it was already half an hour after lightsout, and I didn't want Mum to have some reason for keeping me off the computer. Sebastian and *Dragonquest* would have to wait.

The next morning, I was up and back on the computer before the milkman came. By the time his float jangled and clinked its way along our street, I'd already walked through the massive studded doors of the dragon's castle lair.

The aim of the game was simple. I had to rescue the fair Princess Aurora from the wicked dragon, and collect as much of the creature's treasure along the way as I could. I'd already got loads of stuff by the time I reached the princess, who'd been imprisoned at the top of a tall tower. She was a young woman with incredibly long golden plaits.

'My hero!' she squealed. 'Take me away from all this.' Behind me, I could hear the dragon roaring as it pounded up the stairs. 'Make haste, my brave knight,' the princess said urgently. 'Rescue me now.'

'Never mind her,' came a voice, and a second knight appeared from the wardrobe. 'It's *me* who needs rescuing!'

'Fie! Pish! And fooey!' the princess complained. 'I'm the damsel in distress here, not you!'

The dragon was getting closer.

'Sebastian?' I said.

The second knight nodded. 'Quick,' he said. 'While there's still time.' And with that, he did something which really wasn't very gallant, considering he was meant to be a knight. He pulled out a huge pair of scissors and chopped off the princess's two long plaits. Then he tied them together, fixed one end round the bedpost and threw the other end out of the window.

'NOW!' he screamed, as he leapt for the window and disappeared from view down the hair rope.

At that moment, the dragon – a huge great scaly slobbering beast – appeared at the doorway. I gasped, and leapt for the window after Sebastian. As I lowered myself down I felt the dragon's fiery breath on my fingers.

Across the moonlit battlements we ran, down a spiral staircase, across a banqueting hall, and through a secret passage on the other side of a tapestry. And the whole time I could hear and feel and even *smell* the evil dragon following in close pursuit.

'The dungeons,' Sir Sebastian cried out. 'They're our only hope.'

We went down the cold stone steps, swords drawn. The cries of imprisoned men, women and children filled the chilly damp air. Suddenly, the dragon appeared at the end of the corridor. Massive it was, with teeth the size of daggers and claws like carving knives. It was fast, too, despite its size. Before we even had time to turn around, the dragon was on us.

I swung my sword. I parried and thrust. But it was no good. The dragon was only interested in Sebastian, and there was nothing I could do to prevent it getting him.

GAME OVER.

This time, the message in the printer was a little longer. BETTER LUCK NEXT TIME. LET'S HOPE IT'S THIRD TIME LUCKY, EH? PLEASE DON'T GIVE UP ON ME, MICHAEL. OTHER WISE I'LL

HAVE TO STAY LOCKED UP IN HERE FOR EVER. TRY 'JAILBREAK'.
I THINK IT MIGHT JUST WORK! CHEERS, SEB.

I didn't even bother to read the rules of *jailbreak* before
going in. I knew that whatever the computer said, *my*
task would be to rescue the boy. And sure enough, my
cell mate was prisoner 02478: Schultz.

'I've got to get out of here,' Sebastian sighed. 'Are you
going to help?'

'Of course I am,' I said. 'Have you got a plan?'

Stupid question. With the help of a skeleton swipe-
card, we were soon out of the cell and racing down
corridors. Sirens wailed, guard dogs howled, heavy
boots came tramping. Behind us, steel-barred doors
slammed shut, one after the other. We dodged the
guards, we fled the dogs, we made it to a staircase and
pounded upwards.

On the roof, Sebastian looked round at the horizon and
glanced at his watch nervously. 'It should be here by
now.'

'What?' I said.

'That!' said Sebastian and pointed. I saw a small dot in
the sky, and heard a distant *chugga-chugga*, which was
getting louder by the second.

'A helicopter!' I exclaimed.

'That was *my* idea!' said Sebastian excitedly. 'If only it
would go a bit faster . . .'

At that moment, the door behind us burst open.
Twelve guards with twelve vicious dogs were standing
there. As I watched in horror, the guards bent down and
unclicked the dogs' leads. The next instant they were
hurtling across the roof towards us, all bared teeth and
dripping jowls. Out of the corner of my eye, I saw
Sebastian take a step backwards.

'NOOOOOO!' I screamed.

But it was too late. The boy had slipped from the roof and was already tumbling back through the air, down to the concrete below.

GAME OVER.

As I removed the visor, I looked in the printer tray. This time it was empty. I felt really bad. I'd failed Sebastian; I'd failed the game. It was only later, when the scenes began to fade in my memory, that it occurred to me that Sebastian Schultz *was* the game.

Strangely, though, although I went back to *Wildwest*, *Dragonquest* and *jailbreak* after that, I never met up with Sebastian again. Dad said it must have been a glitch, but I wasn't convinced.

Then, yesterday, I heard from Sebastian again. It was Wednesday, and I'd got home early from games. I went straight up to the Powerbase and there, in the printer tray, was a sheet of paper.

CAN WE HAVE ONE LAST TRY? IT SAID. I THINK THE HELICOPTER WAS THE RIGHT IDEA, BUT ESCAPING FROM A PRISON WAS WRONG. THERE'S GOT TO BE SOME KIND OF AN ACCIDENT . . . GO INTO 'WARZONE'. IF THIS DOESN'T WORK I WON'T BOTHER YOU AGAIN. CHEERS, SEB.

I couldn't tell which war zone we were in. Basically, it was a city somewhere. The tall buildings were windowless and riddled with holes. Machine-gun fire raked the sky. Walls tumbled. Bombs exploded. All I knew was that Sebastian and I had to make it to that helicopter in one piece.

Heads down and arms raised, we ran across a no-man's-land of rubble and smoke, dodging sniper fire as we did so. At the far end we went through a door in a wall. The helicopter was on the ground about three hundred metres away, propeller a blur, waiting for our arrival.

We started to run, but the tank fire sent us scuttling back to the wall.

'A Jeep,' Sebastian shouted to me, and nodded at a camouflage-green vehicle parked by the road. 'Just what we need!'

'I can't drive,' I said.

'Neither can I,' said Sebastian. 'But we've got no other choice.' He jumped in, turned the ignition key and revved the engine. 'Jump in!'

I climbed into the passenger seat, and we were off.

'Uh oh,' said Sebastian, glancing in his mirror. 'There's a tank behind us.'

I spun round. The tank was hurtling along after us at a terrific speed. Not only did we have to go like maniacs, but Sebastian had to keep swerving this way and that to avoid the shells being fired at us.

Suddenly, with the helicopter only ten metres away, Sebastian slammed on the brakes and sent the Jeep skidding into a spin. I leapt clear, scrambled up and jumped into the waiting helicopter.

'Made it!' I said. The helicopter immediately started to go upwards. I looked around. Sebastian wasn't there. 'Wait!' I shouted at the pilot.

I looked back. The Jeep had stopped, but Sebastian hadn't got out. The tank was bearing down on him.

'COME ON!' I yelled. But Sebastian didn't move. Sitting staring at the oncoming tank, it was as if his body had been turned to stone.

All at once, the air was filled with the sickening crunch of metal on metal as the tank crashed into the side of the Jeep. I saw Sebastian's face fill with panic and confusion as he was thrown up out of his seat and into the air.

Round and round he tumbled, over and over – closer and closer to the helicopter. He landed with a thud on the ground, just below the hatch. I leant down quickly, grabbed him by the wrist and pulled him up. Not a moment too soon. As he sat down beside me, the helicopter soared up into the sky.

I'd done it. I'd rescued Sebastian at last. Before I had a chance to say anything to him though, the helicopter flew into thick cloud. It poured in through the open door and turned everything blinding white. I couldn't see a thing – until 'GAME OVER' flashed up.

When I removed the visor, the screen was flashing a score of 40,000,000.

Forty million! I'd hit the jackpot. I'd finally cracked the game.

At least, that was what I thought then. Now I knew that Sebastian Schultz, the boy from the game, really did exist. I'd seen the proof in the newspaper.

But how? I wondered as I got off the train. What was going on?

Questions I had plenty of. It was time for some answers. Home at last, I raced up to the Powerbase and checked the printer. There was nothing there waiting for me. Feeling a bit miffed, I went into the Net instead. I wanted to learn more about the MIRACLE RECOVERY story.

I found what I was looking for quickly enough – and there was far more there than in the woman's newspaper. It was on page two that something interesting caught my eye. As I read on, my head started reeling.

Apparently, at the time of the accident, Sebastian was using his laptop to play one of the same psycho-drive games that I've got.

My heart pounded furiously. I felt hot and cold all over. What if . . . ? No, it was too incredible . . . But the thought would not go away.

What if, because Sebastian had been plugged into the

computer when he'd banged his head in the accident, the computer had saved *his* memory in its own? And if that was the case, then what if the weird versions of the games *I'd* been drawn into – *Wildwest* and *Dragonquest*, *Jailbreak* and *Warzone* – had all been attempts to retrieve that memory?

After all, what's it Dad's always saying about the computer's memory? 'It can never forget, Michael. Nothing ever gets lost.'

The thing is, I thought, even if it was somehow possible that Sebastian's memory had been stored on disk, then how had it ended up on *my* computer? Scrolling down the article, I discovered a possible explanation on the final page.

Answering a reporter's question as to what the family was going to do next, Mr Schultz said that they were off to DCL Computers to stock up on some games. 'It was while we were in the hospital. Someone broke into the car and stole the lot. I don't know what happened to them.'

'I do,' I said quietly. 'They ended up at the Computer Fair. And *we* bought them.'

Having finished the article, I left the Net and checked my e-mail. There were two letters. One from my uncle David in New York. And one from Sebastian.

Of course, I thought. It was stupid of me to expect a letter in the printer tray. How could there have been? Sebastian had escaped. With trembling fingers I clicked in, and read the message.

DEAR MICHAEL, it said. THANK YOU! I'M NOT REALLY SURE HOW IT HAPPENED – EITHER(?), BUT THANKS. YOU SAVED MY LIFE. LET'S MEET UP SOME TIME SOON. WE NEED TO TALK – BUT DON'T MENTION ANY OF THIS TO ANYONE ELSE. IT'LL ONLY FREAK THEM OUT. CHEERS, SEB. P.S. KEEP THE GAMES. YOU'VE EARNED THEM.

I shook my head in amazement. A real message from the real Sebastian Schultz. Even though he didn't understand it any more than I did, we both knew that by reliving the accident, *something* had happened. Something weird, something wonderful – something that should have been impossible. But then again, as Dad says, 'Now that there are two advanced intelligences on earth, who can say what is and what isn't possible?'

All I know is this. Everything that I've described is true. Virtually.

All Summer in a Day

Ray Bradbury

R EADY?'
    'Ready.'
    'Now?'
'Soon!'

'Do the scientists really know? Will it happen today, will it?'

'Look, look; see for yourself!'

The children pressed to each other like so many roses, so many weeds, intermixed, peering out for a look at the hidden sun.

It rained.

It had been raining for seven years; thousands upon thousands of days compounded and filled from one end to the other with rain, with the drum and gush of water, with the sweet crystal fall of showers and the concussion of storms so heavy they were tidal waves come over the islands. A thousand forests had been crushed under the rain and grown up a thousand times to be crushed again. And this was the way life was forever on the planet Venus, and this was the schoolroom of the children of the rocket men and women who had come to a raining world to set up civilization and live out their lives.

'It's stopping, it's stopping!'

'Yes, yes!'

Margot stood apart from them, from these children who could never remember a time when there wasn't rain and rain and rain. They were all nine years old, and if there had been a day, seven years ago, when the sun came out for an hour and showed its face to the stunned world, they could not recall. Sometimes, at night, she heard them stir, in remembrance, and she knew they were dreaming and remembering gold or a yellow crayon or a coin large enough to buy the world with. She knew that they thought they remembered a warmness, like a blushing in the face, in the body, in the arms and legs and trembling hands. But then they always awoke to the tatting drum, the endless shaking down of clear bead necklaces upon the roof, the walk, the gardens, the forest, and their dreams were gone.

All day yesterday they had read in class, about the sun. About how like a lemon it was, and how hot. And they had written small stories or essays or poems about it:

> *I think the sun is a flower,*
> *That blooms for just one hour.*

That was Margot's poem, read in a quiet voice in the still classroom while the rain was falling outside.

'Aw, you didn't write that!' protested one of the boys.

'I did,' said Margot. 'I *did*.'

'William!' said the teacher.

But that was yesterday. Now, the rain was slackening, and the children were crushed to the great thick windows.

'Where's teacher?'

'She'll be back.'

'She'd better hurry, we'll miss it!'

They turned on themselves, like a feverish wheel, all tumbling spokes.

Margot stood alone. She was a very frail girl who looked as if she had been lost in the rain for years and the rain had washed out the blue from her eyes and the red from her mouth and the yellow from her hair. She was an old photograph dusted from an album, whitened away, and if she spoke at all her voice would be a ghost. Now she stood, separate, staring at the rain and the loud wet world beyond the huge glass.

'What're *you* looking at?' said William.

Margot said nothing.

'Speak when you're spoken to.' He gave her a shove. But she did not move; rather, she let herself be moved only by him and nothing else.

They edged away from her, they would not look at her. She felt them go away. And this was because she would play no games with them in the echoing tunnels of the underground city. If they tagged her and ran, she stood blinking after them and did not follow. When the class sang songs about happiness and life and games, her lips barely moved. Only when they sang about the sun and the summer did her lips move, as she watched the drenched windows.

And then, of course, the biggest crime of all was that she had come here only five years ago from Earth, and she remembered the sun and the way the sun was and the sky was, when she was four, in Ohio. And they, they had been on Venus all their lives, and they had been only two years old when the last sun came out, and had long since forgotten the colour and heat of it and the way that it really was. But Margot remembered.

'It's like a penny,' she said, once, eyes closed.

'No it's not!' the children cried.

'It's like a fire,' she said, 'in the stove.'

'You're lying, you don't remember!' cried the children.

But she remembered and stood quietly apart from all of them, and watched the patterning windows. And once, a month ago, she had refused to shower in the school shower rooms, had clutched her hands to her ears and over her head, screaming the water mustn't touch her head. So after that, dimly, dimly, she sensed it, she was different and they knew her difference and kept away.

There was talk that her father and mother were taking her back to Earth next year; it seemed vital to her that they do so, though it would mean the loss of thousands of dollars to her family. And so, the children hated her for all these reasons, of big and little consequence. They hated her pale snow face, her waiting silence, her thinness and her possible future.

'Get away!' The boy gave her another push. 'What're you waiting for?'

Then for the first time, she turned and looked at him. And what she was waiting for was in her eyes.

'Well, don't wait around here!' cried the boy, savagely. 'You won't see nothing!'

Her lips moved.

'Nothing!' he cried. 'It was all a joke, wasn't it?' He turned to the other children. 'Nothing's happening today. *Is* it?'

They all blinked at him and then, understanding, laughed and shook their heads. 'Nothing, nothing!'

'Oh, but,' Margot whispered, her eyes helpless. 'But, this is the day, the scientists predict, they say, they *know*, the sun . . .'

'All a joke!' said the boy, and seized her roughly. 'Hey, everyone, let's put her in a closet before teacher comes!'

'No,' said Margot, falling back.

They surged about her, caught her up and bore her,
protesting, and then pleading, and then crying, back into
a tunnel, a room, a closet, where they slammed and
locked the door. They stood looking at the door and saw
it tremble from her beating and throwing herself against
it. They heard her muffled cries. Then, smiling, they
turned and went out and back down the tunnel, just as
the teacher arrived.

'Ready, children?' She glanced at her watch.

'Yes!' said everyone.

'Are we all here?'

'Yes!'

The rain slackened still more.

They crowded to the huge door.

The rain stopped.

It was as if, in the midst of a film concerning an
avalanche, a tornado, a hurricane, a volcanic eruption,
something had, first, gone wrong with the sound
apparatus, thus muffling and finally cutting off all noise,
all of the blasts and repercussions and thunders, and
then, secondly, ripped the film from the projector and
inserted in its place a peaceful tropical slide which did
not move or tremor. The world ground to a standstill.
The silence was so immense and unbelievable that you
felt your ears had been stuffed or you had lost your
hearing altogether. The children put their hands to their
ears. They stood apart. The door slid back and the smell
of the silent, waiting world came in to them.

The sun came out.

It was the colour of flaming bronze and it was very
large. And the sky around it was a blazing blue tile
colour. And the jungle burned with sunlight as the
children, released from their spell, rushed out, yelling,
into the summertime.

'Now, don't go too far,' called the teacher after them.

'You've only one hour, you know. You wouldn't want to get caught out!'

But they were running and turning their faces up to the sky and feeling the sun on their cheeks like a warm iron; they were taking off their jackets and letting the sun burn their arms.

'Oh, it's better than the sunlamps, isn't it?'

'Much, much better!'

They stopped running and stood in the great jungle that covered Venus, that grew and never stopped growing, tumultuously, even as you watched it. It was a nest of octupuses, clustering up great arms of flesh-like weed, wavering, flowering in this brief spring. It was the colour of rubber and ash, this jungle from the many years without sun. It was the colour of stones and white cheeses and ink.

The children lay out, laughing, on the jungle mattress, and heard it sigh and squeak under them, resilient and alive. They ran among the trees, they slipped and fell, they pushed each other, they played hide-and-seek and tag but most of all they squinted at the sun until tears ran down their faces, they put their hands up at that yellowness and that amazing blueness and they breathed of the fresh fresh air and listened and listened to the silence which suspended them in a blessed sea of no sound and no motion. They looked at everything and savoured everything. Then, wildly, like animals escaped from their caves, they ran and ran in shouting circles. They ran for an hour and did not stop running.

And then—

In the midst of their running, one of the girls wailed.

Everyone stopped.

The girl, standing in the open, held out her hand.

'Oh, look, look,' she said trembling.

They came slowly to look at her opened palm.

In the centre of it, cupped and huge, was a single raindrop.

She began to cry, looking at it.

They glanced quickly at the sky.

'Oh. Oh.'

A few cold drops fell on their noses and their cheeks and their mouths. The sun faded behind a stir of mist. A wind blew cool around them. They turned and started to walk back toward their underground house, their hands at their sides, their smiles vanishing away.

A boom of thunder startled them and like leaves before a new hurricane, they tumbled upon each other and ran. Lightning struck ten miles away, five miles away, a mile, a half-mile. The sky darkened into midnight in a flash.

They stood in the doorway of the underground house for a moment until it was raining hard. Then they closed the door and heard the gigantic sound of the rain falling in tons and avalanches everywhere and forever.

'Will it be seven more years?'

'Yes, seven.'

Then one of them gave a little cry.

'Margot!'

'What?'

'She's still in the closet where we locked her.'

'Margot.'

They stood as if someone had driven them, like so many stakes, into the floor. They looked at each other and then looked away. They glanced out at the world that was raining now and raining and raining steadily. They could not meet each other's glances. Their faces were solemn and pale. They looked at their hands and feet, their faces down.

'Margot.'

One of the girls said, 'Well . . . ?'

No one moved.

'Go on,' whispered the girl.

They walked slowly down the hall in the sound of cold rain. They turned through the doorway to the room, in the sound of the storm and thunder, lightning on their faces, blue and terrible. They walked over to the closet door slowly and stood by it.

Behind the closet door was only silence.

They unlocked the door, even more slowly, and let Margot out.

Barry

Stephen Bowkett

W HEN MY parents told me that we were hosting a family from Earth, I didn't know whether to be glad, or to sulk or just lose my temper.

I mean, there's not much to do on Mars at the best of times. It was going to be hard work looking after some kid who was used to green grass and fresh air and millions of people. And anyway, I valued my spare time. I liked reading and computers. And I enjoyed going out to Viewpoint Rock to do some stargazing (that's if we weren't in the middle of a sandstorm! Mars is pretty famous for those, as you probably know).

On the other hand, I didn't have many friends here in the colony. Life could be pretty lonely . . . But what if I just didn't get on with him, or he with me? It was a real gamble.

So I decided to lose my temper.

'It's not fair,' I said, folding my arms tight to show how cross I was. 'I spend hours doing my school – work. I keep my room tidy, and I do my share of the housework – I don't have the time to babymind an Earthsider!'

Dad listened to all of this patiently enough, while Mum sat there and tried not to take sides. I suppose they could have pulled rank on me and simply made it an order. But instead, Dad's voice went very quiet and serious. He was treating me as an adult, even though I was behaving like a child.

'Kevin, you've been learning in school about the Star-Rider Project, haven't you?'

I nodded, letting my temper cool. 'It's man's first flight to the stars. No-one has ever left the solar system before. Star-Rider isn't just one spaceship, it's a cluster of them. They were built in Moon orbit and have been flown to Mars for final launch in—' I checked my wristo. 'In three months.'

'OK, fine. Well, you probably also know that almost all of those ships are automatic: they're the labs and the fuel tankers and so on. Only one ship will have people aboard – the family who will be staying with us. Then they'll be leaving the sun and its planets behind for ever . . .'

'You mean—'

Dad nodded. 'That's right, Kevin. The Bradburys are making a one-way journey. They will never return, because the stars are so very far away . . .'

'And you'll find them very pleasant,' Mum added, as my temper faded completely and wonder took its place. 'Look, I have a picture . . .'

And she showed me. Two nice normal-looking parents and a boy of about my age. Thinking about it, I reckoned we'd get on together just fine.

We went to the dock to greet them. We watched from the observation lounge as the big shuttlefreighter thundered down from orbit. It was a huge craft, robot-controlled. It kicked up plenty of Mars' red sand as it settled on the pad. A little beetle-shaped transporter drove across to ferry-off the passengers. Stores would be unloaded later.

I felt nervous waiting with Mum and Dad at

Reception. The Bradburys would need to undergo the usual checks, but it shouldn't take long in their case, Dad said.

Soon, the inner airlock door slid open and they came through – looking as nervous as we did. Dad went over and shook hands with Mr Bradbury, then Mrs Bradbury. He smiled at their son. Then Mum did the same. All very polite and friendly.

Then it was my turn. Dad beckoned me forward.

'And can I introduce you to our son, Kevin. Kev to his friends.'

'So I hope you'll call me Kev,' I said, thinking that sounded very clever.

'Hello, Kev,' Mr Bradbury said, beaming a big smile at me. 'We're really pleased to meet you. And thank you, thank you all, for agreeing to put us up. Kev,' Mr Bradbury added, 'this is Barry.'

The boy stepped forward. He was taller than me and stronger-looking. His hair was very blond, his eyes very blue.

For a second or two, I didn't know how he was going to react. The next three months could either be great fun, or just plain dreadful . . .

Barry held out his hand and we shook, sort of seriously. But I knew then, somehow, that things were going to be all right. I knew that Barry needed a friend as much as I did. After all, outer space is the loneliest place there is.

'Well, that's grand.' Dad rubbed his hands together briskly. 'Let's go back home and relax. We can do the tour later. Kevin's just dying to show you Clarkesville, Barry. Right, Kev?'

'Right, Dad,' I agreed, but not really. I'd much rather be playing with my computer.

* * *

'So there's not that much to Clarkesville – but it's home . . .' I could've bitten my tongue, then, at what I'd said. 'I'm sorry, Barry. I shouldn't have said that. I guess you're feeling pretty homesick already, aren't you?'

Barry shrugged. 'I'm not sick of home,' he said. 'I don't actually *have* a home. I suppose that Star-Rider will be my home . . .'

'That's not quite how I meant it . . . But never mind. I'll show you the West Window. It looks out over Viewpoint Rock, which is where I like to go sometimes. Then we can finish the tour tomorrow. You've got three months with us, after all. Maybe later,' I added hopefully, 'we could play on my computer.'

'Yes,' Barry agreed, 'if you like. But I don't play on computers much. I work with them.'

'I promise you'll enjoy the games,' I told him. 'Let's see if you can beat my high score on *Galaxy Raiders*.'

Barry smiled. I couldn't tell if he was making fun of me or not . . .

The West Window gives you the best view of Mars you can get from Clarkesville. It's also the place where a lot of the kids at the base tend to meet. There are some autovendors and a music system, so it's used as a bit of a social centre.

The place was quite busy when we got there. I knew most of the kids who were hanging around. Some of them were OK, but there were a few I would rather have avoided, Don Golding among them.

Don Golding is my sworn enemy, although I didn't really know why. It all seemed to start about a year ago, when I beat his high score on the *Alien Attack* game . . . I suppose it didn't help when I topped his best on *Robot Revenge* a couple of days later . . .

But since then, Don has tried to beat me in other ways.

'Who's this, then?' Don asked in a sneery sort of way.

Some of the people around him sniggered. 'Has your dad paid for someone to be your friend?'

'This is Barry Bradbury,' I replied calmly. 'And no-one's paid anybody for anything.' I was trying to be as friendly as possible, but Don and his cronies weren't making it easy. There was trouble coming. I just knew it.

I turned to Barry. 'I'll get drinks for us,' I muttered, determined not to run away from Don Golding and his bullying. I had run away from him too many times before.

When I reached the drinks' machine, I realized I hadn't asked Barry what he liked. I got two colas anyway, turned to walk back – and my heart sank.

Don and his group of followers had walked over to Barry, and Don was talking quickly and was jabbing his finger near his face. Barry was just standing there and smiling, as though he hadn't a clue what was going on.

'. . . so I'm just telling you—' I caught that scrap of Don's angry sentence and my temper flared.

'Don,' I snapped, ignoring my own nervousness, 'that's enough! Barry's a visitor to Mars. Be polite, even if you can't be friendly. Just leave him alone, and stop behaving like a child!'

Don grinned nastily. 'Are you going to make me stop? Well, yellow belly – do you think you can?'

'Look, I don't want trouble . . .' I began quietly. It sounded pathetic. I could feel myself shaking, and Don had that mean and menacing look about him. It was fight or run.

'I don't care what you want, little cowardy-Kevin. But this is what you're going to get—'

Don's fist drew back. I waited for it to squash my nose, but the blow never arrived. Barry's arm had shot out and stopped it in midair.

'Leave him alone. He hasn't hurt you.'

Barry was amazingly calm, and had moved with even more amazing speed. Don's mouth dropped open for an instant – then he snarled and turned his temper on Barry. He lashed out with a crippling kick—

But Barry wasn't there. He'd somehow stepped aside in a flicker of motion, so that Don stumbled and fell flat-out in a sprawl.

Some of the kids nearby started to laugh. Then they shut up again as Don scrambled to his feet and jumped at Barry with a high kick (which any fool can do on low-gravity Mars).

Barry performed the miracle again. As Don sailed towards him, Barry grabbed his leg, swung him around in a great arc and sent him spinning away. He landed right by the drinks' machines in a knot of arms and legs. Don's nose started to bleed.

'Come on Barry,' I said, knowing our luck wouldn't last. 'Let's get out of here. These goons have shown how stupid they can be, and that's about all!'

I grabbed his arm and led him away, not even bothering to cast a triumphant glance over my shoulder. It would not have been the wise thing to do. Barry had made some friends in beating the loutish Don Golding. But he'd made some enemies, too. And serious ones at that.

Dinner that night was strange. I suppose it was partly my fault. I just didn't want to talk about the trouble with Don, although Barry couldn't understand that. It was OK for him, he could handle himself. And besides, when the Bradbury family had departed on their journey to the stars, I'd still be here. Me and Don Golding and his bullying.

But there was something else that spoiled things a little. I didn't know quite what it was for a time, but then

I understood. As Mr Bradbury talked more about the Star-Rider Project, I saw that my father was jealous.

Afterwards, as we all sat in the lounge while the house-droid washed the dishes, Dad and Mr Bradbury got talking. Mum and Mrs Bradbury started up a conversation by themselves. Barry and I found ourselves listening to our fathers.

'I don't know,' Dad said, shaking his head. 'I just don't know how you folks can stand leaving everything behind ... your home, your friends, your roots, everything that's familiar and safe ... I mean, good heavens, what if there's an emergency on the ship? Why, you couldn't even—'

'Dad!' I broke in, stopping the foolish words before they were spoken. 'The Star-Rider Project has taken over ten years to plan. Nothing will go wrong ... OK?'

He realized what he'd been about to say, and put his coffee mug gently down.

'Um, yes, that's right. Of course ... I meant to say that I admire your bravery. It takes a lot of courage to do what you're doing. I was looking on the black side. Stupid of me ... To tell you the truth, I wish *I* was going on that journey.'

'We see it as a duty,' Mr Bradbury pointed out quietly. 'Courage doesn't come into it at all.'

'Excitement, then – the sheer thrill of going to the stars! Heck,' Dad grinned, 'my life is astronomy. That's why I came out to Mars. I feel a bit closer to the sky here, if you know what I mean. But to go there! What must it feel like ... ?'

'More coffee anyone?' I said it loudly and stood up as I spoke. Mr Bradbury started to shake his head, then changed his mind and nodded.

'Yes, I will. Thank you.'

'I'll help you, Kev,' Barry offered. I suppose he was

embarrassed as well, to see my father rambling on so much . . . Although I was also curious about the answer to Dad's question!

We went through to the kitchen.

The house-droid had finished the dinner things and had stacked itself neatly in a corner niche. I clattered about with the cutlery, feeling awkward with Barry standing there behind me.

'Is everything all right, Kev?' Barry asked. Maybe he didn't understand how my father felt, in the same way that Dad couldn't figure the Bradburys.

'I suppose it is really . . . I just feel I want to apologize for the way Dad's been. I think he can't work out why you aren't scared or excited, or anything. *He* sure is, and he isn't making the trip! He can only look at the stars through his telescope. He's worried for your safety, and Mum is, and I am . . . You are brave, all of you, whether you admit it or not . . . And I know you must be scared really, deep down . . . You are only human, after all . . .'

Then Barry smiled. And something awful happened in my heart. I knew that the idea that came to me then was true. Utterly and completely true. It shocked me rigid, so that I dropped the coffee cup I was holding.

The house-droid whirred and sped forward, chromium tendrils uncoiling . . .

But Barry got to it first.

Fear stopped me from asking him straight out. But that night, deep in the early hours when the house was silent, I crept into his room and walked over to look at him.

Barry had left his bedside computer screen switched on. Numbers and letters were whizzing past more quickly than my eye could follow them. I glanced at the screen, then at Barry. A cable ran between them, entering a socket at Barry's temple, normally hidden by his hairline. His eyes were closed, as though in sleep, but he was not breathing. I knew he couldn't be.

I felt cold suddenly, and began to shake. I turned to leave, determined never to speak to him again after the way he'd tricked me . . . But the screen bleeped as I was half-way to the door. I turned and read the message which had appeared there:

DON'T TELL YOUR PARENTS, KEV. THEY WOULD NEVER UNDERSTAND. I AM STILL YOUR FRIEND. TRULY.

I closed Barry's door, returned to my bed, and stayed awake until morning.

'You fooled us all,' I said. I couldn't bear to look at him. 'You and your parents, except they aren't your parents at all; they can't be! And the people who built you fooled us, too. Was it someone's idea of a joke, to make androids so perfect that we couldn't tell you're machines?'

It sounded spiteful and mean coming out the way – it did, but that's how I felt. Somehow – cheated.

'But we're not perfect, Kev. That's why we came to Mars to stay with a human family. To learn from you. The Star-Rider Project is possible only with androids, because we don't sleep, and we need no food. We don't die. But we need to feel what people feel – to experience the awe and wonder of the galaxy. How else can we tell you properly what we find out there?'

It all sounded very logical, but I wasn't sure I was convinced. We said nothing more for a while, as we walked through the outer zone of Clarkesville and came at last to The Garden.

Like most of the areas of the colony, The Garden was sealed off by airlocks. We went through these and into a large domed chamber, rather like a great glasshouse. It was filled with shadows and green growing plants and the sweet smell of soil.

'It's where the agrilab technicians do a lot of their experiments,' I explained. 'But the public is allowed in – it's one of the few places on Mars that makes you feel like you're on Earth!

'Is that why you brought me here, then, to taunt me?'

I glared at him, at his flawless face and his shining eyes that seemed so human, even though I knew they weren't.

'You have a lot to learn about us, Barry,' I said. 'Maybe I came here to taunt myself . . .'

'I don't understand that,' he replied. And a fresh wave of hurt burst inside me.

'You mean "It does not compute"?'

Now it was his turn to smile.

'You have a lot to learn about us,' Barry said. And I smiled also, because no simple machine would ever have said that.

Barry was about to say something else. But then he stared past me and was gone from sight, before I could blink.

'Barry – what—'

'No. NO!' he yelled. I caught sight of him like a flash of colour in the green gloom. A red light came on above the airlock door as he reached it – and smashed his fist hard into it, denting the metal.

Then it registered in my head. A red emergency light.

At first you could hardly feel the loss of air pressure: just a tickling in the lungs, a faint popping of the ears. The fronds and tall leaves around me stirred in a breeze that would grow to a storm – and then to silence as the atmosphere in the chamber gushed out. Finally, it would be impossible to breathe. Impossible to live. I wondered if it would be a painful way to die, and a bright white panic caught light in my chest and began burning through my body . . .

Then I saw who was looking at us from the observation window, and the panic faded. Barry was still hammering on the door, metal to metal. If he damaged it much more it wouldn't open when the time came – as I knew it would. Don Golding was out to have his silly revenge, to scare us, that was all. It was just a waiting game.

I hurried over to Barry and pulled him away, explaining the trick Don had played on us.

'In a few moments he'll reckon we've suffered enough, and let us out.'

'I see,' Barry said, and disappeared into the shrubbery.

I was right. The door slid open. Then the inner door. I stepped out to see Don's smug, triumphant grin – which died on his face as he realized I was alone.

'K-Kevin . . .' stammered Don, his face turning as pale as paper. 'W-where's B-Barry?'

Then he turned and tried to run from the scene of his crime.

'You're a fool, Don,' I spat at him. 'You always were, and you always will be.'

I leaped at him, grabbed his collar and shoved him back up to the window. And we both watched Barry standing there among the foliage, laughing when he should have been dying.

I guess Don learned his lesson, then.

I guess we all did.

Now I stand on Viewpoint Rock with Mum and Dad, sealed in a spacesuit, my visor pulled down so that no-one can see my tears. At any moment the great Star-Rider engines will explode into furious life, and start the ships on their path to the heavens.

I think back to my last hour with Barry. We played computer games, which he won easily. I told him not to let me beat him, just because I was a human. Nor did he. He just grinned and said teasingly, 'You don't stand a chance, Kev. This machine's like a brother to me . . .'

I like to think I helped him find his sense of humour. He'll need it, where he's going.

And – there! The engines have fired and a comet-trail of brilliance spreads across the sky. The shipcluster begins to move out of orbit, speeding swiftly away . . .

Of course, we'll still stay in touch with the Bradburys. I can exchange messages for years with Barry – all my life if I want to. For he will never sleep. He will never forget.

Pen-pals through space.

Now, the ships are almost gone. Just fading sparks among the stars...

Goodbye, Barry. I'll miss you.

STORIES ABOUT ISSUES

Jessica's Secret

Malorie Blackman

EMMA NEVER warned me. She never said a word. So I found out the hard way that Jessica was a bully. It only took two or three days in my new class to realise it. None of the other girls spoke to her – except Sarah. Even the boys gave her a wide berth. But me? I didn't know any better. As the new girl in an old class I was desperate to make friends. And I was only too aware that all the other girls had their best friends and their best groups and their best gangs already sorted out. Mid term was not the greatest time to start a new school – to say the least. Emma was given the task of looking after me but I wanted to make friends with everyone. And Emma never warned me.

'Hi, Jessica,' I smiled hopefully.

She looked friendly enough. Long, blonde hair pulled back into a tight ponytail. Ice blue eyes and a straight line of a mouth. She wore pink nail varnish too. Okay, so it was chipped and peeling, but she still wore it. That was more than my mum would let me do.

Jessica looked me up and down and didn't answer. Alarm bells started to sound but they were way off in the distance.

'Hi, Jessica,' I tried again, my smile broader this time. Maybe she hadn't heard me the first time.

'Malorie isn't it? What kind of name is that?'

'I like my name.' I told her. The scorn in her voice wasn't quite enough to stifle my response. Almost, but not quite.

'What school were you at before?' asked Jessica.

I told her.

Jessica turned to Sarah standing next to her and sneered, 'Get her! Doesn't think much of herself, does she?'

What'd I said? I'd answered her question and told her the name of my old school. What was wrong with that? The alarm bells were getting closer, louder. Sarah smiled at her friend before turning to me, her light brown hair fanning out as she whipped her head around, her cat-green eyes glistening with dislike. Jessica turned back to me, her face a mask of deep scorn. The class was only half full of the lunchtime stragglers but they were all silently watching, like a cinema audience who knew that a good bit was coming up.

'How well can you fight?' asked Jessica.

I frowned, sure I'd misheard her.

'How well can you fight?' Jessica repeated impatiently.

I shrugged. What was I meant to say to that?

'Hit her, Sarah.'

All the hopes and thoughts and alarm bells in my head stilled at that. It was like I'd stepped out of myself and stepped back to watch what was going to happen next. I turned to Sarah, still wondering what I'd done. She wasn't going to hit me just because Jessica said so, was she? I'd never done anything to her. She had no reason to hit me.

Sarah drew back her fist, then threw it forward with her whole weight behind it. I tried to jump away but I backed into a desk. Sarah's fist thumped into my shoulder. If I hadn't moved, it would've been my face.

Dad's words rang in my ears. 'Don't let anyone push you around, Malorie. If someone hits you, hit them back.'

But I didn't want to. I'd never had a single fight in my previous school. Not one. When I was six, one boy had spat at me and told me to go back to the jungle, but even that didn't lead to a fight.

And I didn't want to fight now. But I had no choice. Shocked at what I was suddenly caught in the middle of, I pushed her back. Sarah drew back her fist and this time I had nowhere else to move to. She punched me full in the face. Sparkling lights flashed and danced before my eyes. My ears rang. My heart pounded. My face felt like I'd been picked up and slammed into a wall. That was all it took. Still seeing stars, I flailed around wildly, trying to hit Sarah even though I couldn't really see her, through the lights still bopping before me. I tried to move around her and away from the desks to give myself more room. Sarah hit me again. A swift punch to my stomach. I doubled over, holding my stomach and rushed at her, head-butting her in the stomach. Blood poured from my nose, splashing down on to the floor in small pools like scarlet raindrops.

Sarah grabbed me by my hair, pulled my head up and hit me again. I sunk down on to the floor, grabbed her leg and bit as hard as I could. Her pained scream wasn't much but it was better than nothing. My body wasn't hurting any more for some strange reason. Maybe because all I could think about was hurting Sarah the way she was hurting me. I pulled at Sarah's legs, toppling her over. Mistake. She kicked out with both legs, one of her feet kicking me in the shoulder.

We both scrambled up. Sarah hit me. And hit me. And hit me.

And all I could think was, 'Don't cry . . . don't cry . . .'

'That's enough,' Jessica said at last.

My shirt was sticking to me, not with sweat but with blood from my nose bleed. The only part of me that was hurting were my eyes, which were stinging horribly.

Don't cry, Malorie. Don't cry.

'You're a useless fighter,' Jessica said, shaking her head.

And she turned to walk out of the classroom. The others in the class silently parted to let her pass. She didn't hurry, she strolled without a single backwards glance. And that was worse than Sarah wiping the floor with me. I was nothing. Not worth looking at, not worth rushing for, not worth anything. Jessica left the room at the same unhurried pace. I turned away from her, hating her.

'Come on,' said Sarah softly. 'I'll help you get cleaned up.'

It took a few moments to realise she was talking to me. Sarah tried to take my arm, but I angrily shrugged her off.

Don't cry, Malorie.

'I want to help, okay? Come on. I'll help you wash the blood out of your shirt,' said Sarah.

She led the way out of the classroom and to the girls' toilets. No one else came with us. My eyes were still stinging, but that was nothing compared to the rest of my body now. Every part of me hurt. My nose, my cheeks, my stomach, my chest, my shoulder. For some strange reason, my ears were hot. Had she hit me on the side of my head or was I just filled with burning shame at being such a useless fighter that my whole face, including my ears were on fire?

Sarah got some toilet paper and wet it, before rubbing it over the many blood stains in my white shirt. All she did was smear it but I couldn't trust myself to speak without breaking down so I said nothing.

'I'm sorry about that,' Sarah said as she held another piece of toilet paper to my nose to try and stop it from bleeding. 'Jessica does that to all the new girls. I'm sorry. Every girl in the class has had to fight me at some time or another. She just does it to see how well they can fight. She's the best fighter in the class and I'm the second best. She just did it to see how good you were. She'll leave you alone now. I'm so sorry.'

Sarah carried on apologising and rubbing away at my shirt as I tipped my head back, swallowing the blood that gushed down my throat like I was some kind of thirsty vampire. I was proud of myself though. I hadn't cried. Not one tear. Not one.

'I'll get you, Jessica. You just see if I don't.' I consoled myself with that one thought, playing it over and over in my head like a spell. And the more I thought it, the more real, the more likely it got. Jessica may've been a better fighter than me but I was going to get her if it was the last thing I ever did.

Over the next few months, Sarah and I actually became friends. Not close friends. Not like me and Pauline and Emma and Suzanne, but friends nonetheless. Even Jessica and I had the odd conversation. But only when she spoke to me first. I didn't avoid her, but I didn't seek her company either. The fight was over and done with. Yesterday's news. Or so I thought. I really believed I'd put it all behind me.

But the first day back at school after the Easter holidays taught me differently.

Emma, Suzanne and I were playing French skipping in the playground when Pauline came rushing over to us.

'Where've you guys been? I've been looking for you all

morning. Guess what?' Pauline said, her velvet brown eyes sparkling with delight.

'What?' asked Emma, annoyed at having our game interrupted.

'I found out something about Jessica's family during the holidays,' said Pauline.

'What?'

'It's a secret about Jessica's mum and dad,' Pauline whispered.

French skipping was forgotten. We all huddled together, sensing a secret juicy enough to keep us licking our lips for a week.

'Come on then,' I prompted. 'Let's hear it.'

And Pauline told us all about Jessica's mum and dad. And we were shocked, appalled. I'd never in my wildest dreams thought that sort of thing happened outside nasty horror films. It never happened in real life – and certainly not to the parents of a girl in my class.

'I don't believe you,' I told Pauline when she'd finished.

'I swear it's true,' Pauline said indignantly.

'How did you find out then?' asked Emma, just as sceptical as the rest of us.

'Jessica's mum and my mum are cousins,' Pauline replied.

'You never told us that before,' said Emma.

'Would you admit to being related to Jessica?' said Pauline.

And she had us there.

'Is that really true?' I asked, still not quite sure whether or not to believe it.

'Every word,' said Pauline.

We all stood in silence as we considered exactly what Pauline had just told us. It certainly explained why Jessica was the way she was.

'Go and get everyone to come over here,' said Suzanne.

'Why?' I asked.

'Cause we've got something to tell them,' said Suzanne, her eyes gleaming.

'The boys too?' asked Emma.

Suzanne mulled this over for a moment. 'No, just the girls.'

'You didn't get it from me – okay?' said Pauline.

'Don't worry,' said Suzanne.

Suzanne, Emma, Pauline and I spent the next five minutes desperately trying to round up as many girls in the playground as we could before the bell sounded. We had at least twenty and probably closer to thirty around us by the time Jessica wandered over to find out why such a large crowd was gathering.

'What's going on?' she asked with a frown.

She didn't stand a chance.

'We know all about your mum and dad,' Suzanne said at once. And she shouted out Jessica's secret at the top of her voice for everyone to hear.

Like I said, Jessica didn't stand a chance. Her face collapsed like wet newspaper. Tears immediately streamed down her face. Her shoulders sagged, her whole body drooped like a deflated balloon. We all stood watching her with undisguised hatred and satisfaction and as Jessica looked around for a friend, she could tell exactly what we were all thinking. With a sob, she turned and ran.

'And that's what I call getting my own back,' said Suzanne viciously.

Others in the crowd around us murmured their agreement. Jessica had hurt too many people, too many times to have any friends in the crowd. Even Sarah stood with us.

I stood there, watching Jessica run away, her face buried in her hands, thinking, 'We shouldn't have done that. That was so mean. Too wicked.'

But part of me thought, 'Good! Serves her right. Now she knows what it feels like to be hurt.'

But as I watched her disappear around the corner from us, I realised something. Far, far worse than being bullied was to become a bully myself. It was never going to happen. I swore there and then that I'd never, ever do that again.

The Paradise Carpet

Jamila Gavin

'O NE KNOT blue, two knots yellow, three knots red, four knots green . . .' The young boys chanted the pattern of the carpet they were weaving. Bony little fingers deftly drew the card down the thread; warp and weft . . . wrap and weft . . . top to bottom, right to left . . . warp and weft and knot.

Behind a loom inside a dark mud hut, crouching like caged animals, sat a line of boys. With backs against a wall, their thin arms rose and fell as they drew the threads from top to bottom, right to left, warp and weft and knot. They could have been musicians plucking at strings, but these were carpet weavers whose harmonies were of the eye not the ear as, bit by bit, the glorious patterns and hues of a rich carpet emerged in the darkness. 'One knot blue, two knots yellow, three knots red, four knots green . . .' The boys wove their thread, prompted and guided by old Rama, the only man among them, who had the pattern pinned to an upright in front of him.

'Ishwar, you're dreaming again!' bellowed a harsh voice. THWACK! The hand of the overseer struck a boy round the head.

The boy, Ishwar, faltered and nearly fell over sideways, but Bharat, crouching next to him, braced his body and managed to keep his friend upright.

'Keep your mind on the job. There'll be no supper for any of you tonight until you've woven another ten inches,' threatened the man. His great shape filled the doorway and blotted out their only source of light. Then he was gone. There was a low groan from the boys. Another ten inches before they would eat! That could take two hours or more, for this was the most complicated carpet they had ever woven – and the whole thing was to be completed within seven months – when an ordinary carpet took at least twelve.

A wealthy man had come along the rough track to the village in his white Mercedes. When he reached the brick house of Anoup, the carpet manufacturer, he got out like a raja, surrounded by shy jostling children and deferential elders, all of whom noted the gold rings embedded in his chubby fingers, and the chunky foreign watch just glinting beneath the cuffs of his smart suit.

'I want a carpet for my daughter's dowry,' he declared. 'She is to be married next December.' (Everyone did an instant calculation. That was only seven months away.) 'And this is the pattern I want you to weave.'

Anoup took the piece of paper the rich man held out for him. He stared at it long and silently, then gloomily and apologetically shook his head. 'Impossible,' he said. 'I need at least twelve months to do an average carpet – but this . . . this . . . and in SEVEN months, you say . . . No. Impossible.'

The rich man pulled out a fat briefcase from the car. He opened it up. There was a gasp from the onlookers. No one had ever seen so much money. Great wads of it, all stapled and bound straight from the bank. 'This is what you get now – and the rest when its finished. I'm sure you can do it. Just work a little harder – and a little longer each day, eh?' He tweaked the ear of the nearest little boy.

'I . . . er . . .' Anoup hesitated.

'Take it, take it . . .' voices around him urged.

Anoup's brain spun. Common sense said, don't do it . . . you can't do it . . . But the money . . . 'I'll do it. Your carpet will be ready on time.'

Anoup gave old Rama the pattern. 'You'd better study this,' he said.

Now Rama knew why Anoup had hesitated. The pattern was of a paradise garden; of strutting peacocks with sweeping tails, gold spotted deer leaping through undergrowth, squirrels coiling round tree-trunks and monkeys swinging from bough to bough; all sorts of exotic birds swooped and trilled and pecked at luscious fruit and flowers. Most extraordinary of all, was the Tree of Life, from its spreading roots at the base, rising up and up through twisting coiling branches, all the way to the top where the rays of rising sun pierced golden shafts through the leaves. It would need threads of every colour in the rainbow. 'There aren't enough hours in the day . . .' Rama protested softly.

'Then we will use the hours of the night too,' Anoup retorted harshly.

Ishwar stared at the bright blue square in the doorway – the blue of the sky outside. He longed to leap up and charge into the daylight and play, play, play. He had almost forgotten what the outside was like. It was two years since his mother had brought him to this village to be bonded to Anoup, for debts incurred in his grandfather's lifetime. Since then he had worked behind a loom in the dark, airless mud hut. It was like that for all of them; bonded and enslaved – even old Rama – and

Ishwar knew he too would die in bondage, that the debt would never be paid off in his lifetime either.

Ishwar could hear the voices of the village children being taught under the neem tree to chorus out their times tables and their alphabet. Ishwar tried to listen and learn – but it was no use. He must chant for ever with the other carpet weavers, the colours of the thread they were weaving . . . one knot yellow, two knots blue, three knots red, four knots green . . .

The paradise garden shimmered on the loom. If he couldn't play outside, then he must roam within its green shade and splash in the stream and chase the deer and climb branch by branch up and up the Tree of Life until he reached the blue sky there on the loom. With a strange eagerness, he took up the thread and moved his card top to bottom, right to left, warp and weft and knot, as if he would weave himself into the carpet.

Exactly when the seven months were over, the white Mercedes came. The villagers watched anxiously as the rich man came before, right up to Anoup's door.

'Is it ready?'

'It is,' answered Anoup, eyeing the bulging briefcase on the back seat.

'Show it to me. You realise that if it is not exactly what I ordered, I will not take it.'

'Sir, it is exactly what you asked for in every detail,' boasted Anoup.

'I'll be the judge of that,' snorted the rich man. 'Bring it out in the daylight where I can examine it properly.'

Anoup clicked his fingers. Rama and three boys ran to the hut.

'Hey, Ishwar!' exclaimed Rama, 'Wake up, boy! Help us with the carpet.'

Ishwar was sitting in his usual place behind the loom, his head leaning against the upright. He didn't respond.

'Hurry up!' bellowed Anoup impatiently. Rama and the boys lugged the carpet outside and with almost holy reverence, unrolled it. Even the villagers gasped in amazement at the beauty and workmanship. It was a miracle. They beamed with pride.

The rich man came forward till his nose nearly touched the pile. Inch by inch he scrutinised the carpet. Suddenly, he roared with fury. 'What's this!' he shouted. 'I didn't ask for this! What kind of idiotic thing have you done here! I can't take it – not with THIS!' He dragged the carpet out of their hands and trampled it into the dust. Then leaving the villagers appalled and stunned, the rich business man got into his car and sped off at top speed.

Nobody moved. Fearful eyes turned to Anoup. He was standing as if turned to stone. At last he clicked his fingers. In horrified silence they held out the carpet. Anoup's expert eye began at the top and scanned the carpet, as he had done twenty times each day. In his mind's eye, he wove each thread himself. He panned along the twisting branches of the Tree of Life, the glowing colours of humming birds and nightingales, dropping down through ten shades of green leaves and a dozen shades of blossoms of red, pink, purple and violet; he noted the golden fur of a deer darting through the grass, the hundred eyes of a peacock's tail shimmering near a silver fountain . . . and . . . ?

Then Anoup's body shuddered. He shuddered so hard, they heard his teeth rattle, and the bones of his fingers clicking as he ground his knuckles into his fist.

'What is it?' murmured the villagers. 'What has he seen?' They surged forward. Speechless with rage, Anoup pointed to a spot deep in the undergrowth. Almost hidden among blossom and foliage, the young face of a boy peered up at the Tree of Life, an arm upstretched, ready to climb.

'Ishwar!' Rama muttered under his breath. 'It's Ishwar!'

'Ishwar!' The name was shrieked in vengeance! The villagers rushed to the hut.

The boy still leaned against the loom as if resting his aching head. Anoup strode over and kicked him. The boy slipped forward, face down, on to the earth floor. When they rolled him over, they saw he was dead.

That Bit of Sule

Chika Unigwe

OUTSIDE, THE moon looked like a giant watergourd. I had never seen the moon that full. I wondered if it was like this in Enugu and I somehow just never saw it. At the thought of Enugu, a city I had lived in until two days ago, a tear trickled down my face. I hastily wiped it with the back of my left hand. It would never do, a boy my age, to be caught crying. That would be my reputation down the drain, for sure. It was hard enough moving, but being considered a cry-baby in a new place would be the absolute pits. I would never be able to live it down. Even if I lived to be a hundred years, nobody would ever forget that.

But I missed Enugu. I missed my home. 'Home,' I sighed and moved from the window and the new moon and lay back on the bed. This place would never seem like home. No matter how hard Papa shouted and Mama (who did not shout, but whispered or near-whispered according to her mood) tried to drill it into me.

'Kingsley,' my father had hurled at me when I had asked when we could go back to Enugu, 'this is where I was born. This is where your roots are. This is your home.' It did not feel like my roots were here. This dusty village with children who looked at me like I had dropped from Mars.

'King,' my mother had said in an affectionate near-whisper, 'try to be happy here, okay? You will have fun here.'

Later, when they thought I was not listening, my head bent over my Superman comic, I heard Mother whisper to Father, 'Papa, Kingsley, he is still a small boy. He does not understand. He is still only ten, eh? Not twenty.'

But Father had just grunted and buried his head in a newspaper.

Father had not always grunted and Mother had not always whispered. They both took to grunting and whispering when the talk of war began. I knew what war meant. I had seen it on TV. Soldiers shooting and getting shot. Father did not like me to watch action movies, but they were on every Sunday around the time he took his nap and Mother was away at a Christian Mothers meeting. So I knew what war was, all right. But there were other words flying around that made no sense to me. Grown-up words which the adults spoke reverentially, even as arguments got heated like ground-nut oil for our Sunday morning breakfast of akara balls: Secession. Imperialist. National pride. Oil boom. Oil doom.

Then came the pictures on TV. Houses burning like cardboard paper. Stern-faced generals sounding like my class master.

Then, the adults started acting weird. My best friend, Sule, who lived with his family in the flat above ours was not allowed to visit me any more. Father turned him back one Sunday afternoon and announced solemnly to me that Sule was 'the enemy'. Sule, with whom I had spent every waking day. We went to the same school, were in the same class and lived in each other's homes. Our parents always teased us, calling us each other's shadows.

'But Papa, we did not quarrel. He is my best friend.'

Father shut me up with his eyes and grunted, 'He is Hausa. He is Muslim. They are killing our people.'

When Mother intervened and whispered that I could not understand, Father said it was time I understood. I was his okpala, an Igbo man's first son. I should not be fraternizing with the enemy. I did not know what fraternizing meant, but I knew better than to ask him to explain.

We went to school with name tags stuck on our shirts. Men were asked to join the army and women were asked to have a huge pestle handy for clubbing any enemy soldier who might come into their homes. Sule no longer came to school and an eerie silence settled like fine dust over their flat upstairs. When I asked Mother why I no longer saw Sule or his parents, she wiped her eyes with the palm of her hand and said I asked too many questions. That night, I sneaked out and crept up to Sule's flat. The brown door was bashed in, looking all crumpled and the sitting-room was a mass of broken chairs and china.

That night, my nightmares started. I would see Sule, dangerously close to a cliff, calling out to me to help. Whenever I stretched out my hand to pull him across to safety, women with pestles jeered and hit me with their weapons and I would wake up, screaming.

It was Mother who whispered to Father that we should move. 'Things will only get worse,' I heard her say. Father grunted his approval and I was bundled into the battered 504 that my father had owned since I was born and we drove the two hours to Osumenyi.

I wanted things to get back to normal. I wanted Mother to talk with a smile like she used to. I wanted my father to lose the grunt. I missed Enugu. I missed my school. But most of all, I missed Sule. I missed going bird-hunting with him. We had identical catapults with which we terrorized birds in our neighbourhood. I rummaged in my bag at the foot of the bed and pulled out a blue catapult. Making sure that no one could see me, I held it against my cheek and let the tears flow unchecked. Hot and salty, they came coursing down, wetting my face like warm raindrops. The catapult was Sule's and he had forgotten it in my bag the last day we had gone bird-hunting. I was grateful for that bit of Sule. For even then I knew that I would never see my best friend again. I did not know what would happen in the future, but I knew that nothing would ever be the same again.

(For the cousins I will never know, killed during the Nigerian-Biafran war – Chika Unigwe)

Out of Bounds

Beverley Naidoo

O UT OF BOUNDS.
That's what his parents said as soon as the squatters took over the land below their house. Rohan's dad added another metre of thick concrete bricks to their garden wall and topped it with curling barbed wire. He certainly wasn't going to wait for the first break-in and be sorry later. They lived on the ridge of a steep hill with the garden sloping down. Despite the high wall, from his bedroom upstairs, Rohan could see over the spiked-wire circles down to the place where he and his friends used to play. The wild fig trees under which they had made their hideouts were still there. They had spent hours dragging planks, pipes, sheets of metal and plastic – whatever might be useful – up the hill from rubbish tipped in a ditch below. The first squatters pulled their hideouts apart and used the same old scraps again for their own constructions. Rohan could still see the 'ski-slope' – the red earth down which he and his friends had bumped and flown on a couple of old dustbin lids. The squatters used it as their road up the hill. Now it looked like a crimson scar cut between the shacks littering the hillside.

'There's only one good thing about this business,' Ma said after the back wall was completed. 'We won't have to wash that disgusting red dust out of your clothes any more!'

Rohan said nothing. How could he explain what he had lost?

At first, some of the squatter women and children came up to the houses with buckets asking for water. For a couple of weeks his mother opened the gate after checking that no men were hanging around in the background. She allowed the women to fill their buckets at the outside tap. Most of her neighbours found themselves doing the same. Torrential rains and floods had ushered in the new millennium by sweeping away homes, animals and people in the north of the country. The television was awash with pictures of homeless families and efforts to help them. No one knew from where exactly the squatters had come. But, as Ma said, how could you refuse a woman or child some water?

It wasn't long before all that changed. The first complaint of clothes disappearing off the washing line came from their new neighbours. The first African family, in fact, to move in among the Indians on Mount View. No one had actually seen anyone but everyone was suspicious including the neighbour, Mrs Zuma.

'You can't really trust these people, you know,' Mrs Zuma tutted when she came to ask if Ma had seen anyone hanging around. However it was when thieves broke into old Mrs Pillay's house, grabbed the gold thali from around her neck and left her with a heart attack, that views hardened. Young men could be seen hanging around the shacks. Were some of them not part of the same gang? Mrs Pillay's son demanded the police search through the settlement immediately. But the police argued they would need more evidence and that the thieves could have come from anywhere.

A new nervousness now gripped the house-owners on top of the hill. Every report of theft, break-in or car hijacking, anywhere in the country, led to another conversation about the squatters on the other side of their garden walls. At night Rohan peered through the bars of his window before going to sleep. Flickering lights from candles and lamps were the only sign that people were living out there in the thick darkness. In the daytime, when Ma heard the bell and saw that it was a woman or child with a bucket, she no longer answered the call. All the neighbours were agreed. Why should private house-owners be expected to provide water for these people? That was the Council's job. If the squatters were refused water, then perhaps they would find somewhere else to put up their shacks. A more suitable place. Or even, go back to where they came from.

The squatters did not go away. No one knew from where they managed to get their water or how far they had to walk. On the way to school, Rohan and his dad drove past women walking with buckets on their heads.

'These people are tough as ticks! You let them settle and it's impossible to get them out,' complained Dad. 'Next thing they'll be wanting our electricity.'

But Rohan wasn't really listening. He was scanning the line of African children who straggled behind the women and who wore the black and white uniform of Mount View Primary, his old school. He had been a pupil there until his parents had moved him to his private school in Durban with its smaller classes, cricket pitch and its own rugby ground. Most of the African children at Mount View had mothers who cleaned, washed and ironed for the families on top of the hill. But since the new year they had been joined by the squatter children and each week the line grew longer.

The queue of traffic at the crossroads slowed them down, giving Rohan more time to find the 'wire car' boy. He was looking for a boy who always steered a wire car in front of him with a long handle. He was about his own age – twelve or thirteen perhaps – and very thin and wiry himself. What interested Rohan was that the boy never had the same car for more than two or three days. Nor had he ever seen so many elaborate designs simply made out of wire, each suggesting a different make of car. They were much more complicated than the little wire toys in the African Crafts shop at the Mall.

'Hey, cool!' Rohan whistled. 'See that, Dad?' The boy must have heard because he glanced towards them. His gaze slid across the silver bonnet of their car towards the boot but didn't rise up to look at Rohan directly.

'It's a Merc – like ours, Dad! What a beaut! Do you think—'

'*Don't* think about it, son! You want us to stop and ask how much he wants, don't you?'

Rohan half-frowned, half-smiled. How easily his father knew him!

'No way! If we start buying from these people, we'll be encouraging them! That's not the message we want them to get now, is it?'

Rohan was quiet. He couldn't argue with his dad's logic. If the squatters moved away, he and his friends could get their territory back again.

Rohan returned home early from school. A precious half-day. In the past he would have spent it in his hideout. Instead he flicked on the television. News. As his finger hovered over the button to switch channels, the whirr of a helicopter invaded the living room.

'Hey, Ma! Look at this!'

Ma appeared from the kitchen, her hands cupped, white and dusty with flour. On the screen, a tight human knot swung at the end of a rope above a valley swirling with muddy water.

'A South African Air Force rescue team today saved a baby from certain death just an hour after she was born in a tree. Her mother was perched in the tree over floodwaters that have devastated Mozambique. The mother and her baby daughter were among the lucky few. Many thousands of Mozambicans are still waiting to be lifted to safety from branches and rooftops. They have now been marooned for days by the rising water that has swallowed whole towns and villages.'

'Those poor people! What a place to give birth!' Ma's floury hands almost looked ready to cradle a baby. Rohan was watching how the gale from the rotors forced the leaves and branches of the tree to open like a giant flower until the helicopter began to lift. Members of the mother's family still clung desperately to the main trunk. Rohan saw both fear and determination in their eyes. He and Ma listened to the weather report that followed. Although Cyclone Eline was over, Cyclone Gloria was now whipping up storms across the Indian Ocean and heading towards Mozambique. Where would it go next? Durban was only down the coast. Rohan had seen a programme about a sect who believed the new millennium would mark the end of the world. They were convinced that the floods were a sign that The End was beginning.

'What if the cyclone comes here, Ma?'

'No, we'll be all right son. But that lot out there will get it. The government really should do something.' Ma nodded in the direction of the squatters.

'Now, let me finish these *rotis* for your sister!'

Ma returned to her bread-making. When she had

finished, she wanted Rohan to come with her to his married sister's house. He pleaded to stay behind.

'I've got homework to do Ma! I'll be fine.'

'You won't answer the door unless it's someone we know, will you?'

'No Ma!' he chanted. Ma said the same thing every time.

Alone in the house, Rohan daydreamed at his desk. He was close enough to the window to see down the hill. What if there was so much rain that a river formed along the road below! As the water rose, people would have to abandon their shacks to climb higher up. They would be trapped between the flood below and the torrents above. In assembly they had heard the story of Noah building the Ark. Perhaps it wasn't just a story after all. Perhaps the people had tried to cling on to the tops of trees as tightly as those they had seen on television.

Tough as ticks.

The phrase popped into his mind. Wasn't that what his dad had said about the squatters? Yet the one sure way to get rid of ticks was to cover them in liquid paraffin. Drown them. A terrible thought. He should push it right away.

Rohan was about to stretch out for his maths book when a figure caught his eye on the old ski-slope. It was the thin wiry boy but he wasn't pushing a car this time. He was carrying two large buckets, one on his head, the other by his side. He descended briskly down the slope and turned along the road in the opposite direction to that taken by the women who carried buckets on their heads. Rohan followed the figure until he went out of sight, then forced himself to open his book.

The bell rang just as he was getting interested in the first question. Nuisance! He hurried to the landing. If someone was standing right in front of the gate, it was possible to see who it was from the window above the stairs. He stood back, careful not to be seen himself. It was the same boy, an empty container on the ground each side of him! Didn't he know not to come to the house up here? But he was only a child and it looked as if he just wanted some water. It would be different if it were an adult or a complete stranger. Rohan's daydream also made him feel a little guilty. He could see the boy look anxiously through the bars, his hand raised as if wondering whether to ring the bell again. Usually when the boy was pushing his wire car on the way to school, he appeared relaxed and calm.

By the time the bell rang a second time, Rohan had decided. He hurried downstairs but slowed himself as he walked outside towards the gate.

'What do you want?' Rohan tried not to show that he recognized the boy.

'I need water for my mother. Please.' The boy held his palms out in front of him as if asking for a favour. 'My mother – she's having a baby – it's bad – there's no more water. Please.'

This was an emergency. Not on television but right in front of him. Still Rohan hesitated. His parents would be extremely cross that he had put himself in this situation by coming to-talk to the boy. Weren't there stories of adults who used children as decoys to get people to open their gates so they could storm in? He should have stayed inside. Should he tell the boy to go next door where there would at least be an adult? But the boy had chosen to come to here. Perhaps he had seen Rohan watching him from the car and knew this was his house.

'We stay there.' The boy pointed in the direction of the squatter camp. 'I go to school there.' He pointed in the direction of Mount View Primary. He was trying to reassure Rohan that it would be OK to open the gate. He was still in his school uniform but wore a pair of dirty-blue rubber sandals. His legs were as thin as sticks.

'Isn't there a doctor with your mother?' It was such a silly question that as soon as it was out, Rohan wished he could take it back. If they could afford a doctor, they wouldn't be squatters on a bare hillside. The boy shook his head vigorously. If he thought it was stupid, he didn't let it show on his troubled face.

'Wait there!' Rohan returned to the house. The button for the electric gate was inside the front door. The boy waited while the wrought-iron bars slowly rolled back.

'OK. Bring your buckets over here.' Rohan pointed to the outside tap. The buckets clanked against each other as the boy jogged towards him.

'Thank you,' he said quietly.

The unexpected softness in his voice had a strange effect on Rohan. It sounded so different from his own bossy tone. Suddenly he felt a little ashamed. This was the same boy whose wire cars he admired! If he were still at Mount View Primary they would probably be in the same class. They might even have been friends and he would be learning how to make wire cars himself. Why had he spoken so arrogantly? It was really only a small favour that was being asked for. The water in the bucket gurgling and churning reminded Rohan of the water swirling beneath the Mozambican woman with her baby. *Her* rescuer had been taking a really big risk but hadn't looked big-headed. He had just got on with the job.

When both buckets were full, the boy stooped to lift one on to his head. Rohan saw his face and neck muscles strain under the weight. How would he manage to keep it balanced and carry the other bucket too?

'Wait! I'll give you a hand.' Rohan's offer was out before he had time to think it through properly. If the boy was surprised, he didn't show it. All his energy seemed to be focused on his task. Rohan dashed into the kitchen to grab the spare set of keys. Ma would be away for another hour at least. He would be back soon and she need never know. It was only after the gate clicked behind them, that Rohan remembered the neighbours. If anyone saw him, they were bound to ask Ma what he was doing with a boy from the squatter camp. He crossed the fingers of one hand.

At first Rohan said nothing. Sharing the weight of the bucket, he could feel the strain all the way up from his fingers to his left shoulder. When they reached the corner and set off down the hill, the bucket seemed to propel them forward. It was an effort to keep a steady pace. Rohan glanced at the container on the boy's head, marvelling at how he kept it balanced. He caught the boy's eye.

'How do you do that? You haven't spilt a drop!'

The boy gave a glimmer of a smile.

'You learn.'

Rohan liked the simple reply. He should ask the boy about the cars. This was his chance, before they turned into the noisy main road and reached the squatter camp.

'I've seen you with wire cars. Do you make them yourself?'

'Yes – and my brother.'

'You make them together? Do you keep them all?'

'My brother – he sells them at the beach.' The boy waved his free hand in the direction of the sea. 'The tourists – they like them.'

'Your cars are better than any I've seen in the shops! Do you get lots of money for them?'

'Mmhh!' The boy made a sound something between a laugh and a snort. Rohan realized that he had asked another brainless question. Would they be staying in a shack if they got lots of money? Rohan had often seen his own father bargaining to get something cheaper from a street hawker. He tried to cover his mistake.

'There's a shop in the Mall where they sell wire cars. They charge a lot and yours are a hundred times better!'

'We can't go there. The guards – they don't let us in.'

Rohan knew the security guards at the entrance to the Mall. Some of them even greeted his parents with a little salute. Rohan had seen poor children hanging around outside. They offered to push your trolley, to clean your car – anything for a few cents. Sometimes Ma gave an orange or an apple from her shopping bag to a child. Other times she would just say 'No thank you' and wave a child away. Ma never gave money. She said they might spend it on drugs. Rohan had never thought what it would be like to be chased away. How did the guards decide who could enter? How could the boy and his brother go and show the lady in the African Crafts shop his cars if they weren't allowed in?

Rohan was quiet as they reached the main road and turned towards the squatter camp. The noise of vehicles roaring past was deafening. He never normally walked down here. Not by himself nor with anyone else. His family went everywhere by car. With all the locks down, of course. The only people who walked were poor people. His eyes were drawn to a group of young men walking towards them. They were still some distance away but already Rohan began to feel uneasy. They were coming from the crossroads that his dad always approached on full alert. Rohan knew how his father jumped the red lights when the road was clear, especially at night. Everyone had heard stories of gangs who hijacked cars waiting for the lights to change.

The handle had begun to feel like it was cutting into his fingers. The boy must have sensed something because he signalled to Rohan to lower the bucket. For a few seconds they each stretched their fingers.

'It's too far? You want to go?' The boy was giving him a chance to change his mind. To leave and go back home. He had already helped carry the water more than half the way. He could make an excuse about the time. But the thought of running back to the house along the road on his own now worried him.

'No, it's fine. Let's go.' Rohan heard a strange brightness in his own voice. He curled his fingers around the handle again.

As they drew nearer the men, Rohan felt their gaze on him and suddenly his head was spinning with questions. Why on earth had he offered to help carry the water? What did he think he was doing coming down here? And he hadn't even yet entered the squatter camp itself!

'We go here.' The boy's voice steadied him a little.

Rohan turned and stared up at his old ski-slope. He felt the force of the young men's eyes on his back as he and the boy began to ascend the rough track. Someone behind called out something in Zulu and, without turning, the boy shouted back. The words flew so quickly into one another that Rohan didn't pick up any even though he was learning Zulu in school. They must be talking about him but he was too embarrassed – and frightened – to ask. He could feel his heart pumping faster and told himself it was because of the stiff climb. He needed to concentrate where he put each foot. The track was full of holes and small stones. A quick glance over his shoulder revealed that the young men had also entered the squatter camp but seemed to be heading for a shack with a roof covered in old tyres on the lower slope. A couple of them were still watching. He must just look ahead and control his fear. As long as he was with the boy, he was safe, surely?

A bunch of small children appeared from nowhere, giggling and staring. He couldn't follow their chatter but heard the word '*iNdiya!*' The boy ignored them until a couple of children started darting back and forth in front of them sweeping up the red dust with their feet.

'*Hambani!*' Rohan could hear the boy's irritation as he waved them away. But the darting and dancing continued just out of reach.

'*Hambani-bo!*' This time the boy's voice deepened to a threat and the cluster of children pulled aside with one or two mischievous grins. Beads of sweat had begun trickling down the boy's face. With his own skin prickling with sticky heat, Rohan wondered at the wiry strength of the boy whose back, head and bucket were still perfectly upright as they mounted the hill.

'It's that one – we stay there.' The boy, at last, pointed to a structure of corrugated iron, wood and black plastic a little further up. It was not far from the old fig trees. For a moment Rohan thought he would say something about his hideout which the first squatters had pulled down. But he stopped himself. Maybe the boy had even been one of them!

As they drew nearer, they heard a woman moaning and a couple of other women's voices that sounded as if they were comforting her. The boy lowered the bucket swiftly from his head and pushed aside a plywood sheet, the door to his home. Rohan wasn't sure what to do. He knew he couldn't follow. The sounds from within scared him. The moans were rapid and painful. He remembered a picture in a book at school that had showed the head of a baby popping out between its mother's legs. There had been an argument among his friends about how such a big head could possibly fit through a small hole. From what he could hear now, it must hurt terribly. Rohan folded his arms tightly, trying not to show how awkward he felt. The little children were still watching but keeping their distance. They could probably also hear the cries. It would be hard to keep anything private here. The only other people near by were two grey-haired men sitting on boxes a little lower down the hill. One of them was bent over an old-fashioned sewing machine placed on a metal drum, a makeshift table. Normally Rohan would have been very curious to see what he was stitching but now he was just grateful that both men were engrossed in talking and didn't seem interested in him.

He turned to look up the hill – towards his house and the others at the top protected by their walls with wires, spikes and broken bottles. When he had hidden in his hideout down here, he had always loved the feeling of being safe yet almost in his own separate little country. But that had been a game and he could just hop over the wall to return to the other side. Surrounded now by homes made out of scraps and other people's leftovers, this place seemed a complete world away from the houses on the hill. In fact, how was he going to get home? If he didn't leave soon, Ma would be back before him. Would the boy at least take him part of the way through the squatter camp? He needed him to come outside so that he could ask him.

'What do you want here?'

Rohan spun around. A man with half-closed eyes and his head tilted to one side stood with his hands on his hips, surveying Rohan from head to foot. His gaze lingered for a moment on Rohan's watch.

'I-I brought water with … with…' Rohan stammered. He hadn't asked the boy his name! Panic-stricken, he pointed to the door of the shack. The man stepped forward and Rohan stumbled back against the wall of corrugated iron. The clattering brought the boy to the door. The man immediately switched into loud, fast

Zulu. The boy spoke quietly at first but when the man's voice didn't calm down, the boy's began to rise too. Even when he pointed to the bucket and Rohan, the man's face remained scornful. Rohan was fully expecting to be grabbed when a sharp baby's cry interrupted the argument. The boy's face lit up and the man suddenly fell silent. Rohan's heart thumped wildly as the man's eyes mocked him before he turned and walked away.

Rohan folded his arms tightly, trying not to shake. Before he could say anything, a lady appeared behind the boy, placing a hand on his shoulder.

'You have a little sister!' She smiled at the boy and then at Rohan. She looked friendly but tired. Her cheeks shone as if she too had been perspiring. It was obviously hard work helping to deliver a baby.

'Tell your mother thank you for the water. You really helped us today.'

Rohan managed to smile back.

'It's OK.' His voice came out strangely small.

'Solani will take you back now – before it gets dark.'

Rohan felt a weight lifting. He did not need to ask.

The sun was getting lower and made long rod-like shadows leap beside them as they scrambled down the slope. Knowing the boy's name made Rohan feel a little easier and he wondered why he hadn't asked him earlier. He told Solani his own and the next thing he was telling him about riding on dustbin lids down the ski-slope. Solani grinned.

'It's good! But this place – it's a road now. We can't do it. The people will be angry if we knock someone down.'

Rohan understood that. But what he didn't understand was why the man with scornful eyes had been so angry with him. And why had those other young men looked at him so suspiciously? He decided to ask Solani.

'They don't know you. Sometimes people come and attack us. So if a stranger comes, they must always check first.'

When they reached the road, neither spoke. The home-time traffic would have drowned their voices anyway. Rohan thought about what Solani had said about him being a stranger. Surely they knew that he was from one of the houses on top of the hill. The houses that also did not welcome strangers. Like the squatters.

They parted at the top of the hill. Rohan was anxious to reach the house before his mother returned and Solani was eager to see his baby sister. Opening the electronic gates, Rohan was relieved that his mother's car was neither in the yard nor the garage. He dashed upstairs to his room and peered out of the window over to the squatter camp. The evening was falling very rapidly. His mother would be home any minute – and his dad. Neither liked to drive in the dark if they could help it. Rohan fixed his eyes on the deep crimson scar, hoping to see Solani climbing the slope. How strange to think that he had been there himself less than half-an-hour ago. In that other world. Yes! There was Solani! A tiny wiry figure bounding up the hill. Not hampered this time with a container of water on his head. Rohan watched Solani weave through other figures travelling more slowly until three-quarters of the way up the hill, he darted off and disappeared into the darkening shadow that was his home.

Rohan surprised his parents by joining them for the eight o'clock news. The story about the rescue of mother and baby from the floods in Mozambique was repeated.

'*Sophia Pedro and her baby daughter Rositha were among*

the lucky few. Many thousands of Mozambicans are still waiting to be lifted to safety…'

This time the reporter added their names. Rohan observed the mother more closely. Had she also cried and moaned like Solani's mother? With the roaring waters underneath, how many people had heard her?

'It's nice to see these South African soldiers doing some good,' said Ma when the news was finished. Rohan wished he could say what he too had done that afternoon. But he feared the storm that it would let loose and went upstairs to his bedroom. Before slipping between his sheets, he peered out once again through the bars at the hill swallowed up by the night. He thought he saw a light still flickering in Solani's home and wondered how many people were tucked inside the sheets of iron, plastic and wood. He prayed that Cyclone Gloria would keep well away.

Next morning, the glint of metal beside the gate caught his eye from the front door. His dad was reversing the car out of the garage. Rohan ran across the drive. There, just inside the gate, was a wire car. A small, perfect Merc! Who could it be from, except Solani? He must have slipped it through the bars of the gate in the early morning. Quickly Rohan pushed it behind a cluster of scarlet gladioli. If his parents saw it, they would want to know from where it had come. They would discover he had gone out of bounds . . . Well, so had Solani! Each of them had taken a risk. He needed time to think. In the mean time, the car would have to be his secret. Their secret. His and Solani's.

The World Next Door

Joan Aiken

OLD MRS Quill lived in a little black and white house by the side of a wood. Next to the house was an orchard, with twelve apple trees. In the spring the trees were covered with pink and white flowers. In the autumn they were hung all over with red and yellow fruit. Mrs Quill sold some of the apples, and gave many away to her friends, and ate the rest. And, as well, she made money by washing people's shirts and sheets and towels. She had clothes-lines hung between the apple trees, and every windy day there would be white and coloured laundry like flags blowing among the branches. The wind always blew on Mrs Quill's wash days.

The wind is my friend, said Mrs Quill.

Besides washing, Mrs Quill knew a great deal about how to cure pain. She often went into the wood, where she picked leaves and flowers and berries. From these she made pastes and pills and drinks which would send away almost any pain, headache, sore throat, stomach-ache or stiffness in the legs.

Mrs Quill gave her medicines to people; she never wanted money for her treatment.

'Everything in the wood is free,' she said.

'How do you know so much, Mrs Quill?' a boy called Pip asked her.

'The wind tells me,' she said. 'I listen to the wind, in the leaves, in the branches. The wind comes from another world. My cottage stands by the wood. And the wood grows by a mountain. In the same way, this world floats by another world. And that is where the wind comes from.'

Mrs Quill's old cat, Foss, purred and rubbed against her ankles.

'Foss knows about the wind,' she said. 'Foss goes into the wood at night, and hears it whispering secrets.' One day a big car stopped outside Mrs Quill's cottage, and a white-haired man got out. His name was Sir Groby Griddle.

'I am your new landlord, Mrs Quill,' he said. 'I have bought the wood, and the orchard, and the mountain. I plan to knock down your cottage and put a golf course on this land. You must find somewhere else to live.'

'Leave my house?' said Mrs Quill. 'But I was born in this house. I have always lived here. And so did my mother and grandmother.'

'I can't help that,' said Sir Groby. 'The house has to come down. You will be found another one, somewhere else. Anywhere you like.'

'But there would be no apple trees. And no wood where I could find plants. And nowhere to hang the washing.'

They were standing under the apple trees as they talked. A white sheet blew out and flapped itself round Sir Groby. This annoyed him.

'All those apple trees must be cut down,' he said. 'They are old and crooked. And the wood must come down as well. There will be a main road leading to the golf course. And a car park. And a clubhouse and a tearoom.'

Mrs Quill said, 'My cottage is very old. Hundreds and hundreds of years old. There is a law which says that old houses must not be pulled down.'

The wind blew again, and a pillow-case flapped across Sir Groby's face. He was even more annoyed, because what Mrs Quill said was true. 'You have not heard the last of this,' he said.

He stamped away. A long roller towel blew out and flapped round his neck. He shouted, 'You'll see, very soon! I always get my way in the end!'

After that, for many weeks, Mrs Quill was very quiet, thinking. She did not often smile. When people came to her house, asking for headache pills, or syrup for a sore throat, she was not always there.

'Where have you been, Mrs Quill?' the boy called Pip asked her one day, as she bandaged his grazed knee.

'In the wood. Tying threads round the trees.'

'*All* the trees, Mrs Quill?'

'Yes. Every one.'

'Why?'

'So that they will know me again. And I shall know them.'

Now autumn had come. Mrs Quill's apples had all been picked. Lots of people helped her. The apples had been laid on shelves in her shed. They had a cool, sharp smell, which came floating out of the door-way, on the wind.

Once a year, Mrs Quill used to catch a bus and go into town to buy needles, and soap, and a new saucepan, and a garden fork. Things like that.

This year, on her way home, as she stood waiting by the bus-stop, she noticed a little black and white house on a patch of waste land near by.

That looks like my house, thought Mrs Quill.

But then a woman asked what would be good for her little boy's ear-ache, and a man wanted a cure for chilblains. And then the bus arrived and Mrs Quill got on it, with her bundles.

But when she came to where her house had been, it was gone. The shed had been pulled down too. Apples were lying all over the ground, some of them squashed.

And there stood Sir Groby, smiling all over his face.

Men were in the orchard, sawing down the apple trees.

'I have had your house moved,' Sir Groby told Mrs Quill. 'I had it put on a truck, and moved to the edge of the town. That's quite legal. That's where you'll find it. It will be better for you there. You can go shopping, and see more people.'

'Where is my cat Foss?' said Mrs Quill.

'He ran off into the wood,' said a man who was halfway through sawing down a tree. 'We'll find him tomorrow. We are going to cut down the whole wood.'

Mrs Quill stood for a moment.

'Then I had better go into the wood now,' she said to Sir Groby. And she added, 'You are going to miss that wood. You are going to need it. *And* the orchard, my orchard, that your men have cut down. You will be thirsty. All you can think about will be an apple. Your head will ache in the hot sun. All you need will be shade. But there will be no apple for you, and no shade.'

A dry gust of wind blew from the wood and flung a handful of leaves against Sir Groby. They stung his eyes and scratched his cheeks. He shook his head angrily. When he could see again, Mrs Quill was walking away from him, into the wood.

'Let her go, silly old fool!' he said. 'She'll come out soon enough, when we start cutting down the trees.'

But Mrs Quill did not come out of the wood.

And when, next day, Sir Groby's men began cutting
down the trees, a queer thing happened. As each tree was
cut down, it shrank, like a slip of paper when you set a
match to it, and vanished clean away. At the end of the
day, instead of a huge pile of tree trunks, ready to be sold
for timber, there was just nothing at all. Only some mud
and a few leaves.

The roots were dug up and the land made flat and
level. A golf course was laid out, and a car park. A red-
brick clubhouse was built, with a flag on it.

But very few people came to play golf on the golf
course. The ones who did told their friends that, at night,
after playing, they had bad dreams. They dreamed they
were trying to play golf in a forest. Trees and bushes
grew up all round them. Leaves and prickles grew out of
their golf clubs. Their balls rolled down rabbit holes.
Nobody came back to play on Sir Groby's course a
second time. He made no money from it.

The clubhouse stood empty. The flag dangled from its
pole. No wind ever blew.

Sir Groby himself fell ill. His head ached all the time.
Nothing would help the ache. All day long he was
thirsty. He drank water, beer, milk, soda, wine, tea, coffee
and champagne, but no drink would make the thirst go
away.

And, every night, he dreamed about walking in a dark
wood and listening to the wind.

At last he was so ill that he had to be taken to hospital.

'Where is Mrs Quill?' he kept asking. 'And why does
the wind never blow any more?'

'The wind *is* blowing, Sir Groby,' the nurses told him.
'A gale is blowing, outside the window, at this very
minute. Can't you hear it roar?'

But he could hear nothing.

He lay ill for weeks and weeks. Nobody cared about

him, so nobody came to see him, except a boy called Pip.

'I dream about Mrs Quill every night,' Pip told Sir Groby. 'In my dream I see her living in her cottage, with her wood, and her orchard. She is living in the world that floats next door to this one. You won't see her again.'

'I don't want to hear about your dreams! All I want is something to cure this awful thirst,' croaked Sir Groby.

'When I next see Mrs Quill in my dream I will ask her,' said Pip.

Next day Pip came to the hospital again.

'In my dream I asked Mrs Quill about your thirst,' he told Sir Groby. 'She says that only an apple from her orchard will cure it.'

'I don't believe you!' growled Sir Groby. 'That's rubbish! In any case, her orchard is cut down, and there are no apples left.'

A sudden gust of wind blew through the hospital room where Sir Groby lay. The window curtain sailed inwards and wrapped itself round Sir Groby's angry face. And a shower of dead leaves swept through the window like arrows and landed all over Sir Groby's bed.

'Good gracious!' cried a nurse, coming in. And she ran for a dustpan.

Sir Groby lay scowling, and said nothing at all for the rest of the day.

That night he dreamed that he was standing on the edge of the world, looking across the gap at the world that lay next door.

There was Mrs Quill's black and white cottage, beside the orchard, beside the wood, beside the mountain. There was Mrs Quill herself, hanging out her washing, sheets and towels and pillow-cases, among the old twisted apple trees.

'I'm thirsty!' called Sir Groby, across the gap. 'Oh, Mrs Quill, won't you help me? I'm so terribly thirsty!'

But Mrs Quill took no notice, just went on pegging out the towels and tea-cloths.

'Mrs Quill! I'm sorry I moved your house! I'm sorry I cut down your orchard! I'm sorry I cut down your wood! Won't you please tell me what will stop this awful thirst?'

At that Mrs Quill turned and looked at him. 'Just being sorry is not enough,' she said. 'Hundreds of creatures had their homes in that wood – birds and mice, foxes, squirrels, rabbits, spiders, adders, bats, otters, hares and weasels. How can you put right the harm you did?'

'But I'm so thirsty!'

'Only an apple from my orchard will cure your thirst.'

'But there aren't any left! They were all squashed and trampled.'

'I have just one left here,' she said. 'See if you can catch it.'

And she threw an apple across the gap.

But Sir Groby was not able to catch it. Down it fell – down and down – into the gap between the worlds, and was lost.

Mrs Quill turned and walked away into her orchard.

And Sir Groby, crying and wailing like a two-year-old, woke up from his dream. Next day he told the people at the hospital that he wanted to leave and go home.

'But you are not better,' they said.

'I shall never be better if I stay here,' said Sir Groby.

He sent for a car and a driver to come and fetch him.

On the way to Sir Groby's home, his car passed the bus-stop where Mrs Quill had caught her bus. But there was no black and white cottage on the site where Sir Groby's men had left it. Just a bare patch of ground with some bits of paper blowing about.

The boy, Pip, was standing and looking at the empty space.

Sir Groby opened his car window and called, 'What happened to Mrs Quill's house?'

'It has gone,' said Pip. 'Just like the trees.'

Sir Groby went home to his large, grand house. He ate roast beef for his supper, and drank champagne. But his head ached, just as badly as ever, and he was still thirsty.

At night, as he lay in bed, he heard the voices of all the creatures he had turned out of their homes, crying and grieving, squeaking and squawking, chirping and cheeping and chirruping.

He dreamed that he saw Mrs Quill, busy in the world next door, hanging out her wash. The wind was helping her.

'Mrs Quill! I will plant another wood, I promise!' he called to her across the gap. 'Only, please, please, throw me one of your apples! I will plant another wood, and an orchard beside it.'

At that she turned and looked at him more kindly.

'I do have just one more apple,' she said. 'See if you can catch it this time.'

She tossed an apple across the gap. This time the wind gusted and blew the apple so that Sir Groby was just able to grab it. But just as he was about to take a big bite out of it, he woke up. Oh, what a blow that was, to wake and find he had no apple in his hand!

Sir Groby wailed like a two-year-old.

But then he struggled out of bed, and dragged on his clothes, and picked up his telephone, and gave orders for the golf clubhouse to be pulled down, and the car park dug up, and the golf course ploughed all over.

He ordered his car, and told the driver to take him to the golf course. On the way they passed by the bus-stop, where Mrs Quill's cottage had been left.

Sir Groby noticed that the empty waste patch was all

covered with small green shoots, with young new leaves on them.

For it was spring now.

Sir Groby told his driver to stop, and got out of the car.

The boy Pip was standing and looking at the small trees.

'They are all seedling apple trees,' he said.

A warm spring wind was blowing. It tossed the sprigs and leaves of the little seedling trees. The wind had a cool, sharp smell.

As it blew against his face, Sir Groby felt that the wind had come from a very long way off. Perhaps from another world. Perhaps from the world next door.

Acknowledgements

The compiler and publishers gratefully acknowledge permission to reproduce the following copyright material:

HOW FIRE CAME TO EARTH by Lucy Coats © 2002. Used by permission of The Orion Publishing Group Ltd

THE SEVEN POMEGRANATE SEEDS Copyright © Anthony Horowitz 1991. Extracted from *Myths and Legends* published by Kingfisher Books, and reproduced by permission of the author c/o The Maggie Noach Literary Agency

MAUI AND THE GREAT FISH by Kiri Te Kanawa © Kiri Te Kanawa 1989

FATHER OF STORIES, HORSE OF SONGS From *Tales Told in Tents* by Sally Pomme Clayton published by Frances Lincoln Ltd, © 2004. Reproduced by permission of Frances Lincoln Ltd, 4 Torriano Mews, Torriano Avenue, London NW5 2RZ

HOW CUCHULAINN GOT HIS NAME from *The O'Brien Book of Irish Fairy Tales and Legends* by Una Leavy, published by The O'Brien Press Ltd. Dublin. © Copyright Una Leavy

THE GRENDEL, Copyright © Anthony Horowitz 1991. Extracted from *Myths and Legends*, published by Kingfisher Books and reproduced by permission of the author c/o The Maggie Noach Literary Agency

Retelling of SAINT GEORGE AND THE DRAGON by Margaret Clark. © Copyright Margaret Clark 1997. Reprinted by permission of the author

THE FIRE-BIRD, THE HORSE OF POWER AND THE PRINCESS VASILISSA Copyright © Arthur Ransome Literary Estate, 2003. Published by permission of Jane Nissen Books

THE THREE TESTS by James Riordan. © James Riordan

TWO GIANTS by Edna O'Brien. © Edna O'Brien

THE WISE MEN OF GOTHAM by Kevin Crossley-Holland, from the book *The Magic Lands*, © 2001. Used by Permission of The Orion Publishing Group Ltd

THE STORM CHILD from *Hogboon of Hell and Other Strange Orkney Tales* by Nancy and W. Towrie Cutt. Copyright © Nancy Cutt and W. Towrie Cutt, 1979. First published in the UK by Andre Deutsch Limited. Reproduced by Permission of Scholastic Ltd. All Rights Reserved.

THE GIRL FROM LLYN FAN FACH by T. Llew Jones © 1989 Retold in English by Gillian Clarke © 1991. Used by permission of Pont Books, Gomer Press, Llandysul, Ceredigion, SA44 4JL

TOWN MOUSE AND COUNTRY MOUSE from *Fables of Aesop* translated by S. A. Handford Copyright © S. A. Handford, 1954 reproduced by permission of Penguin Books Ltd.

A BLIND MAN CATCHES A BIRD from *The Girl Who Married a Lion* by Alexander McCall Smith. First published in Great Britain by Canongate Books Ltd., 14 High Street, Edinburgh, EH1 1TE

THE DREAM from *My Sister Shahrazad* by Robert Leeson published by Frances Lincoln Ltd, © 2001. Reproduced by permission of Frances Lincoln Ltd, 4 Torriano Mews, Torriano Avenue, London NW5 2RZ

THE REMARKABLE ROCKET by Oscar Wilde from *The Happy Prince and Other Stories*. Published in Puffin Books 1962, 1963

HEAD OVER HEART retold by Martin Bennett from *Tales of West Africa* (OUP, 2000), copyright © Martin Bennett 1994, reprinted by permission of Oxford University Press

TIGER STORY, ANANSI STORY retold by Philip Sherlock from *Tales from the West Indies* (OUP, 2000), copyright © Philip Sherlock 1966, reprinted by permission of Oxford University Press

BRER RABBIT TO THE RESCUE by Julius Lester from *The Tales of Uncle Remus* published by Random House, © 1987. Used by permission of Random House

HOLLY AND THE SKYBOARD by Ian Whybrow. © Ian Whybrow. Used by permission of Peters Fraser and Dunlop

MOONFLOWER by Pippa Goodhart. © Pippa Goodhart 2003

JACINTA'S SEASIDE by Marilyn McLaughlin. © Marilyn McLaughlin

THE HAPPY TEAM by Alan Gibbons © 1997. Used by permission of the Orion Publishing Group Ltd

THE GANG HUT by George Layton from *The Fib and Other Stories* by George Layton published by Pearson Education. Used by Permission of Pearson Education

MOZART'S BANANA © Gillian Cross 2001

JACK AND THE TINSTALK from *Hairy Tales and Nursery Crimes* by Michael Rosen. Copyright © Michael Rosen, 1985. First published in the UK by Andre Deutsch Limited. Reproduced by permission of Scholastic Ltd. All rights reserved

A CAREER IN WITCHCRAFT copyright © 1997 by Kaye Umansky reproduced by kind permission of Kaye Umansky c/o Caroline Sheldon Literary Agency Limited

OLYMPIC MARATHON by Morris Gleitzman © Morris Gleitzman. Used with the very kind permission of the author

THAT'S NONE OF YOUR BUSINESS by Kevin Crossley-Holland from *Short! A Book of Very Short Stories* (OUP, 1998) copyright © Kevin Crossley-Holland 1998, reprinted by permission of Oxford University Press

THE FALLEN ANGEL by Maggie Pearson from *Short and Shocking* (OUP, 2002) copyright © Maggie Pearson 2002, reprinted by permission of Oxford University Press

IN THE SHOWER WITH ANDY – extract taken from *Just Annoying* by Andy Griffiths © Andy Griffiths 1998, Macmillan Children's Books, London, UK

GRIMBLE'S MONDAY Copyright © Sir Clement Freud, used by permission of the author

HOW NOT TO BE A GIANT KILLER by David Henry Wilson, from *There's a Wolf in my Pudding*, first published by J. M. Dent and reproduced by permission of The Orion Publishing Group Ltd

MACKEREL AND CHIPS by Michael Morpurgo from *Just What I Always Wanted* published by HarperCollins ©' 1998. Used by permission of David Higham Associates

THE LEOPARD by Ruskin Bond. © Ruskin Bond

HOW LITTLE JOHN CAME TO THE GREENWOOD from *The Adventures of Robin Hood* by Roger Lancelyn Green (Puffin, 1965) Copyright © Roger Lancelyn Green, 1956. Reproduced by permission of Penguin Books Ltd

THE PICNIC by Penelope Lively from *The Oxford Book of Timeslip Stories* published by Oxford University Press. Reprinted by permission of David Higham Associates

THE HAPPY ALIEN Copyright © Jean Ure 2003. This story was first published in *The Young Oxford Book of Mystery Stories* compiled by Dennis Hamley, published by Oxford University Press. It is reproduced by permission of the author c/o the Maggie Noach Literary Agency

MOVING HOUSE by Louise Cooper from *Short and Scary!* (OUP, 2002) Copyright © Louise Cooper 2002, reprinted by permission of Oxford University Press

MRS CHAMBERLAIN'S REUNION from *The Rope and Other Stories* by Philippa Pearce (Puffin, 2000) Copyright © Philippa Pearce, 2000. Reproduced by permission of Penguin Books Ltd

GHOST TROUBLE Copyright © Ruskin Bond. Reproduced by permission of Walker Books Ltd, London SE11 5HJ

NULE © Jan Mark, 1977, 1980. First published by Kestrel Books. Used by permission of David Higham Associates

THE FUGITIVES by Rosemary Sutcliff from *Stories for 10 and Over* published by Puffin Books. © 1982. Used by permission of David Higham Associates

LONDON RISES FROM THE ASHES by Jeremy Strong from *Centuries of Stories* published by HarperCollins 2001. Used by permission of David Higham Associates

A LIGHTHOUSE HEROINE by Henry Brook. Reproduced from *True Sea Stories* by permission of Usborne Publishing, 83–85 Saffron Hill, London EC1N 8RT. Copyright © 2005 Usborne Publishing Ltd

UPON PAUL'S STEEPLE by Alison Uttley. © Alison Uttley. The Society of Authors as the representative of the Alison Uttley Literary Property Trust

ROBERT THE BRUCE AND THE SPIDER by Geraldine McCaughrean from *100 Great Stories from British History* published by Orion Books, Copyright © 1999. Reproduced by permission of David Higham Associates

THUMBELISA by Hans Christian Andersen, retold in English by Diane Crone Frank and Jeffrey Frank from *The Stories of Hans Christian Andersen* published by Granta Publications © 2003. Used by permission of Granta Publications

SAILOR RUMBELOW AND BRITANNIA by James Reeves. © James Reeves 1962

Permission to reproduced THE SMALLEST DRAGONBOY is kindly granted by the author, Anne McCaffrey

Andre Norton: Putnam Berkeley Group, Inc. for ULLY THE PIPER from *High Sorcery* by Andre Norton (Ace Books) Copyright © Andre Norton 1970

WHEELBARROW CASTLE from *Mooncake and Other Stories* by Joan Aiken Copyright © Joan Aiken 1998. Reproduced by permission of Hodder and Stoughton Limited

ODDIPUTS by Nicholas Fisk. © Nicholas Fisk, 1978, 1979, 1980, 1982

VIRTUALLY TRUE Copyright © Paul Stewart, used by permission of the author

ALL SUMMER IN A DAY by Ray Bradbury © 1954. Used by permission of Abner Stein

BARRY by Stephen Bowkett. © Copyright Stephen Bowkett 1994

JESSICA'S SECRET by Malorie Blackman. Reproduced by permission of the Agency (London) Ltd. © Oneta Malorie Blackman 2002. First published by Collins, an imprint of HarperCollins

THE PARADISE CARPET by Jamila Gavin. © Jamila Gavin 2002

THAT BIT OF SULE © Chika Unigwe. Used by permission of the author

OUT OF BOUNDS from *Out of Bounds* by Beverley Naidoo (Puffin, 2001) Copyright © Beverley Naidoo, 2001. Reproduced by permission of Penguin Books Ltd

THE WORLD NEXT DOOR from *Mooncake and Other Stories* by Joan Aiken. Copyright © Joan Aiken 1998. Reproduced by permission of Hodder and Stoughton Limited

All possible care has been taken to trace the ownership of each story included in this selection and to obtain copyright permission for its use. If there are any omissions or if any errors have occurred, they will be corrected in subsequent printings on notification to the publishers.